The author writes novels with emphasis on history, travel, and the actual environment, six of which have been published, or are in the process of being published. He also provides services as a consulting geologist.

This book is dedicated to those involved in wildlife conservation worldwide.

David T. Sanders

LAUTARO LODGE

AUSTIN MACAULEY PUBLISHERS™

LONDON • CAMBRIDGE • NEW YORK • SHARJAH

Ordering Information
Quantity sales: Special discounts are available on quantity purchases by corporations, associations, and others. For details, contact the publisher at the address below.

Publisher's Cataloging-in-Publication data
Sanders, David T.
Lautaro Lodge

ISBN 9781645758068 (Paperback)
ISBN 9781645758051 (Hardback)
ISBN 9781645758075 (ePub e-book)

Library of Congress Control Number: 2022922181

www.austinmacauley.com/us

First Published 2023
Austin Macauley Publishers LLC
40 Wall Street 33rd Floor, Suite 3302
New York, NY 10005
USA

mail-usa@austinmacauley.com
+1 (646) 5125767

The assistance of Joy Jennings Danziger, as a proof-reader and advisor, and the administrative services of Amar Dhariwal are hereby acknowledged.

Table of Contents

Chapter One
Continental Shift

There were still hours before sunset on a long summer day in the Southern Hemisphere when Derek Lugard departed a boat at the dock in *Puerto Natales*. The tourist vessel on which he had traveled for nearly a week from *Puerto Montt*, through spectacular scenery in the Los Lagos Region of Patagonia, was his last mode of travel. He arrived in Chile by air, following short visits to several South American cities on his way from southern Africa where he had spent more than a decade working as a Wildlife Conservation Officer and a hunting guide.

Reluctantly, he had accepted a job in Chile offered by an Englishman he had guided on three big-game hunts. He became aware during the sail along the inland waterway from *Puerto Montt* that if he was to work in the rugged, mountainous terrain, fjords, glaciers, and rivers he had seen from the boat, this was going to be a tremendous challenge, and Roger Richardson, his new employer, had told him that the land he had purchased on which he wanted Derek to work was typical of the region. With a full understanding that the geography, geology, flora, and wildlife of this country was vastly different from that with which he had become so familiar, living in South Africa and studying at a university in Pretoria, he had been trying to learn all he could in preparation for the new job since he accepted it.

He spoke several languages fluently, but not Spanish. He thought his studies of that language were progressing very well until arriving in Santiago to find that the dialect spoken in Chile was much different from the Castilian version he was learning, causing him to make the many adjustments.

Derek seldom stayed in hotels if there was an alternative. He had booked a room in a bed and breakfast inn in the outskirts of this quaint, waterfront community. Having brought with him most of his belongings in a large leather suitcase and a backpack, it was necessary to hire a vehicle to take him from the dock to that inn. The driver he secured said little on the way there, but Derek was able to get directions from him to the vehicle rental company where Mister Richardson had informed him, by a telegram he received before leaving Johannesburg, that a prepaid rental vehicle was to be held for him there. The inn was old, but the room assigned to Derek was large, well-furnished and clean.

After checking-in, he walked through the city to the rental establishment and signed for a new Range Rover Defender, with a body style the same as the six-seat, older vehicle he had sold in Johannesburg. The money received from that sale and most of his savings, in the form of Krugerrand gold coins, he carried in a money-belt he was wearing beneath his shirt and down jacket. The vehicle was a welcomed surprise. At the inn, he transferred most of his belongings to the rear compartment and locked it. There was nearly another hour before the dinner-time he was informed of when he checked-in, so he walked back into the city, looking for a pub.

He found a café serving drinks and sat at a small patio table, illuminated by a setting sun. He ordered a beer from a pretty European girl. Sipping the beer, Derek told himself he was going to like Patagonia in the summer months, but having never lived in a cold climate, hae was uncertain about the winter months of cold and long hours of darkness.

The dinner served at the inn was not unexpected in a region with extensive grazing lands that were once the center of a huge sheep industry: lamb stew.

Those at the dinner table with him were all young German men who had come to engage in trekking into the glaciers and high mountains. They did not involve him in their discussions. However, he spoke German, so he was able to share their enthusiasm for the area. The woman who served them spoke German, also. In response to Derek's question after dinner, she told him that many German's had emigrated to central and southern Chile in the middle 1800s.

Brandy was served after dinner. Derek drank one glass and went to the reception area to pay for the room, telling a man at a counter that he would be leaving early in the morning and would leave the key in the room. He showered and went to bed as soon as he got to the room, which was located on a wing of the building with a door facing a parking space into which he moved the vehicle. He quickly fell asleep.

He was awakened by the shaking of the entire room and the crashing of a lamp to the floor from a nightstand. Trying to stand, he fell back on the bed. The motion continued for a couple of minutes. Derek had experienced earthquakes before, but nothing like this. He moved to a switch to the overhead light-fixture near the door. The room remained dark and he threw open the door to more total darkness. He found his trousers and slipped into them. Leaving the door open, he went to the Range Rover and turned on the headlights. In that light, he finished dressing, grabbed his jacket and rushed from the room.

Driving eastward through a darkened city, he saw no one. At the first intersection of roads, he stopped and retrieved from his backpack a map to the Richardson property he had been provided. The markings on the map showed that he should turn left and go beyond the airport. He glanced at his watch. It was four a.m.

A sign announcing the Teniente J. Gallardo Airport was passed and faint lights could be seen in the direction an arrow on the sign pointed. Derek turned onto a road leading that way. Car headlights, pointed in his direction, were turned on and a man with a flashlight waved for him to stop. The man, a security guard in uniform, came to the window that he rolled-down and informed him the airport was closed. Derek asked if with emergency power, anything about the earthquake had been learned by radio. He was told that a major earthquake, centered off-shore Santiago, had done major damage, killed many people, and disrupted electric power to nearly the entire country. Thanking the man for the information, Derek turned his vehicle around and returned to the main road.

At the next intersection, a decision was made to wait there for daylight before undertaking a search for the property. The wait lasted until the sun rose over a steep escarpment, several hundred feet high, located a few miles away. Derek got out of the vehicle to take-in another enthralling view, a view that was overshadowed by scenery that included high, snow-capped mountains he saw as he turned to look to the northwest. It was toward that region he was headed.

The ground shook violently again before Derek got back into the vehicle. *A very strong aftershock*, he thought, as he tried to imagine the destruction being done throughout the country. He recalled that he had read about such a quake in 1960, 50 years previously, that was centered off-shore Valdivia. That was the largest earthquake ever recorded, killing thousands of people, and destroying cities like *Puerto Montt*, the city he found so appealing when he went there to catch the boat that brought him to Patagonia.

The map he looked at once more indicated that his destination was just beyond *Cueva del Milodon*, a National Monument. After driving a mile or so, past a road with a sign pointing toward that site, he saw a well-maintained road through scrub brush on a long, south-facing slope of a highland. He had been traveling on that road for only a few minutes, when he saw his first terrestrial wildlife in South America. He stopped to retrieve binoculars, leaned across the hood, and watched a huge Red Stag, followed by six does, called hinds, walking, slowly up a trail. He had seen such deer in Europe, but none having antlers with the spread and thickness of the animal upon which he concentrated his attention.

The watching continued until the small herd disappeared into a thicket of trees. With the binoculars lying on the front passenger-seat, the drive toward a high ridge continued. The roadway made a sweeping curve to the left. The view ahead was another that Derek would not forget. A three-story stone building was at the center of a large compound, with a wide front porch and stone stairway. On one side was an attached, one-story, elongated structure made from the same stone that also had a wide porch. Blooming vines draped the front of that structure from the leading edge of a red-tile roof over the porch to the ground, nearly hiding multiple doorways. On the opposite side of the main building, a garage built of wood housed several vehicles and equipment that were visible through open doors. In front of those facilities, separated by more than forty yards of a gravel surface, stood a two-story barn, and adjacent, wood-rail fences enclosing corrals in which many horses were milling around, nervously.

Derek parked in front of the blooming vines and got out. A man stepped out to greeted him. In Spanish, the man introduced himself as Rios Asensio. Except for brown skin, rather than black, Rios looked like several members of the Zulu tribe with whom Derek had been associated for many years in South Africa, particularly, a young man he considered his best friend. He was very tall, only a few inches less than seven feet, and muscular. Derek kept his six-foot, two-inch body in good condition through regular exercise and running, but he knew that he must have looked small as he shook Rios' hand, introduced himself, and explained way he was there.

14

Rios offered to take the baggage into a room he said was reserved for him. Derek open the rear door of the vehicle and the strength of Rios was displayed. He took the suitcase that Derek had struggled to load in one hand, the backpack in the other, and led Derek into a large, well-furnished suite of rooms. No rearrangement or breakage caused by the earthquake was obvious. Derek ask about that and was told clean-up had been completed in this building but was still underway in the main house.

Headed to the lower level of the main house, Rios pointed out the adjacent doorway that lead to where he stayed. There was a door into the lower level. Before entering, Derek looked closely at the outside of the building, seeing not a stone or roof tile out of place. Going inside, he saw why the building had withstood the earthquake without obvious structural damage. The stone walls were nearly two-feet thick. The lower level was partitioned to create offices, working spaces, and a meeting room. The partitions and furnishings appeared to have been fashioned from rosewood. Their way was illuminated by overhead lights. When Derek asked about the lights, Rios informed him that the compound had a diesel generator for emergency power that he had started early that morning.

A tall, attractive woman, with long blonde hair and trim figure, was waiting for them at the top of a stairway to the second level. She and Rios embraced, and Derek was introduced to Afton Atkins. She apologized for her unkempt appearance, saying she and the domestic help had been working all morning to clean up broken glasses, dishes, fixtures, wall coverings and picture frames. Before more could be said, a boy burst through the front door, rushed to where the three of them stood, and, in a loud, excited voice, informed them of impending danger. Derek did not understand all the boy said, but it was clear to him that he was reporting that a dam was about to wash out.

Derek commented, "We must be certain that anyone living, traveling, or working below that dam, wherever it is, are moved out of the way of flood-waters."

"Why don't you and the boy do that, Rios?" Afton said. "I know a place from where we can view the danger of the dam washing-out from above. Would you come with me, Derek?"

"Lead the way!" Derek said.

Afton went to the front door, put on a woolen jacket hanging on a hat rack, ran down the outside stairs, and onto a trail beyond the compound. The trail led to a deep ravine over which a bridge constructed from rope and narrow planks had been hung. It was tied to large trees on either side. Without hesitation, she jogged across the bridge. Derek followed. The trail on the other side led to a prominent rock outcrop. There they stopped to observe a large reservoir at the mouth of the ravine. It was obvious that waves had washed over the earthen dam and eroded material from around a concrete spillway, but the dam had withstood the main earthquake and the first aftershock.

Derek offered his opinion, "The dam is doomed to fail. The erosion around the spillway has caused it to shift and settle. Even without further aftershocks, the spillway structure will slide away, and the impounded water will flood the land below. Another aftershock will accelerate that. We should go back."

Afton led the way, again. With them on the bridge, another aftershock struck. The bridge first took the shape of gigantic ripples that threw them face-down onto the planks. Then, it began to sway. Derek crawled to where he could grab Afton's ankles, shouted for her to hold-on to the spaces between the planks, and he forced the front of his boots into such spaces. Lying on his money belt was uncomfortable, and Derek envisioned the excitement of the person who found his body in the ravine with it still intact.

As the swaying diminished, Afton commented, "I think the large ropes attached to the trees will hold. We should crawl forward as soon as we can, though, in case a tree is uprooted. The root systems in the shallow soil may give-way."

Derek released his hold on her ankles. She crawled to safety, as did he. They sat on the ravine rim next to each other staring at where their lives could have ended before they even got to know each other.

"I feel certain that last shaking resulted in dam failure," Derek said. "We should get back and survey the flood damage."

They were met by Rios on an all-terrain vehicle. He reported that the dam had, indeed failed, but he and the boy had been able to warn all in danger, and the boy's family members had stopped cars on the highway while the floor-waters flowed over to road. He continued, "We are now faced with a massive clean-up and the construction of a new dam. I hope our earthquake problems have ended."

"I'm concerned about the horses," Derek said. "They were in near panic when I arrived. This last tremor may have driven them through the fencing."

The corrals were empty when they arrived there. A section of wooden fence lay flat.

Rios had a suggestion: "I'll repair the fence, open the gate for their return, and go look for the remuda on the ATV. One of you should saddle Old Thunder in the barn and go into the hills on him. He will find the other horses before I can." Afton and Derek went into the barn. Afton led a small, white stallion from a box-stall to a tie-down rack. "Old Thunder, I presume," Derek commented, and he was told this was the only stallion on the place and the favorite of the handlers.

"Trail-riding must be a popular activity here," Derek said. "Where are the handlers now?"

"At home with their families, they come here only when rides have been organized."

While Afton showed Derek to a large tack room and selected tack for the horse, Derek told her that he would ride to look for the escaped horses. Agreeing, she said that she should return to the main house and see what additional damage had been done, so his was a good idea.

"If you will saddle him, I'll go to my baggage and retrieve riding boots," Derek said.

In his new quarters, Derek removed his money belt. He placed it in-between the mattress and box springs on the bed, changed boots, and returned to the barn just as Old Thunder was being led out. With Derek in the saddle, Afton lowered stirrups as far as possible. Then the big man rode into hills he knew nothing about on the small horse, watching the ground for fresh hoofprints. He spotted what appeared to be those made recently by horses moving up a narrow trail, single file. He followed, realizing the trail through the brush was not wide enough for the ATV.

Soon, he could hear that machine far to his right. Derek reached the top of the slope without seeing the horses. He dismounted, sat on a rock outcrop and savored another magnificent view. The opposite slope of the large hill was very steep, *too steep for the horses to have gone that way*, he concluded. At the bottom of the hill was a lake to the west that appeared to be more than two miles long and at least one-half mile wide. Beyond the lake, the terrain was heavily wooded, forming ridges, plateaus, and steep canyons. In the distance, ice fields, glaciers, and snow-capped mountains were visible. The first glacier appeared to be only a few miles away.

Sitting in awe of his surroundings, Derek forgot the mission he was on until horses approached him from the right, still walking in single file. He remounted and started down the trail in front of them. Seeing Rios on the ATV behind the horses, he waved. Rios waved back, turned his vehicle, and went down the way he had come up the slope. Old Thunder and led the other horses all the way to the corral, where Rios was waiting to close the gate.

Derek removed the tack from the stallion and returned him to his stall. Hearing someone above him when he returned the tack, he climbed a ladder to find Rios throwing grass hay down to the horses. He took some hay to an opening in the floor above a feeder in Old Thunder's stall and filled that feeder. Rios suggested that they go to the main house to check on the clean-up.

Afton met them on the porch. She told them, "There was not much left after the first tremor that could break, so the clean-up job is complete. In inside cabinets, we still have a lot of unbroken dinnerware. Many of the pictures and paintings can be reframed and rehung. The girls do need help in moving the debris to a pile in the back of the building that we started."

Rios said, "I will go help."

As she had not done before, Afton spoke in English. She asked if they could go examine the flood damage. Derek escorted her to the Range Rover where he had left it and opened a door for her. It was a short drive through high grass and low brush to the edge of the area cleared of vegetation by the floodwaters. Some soil had been washed away and what remained had turned to thick mud. A stream of water flowed in a deep, newly incised channel. Walking down a gentle slope at the edge of the erosion, they saw several dead fish. Derek stopped to examine a large one. Ahead of him, Afton called, "Here is a dead fox." He moved on to examine the fox.

"This is a Chili Grey Fox," he told her. "She was nursing a litter. We should look for a den to see if any of her young survived."

Although not expecting to find a fox den on this slope, they walked all the way to a highway where they could see dwellings and farm plots ahead of them. There was minimal mud on the roadway and vehicles had driven through it. Beyond the highway, the removal of vegetation was also minimal. As they walked back to the vehicle, they discussed what could be done with this land and whether, or not, they would recommend rebuilding the dam.

Derek voiced his opinion about the dam. "I believe it would be wise to rebuilt it with a concrete core or build a reservoir at the mouth of the ravine.

The old channel-cut suggests the ravine into which we nearly fell runs a lot of water at times. Without an impoundment, the ravine will expand into useable land."

"What would you suggest be done with the disturbed land?" Afton asked.

"I know little about what Mister Richardson plans to do with any of the ranchland he purchased, land that is here, apparently, called an *estancia,* or what my role will be. However, he did mention a possible fish hatchery. One could be built on that land and I have experience in that area. The species of dead fish I saw suggests that someone was raising fish in the reservoir."

"Like you, I have not been told what my job as a botanist will be." Afton commented. "I guess we will find out."

Derek responded, "Not soon, given the disastrous earthquakes."

They walked passed the vehicle to an abrupt change in the slope and along a drying, rocky edge into a portion of the ravine to the dam site. The center of the dam as gone, but beyond a gap of about twenty feet, through which water flowed, the earthen fill was still in place. Afton pointed to where they had stood above the site. Derek commented that a similar rock outcrop on the other side made this an excellent site for a better dam.

Returning to the gentler slope, Derek said he would search along the change in the topography for a fox den. Afton told him that she had been collecting and pressing all the blooming flowers she had seen since her arrival and she had noticed some new ones on their walk that she wanted to collect while he did that.

A den was found. Two kits were scurrying in and out of a hole. Derek was not able to catch them until he placed a flat rock over the hole when they were both outside. Then, with much difficulty, he was able to catch and hold one in each hand against his chest until he reached Afton at the vehicle. She placed the flowering plants collected on the floor behind the front passenger-seat. Sitting on that seat, she suggested that she would hold the kits beneath her jacket. There, the kits continued to squirm for a few minutes on the drive back to the compound, but, eventually, they settled down.

"Will we be able to keep them alive?" she asked.

"They are old enough to eat solid food. If we have milk to give to them with bits of meat, they should survive."

"The girls milk a goat for white tea and coffee. We can feed them in the way you suggest."

"I have heard you mention the girls several times, but I don't know who they are."

"Heidi and Harriet Meister. They were living on the property when it was sold. They are probably illegitimate children of Ambrose Meister, the previous owner. Their mother was a native, but of a different tribe than Rios. I was told that the mother and a baby died in childbirth on the *estancia* several years ago. The girls are in their late twenties, very pleasant, and speak both Spanish and German. Rooms for their family were added in the rear of the main house. Behind the garage they tend to a few sheep and goats in a pasture. I'm sure you will like them as much as I do."

Derek asked, "Was Rios living on this land previously as well?"

"Most of his life, I believe. No one knows the land better than Rios."

"His size lends support to the observations reported by Ferdinand Magellan's crew and other explorers regarding them seeing giants in this region," Derek said. "I feel small standing next to him, and early Spaniards were as much as a foot shorter than I am, so the contrast would have been greater in Magellan's time. I have learned to like and respect him already. He reminds me a great deal of a Zulu that I have cherished as a friend for most of my life."

Reaching the compound, Derek backed the Range Rover into a vacant space in the garage next to the ATV that Rios had been driving. Getting out, he noticed that vehicle had been customized to accommodate Rios' size.

"Where shall we put our babies?" Afton asked.

"Let's fix a place for them in an empty box-stall I saw in the barn."

In the stall enclosure, Afton knelt and opened her coat. The kits jumped to the floor and ran around, wildly, before cowering in a corner. In an opposite corner, Derek made a home for them with canvas draped over an overturned, wooden box, covered with straw. The box was raised at one end over a length of clay drain pipe to create an entrance. Leaving the box-stall, the two of them closed the door and stood looking inside. Almost immediately, the kits scampered into their first man-made den.

"Let's go to the main house," Afton suggested. "I will workup the formula and come back to feed them."

"Whether or not Roger Richardson envisioned an animal rescue center, we may never know, but we have started one," Derek commented, as they walked to the house. "When I have time, I will build them a proper den on the hill behind the compound."

Derek went with Afton to meet the girls. They were preparing dinner in an elaborate kitchen. The smell of food cooking remined Derek that he had not eaten since the night before. What he saw being cooked was not more lamb stew. Beef steaks were on a counter-top grill and vegetables were boiling in pots on a large range. He was told that dinner would soon be ready. The voices brought Rios up from the lower level where he had been repairing picture frames. He offered to show Derek the remainder of the house. They started in a dining room next to the kitchen, where one end of a large table had already been set. The room in front of that one was a well-furnished living room, with a large fireplace in which logs were burning. A study adjoined that room. Four of the five bedrooms on the upper floor were all furnished for guests. One was a well-furnished master bedroom that Rios told him was reserved for the owners. All had separate bathrooms.

Returning to the kitchen, they met Afton who was headed to the barn with a thin pan of uncooked beef, diced into very small pieces, and warm milk. She explained to Rios what she was doing. Derek suggested it be left near the entrance to the makeshift den where it could be easily watched from outside the stall. He told her not to be discouraged if it took a long time for the kits to get used to eating this new food. He also cautioned her to watch carefully when the door was opened, for they were very quick and would get away at their first chance.

When Afton returned, the others were seated at one end of a dining-room table that could seat twelve, waiting for her. The excellent meal was enjoyed by all. Discussions included the answering of many questions that Derek asked. He answered questions, too, about his years in South Africa, and told the others what he knew about the new master of the *estancia*. At the end of the meal, Rios went back downstairs to the patch and repair work he had started. The girls cleared the table. Afton and Derek moved to the living room with cups of strong coffee, where Afton suggested they begin to get to know each other.

She described how while in graduate school at the University of California, Davis, she had responded to a very strange offer of employment as a botanist that had been published in the school newspaper, not expecting anything to come of it. Yet, a few weeks later, she received a round-trip airline ticket to

London, with a schedule for an interview at the Ritz Hotel where a room was reserved for her. At that interview, she met Mister Richardson for the first, and only time, she told Derek.

"I thought the interview went well," she continued. "But I learned little about the job, except that I would work directly for him as a botanist on a large property in South America, the location of which would be shown on a map to be sent to me with a service contract, if I was hired. I spent several days enjoying the sights in London, and returned to Davis not expecting a job offer, and none was received for over a month. Then, just after last Christmas, I received what had been promised. The map was sketchy, but it gave me a place to start my own research.

"The contract had a first-month retainer attached that was in an amount I never dreamed of making in my chosen profession. Also provided were airline reservations, tickets from San Francisco to Teniente J. Gallardo Airport, and a voucher for a taxicab company to take me to the estate of Ambrose Meister. So here I am, having had no further word from my client, with only a regional map with a circle drawn on it, no property boundaries, and the words, *Estancia Margo*, written inside the circle."

"What was your impression of the man in that one meeting?" Derek asked.

"He was a very pleasant, good-looking, well-mannered gentleman. We met in his suite at the Ritz. As I was leaving, a beautiful woman, much younger than him, emerged from a bedroom. He introduced her as his wife, Margo. I assume she is the one for whom he named the property."

Derek's story was much different. "The wife who accompanied Roger to southern Africa to hunt big game under my guidance was named Marsha, a very nice person. I have heard nothing about her since. I liked her and hope she is still alive. Mister Richardson was my best client. He was friendly, unassuming, and always a gentleman. In our overnight camps, he often questioned me about my degrees in Wildlife Management and Fisheries, and about the work I was doing as a Wildlife Conservation Office when not working as a guide.

"He explained to me his interest in conservation, but never mentioned land he owned, or hoped to own, to advance that interest. Like you, I received a contract by mail that called for payment for my services at a rate I could not refuse. No advance payment was included with the offer, nor travel expenses.

I chose to fly to several cities on my way to Chile and took a tourist boat from *Puerto Montt* to *Puerto Natales*."

Afton responded, "We are both here with no idea of what is expected of us or to what area we are expected to apply our professional knowledge."

"We have already found things that need our attention, so we should do what we think is right until we hear from Mister Richardson. This could become the biggest challenge we will ever face as professionals."

Chapter Two
Estancia Margo

Exhausted after nearly twenty hours that had included intense activity in a new environment, Derek slept very soundly until daybreak. The morning that greeted him when he left his quarters was cold and overcast. Mist or light rain caused him to go back inside for a waterproof wind breaker that he put on over a sweater. He walked along the vine-covered walkway beyond where he and Afton had left each other after their evening by the fireplace, passed the door to a fourth apartment, and went around to the back of the unit. From the end of the building to the pasture confining sheep and goats, there was a wide, nearly flat, grass-covered area with a few large trees.

Near the center of the area was a large propane tank, a modern generator on wheels, a ground-water well, and a water tank. The brush-covered slope up which he had ridden looking for the horses bounded the flat area. He walked to the pasture and spent time looking at the animals. He was to find out later that Rios sheared the sheep, and the girls carded the wool, spun and dyed thick fibers, and wove winter clothes. The walk continued around the compound. In the barn, he saw that the food Afton had left for the motherless kits had been eaten.

Derek had assumed that he was the only one awake in the compound. He found that he may have been the last. Entering the lower level of the main house, he found Afton in one of the work area offices, adding more flowers to a press she had made from pieces of plywood, with cardboard dividers. Newsprint separated the plants: blooms, leaves, stems, and roots. Straps were designed to hold it all together, tightly. Rios was in an adjacent space still repairing and replacing broken picture frames.

"Good morning," Afton said. "Heidi and Harriet have coffee and tea upstairs and breakfast will be ready soon."

"One has to get up early to stay current with activities around here," Derek said.

"I saw you going into the barn on your survey of the compound. Had the little fox eaten?"

"They had and were back in the temporary den. Those are encouraging signs. I think they will grow to be fine adults."

Rios joined Derek, and they walked to the kitchen where they were greeted, in Spanish. Derek decided that this was a good time to let the girls know that he spoke their other language. He returned the greeting in German. With no hint of surprise, Heidi asked, jokingly in that language, if he had milked the goat while out back. He said that he had to confess he had not. That brought laughter and a response from Rios, that may have been intended to show he spoke that language, too: "That's woman's work." That short exchange pleased Derek because he felt more comfortable speaking in German than Spanish. He could continue to improve his Spanish, while speaking more freely with these three in German and with Afton in English.

Harriett asked Rios and Derek to sit at a table in the kitchen and served them breakfast, reporting that Afton ate little for breakfast, so she was going to take a tray downstairs to her. As they ate, Derek told Rios about the Red Stag herd he had seen and asked about that population. He was told that poaching for trophies was a big problem and some native people still killed a few for meat, but where hunting access was limited by the terrain or by the property owners, there were still many in the area.

Derek commented, "That magnificent animal, like so many in Africa, warrants opportunities for tourists to observe them and take photographs, rather than killing them in order to take a trophy back home."

"Such tours, called eco-tours, have been established. Herr Meister had considered one originating here," Rios responded.

"Are you aware of viewing areas in trees and among rocks where *stands* could be created for that purpose?"

"Many."

"You must show me sometime. How about the smaller, Andean deer?"

"There are still a few small herds in the area."

"I have some ideas about how to enlarge those herds, using ways I have perfected for other species of mammals in Africa. With the help of you and Afton, I hope to try that here."

"You can expect my help. Tell me what needs to be done."

Afton joined them at the table with a second cup of coffee and asked what they had been talking about. When Derek told her, she asked for the details of his ideas about the Andean deer, a species she said had been classified as threatened for extinction by governmental authorities.

"There is little anyone can do about habitat-loss in the modern world, but creating reserves and improving the habitat remaining, particularly the food available in those reserves, is something that can be done. Deer are browsers. We need to study existing brush-cover here to determine what that species eats, collect seeds or cutting from those plants, and expand the plant populations."

"Do you have an idea about the type of vegetation they eat?" Rios asked.

"Other deer species I have studied primarily eat small leaves from mahogany and other hardwood bushes and small trees. That may be the case in Patagonia."

"I brought all of the books on plants in the region that I could find," Afton reported. "I will see how many such plants are listed and I recommend we start investigating today."

"If Rios leads us to places where he has seen herds, we can begin looking for evidence of browsing. I suspect we will find some," Derek responded.

"We should take horses to near such places, leave them tied, and continue on foot. If we approach a herd without them knowing we are nearby, we should be able to observe them feeding," Rios suggested. "I will get the horses ready."

Afton and Derek said they would bring binoculars and cameras and meet him at the barn. Even though he did not expect to hear from their employer this soon after the earthquake, Derek decided to attach his satellite telephone to his belt when he went to his room for his camera and binoculars. As he and Afton were walking to the barn, Derek wondered how Rios could adjust stirrups for his long legs on a small horse. They found he rode bareback on the stoutest horse in the *remuda*, with his feet nearly touching the ground. He handed the reins on the bridle of Old Thunder to Derek. The young mare he had saddled for Afton was one he knew she had ridden before.

Rios led them on the trail he had taken on the ATV when looking for the escaped horses. In a grove of trees about halfway up the slope, he stopped, dismounted, and tied his horse. His companions did the same. They separated and crept, silently, through the trees for several minutes.

Beyond the woodland, there was a topographic basin with brush and grass on each enclosing slope and a stream running through it. There was a herd of about twenty deer near the stream. The brush was very thick, but they were able to advance on the herd following widely-spaced game trails. They walked in a crouched posture and crawled until they were only a hundred yards, or so, from the deer. Taking positions with views of individuals or groups, they watched and took many photographs with telescopic lenses for more than an hour. The viewing ended when the deer bolted away after hearing the roar of a cat. Afton and Derek were able to photograph a puma chasing and killing a fawn.

They came together to discuss what to do next. Afton and Derek wanted to examine the plants that they had seen being browsed, but Rios advised against going near the puma without a rifle. On the hike back to the horses, Rios explained what the puma would do. Derek understood very well what he said from this experience with large cats: The puma would eat its fill and bury the remainder, returning from his wide-ranging hunting when necessary. Derek suggested they spend the next day exploring the region further and return to the site the following day.

It was late afternoon when they were back at the barn. Afton asked if Rios would put her horse away while she went for food for the kits. Rios and Derek took care of the horses ridden that day and feed them all. Working together, they spoke Spanish and Derek asked that his words be corrected when Rios heard incorrect usage because he was determined to improve that language skill. Afton returned to feed the kits and three observers stood at the low door to the stall, watching them dart in and out from the den to the food.

As they returned to the main house, Heidi told them that an early supper awaited them, and that Harriet had something to show them. What Harriett had to show them was a list left by Ambrose Meister regarding those they should expect to arrive at the *estancia* to work for the buyer. Afton's and Derek's names were on the list with another, Robert Grayson. Neither Afton nor Derek had heard the name before. While eating they discussed who he might be. It was assumed that he was another professional.

Rios went to his quarters after the meal. Afton retrieved books from her office and she and Derek went into the study where Derek wrote down the names that she provided of plant species from her research that she thought the deer might be eating. Later, they went to sit on the front porch to enjoy the setting sun. At dusk, a vehicle arrived in front of the porch. Afton recognized the driver who got out. He had brought her from the airport. The passenger was an older man with gray hair and beard. He climbed the stairs with the driver behind him, carrying two suitcases and a briefcase. Afton and Derek arose to greet the man. He introduced himself as Doctor Robert Grayson and asked them to call him Bob. Before the driver left, Derek asked him to help carry the luggage to the end apartment in the adjacent structure. He suggested Doctor Grayson sit with Afton while they took care of the luggage and that they would show him to his quarters later. The driver seemed less than pleased until Derek gave him a large tip. Accepting the currency, he rushed to his car and drove away.

Returning to the porch, Derek was informed by Afton that a professional paleontologist had joined them. Bob apologized for arriving so late and explained: "I had to stop at the cave to see the replica of a giant sloth that was known to have lived in that cave during the Pleistocene era. I was hired by a Roger Richardson, whom I have never met, to look for more fossil evidence of the sloths' existence. Skin, hair, and a few bones were the evidence found in the cave."

The story of Doctor Grayson's employment that he told them was as strange as theirs. He had retired from teaching vertebrate paleontology at the University of Kansas when a letter from Roger Richardson arrived with the job offer. The letter was followed by a contract, retainer, airline tickets, directions to the site, and an expense advance. He told them he had recently lost his wife, so he decided to accept the offer.

When asked, he said that he had not eaten since lunch served on a flight from Santiago, so Afton invited him to go to the kitchen with her where the girls would prepare something for him. Afton and Derek waited in front of the fireplace in the living room while he ate, expecting to brief him on their professions. When the doctor joined them, he went into things that would affect his studies, first saying, "From the air, the area around here appeared to be covered by dense vegetation. Outcrops of fossiliferous strata may be hard to find."

Derek responded, "So far, I have seen few rock outcrops in the brush and tree-covered slopes. However, a deep ravine, into which Afton and I nearly fell during an earthquake, has exposed a thick sequence of strata. In fact, a dam was destroyed, and a water impoundment drained, exposing strata had has not been accessible for many years."

"I will start work there tomorrow. Now, if you will kindly show me to my quarters."

Somewhat put out by the self-centered attitude of the new professional, Derek told him that he must have seen where his luggage was taken while he sat on the porch and added: "Yours are the rooms at the end of the adjacent building. The door is not locked."

"I expect you to take me to the ravine in the morning," Doctor Grayson said as he went out the front door.

"This association is going to be interesting, if not trying," Afton remarked. She and Derek went back into the study and continued their efforts until late, then carried the books to the lower level and went on to their quarters.

Afton, Derek, and Rios were finishing breakfast at the table in the kitchen when Doctor Grayson entered from the front of the house. His first comments were, "The accommodations are adequate, but nothing great. I must remember this is a backward country."

Thankful that the Heidi and Harriett did not understand what he said, Afton and Derek wanted to counter his comments. Both considered their rooms very nice and had yet to see evidence of a backward country. Instead, they said nothing and went with Rios to the lower level. There they discussed their plans for the day.

"I'll give the keys to the Range Rover to the "good professor" and point him to the ravine," Derek said. "We might consider another day on horse-back. Rios has a lot more to show us, Afton."

She agreed and asked Rios if he would guide them to other areas of the *estancia.* While Afton and Rios went to the barn with Afton's field equipment in her backpack, Derek got his backpack and went to the kitchen. He gave the keys to Doctor Grayson and explained the way to the nearby ravine. Rios had anticipated a day with Afton and Derek, so he had Heidi and Harriett prepare a lunch and put it in saddle bags for them. Derek kissed each girl on a check and thanked them in German before leaving with the lunches to join Afton and Rios. They had the horses ready.

Rios took them far to the east and up the long slope on a trail that he had been told was near the edge of the property. There were more trees and less brush, but the vegetative cover was still dense. The vegetation changed when they crossed the ridge. A vast grassland lay in front of them, all the way to the shore of the lake that Derek had seen before. Near the shore of the lake, a large herd of guanaco was grazing. As Derek had requested, the three of them had conversed in Spanish all day, with Rios and Afton correcting Derek, regularly. He voiced his amazement at the size of the guanaco herd. Rios responded by telling them they would all be males and that the breeding herds, with a dominant male, were much smaller. As they rode near the herd, the guanaco did not flee, but continued to graze. Rios informed the others that in the grasslands to the north there were many such herds.

A small river entered the lake from the northeast. Derek dismounted, handed the reins of this horse to Afton, and walked along a bank of the river, observing many fish of several different species. Afton and Rios guided the horses through the stream and chose a place in nearby trees to eat lunch. Derek voiced his amazement about the fish populations he had seen when he joined them. Rios informed them that there were many fish in all streams in the grasslands and that in the Dorotea Region, fly-fishing was one of several excursions offered to tourists staying at several resorts. Afton asked if part of the lake was on the *estancia* and was told the entire lake and some of the wooded area behind them was part of Ambrose Meister's land grant, where he raised cattle before selling the stock and the property.

The ride continued after lunch along the north shore of the lake to a point of land from which a highway headed toward the ice fields was visible. Afton dismounted often to collect blooming plants and place them in a plastic bag. Riding south, they crossed the outlet to the lake, a river flowing southwestward, which they forded. Rios now led them into higher terrain. At one stop to take photographs, the inland waterway could be seen into which flowed the river they crossed. Beyond that, the community of *Puerto Natales* was in view. The land they crossed from there back to the compound varied greatly. There were grassland areas, groves of dense trees, and large areas of low brush. The topography varied from broad canyons to low ridges. Heading into one canyon, Afton saw and photographed Red Stag for the first time. Crossing the upper reaches of the ravine across which the rope bridge was suspended, they stopped, once more, to take photographs. The beautiful setting of the compound in early evening was spectacular.

"Our home on the *estancia* needs a name," Afton suggested.

"I recommend Lautaro Lodge," Rios offered. "Lautaro was a hero who fought for the rights of my people many years ago."

Afton and Derek agreed. "A fine name," Derek said. "I think our employer might accept it. We should make that suggestion when we get the opportunity."

The ride ended in the darkness. Only the front porch of the main house was illuminated by an outside light. Everyone still in the lodge had apparently gone to bed. The lights in the barn were switched on and the horses cared for. The three agreed to deposit their things in their apartments and meet in the kitchen to find something to eat.

Meal preparation was not necessary. The girls had left a large pot of stew over a low flame on the stove and freshly baked bread. After eating, three tired companions went to their beds.

When Derek took his morning walk, he noticed the Range Rover was not in the garage. That, obviously, caused him great concern, so he went to Doctor Grayson's apartment and knocked on the door. A sleepy occupant opened the door, not fully dressed. When asked about the vehicle, he said it had bogged down in thick mud. He started to chastise Derek for making him go out alone. Derek walked away. He joined Afton and Rios at breakfast, told them what he had learned, and added, "He tried to drive where he should have walked."

Rios offered, "There is a small motor-grader in the garage that I use to maintain our roads. We can pull the vehicle out of the mud after we finish eating."

Doctor Grayson had yet to appear in the main house when Rios and Derek left to undertake that job. With a chain, they both rode on the grader to the site. As Derek had suspected, Doctor Grayson had driven into the mouth of the ravine where he and Afton had walked. The vehicle was covered with mud from spinning wheels. Rios kept the grader with two wheels still on dry land. Derek waded through the mud to attach the chain to the vehicle and got in. The keys were still in the ignition. Rios backed the grader out of the ravine, pulling the vehicle that Derek had started and put into low gear. Back on the grassland, they stood looking at a mud-covered vehicle and the mud on Derek's trousers and boots, when Derek's satellite telephone rang.

It was not their employer calling, but his wife, Margo. She sounded frantic, asking that she be picked up at the local airport, immediately. Saying nothing more, she hung up. Derek told Rios what he had been ordered to do and expressed how unhappy he was about having to go to the airport in the muddy condition of himself and the vehicle. Rios suggested he stop at a hose connection by the garage to wash the mud from his clothes and the windows. That being done, Derek sped to the airport.

Derek saw a woman, pacing in front of the terminal. Two men stood near her with a large amount of luggage by their side. He drove there, got out and tried to introduce himself to the woman. Without responding to him, she asked if he had come from the Meister property. When he acknowledged that, she got in the front seat. The men introduced themselves as Ted Benson and Ned Willis, pilots of Mister Richardson's plane. They loaded the luggage and got in the second seat. As Derek drove away from the terminal, the woman finally offered her name, Margo Richardson, and said, "You tell our driver what we have been through, Ted. I don't want to relive it."

The events described were totally unexpected and hardly believable: The company plane had dropped-off Mister Richardson at the airport near *Puerto Montt* and flew to Easter Island, where they secured the plane and took rooms in a beachfront hotel. The tsunamis formed by the earthquake did great damage to the hotel but not the airport. Eventually, they were able to get back to the plane with their luggage, have it refueled, and take-off to come to Patagonia.

"We flew over *Puerto Montt*. It was a destroyed city," Ned Willis added. "We have no idea what happened to Mister Richardson. He didn't even tell us where he was going to stay. Has anyone here heard from him?"

"The staff that remained on the property Mister Richardson acquired, two young women and a native man, me and two other professionals are on the place. We have electric power provided by a generator, but the only communication equipment is my satellite telephone. The only call I have received was the one from Missus Richardson that brought me to get you."

"From the looks of this vehicle, it appears as if you have experienced problems, as well."

"A dam burst and flooded a large area. This vehicle was foolishly driven into the resulting mud and I look this way from getting it unstuck. The property suffered no serious, additional damage. The structures were very well built, and we are a long way from the epicenter of the quakes."

Rios was headed into the main house, having taken Doctor Grayson to the ravine on the ATV when he saw the Range Rover approach. He went inside to get the girls. They were waiting to greet the new mistress of the house on the front porch. Margo got out and ordered that she be taken to the best room. Heidi and Harriett escorted her upstairs to the master bedroom.

Looking at the house as he stood by the rear door of the car, Ned commented, "What a magnificent building."

Derek replied, "We call it the Lautaro Lodge." He, then, excused himself to go change clothes.

Rios, carrying most of the luggage, took the pilots to other rooms on the upper floor. The bags shown to him as those belonging in the master bedroom, he took inside that room and placed them where Harriett pointed. Heidi was checking the supplies in the bathroom. Missus Richardson was lying face-down on the bed crying and was left alone. The pilots settled into adjacent rooms, after thanking Rios in English, the only language either spoke.

Derek returned to the main house through the lower level. He entered Afton's work space where she was pressing more plants. She was as shocked as he had been when he told her what he had learned about where the man who had hired them had gone. His impression of the wife was less than complimentary, and he told her about the pilots who he had brought there.

"Heaven knows what this assignment will become. Things don't look good just now," Afton commented.

"Don't be discouraged," Derek told her. "I have hunted with Roger Richardson and found him to be strong, with a strong-will. I believe he survived the earthquake and that he will be here to direct us in what he wants done. Let's continue to do the things that seem right to us."

Rios joined them. He explained how he was ordered to take the "good professor" to the ravine and to return for him in early afternoon.

The three of them went upstairs. They found the pilots sitting in the living room by a fire, drinking whisky. Afton was introduced to them. They all declined a drink and they went to the kitchen. A meal for the young fox had been prepared. Afton and Derek took it to the barn and Derek moved the Range Rover to the hose by the garage. The two of them had started washing the vehicle, when Rios came to help. They discussed how each of them viewed their futures as they worked together. Derek repeated what he had told Afton, earlier: They should continue to do what they thought needed to be done to improve the property. Each voiced how much they enjoined the land and their association with each other.

With the vehicle looking as good as new, Derek backed it into the garage and Rios drove out in the ATV, headed to get Doctor Grayson. Afton and Derek went to their quarters.

At dinner time, everyone was seated in the dining room, except Missus Richardson. Robert Grayson had been introduced to the pilots and they were discussing flying, something that the Doctor had done in the United States Air Force. Wine and dinner were served by Heidi. Harriett had prepared a tray to take to Missus Richardson. Before she left, Margo appeared. She had composed herself and was dressed in attractive clothes that accented a trim figure. Her hair was brushed, and she wore makeup. Standing at the dining room door, she could only be described as stunning. She apologized for her earlier lack of decorum and introduced herself to everyone.

Afton was the first to speak, "We know what you are going through. You should believe what Derek, the only one working here who has been in tough situations with your husband, believes: He survived and will soon be here to direct us in what he hired us to do."

Margo sat next to Afton and thanked her for the thoughts. Derek confirmed what he believed.

"You should be the one to go find my husband, then, Derek. I, too, think he is alive and needs help."

"It is likely that the ferry boats are not yet running to *Puerto Montt* but there was a large motor-boat tied to the dock when I arrived. I'll have Afton take me to *Puerto Natales* to see if I can charter a trip into the devastation. Obviously, it would be foolish for me to make any promises, but I think I will return with Roger, alive and well."

The dinner discussions continued with explanations from Afton about the language situation and the quarters where everyone slept. She explained that Heidi, Harriett, and Rios had worked for the previous owner and described the professional work the others had begun.

The discussion continued in the living room after dinner. Rios served brandy to those who wanted an after-dinner drink. Missus Richardson remained in control of her emotions and was pleasant company.

Early the next morning, Derek packed a small bag and he and Afton started to *Puerto Natales* before the others were awake. Alton drove and expressed her concerns about his mission, telling him that she would pray for his success.

Arranging for a boat was not easy. The owner of the boat that Derek had seen was not anxious to make the trip. Several gold coins that Derek was again carrying in his money-belt finally convinced him. While Juan Aparicio fueled his boat, Derek and Afton sat in the Range Rover. Derek expressed his wish that she had a satellite telephone, too, so they could keep in contact. She gave him the land-line number and promised to pressure the local authorities for a reestablishment of telephone services. He agreed to call that number each evening, until she or someone else at the lodge answered.

The boat owner waved Derek aboard. He and Afton walked to the dock. Before Derek climbed onboard, they embraced. She stood on the dock waving as the boat moved into the inland waterway.

Chapter Three
Survival

The first fall Roger experienced was from his bed to a pitching and swaying floor. He was not even able to get to a position on his hands and knees before the entire floor fell onto a floor below, causing dust to rise that nearly suffocated him. Another attempt to rise from a prone position was thwarted by intensive shaking and more falling of everything around him. Now, the cries of humans and thicker dust deadened his senses and he could see only faint light. His surroundings tilted sharply to one side and he slide into a corner between the floor he was on and a wall of splintered wood. Another wall and debris fell to trap him. The shaking continued for a few minutes longer. When it stopped, he realized that he had lived through a major earthquake, but he could not remember where he was or why he was not in London where such events did not happen.

Death throes continued to be heard that would haunt him through the remainder of his life. He realized that many others were not as lucky as he was, but he also knew that death would take him, too, unless he could extricate himself from this predicament. His body was so tightly wedged between masses of wood and wallboard that he could barely move. The fading light he had seen vanished. He was in total darkness. Blood was flowing, slowly, across one cheek and his head was pounding. His attempts to remain conscious and alert failed. His mind drifted away.

The next thing that entered his mind was an image of him as a young boy, walking with his father in unfamiliar surroundings. They sat in a ring of black men wearing strange clothes. As his father stood to speak, the image faded and was replaced by blackness. Hours passed before he regained consciousness. The new image on this mind was a grave-side service and his mother, dressed in black, crying for someone that could have been him or his father. Eventually, his mind focused on his surroundings. No more human cries could be heard. An attempt to move was met by another severe shaking of his entombment and everything around it.

These times of partial recognition of his surroundings, shaking, and a darkness in his mind continued for a long period. Severe thirst and hunger aroused him, and he began to think again of his entrapment. Still, he could not recall where he was when all of this happened. Turning his body so he could place his feet on the upper wall, he pushed with all his remaining strength, but nothing moved. Having no way to know time as it passed, Roger laid in that place for what seemed to be days. Scenes flashed through his mind that must have been from his past, but he recognized none of them.

Knowing his life was fading away, he vowed to himself to stay alive until he was rescued. Feeling all around, his hand found a pipe. With a piece of wood, he began to strike that pipe, causing a sound. He continued to pound on the pipe with all his remaining strength. The sound was heard by rescuers who began removing debris in that direction, very carefully, with an excavator and hand work. When they reached him, he was alive but not conscious. Medics moved him to an ambulance on a stretcher and he was taken to a hospital where he lay, still unconscious, for two more days, with IV-tubes attached.

When he awoke his response to questions asked by nurses and doctors, in the Spanish language that he understood, was that he did not remember his name or why he was in Chile. When he spoke in the language that he used, regularly, an English accent was detected by the nurse that continued to monitor his condition.

A clerk at the hospital tried, unsuccessfully, to match his name with missing-person reports. The registration records at the hotel where he was found had been destroyed, so the room he was in could not be determined, and personal items retrieved from the ruins of the hotel provided no clues about who this patient was. A specialist was called to try to clear his mind and memory. That effort met with little success. The overcrowded hospital required the administration to transfer him to a very crowded annex building that provided a place to sleep, a mattress on the floor, food, and water, but no medical care.

The earthquake effect on the nearly 1,400 miles of waterway through which the motor-boat, with Derek aboard, was racing to *Puerto Montt* was evident by high-water marks along both banks. There was no other traffic on the water and the surface of the water was calm. It took the entire voyage for Derek to convince Juan to secure a berth, allow him to continue to sleep onboard, take on provisions, and return to *Puerto Natales* with him and his employer onboard when he was found. An unoccupied berth was easy to find. Many held damaged boats, but boats once in other berths had evacuated. The waterfront and the damaged city were nearly deserted.

Derek and Juan walked along the waterfront until they found the remnants of a store selling provisions and restocked the boat. Derek began his search by reviewing a casualty list maintained at a severely damaged city building. Then, he started asking about unidentified patients at hospitals and medic clinics. After two days, he was very discouraged. Few survivors were still being found, but many dead. His description of the Englishman he was looking for finally led him to the building where he saw Roger, looking forlorn and bewildered. At first, there was no recognition expressed by him. His many hours in the wilds of Africa with Derek, eventually, came into focus in Roger's mind and he spoke Derek's name. On a bench, sitting together, Roger's memory began to return. His first question was if Derek knew anything about his wife, Margo.

"She and your pilots are at your new estate in Patagonia and your plane is at the nearby airport." Derek told him. "They survived the tsunamis that hit Easter Island. Margo sent me here to find you."

"You found me, young man, but I don't know how."

"It was not easy. Wait while I get you released. I have a motor-boat waiting to get us out of here."

It required a lot of paper work and written commitments to pay for services rendered at the annex and the hospital before Derek was able to return with release forms. There were showers, soap, towels, and razors at the annex, so except for his clothes, Roger looked more like Derek remembered him when they left. With difficulty, they found a men's clothing store that had reopened. When Roger saw Derek pay for the clothes and boots he had chosen with a gold coin taken from his money belt, he asked if he was paying for the trip with his own money. Finding that was the case, Roger said their next stop would be at a bank. It took a long time to find a bank that was open. Waiting in a long line at a Barclay bank, Derek asked if they should not see if any of his belongings had been recovered from the destroyed hotel.

"No money found would be turned-in. I will have my old debit card cancelled and a new one issued when I get to a teller," Roger told him.

"I'll be just outside, watching the unsavory crowd. Any cash you come out with should be well hidden. Some of them outside look like they would cut our throats for a few pesos."

Fortunately, a police officer dispersed the crowd before Roger came out of the bank. There was no public or private transportation operating and it was a long walk to the harbor through streets littered with mounds of debris. A van serving food was on the remnants of one street. Roger stopped and purchased a large amount of grilled beef rolled in corn tortillas and several bottles of beer. Juan was impatiently waiting when they got to the boat. He backed out of the berth and headed down the waterway as soon as his passengers were onboard, having had to carry cans of fuel over a long distance to re-fuel.

Roger told Derek little about his survival during the following days on the boat, but he did mention his mind wanderings in a semi-conscious state. "On one occasion, I relived the meeting in which father took me with him when he met with the leaders in the black Homelands of South Africa, a meeting in which he was granted mining concessions that proved to contain huge reserves of platinum. That was the beginning of the fortune he left me.

"As a geologist, I have found and developed important mineral reserves elsewhere, but nothing to compare with those platinum reserves on Merenski Reef, the development of which came at a time when the automobile industry began the use of the metal in catalytic exhaust-controls. Now, that industry will soon need major reserves of lithium for batteries. That is my main interest in this part of the world. Chile and Argentina will become major producing countries and my company hopes to become a significant supplier. The property I purchased from Ambrose Meister is a part of my plans. Establishing a reputation as a good steward of the land should help in convincing government officials that we will restore land disturbed by mining and processing lithium.

"Reclamation of vast surface disturbances will be one key to long-term lithium recovery. The acquisition of other large estates by film actors, a television network owner, and European investors has become controversial because they have not considered carefully enough the interest of the natives, local European populations, and the state. We must do that."

Derek responded, "The professionals you engaged have already started working toward the creation of a nature reserve, thinking that was your objective, but not knowing for certain. Those who have lived on the land most of their lives, particularly a near giant named Rios, have been very helpful. In honor of a hero of his people, Rios has suggested we call the beautiful headquarters on the property, Lautaro Lodge."

"That sounds like a great name to me. What is your impression of the other professionals?"

"Afton Atkins is, clearly, a well-qualified professional botanist. She is very personable, and we work well together. Doctor Grayson arrived only recently. He seems qualified and enthusiastic, but his personality and attitude have already caused some problems. It will take some time for me to get used to working with him, but I will."

"My wife, Margo. Do you like her?"

"She was in a terrible state of shock when she arrived but was calmer when she asked me to go find you. She is a beautiful woman. However, I expected to see Marsha, whose company I enjoyed during our time together on safari."

"Marsha, I cherished. Unfortunately, cancer took her from me a few years ago. Margo and I met at an exhibition of wildlife paintings, a fund-raiser for a conservation group. She is a painter of wilderness landscapes. Very good, in my biased opinion."

"I have never before seen so many views of unique lands as I have since arriving in Chile. Margo will have many scenes from which to choose."

"What activities have my retained professionals chosen to occupy their time?"

"Afton and I have asked Rios to ride horseback with us, so we can become familiar with the magnitude of the challenge. Although Rios has never been told the perimeter of the property nor been provided a map, he has taken us over many square miles on which he worked for Mister Meister. Afton has collected a multitude of plants which she is studying, and I am becoming familiar with the native mammals and fish. The three of us have initiated a study intended to improve the habitat for the endangered Andean deer.

"By chance, we have started a wildlife rescue center with Chili fox, temporarily living in your barn. The land has dense vegetative-cover. Except in the nearby national monument where the cave in which skin and a few bones of an extinct giant ground sloth have been found, and an occasional rock feature, the outcrop of potential fossiliferous strata is limited. However, in a ravine, Doctor Grayson has started his studies. Exposures of strata in that ravine were extended when a dam burst due to damage caused by the earthquakes."

"I have an interest in the fossils that may be found. Particularly, mega-fossils in the Cretaceous and Pleistocene strata. I have read reports of large dinosaurs found, as well as giant mammals, like the sloth, and extinct horses. Was there other serious damage done by the earthquakes that nearly took my life?"

"The *estancia* structures were so well built that they were not damaged. A great deal of glass was broken, and many wall-hangings had to be thrown out or repaired, but the total damage was light. You may hear about a rope bridge from which Afton and I were nearly thrown into the deep ravine, but no one was seriously hurt."

"As I expected, Derek, you have taken the initiative to improve on what I purchased in Patagonia. I very much appreciate that, and I can hardly wait to see what I own there for the first time. Ambrose Meister and I closed the transaction in London and he went to the village of his family in Bavaria."

Roger and Derek also discussed their experiences on safari in Africa and the changing of such activity from hunting to observation and photographing. As he had promised Afton that he would do, he called the lodge every evening, hoping for his calls to be answered. One evening that occurred. He asked Harriett to let him speak with Afton. With her on the call, he reported his success and the fact that he was returning with their client. He gave her Juan's estimate of arrival at his berth at *Puerto Natales*. She said she would convey his message to Margo and the others and meet the boat.

When he terminated the call, Roger asked, "Is it going to be necessary for me to learn German?"

"The help at the *estancia* speak both German and Spanish. I choose to converse with them in German because my Spanish is not very good, yet. I spoke with Afton. She will tell the others and drive the Range Rover you had waiting for me to pick us up. You will be to your Patagonian home soon. I know you will like it."

Afton and Margo were standing on the dock when the boat arrived. Roger jumped from the boat and rushed into Margo's arms. Derek followed, carrying his small bag which he asked Afton to hold while he helped Juan tie-down. Roger returned and paid Juan, in currency, including an unexpected large bonus. Both he and Derek expressed their appreciation as they left the dock.

Afton handed Derek the keys when they reached the vehicle and got into the front passenger seat. Roger and Margo slide into the second seat as Margo said, "I was afraid I would never see you again."

He replied, "It will take more than a devastating earthquake to put me away, and you chose the right man to rescue me." Nothing more was said about his survival by either of them. Derek placed his bag in the rear compartment, got behind the wheel, and drove out of the city. Roger asked that they go to his plane first for clothes he had left there.

Fortunately, Margo had anticipated that and brought the pilots' keys. Everyone helped Roger transfer clothes on hangers, shoes, and boots to the third seat of the Range Rover. Roger also retrieved a rolled, wall-size aerial-photograph of the *estancia* on which he had the property boundary plotted and the bag in which he carried his field equipment.

On the way to the lodge, Margo provided Roger with her impressions of the lodge and those working there, formulated from her first few days staying there. She described the horror of the giant waves crashing into the hotel where she was staying on Easter Island and their escape from that island.

Afton told Derek that she and Rios had gone back to the site where the three of them had observed Andean deer browsing and brought back cuttings from bushes that showed browsing. She said that she was studying that plant and other, similar ones, growing in the region. Derek asked about what Bob Grayson had found so far and learned that he had found a fossiliferous bed of shale a few tens of feet above the floor of the ravine and had solicited the help of Rios to build a platform and ladder to allow him to start excavating that layer.

Roger wanted to see the cave where the giant sloth fossils had been found. At the parking lot near the cave, they all departed the vehicle and examined the life-size replica of the huge creature that stood by the entrance. A guided tour was forming, so Roger purchased tickets and they joined the tour. The tour guide explained that excavations were planned to find more bones of the sloth and to establish the fact that humans occupied the cave, with one objective being to determine if the sloth was extinct before humanoids lived in the region. Roger asked the age of early man remains found and was told that in several places in the country the dating of human remains had range from 13,000 to 10,000 years before the present, but theories imply there was much earlier human-like cultures.

The next stop was in front of Lautaro Lodge. They had been expected, so the pilots, the girls, and Rios came onto the front porch. Before joining them, Roger stood with his arm around Margo and looked, in amazement. He said to Margo: "This is a magnificent place."

Afton and Derek transferred Roger's things to the porch where Rios, Harriett and Heidi took them inside. The pilots welcomed Roger with sincere comments about how happy they were to see him again. The group went inside, and Margo introduced Roger to those already moving his things to the master bedroom. Afton got back in the vehicle as Derek moved it to the garage. He said, "You can now tell me how things have really been in my absence."

She replied, "Missus Richardson has proven to be a very moody person. One minute she is pleasant to others. The next minute she is barking unreasonable demands. The pilots do nothing but sleep, eat, and drink. I suspect that Margo drinks too much, also."

"And the 'good professor'?"

"He is as obnoxious as you will remember, very demanding, and shows no appreciation for anything done for him."

"Not a very compatible group. I hope the fox kits have survived life in captivity."

"They need to be moved back to the wild. I have seen where they killed and ate a mouse, so they should be able to feed themselves."

"While the others are providing Roger with a tour of the facilities, let's move the fox. I will take my bag to my quarters. If you will find a shovel and meet me there, we will build a den in the hill behind our rooms."

Tunneling into the base of the hill and excavating rooms and *runs,* later covered over by flat rocks and dirt, a den was constructed. Moving the kits was more of a challenge, but they were able to trap them in the box built into the den in the barn, wrap the box in canvas to keep them inside, and carry the box to the new den, where they were released at the mouth of the tunnel. They scampered inside. Satisfied with their efforts, Derek asked to see the cuttings from the deer forage.

The two of them were seated in Afton's workspace in the lower level of the main house when Rios escorted Roger to that level. Roger commented when he saw them, "You two are back to work already?"

Derek answered, "These cuttings of deer forage are a part of our studies to improve the food base of the Andean deer. I was anxious to see what Afton and Rios had collected."

"Continue on. Rios will show me the remainder of the facility. Lunch will be served soon. Please join us for that. Then, I would like to take a short ride into the hills to see some of our surroundings."

Arrangements for lunch had been made so that everyone in the lodge could sit at the dining room table and get better acquainted as they ate. It was a very pleasant time that lasted more than two hours. Leaving the table, Derek said that he and Rios would saddle horses and asked Roger if others were going to ride. "Just you and me," was the response.

Derek lead his client on the last part of the perimeter route he had ridden with Afton and Rios. Above the upper portion of the ravine where Doctor Grayson was working, he suggested they dismount and take a good look all around. To the southwest the *Ultima Esperanza*, the waterway on which *Puerto Natales* was located, could be seen. Derek explained it was named Last Hope by Juan Ladrilleros who was searching for the Strait of Magellan in 1557. Roger asked about the large structure visible on the shore north of the city and was told it was a cold storage facility when the area was the center of a large sheep industry that was being converted to a luxury hotel, called Singular Patagonia.

Roger walked to the termination of the ravine and studied the drainage channels that converged in that area while Derek held the horses. Returning to rejoin him, Derek pointed out where the dam and reservoir had been before the earthquake and the damage done by the floodwaters. Roger asked what his recommendations were regarding the reservoir site.

"The location of the dam was on trend of bedrock and my first thought was to rebuild the dam with a concrete core for the impoundment of another deep reservoir and create a fish hatchery below where floodwaters removed vegetation and soil. If the paleontologist plans to excavate in the cliffs once beneath the reservoir waters, a shallow reservoir and fish ponds lower down might be more appropriate. We should see what Doctor Grayson has found and talk with him about his plans. The best strata exposures in the area are along the sides of this ravine."

"We will do that tomorrow. Let's continue on the trail we are on for the remainder of this day."

As Derek had hoped, a small herd of Red Stag were seen where they had been seen, previously. The buck was enormous. Positioned where the deer were in plain sight, they watched them for a long time while they browsed through low brush.

"It will take a long time for me to lose my hunter's instinct and my desire for a trophy." Roger remarked. "What a great wall-display the head and antlers of that animal would make."

Derek responded, "It took me a long time to change, but I now prefer to observe and photograph wild animals such as those. If it meets with your approval, I plan to work with Rios in establishing prime places for doing that on your property."

"Do that and start an inventory of the populations of all wild animals that we can use as a baseline for expansion."

Rather than continuing-on the trail along the slope, Derek chose a trail he had not been on before that headed up the slope. At the crest of the highlands, the scene of the ice fields and snow-capped mountains that he had seen on his first day on the property unfolded in front of them. He commented what a fine painting could be created from this and other places along the crest.

"I so wish that Margo would come to places like this to paint," Roger said. "But I'm afraid she will insist on sites accessible by a vehicle."

Derek wanted to ask questions about where Margo had painted landscapes and if she ever traveled with him into the *bush,* as Marsha had, but he said nothing. They sat there, enthralled by the scene, for many minutes before starting back down the trail.

It was nearly dark when they returned to the barn. Derek offered to take care of the horses, and suggested Roger go to the house to meet with Doctor Grayson, who should be there ready for dinner.

When the horses they had ridden were put away and all fed, Derek went to his quarters to shower and dress for dinner. He had removed his jacket and shirt when there was a light rap on his door. He slipped his shirt back over his shoulders and open to door to find Afton. He invited her inside.

"You might consider taking your time to change," she said. "There is a bad scene in the main house."

Derek asked her to sit across from him at a small table and explain. She said that Roger had returned to find his wife very drunk, shouting at the girls over something she thought they had done wrong. Heidi and Harriett retreated to their quarters while Rios stood in the kitchen doorway, not knowing what to do, she told him.

"Were the pilots there? What did they do?" Derek asked.

"They were sitting in the living room with Bob Grayson. None of them said anything and did nothing. When Roger tried to calm his wife and guide her upstairs, she shouted foul language at him. I slipped down to the lower level and came to see you."

"Why don't you go to your quarters while I shower and change? I will join you there with a bottle of wine I brought back from up north. We will see if it is any good and allow time for things to settle down. We did not sign-on as referees in household or marital squabbles. If you see Rios, ask him to join us."

Afton had placed two wine glasses on her small table before she answered Derek's knock at her door. Her first comments were that Rios was trying to console Heidi and Harriett in his quarters, and that the girls were planning to leave and walk to the home of a neighbor beyond the highway.

Derek poured the wine, held a chair for Afton, and sat opposite her. Neither said anything more for several minutes as they sipped wine.

"Roger proved to be a fair cook on safari." Derek, eventually, commented. "We should sit tight and see what our leader does about dinner and the potential loss of some very good help. I feel terribly sorry for two lovely young women.

Hearing footsteps on the walkway, Afton and Derek sat quietly as Bob Grayson returned to his quarters. Afton opened her door to a gentle knock a few minutes later and invited Rios to join them. He refused a glass of wine. Afton took hers from the table, asked him to sit with Derek, and she sat on the edge of her bed.

Rios told them that he had convinced Heidi and Harriett not to leave that night, but they refused to go back to their quarters, so he had told them they could sleep in his bed. He would sleep on the floor. Derek asked if it was known what the girls had done to set Margo off the way it was explained to him. Neither had any ideas.

Knocking was heard. This time it sounded as if the knock was on his door, so Derek went to the walkway, followed by Afton and Rios. Roger was there holding a box.

"Rios showed me your unit, Derek," he said. "I have gathered up all the booze I could find, and I want you to keep it locked up for now. I considered pouring it all out but decided that sensible drinkers need not be deprived of a drink, now and then."

"We three were discussing what happened and if there was something we could do to help. I will open my door, and Rios can bring the box inside," Derek said, motioning to Rios.

Roger stood in silence next to Afton until the box was placed in a closet and Derek and Rios rejoined them. He then commented, "I prepared a hunter's stew in a large pot that should be ready to eat by now. I want you all to come to the dinner table and bring the young ladies who normally cook and Doctor Grayson. Eating together, we need to put this incident behind us, right away, or what has been initiated at this lodge will have been for naught."

Afton went back to the main house with Roger, set the table, filled bowls with the stew, and added plates of sliced bread and butter to the table. When Rios arrived with the unhappy girls, hanging their heads, the pilots were seated. Derek and Bob arrived and sat on each side of Afton. Roger took the chair at the head of the table. He commented, "My wife is sleeping it off. I have asked her to apologize to each one of you that she offended, personally, and informed her this was the beginning of her rehabilitation. Her drinking has been getting progressively worst over the past few months. It was booze that caused her to act as she did, nothing any of you did wrong. She is really a fine person when sober. You will all learn that over time."

As they ate, Roger made a point of speaking with each person at the table, asking them for suggestions on improving the household routine and their thoughts on improving the surroundings. He asked Rios about the power and was informed that public power had been restored and he had ordered propane, so they would be prepared for the next emergency.

Afton suggested that Heidi and Harriett go to their quarters after the meal, saying she would clear the table and wash up. All, except she and Derek, when to their rooms. The two of them cleaned up the dining room and kitchen before walking, together, to their quarters. An emotional evening ended in a sense of harmony.

Chapter Four
Mega-Fossil

Roger and his consultants were the only ones in the kitchen for an early breakfast. Afton ate her normal, small meal of juice, coffee, and toast. The others had pancakes, German-style, and sausage served to them by Heidi, with coffee and tea. Discussing the day's activities, Roger said he planned to go with Bob to examine the strata exposed in the ravine.

Derek remarked, "You should take the Range Rover. I was hoping that Afton and Rios could accompany me in gathering seeds from deer forage and begin planning a hothouse to propagate new plants to be set out in the spring."

Harriett said they should return to the kitchen before they left the compound, because she and Heidi would have lunches prepared for them. Derek and his team went to the barn and prepared horses. The Range Rover drove away as Afton went for the lunches. She found that the pilots were eating breakfast. Ted asked if there was something they could be doing.

Afton replied, "You two should consider your stay as a vacation and begin to enjoy the activities people spend real money to do down here. The girls will show you a closet in the back that contains a lot of fishing gear. Organize some of it and I will ask that you be taken to a stream *teaming* with fish as soon as the Range Rover is available. Derek is anxious to investigate the fish populations, so he may be excited about taking you. If you ride, Rios or one of the horse handlers that are on call, will take you to see some of the most beautiful scenery on earth, or you can hike."

Rejoining her team, Afton told them what she had told the pilots. "Excellent," Derek said. "I see more for us to do that needs the approval of our client, so I hope the pilots don't pressure him into moving-on too soon."

Roger was directed to park the vehicle at the mouth of the ravine. A short walk brought him and Doctor Grayson to scaffolding made of recently cut logs, tie together with rope, and a ladder to a working platform. The Doctor commented, "I spotted bone fragment in that three-foot bed of sandy clay above the platform through binoculars and that tall native built a way for me to examine it. I have had only a short time to examine the layer. I left my tools on the platform. Do you want to climb up and look?"

Roger replied, "The strata dip into the hill. I'll go up the ravine to where I can pick at the layer from the floor of the ravine and join you later."

Doctor Grayson climbed to the platform and began removing material in earnest. Roger walked further up the drainage, carrying a rock hammer, and examined the same bed at a lower level. Suddenly, he heard a loud scream and quickly turned to see his paleontologist fall backwards from the platform in a cloud of dust. He ran back to where he had fallen and found the doctor unconscious, but as soon as he raised him to a sitting position, consciousness returned, and he asked what had happened.

"It appears as if strata above where you were digging broke loose, fell against your chest, and pushed you from the platform. Are you all right?"

"Help me up to see!"

Standing, Bob replied there was pain in his back. That, he said, was to be expected, but he did not have any broken bones.

"I'll help you back to the vehicle and get you to your bed. Maybe there are some pain pills in the lodge. You stay down until the pain has subsided. Fossils can wait a bit longer to be discovered."

After he had helped Bob to his bed, Roger went to the kitchen. Harriet told him there was aspirin and pain-relief ointment in a medical kit. She would take care of the doctor.

Roger went back to the ravine and climbed the ladder to the excavation that Bob had started. In a layer of hard clay above where the sandy clay was being removed, exposed by the rock fall, was an astoundingly large bone. He was able to reach the lower part of the fossil. He tapped it with his rock hammer and removed some clay beneath it. Knowing that a mega-fossil that had been found was very important and that it would require removal by more than one person from a higher platform, he climbed down and returned to the compound. When Roger went to report his find to Bob, he took him his lunch, and suggested that as soon as he was able to supervise, a team should be organized to continue his excavation.

Heading back to take the vehicle to the garage, Roger saw his pilots on the porch of the main house. As a surprise to him, it appeared as if they were practicing casting with a fly-rod. He stopped to find out. Ned commented as he came to the steps, "I haven't fished since I was a boy and Ted never has, but Afton suggested we become like tourists and try it out."

"Fly-fishing is my favorite pastime," Roger responded. "I'll take you, if you found a rod for me and if someone told you where we should go."

"We were hoping you would volunteer, so we took a rod for you when we got one for ourselves and a tackle-box from a storage closet. Harriett said Herr Meister's friends preferred to fish on a river that crosses beneath the road we came on, closer to the ice fields."

"Have you seen Margo?" Roger asked.

"She is still in your room, as far as we know." Ted replied. "Heidi was preparing lunch to take up to her when we finished ours," Ned answered.

"I think we should give her more time by herself. Load up! Let's find a place to wet a fly."

Afton, Derek, and Rios rode to where they first saw the herd of Andean deer. There, the horses were tethered. The collecting of seeds from growth of deer forage was accomplished by the three of them traversing into a topographic basin through dense growth, each with a cloth sack. It was difficult work. The thick brush was almost impossible to walk through and the game trails were few. The clusters of seed were hard to free from the plants, but there were many individual seeds in each cluster, so the sacks they eventually filled held many hundreds of seeds.

Near where they had seen the puma kill a fawn, they sat in a grassy area and ate the lunch the girls had prepared for them and drank from a small stream of crystal-clear, rapidly flowing water. Derek had not brought a rifle with him from South Africa and had not located one in the compound. Rios, however, had the rifle he often took with him, carried on a sling over one shoulder. They felt safe.

The climb back to the horses took more than one-half hour. They had seen no deer, but the signs that a herd was still feeding in the area were seen everywhere. The sacks of seeds were tied to the saddles on the horses that Afton and Derek were riding. As Afton and Derek were transferring the sacks from the horses to the lower level of the main house, Heidi approached them, saying she had just finished making up their rooms. She explained the fall Bob had taken and her treatment of the pain in his back. Afton asked about Missus Richardson and was told that her sister had taken her a tray with lunch and found the breakfast she had taken to her room had not been touched.

"Others may think Margo should be left alone to contemplate her actions," Afton remarked. "I believe that is the worst thing for her. Let's leave the horses saddled, Derek. I will go invite her to take a ride with me."

It took several taps on the bedroom door before Margo opened it. Afton told her that she wanted to talk with her. With reluctance, Margo invited her inside and to a table from which she removed the uneaten meal.

"I understand that it is none of my business," Afton said. "But you should not stay cooped up in this room by yourself. You are in a magnificent setting and those in the lodge have forgiven you for anything you have done or said that may have caused them concern. I would like to take you on a horseback ride and show you some on the amazing botany that has so excited me. I assume you ride and have brought riding clothes."

The response was, "I have ridden since childhood and I have appropriate clothes and boots with me."

"Then, you should join me. Two horses stand saddled out front."

"I will. Thank you for asking."

"Great! I will have the girls prepare us lunch," Afton said, ignoring what she had seen on the tray and the fact she had eaten a lunch already.

She had fruit for two, sandwiches, a thermos of tea and tin cups placed in a sack by Harriett, who voiced her feelings that Afton was doing the right thing. She put the lunch in a saddle-bag and was waiting for Margo when she came to the front of the porch. The beautiful woman joined Afton with a smile on her face and mounted the horse that Derek had ridden, and Afton adjusted the stirrups for her. Derek and Rios were in Afton's workspace starting to separate seeds.

Afton led the way along the access road for a time, then they descended into the lower portion of the basin where the seed gathering took place. On the slope ahead of them was a mass of late-blooming flowers, forming a carpet-like appearance, framed by tall, dense ferns. The stream cascaded through large boulders, creating deep, clear pools. Alton suggested they dismount and savor the view from a large boulder adjacent to the trail. Margo referred to the view as enthralling as she climbed to sit on the boulder. Afton tied the horses to a tree and sat beside her. Over the next two hours, a friendship began to develop between these two young women in a setting new and strange to them both.

They discussed meeting each other, briefly, in London. Margo provided Afton with the story of her life prior to that: She was born into a wealthy, titled family in central England and attended the best private schools. She had never had to work, except as a charity worker. Boredom caused her to take lessons from an artist friend of her mother. Painting with oil on canvas had been her only escape from a tedious existence until she met Roger. She had hoped to become a part of his busy business career and help him, but he made no room for her in that part of his life. It was as if she had become what was being referred to as a "trophy wife." She longed to do something meaningful with her life.

Her drinking was not mentioned. Afton thought it would help her cope if that was discussed, but she decided not to mention that. They eat and drank tea as they enjoyed the settling.

"I have taken hundreds of photographs of settings like that before us, wishing I had the talent to capture such scenes on canvas." Afton commented. "You should pursue your painting and I have never been to a place where the scenes that need to be painted are so numerous."

Margo said, "Roger told he how he chose you to come here to work for him. Have you always had interest in botany?"

"It's my passion, really. I am happy working every hour, each day, with plants. My collection since arriving here now numbers in the hundreds, including all the species you can see from here."

Their discussions turned personal. When asked, Afton told Margo that she had never been married but had dated several men, none of whom seemed right to her. Margo's next question was her feelings about Derek. Her reply was, "Derek is a very handsome, kind, personable young man. We have become good friends and I enjoy being with him a very much. Whether or not my feels lead to love is unknowable."

"Roger, a widower, was my first love. My love for him has never faded," Margo said. "I know he misses his first wife deeply. I must work harder to hang-on to his love for me."

The sun was low in the sky when Afton and Margo started back. The only discussion as they rode side by side, was about the episode the day before. Margo asked if Afton thought those at the lodge would ever forgive her. She was told that they had already forgiven her, and Afton suggested she become involved in what has happening on the *estancia* named for her.

The fishermen had returned in the early evening. While Ned and Ted were delivering their catch to the kitchen and bragging about those fish, Roger went to see to his wife. He found the bedroom in proper order, but no Margo. He rushed back to the kitchen to learn from Harriett that she had gone horseback riding with Afton. That pleased him.

Roger and Derek were sitting on the porch where Afton and Derek sat, most evenings, when the horsewomen were seen coming up the road. They had devised a plan to have lumber brought from the city to expand the scaffold at the ravine excavation and start the construction of a hothouse. Margo dismounted when they reached the porch and rushed up the steps into Roger's arms. Derek left the two of them alone and walked to the barn with Afton, leading one horse. Putting the horses away, Derek asked about the ride and received a response: "We had a good time and learned a lot about each other. Margo is a fine person. We should try to help her fit-in here."

All those at the lodge were together when dinner was served that evening. With great difficulty, Doctor Grayson had walked, stiffly, still in pain, from his quarters and was helped to a chair at the head of the dining room table by Heidi. Roger and Margo sat across from Afton and Derek. The pilots, still bragging about catching the salmon that was being served, sat next to each other, across from Rios. A lot had happened that day and those events were discussed. The highlight mentioned, after exaggerated stories about fly fishing, was Roger's discovery of a mega-fossil in the excavation that Bob had started.

The dimension of the bone he described was amazing. The paleontologist conveyed his excitement and the fact he could hardly wait to examine it, saying it was likely a leg bone of a giant sloth. Margo described the beautiful wildflowers that she had been shown on her ride. Afton asked about the success that Derek and Rios had with sorting the brush seeds they had collected and was told by Derek that they had many hundreds, but the seeds had a hard shell that might have to be parted for the seeds to germinate. Rios and the girls listened to those discussions conducted in English, understanding very little.

Roger spoke in Spanish when he discussed the events planned for the next day: He and Rios would take the flat-bed truck in the garage to the city to purchase wood for expanding the scaffold at the excavation and items necessary to construct a hoisting system that would allow the lowering of large fossils to the bottom of the ravine. They would also buy bags of concrete-mix for supports for a hothouse and return with two of Rios' friends to help in construction efforts and in excavating. The new-hires would be allowed to commute in the truck in the garage and would bring other supplies as needed each day.

At the end of the meal, Margo stood. She asked Heidi and Harriett to come back to the table from the kitchen. With tears in her eyes, she apologized for her earlier actions and promised that it would not happen again. Those leaving the dining room did so with good feelings for the owner's wife.

Roger and Rios ate an early, light breakfast the next morning and were getting in the truck that Rios had brought in front of the porch when Margo joined them and asked to go with them. Roger held the door as she slid into the middle of the bench seat next to Rios and he sat next to her. It was a crew-cab, so there would be room for the two men they planned to pick up on the second seat. Before they reached the road to the airport, Margo asked if they could go to the plane to pick up her easel, canvas, and paints, telling them that she had brought the pilots' keys. She was let out next to the plane and within minutes she returned with a large leather case she placed between the seats.

Rios' friends, Raoul and Luis, were neighbors, living on adjacent farms not far from the airport. Rios explained that they had often helped Herr Meister and worked as horse handlers at times. The two of them were waiting in front of a small home surrounded by flower and vegetable gardens when Rios stopped there. They were somewhat shorter than Rios, but also husky, handsome young men, with brown skin and black hair. Both spoke Spanish. Rios introduced them as they got into the truck.

Harriett had asked Roger to go to the market that delivered food and supplies ordered by her; things that were delivered weekly. She wanted him to make sure that continued. The market was the first stop in town. Roger went inside, paid an overdue bill, and changed the account name. Margo walked around the well-stocked market. The others stayed in the truck.

At a lumber and supply store, the native men began loading the things listed by Roger in a notebook he gave them. Roger and Margo walked around the business district noting the types of businesses and looking for a bank. The bank they found was not yet open, so they went to a café for coffee and tea. There were many people in the café, including Juan Aparicio, the boat owner. He acknowledged Roger and told the others who Roger was and about his arrival on his boat, so several stopped to welcome the couple to town. Both Roger and Margo voiced their appreciation.

When the bank opened, they went inside. Margo waited on a front bench while Roger was ushered into the manager's office. Returning to where Margo sat, Roger informed her that the telegraph was back on line, so he was able to have money wired here from their London bank, with which he opened an operating account, and he had received bank drafts to pay for things they needed for the improvement of *Estancia Margo*.

The truck was loaded when Roger and Margo returned to the lumber and supply store to pay for the material. Although, it was not yet lunchtime, Roger suggested that they eat at a restaurant in town, because it would be afternoon before they got back to the lodge and the girls would not be expecting them. Rios chose a roadside restaurant near the edge of town. Seated at a corner table, they were soon attended to by two girls who obviously knew the young men. Friendly chatter soon began in a native language. It was some time before the ordering of lunch was addressed. Roger commented that they were, obviously, where he and Margo could be assured of a good meal and asked Rios to order for them.

The meal served was spicy pork loin slices, fried potatoes and greens. Leaving the restaurant, Margo commented that their companions were, obviously, popular, illegible bachelors. On the way to the lodge, the young men were asked if all of them were of the Tehuelche tribal group and where most of their people lived. Raoul said he was of the Mapuche tribe, some of whom still lived in groups outside the cities and were well-known for their crafts.

The sacks of concrete mix were unloaded near the barn, at a place Roger and Derek thought the hothouse should be built to receive the most sun. Margo left them and carried the leather case with her art equipment and supplies to the main house.

There was still too much mud at the previous reservoir site to drive into the ravine, so the lumber for that job had to be carried some distance. However, as Raoul and Luis did that, Rios and Roger began the required work, using the tools from the box that Rios had tied on the bed of the truck. The working platform was raised to the level of the exposed, large bone. Planks, rather than logs, were placed to form a working space. Roger realized that, eventually, the strata from that level to the rim of the ravine would have to be removed and examined for additional fossils before the excavation was expanded, but with the hoist they installed, all fossils could be lowered to the ravine floor. The material removed, he reasoned, could be used in the dike of a new reservoir that Derek had suggested. By the time daylight began to fade, the excavation site was ready for the resumption of work when Doctor Grayson was able to do that.

With Raoul behind the wheel, the truck was driven to the front of the lodge where Rios and Roger got out and the new help started for home. Roger went through the main door and Rios to the door into the lower level to see how Afton and Derek were doing with the seeds. Rios found them with baskets full of seeds, but they were pondering a problem, which Afton explained: "As Derek mentioned, the seeds have a hard shell that in nature is spilt by fire to allow germination. We must find a way to do that, manually, before planting the seeds in the new hothouse."

Rios had a suggestion, "My people ground maize for centuries between two pieces of sandstone. That would be a slow process, but it should work."

She asked, "Could you find such pieces of sandstone?"

"There are those that are used to make coarse-ground meal for some recipes, behind the kitchen."

"That's great! Could you get them for us?"

Rios went to the kitchen where he found Margo helping with dinner. "These young ladies are teaching me to cook," she told him. "Dinner will be ready soon." He continued-on to get the grinding-rocks, explaining how they were going to be used.

Returning to Afton's workspace, Rios reported what he had learned in the kitchen. "Let's see if we can break-down some seed coverings before we go to dinner," Afton suggested.

Afton rolled a rounded piece of sandstone over a hand-full of seeds laid on a heavily-wore flat rock. Taking a few seeds to view with her microscope, she announced that this old-fashioned technique was going to work.

The three of them went to their quarters to wash up and change for dinner. Having heard Afton in the adjacent unit, Bob was waiting for her on the walkway. They walked together to the dining room. He no longer walked in a crouch to lessen the pain and told her that he would be able to resume his work the next day.

Setting out the meal, Harriett told everyone gathered that Margo had prepared the chicken dish. Kissing Roger on the forehead before she did, Margo sat next to him. The day's accomplishments were discussed, and Margo was complimented. She responded by saying that she hoped that they would like the first dish she had ever made and gave credit to Harriett for her instructions. She told them she would continue to learn to cook.

The next morning, Raoul and Luis returned with panels of glass and more lumber. They helped Rios cut straight logs, thinning a wooded area near the road, dug holes for the hothouse supports and set the logs in concrete. Roger and Bob went to the ravine excavation in the Range Rover.

From the new platform, more clay was carefully removed from the large fossil. Bob announced that, as he has expected, it was a leg bone of a *Milodon*, and expressed his opinion that more of the creature would be found at this site. As they worked, they discussed the expected final shape of the excavation. Bob was insistent that a screening system be established before more than the material immediately around the leg bone was removed, because all fossil evidence from the site needed to be preserved. They stopped work when the huge fossil was nearly free, to await others to help. Climbing down from the platform, they took their tools and began to examine the fossiliferous layer where it could be reached, heading up the ravine. They found no other fossils, but walking back, looking at the scaffold, Roger realized that high water in the channel could undermine the legs and destroy it. He left the paleontologist to his work and drove back to the compound.

Unexpectedly, he saw his pilots were dressed in warm clothes and were headed on a hike, they told him that they were planning to go beyond the woodland where Rios harvested timber. For their safety, Ned carried Rios' rifle over his shoulder. Roger asked about Margo and was told she was in the lower level working with Afton. *My love has taken the advice she said she was given by Afton,* Roger thought. *"And plans to make herself useful."* He chose not to bother Afton and Margo and walked to where the work on the hothouse was progressing. Hearing more hands were needed to move the huge fossil, that crew moved to the ravine. Rios, as he was asked to do, drove there in the motor-grader.

At the base of the scaffold, Derek constructed a box into which the fossil could be placed. Raoul and Luis climbed to the platform to help Bob. Roger directed Rios in the grader work to move the stream-channel away from the legs of the scaffold and to build a berm around the legs.

When the bone was free from strata that was several tens of thousands of years old, and it was laid on the platform, Derek raised the hoist attached to a sling he had fashioned from canvas. With the bone in the sling, it was lowered into the box he had built. Roger came to provide guidance and released the hoist clamp. The others stood around the box, in awe of the fossil, as Raoul backed the truck on a roadway Rios had cleared of mud to the flowing steam. With two on each side of the box, holding straight limbs that Derek had placed beneath the box, it was carried to the flatbed and slide onto the truck. The first discovery from an excavation that was to become well-known was taken to the compound. All from the ravine followed the truck back there.

The largest work area on the lower level of the main house was set-side for the fossil collection. Through the doorway leading from the walkway in front of the living quarters, the box was moved there and placed on the floor, to be moved again when a work bench and shelves were built. Afton and Margo joined the others as this was accomplished. Heidi and Harriett had prepared lunch for everyone.

The work crews ate in the dining room. As they ate, Bob asked Rios if there was any coarse screen on the place from which material from the excavation would be screened in search of fine fossils or artifacts. Roger commented that he had anticipated such a need and a roll of one-quarter-inch screen had been brought with the last load, so after lunch, the needed screen-frames and supports were built. When Derek asked how the seed preparation was progressing, Afton reported that with Margo's good help, they would have deer forage seeds ready to plant as soon as the hothouse was finished.

Everyone was busy all afternoon. Roger and Bob drove back to the ravine, climbed to the excavation, and began to examine the layer behind where the fossil was removed. Afton and Margo went back to grinding-off seed shells and the others worked on a screening system and framework for glass panels.

At the end of the day, Raoul and Luis drove home in the truck with a list of things that would be needed the next day. Rios fed the horses and went to his quarters. Work with the seeds was still underway, so Derek went to Afton's workspace before going to his rooms. Roger joined them there and asked if the pilots had returned. No one had an answer for him, so he went to the second floor. Returning a few minutes later, he reported that Ted and Ned had not returned and asked Derek to go with him to look for them.

Derek drove the Range Rover to the woodland where trees were harvested. He and Roger got out and started into the area. They had not gone far before they met the pilots. Both began to explain, excitedly, the day they had experienced, saying they had seen magnificent scenery and many wild animals, including a puma and giant, flightless birds. Their descriptions continued during the drive back to the compound, and through dinner that evening. They listened to discussions of the things that the others at the table had accomplished that day, but Ned remarked that being a tourist was much more exciting.

Chapter Five
Near Disaster

Doctor Grayson, with Luis to help him, continued the work at the fossil excavation for the next two weeks, without any additional discoveries. Work on a small hothouse was completed and benches were built upon which flats containing seeds planted in potting soil were placed. Most of the seeds planted where those collected from deer forage, but seeds of flowering plants that Afton had collected were also planted. Raoul joined the work in the ravine when the hothouse construction was completed.

Since arriving in Patagonia, Afton had wanted to study areas along the retreating ice fields for any plants emerging from centuries being covered by thick ice. With permission from Roger and agreement from Rios to take her there, she planned a trip. Derek planned to go to the place where the pilots told him they had seen rheas, a bird he had yet to observe. Roger decided this would be a good time for him and Margo to observe the ice fields and glaciers from the air.

Derek's journey was by far the shortest. He needed only to get to the grasslands, northeast of the lodge. By referring to the books on wildlife he had purchased, he hoped to be able to identify the species that had been seen, one of three that were prevalent in the country. Two of those species were considered threatened of extinction due to hunting to obtain skins for leather, feathers, and meat. He chose to make the journey on Old Thunder.

Rios was going to drive Afton in the truck, and they prepared for a two-day trip. The plan was to spend time at Patagonia Camp, stay one night there and go on a southeast arm of the ice field. Rios showed Roger, on a regional map, where those in the plane could look for them on the day they had decided to fly.

The pilots, Margo, and Roger started for the airport in the Range Rover early on that day, with Roger driving. At the terminal parking lot, Roger received a call on his satellite telephone from Harriett to inform him that a government official from *Ultima Esperanza* Province had come to see him. Postponing the flight was discussed, but Roger made the decision that the others should make the flight while he returned to meet with the government man and called Harriett back and asked her to entertain the man until he arrived. They had left the lodge without breakfast, expecting to eat at a café in the terminal, so the pilots escorted Margo there. She ate only a croissant with her coffee. Ted and Ned had a full meal that included eggs and spicy sausage that was advertised as a special.

At the plane, Margo got onboard and strapped herself in a seat just behind the copilot-seat. The pilots completed a pre-flight check and what was to be a sightseeing flight began. The low clouds and fog had lifted when they flew over Patagonia Camp, located above a sparkling turquoise-colored lake just outside *Torres del Paine* National Park. As the plane approached the ice field, it descended to a low altitude, so they could look for Afton and Rios, but no one saw them. The hikers noticed the plane some distance away. Afton was on her hands and knees collecting plants and placing them in a plastic bag. Rios had hiked to the edge of the ice and was astounded by the flow of water. The flight continued northward, circled around a high mountain and descended for a look at hikers on the ice sheet once more.

One of the engines on the Beechcraft Baron sputtered and appeared to be dying. Naturally, Margo was near panic, but she was told that they would make it back to the airport, safely, when the engine began to run smoothly again. They would have made it back without a serious incident if not for the reaction of the pilots to what they had eaten. Ted, in the pilot's seat, was the first to become sick. He left his seat and went into the head, where he vomited. Trying to return to his seat, he became dizzy and collapsed. Margo tried, in vain, to move him.

Ned asked her to take over the plane while he got his companion to a reclined seat. She had spent a lot of time relieving one of the pilots on long flights, so she did as asked. That required her to move into the pilot's seat. Before Ned could return to the cockpit, food poisoning hit him. He, too, vomited in the head and became very dizzy, but he did not pass out. Back in his seat, Ned realized that in his condition he could not function properly and told Margo she would have to land the plane.

Panic now overcame Margo. She had never performed a landing. Ned told she could do it, with his constant directions. His direction for her to line up the plane with the runway on a gradual descent was given after Ned had reported to the control tower the emergency and the need for an ambulance. The right engine again began to sputter.

"What do I do, now?" Margo exclaimed.

Ned responded, "Say focused on the runway. We can only hope the engine does not die."

"Are you not able to take over?"

"I can focus on nothing. My whole body is shutting down. You can do this. When the wheels touch, push down the throttle all the way and let the plane roll to a stop. This is a long runway." He showed her how to shut-down the engines and told her to do that when the plane stopped.

By the time the plane rolled to a stop, Ned had passed out and the right engine had died. Margo shut the other engine down, released herself from the restraints over her shoulders, and rushed to open the door to let two paramedics inside. Collapsed in a passenger seat, she watched as the pilots were taken to an ambulance.

The official that Roger met with at the lodge was Juan Ledesma. He was making a tour of the province to document damage from the earthquakes. The absence of significant damage at *Estancia Margo* was a surprise to him. Roger took the opportunity to determine the proper procedures and channels that would be important in obtaining government approval of improvements and changes in land use that he anticipated. After the meeting, Roger drove back to the airport. He was in a lounge watching the sky for his plane when he saw emergency vehicles on the move. Rushing to the control tower, he was told about the emergency.

The airport director was headed to the runway. When Roger told him that it was his plane that had the emergency, the director offered to take Roger with him to the runway. They arrived to see the pilots taken to the ambulance. Roger ran to the plane and climbed onboard and found Margo, still in a rear seat. She stood, and they embraced, as Roger asked what had happened. After hearing Margo's report, he exclaimed, "You took the controls and made the landing, my love?"

"I did, but I don't know how I did it. It was the most frightening time of my life."

"Come. The airport director is outside. I will ask him to take us to the terminal and have the plane towed to a maintenance hangar."

The director was as amazed as Roger had been when he learned that Margo had landed the plane for the first time in her life. He complimented her for her courage when he dropped them at the Range Rover.

At the hospital in *Puerto Natales*, they learned that the stomachs of the pilots had been pumped and they were conscious, lying in beds in the same room. A doctor told them that he thought they should stay overnight for observation.

The pilots were discussing the ordeal when Margo and Roger went to their room. Ted said he could remember little about what had happened. Ned told Margo that she had saved their lives, and hers. Both pilots swore they would never again eat in a strange place before a flight. Leaving the room, Roger told them he would come to take them to the lodge the next morning.

Back at the maintenance hangar, Roger instructed the maintenance manager to overhaul or replace the engine on his plane that had been an added problem on what was to have been a short sightseeing flight. Margo suggested, when Roger returned to the vehicle, that they drive to Patagonia Camp. She said it had been a magnificent sight from the air, and that she needed to clear her mind. The trip there took nearly an hour. What they found was a resort community with paved roads, traffic lights, shops, and a hotel, in addition to the igloo-shaped kurts scattered among dense vegetation in the hills. The views of the lake and waterfalls were extraordinary. A brochure provided the reason that Afton had wanted to stop there before going to the ice fields. There was a forest of southern Beech trees, *Nothofagas antartica*, unique to parts of the southern hemisphere and other rare plants growing in the area.

They went to the hotel restaurant for dinner where they encountered Juan Ledesma eating alone. He invited them to his table, explaining that he was continuing his examination of earthquake damage. Roger introduced Margo, as they sat with him, and Roger explained the near tragic event he had missed while meeting with him earlier. The discussions at the table included the topic of the electric-power grid of the country that led to nearly complete loss of electricity for general uses. Mr. Ledesma told them about government programs to expand hydroelectric facilities in several parts of the country and the opposition by environmental groups that delayed such projects. He summarized the situation, "Under one national administration, some projects are advanced, only to be stopped again by an administration of a different political party."

Roger replied, "The melting ice sheets and the huge variation in elevations provide tremendous opportunities for hydroelectric projects. I have been involved in the development of small power-producing hydro-plants to serve local communities in several parts of the world. In none of those areas has there been an expanding supply of free-flowing water and such elevation drops. Your country should seriously consider such projects."

The response from Juan was, "I don't know about the country, but I think I can convince my provincial government to look into such potential. Would you provide your expertise?"

"I would be happy to do so. I am now a part-time resident in the province."

Leaving the table, the three shook hands and Mr. Ledesma told Roger to expect him and others in the local governments to visit him to discuss this and other matters in the future. Juan insisted that Roger and Margo had been his guests and paid the bill. Part of the drive back to the lodge was in the dark. Those who had been involved in other activities that day had returned before them and eaten. Afton and Rios had returned in time for those helping Doctor Grayson, who had spent one night in Rios' quarters, to take the truck home. Afton and Derek were sitting in the living room. Margo and Roger joined them.

The wonderful country each had seen that day was discussed by them. Nothing concerning the near disaster was mentioned. The topic of hydropower generation was brought up by Roger. "It is ironic that you should bring that up," Afton commented. "I once worked on an Environment Impact Statement involving a pipeline from a high-elevation lake in Idaho to a hydro-plant to generate more than a mega-watt of electricity for a small community. Throughout my travels this day, thinking about the massive blackout, I asked myself why such facilities, on steep slopes in this region, had not been built."

"Probably due to the lack of foresight by politicians," Roger responded.

Derek had a contribution to make: "It seems to me that natural depressions filled by underflow from the melting of the massive ice and lakes impounded by marginal moraines, the overflow from which flows down steep drainages, causing erosion, would be logical water sources to pipe to generators and limit erosion. If the intake to the pipe is situated below where such standing water freezes, the generation could be year-around."

"Keep those thoughts in mind," Roger said, as he and Margo left to go up to their bedroom. "We may have installed similar thoughts in the mind of a politician this evening who might ask us to undertake such projects."

Margo was still not able to get the events of the flight out of her mind. When they went to bed, Roger sensed that and told her, once again, how brave she had been and how proud he was of her. Jokingly, he suggested she should consider flying lessons and a license. To his surprise, she replied that she would like to do that, telling him that her biggest fear during the entire event was not knowing what she would do if Ned passed out during the decent. She added, "I felt confident that I would be able to get us on the runway with instructions from him, but if the plane touched down and an engine failed, completely, and he was not able to advise me, I envisioned disaster."

As they fell asleep, Roger held her, tightly. He told her that he had married an amazing woman.

The activities of all working on *Estancia Margo* were underway after Margo and Roger finished breakfast the next morning. Roger made the rounds to all of them and Margo stayed with the girls and explained to them how the pilots had eaten bad food at the airport that required overnight hospitalization. She said nothing about her landing the plane.

Rios was installing sprinkler irrigation in the hothouse and a buried, water-line extension from the barn. Doctor Grayson and his commuting helpers were busy in the fossil excavation and he reported that they were removing clay from around what could be another large bone. Derek was doing research in his workspace next to Afton's on his laptop computer. Afton had the most interesting things to show and tell him: "If you look carefully at these dead-looking clumps of moss I collected at the edge of the retreating ice," she said. "You will see new growth, meaning the plants are not dead but have survived under the ice for at least several hundred years. The last advance of ice to cover them probable occurred during the Little Ice Age from the 1500s to about 1850. I have a lot more plants to examine that I collected, yesterday, but it is likely that such regeneration has occurred in species of lichen, as well."

Roger responded, "That is an amazing discovery, worthy of further study and the publication of your findings."

"I plan to see if I can grow clones from my collected plants to further document my findings. This could add greatly to our knowledge of glaciation. I will do research to see what other botanists are finding. I'm certain studies like mine are going on elsewhere, in the Arctic, the Antarctic, and in other parts of Patagonia."

"What I see is a better understanding of natural land restoration. These and other plants re-establishing ground cover will reduce erosion of the soil profile over which advances of ice occurred, allowing earlier, beneficial use of the land. That is one positive element of climate change that would be important in sparsely populated agrarian areas on the earth and might create investment opportunities. You are involved in important scientific research, Afton. I am very proud of you."

The next morning, Roger and Margo went to pick up the pilots. They had been released from the hospital and were sitting in a reception area, anxious to leave. It was a happy reunion. Margo escorted them to the vehicle while Roger made payment for the hospital services and was told payment for the ambulance services had to be paid at the airport. On the drive to the airport, Roger announced that Margo had decided that she wanted to take flying lessons. "I need to be better prepared to help you gentlemen," Margo commented. "We were very lucky, yesterday. As much as we all fly, an extra qualified pilot would be a good thing. I dread to think about the outcome of the last flight had both of you passed out at once."

Ned reminded them that he was a qualified instructor pilot, with international credentials, and said he would be very receptive to giving Margo lessons. Adding, "You proved you have what it takes to be a great pilot: courage, quick-thinking, and common sense."

From the parking lot at the airport, Roger went to the terminal to pay for the ambulance services and to discuss the food poisoning with the Airport Director. The others walked to the maintenance hangar. The director informed Roger that several people had become ill after eating in the airport café before it was determined that contaminated, imported sausage was the cause and another, local supplier was found.

Learning the recommendation of the mechanics was that an engine should be replaced, Ned informed the maintenance manager that the owner of the plane would arrive, soon, to discuss that with him and asked about rental planes. They were shown a Diamond Aircraft, single-engine, Turbo Star, parked outside, and were examining the plane when Roger arrived. The decisions were made that the engine replacement was the prudent thing to do and that Ned should give Margo lessons in the rental plane while that was being done. A schedule of rental times was created, and on their way back to the lodge, Roger asked Ted to look-into the lease of a helicopter, with a pilot. The possible need for such an aircraft was discussed.

A few days later, Juan Ledesma and three other officials of the provincial government arrived at the lodge to talk with Roger and his people about small hydroelectric power plants. Roger escorted them to the conference room on the lower level, where the girls served them tea and coffee, and he asked Afton and Derek to attend an informal meeting.

After making introductions, Roger initiated the discussions: "My company has invested in small power plants like those that I envision for your country. One that proved very successful was in an area of high mountains with a limited water supply. At that plant, water flows down less than four-hundred vertical meters in a pipe-line from a lake, generates power consumed in the near-by mountain community, and discharged into a reservoir. In off-peak hours, an electric pump raises the water back to the lake and the process is repeated. Here, with the retreating ice sheets and mountain glaciers, you have huge volumes of water and elevation drops like few places on earth. Power could be generated in your province by water flowing in pipelines or natural channels to the sea."

Mister Ledesma replied, "That is an intriguing concept."

"My associate showed me his research that I would like him to present to you."

Derek made a presentation: "The concept is not new. A plant operated in Telluride, Colorado in 1895 and one build in 1929, outside Ottenbach, Switzerland, is still operating. There are more than 45,000 in China, several more in other parts of Asia, five in the United States, two in Europe, and one in Africa. The generating capacities range from about one megawatt to more than fifty. As Mister Richardson indicated, your country has the free-flowing water and elevation differences for this to become an important part of your overall energy structure."

"Why are there not more such plants in the United States?" one of the men asked.

The answer Roger gave, was, "The permitting and regulatory processes are too lengthy and costly, even though no other source of energy can be developed with so little damage to the environment. Furthermore, huge investor-owned and government-owned entities want to see return on the massive projects they have funded."

"Would your company we willing to undertake feasibility studies for our province?" Mister Ledesma asked.

Roger responded, "I assembled my professional group to conduct evaluations and to devise improvements to the land I purchase, but I see such studies as an extension of the work that they have begun, particularly related to environmental issues. Furthermore, the young lady with us has made some discoveries that will affect land use in areas of retreating ice sheets. We could concentrate feasibility studies in areas where both power generation and future land use can be considered."

"In choosing possible project sites," the government-man who had not yet spoken commented, "You should remember the people who need reliable electricity are widely separated in our province, so transmission of power must be a major consideration."

"You are certainly right about that," Roger replied. "Do you gentlemen want me to prepare a proposal for our assistance to you?"

"Please do," Juan said as he and the others stood to leave, "and we thank you very much for what we have learned this day."

Roger walk with the government officials to their vehicle. Afton and Derek were still in the room discussing what had transpired when Roger returned and suggested they begin a search for a possible site for a 50-megawatt hydroelectric plant within a hundred miles for *Puerto Natales*, telling them that as soon as an engine on the company plane had been replaced or a helicopter lease arrangement secured, they could begin aerial reconnaissance.

"Did engine trouble develop on the flight a few days ago?" Afton asked. "We had heard the problem was bad food eaten by the pilots."

That question was answered by Roger. He explained the entire event and the heroic efforts of Margo in saving herself, the pilots, and the plane. Both Afton and Derek voice their astonishment and pride in Margo. At dinner that night, the story was repeated for the benefit of the others. Margo blushed at the compliments she received.

Activities on the *estancia* continued and Afton and Derek began research on possible hydroelectric sites in the region. Roger decided he should begin to look more closely at the land he had purchased. That began by placing the large aerial photograph he had acquired on the wall in the conference room and studying the features shown. On a series of daytime hikes he took, Ted went with him.

The routes Ned chose during the flights in the smaller, rented airplane, while giving Margo instructions, did not take them over the ice fields or high-mountain terrane, but on the days when the weather was clear, they were able to see the majesty of much of southern Patagonia. They flew the entire waterway that was referred to as the Strait of Magellan, from the Pacific Ocean inlet to a connected narrow, rock-bound channel, above a series of bodies of water of various dimensions that connected to the Atlantic Ocean. Both were amazed that a sea route with so many narrow passageways could have been used by ocean-traversing ships for so many centuries. The size of the city of *Punta Arenas*, on the straits, was a surprise to them.

Margo had made many landings on the runway where she had adverted disaster. She was asked to land at the airport near *Punta Arena* on a windy, foggy day, which she did with confidence. In a taxi, they took the opportunity to tour a part of the city, some 20 kilometers from the airport. Upon leaving the area, they flew over coal-mining operations to take many photographs, as Roger had asked them to do. For the cross-country phase of her instructions, they flew across the pampas to *Bahia Blanca* in Argentina. Returning, they flew-over and photographed more coal mines for Roger, in the *Rio Rubio* region.

On the day chosen for Margo's first solo flight, Roger and Ted went with the instructor and student to the airport. The observers watched from the maintenance hangar, where Roger also checked on the progress of the engine replacement. Margo flew over *Puerto Natales* and in a wide circle headed across the highlands and pampas to the northeast, out of their sight. The observers moved to their plane. Ned told Roger that Margo had been the best student he had ever worked with, telling him that she had exceptional eye-hand coordination and a was very quick learner. He said she developed nearly unbelievable confidence, in part, he thought from her success in avoiding disaster on her first landing. Ted took the opportunity to straighten out everything in the plane cabin while Roger and Ned waited in reclined seats. A low pass over the hangar alerted them to Margo's return. The three of them went to the front of the hangar to watch a perfect landing.

Gleeful would describe Margo's bearing after she parked the plane next to the hangar, climbed down, and joined them. She received embraces from each of them with words that reflected their feelings of a job well done. Ned signed her flight record and they all walked to the Range Rover. Roger announced that this day should be celebrated, and he drove to a waterfront restaurant in *Puerto Natales*. They each ordered a seafood dinner. Margo declined the offer of champagne. Even though she told them that if they chose to have a drink that would not tempt her, they all had tea with their meals.

A man came to their table when they were preparing to leave and announced, "My name is Henry Morrison. I represent a company in Australia and I am on a fact-finding mission here. Would you be able to give me a few minutes of your time?"

Roger replied, "Pull up a chair. What facts might we be able to offer you?"

"My company is considering expanding fish-farming in the sound and I am trying to determine local support for that. I was told you are from a nearby *estancia*, so I thought you might have opinions about such plans."

"Aquaculture is an industry that I have investigated for investment opportunities," Roger responded. "For an industry engaged in increasing the food supply and taking pressure off ocean harvests of fish, the amount of opposition from environmental groups I find astounding. Every organized group will oppose your plans, use every tactic, including spreading false information, to prevent any such development. If, heaven forbid, there is an accidental release of fish or a disease spreads to natural populations at any of your other operations, your chances of securing support and permits will be close to nil."

"Our record of sound practices in other areas of subsea-pen development has been good, Mister Morrison offered.

"Let's hope it remains so. I would be in support of pens in the sound, if your studies prove they can be installed and operated in a proper way. I am considering raising fresh-water-fish on our *estancia*. We might engage in joint marketing efforts."

"I appreciate what you have told me," Mister Morrison said as he got up to leave the table. The others walked with him from the restaurant.

Chapter Six
Power-Plant Planning

A few days later, Margo asked Roger if they could drive to *Punta Arenas*, telling him that she was so surprised and impressed by this European-like city at the end of the earth when she visited, briefly, during flight training and that she would like to spend more time there. She told him that Rios had told her it was a three-hour drive, but the only road crossed a part of Argentina. Roger agreed, and they left Lautaro Lodge early one morning. The drive was in exceptionally clear and sunny weather through grasslands. They crossed into and out of Argentina without incident or delay. The waterway extension of the Strait of Magellan and the shore-side city were seen some distance away, with the Brunswick Peninsula in the background.

As they entered the city, Margo commented that she had read that the more than 120,000 citizens made it the largest city south of Parallel 46. They secured a room in a two-story hotel with a red roof, a roof-color like many of the predominant single-story homes and businesses. The hotel was owned and operated by a Croatian family. They were to learn that more than on-half of the citizens were of that nationality whose ancestors had emigrated there during a gold rush or during the time when the southern pampas was a leading sheep-grazing region.

During lunch in the hotel, Margo informed Roger of other facts she had learned about the city: She told him that it was a penal colony for criminals and rouge military personnel in the mid-1800s; sheep dominated the economy between about 1890 and 1940 with one company, *Sociedad Explotadora de Terra del Fuego*, controlling more than 3,900 square miles at one time; and it had been an important coaling station for steam ships.

On a walking tour after lunch, they saw restored mansions of sheep company owners, many other historic buildings, a monument depicting

Ferdinand Magellan, and a replica of Magellan's ship, *Victoria*. They also passed the building housing the Magallanes Provincial government. The wind they had faced all day grew very strong in late afternoon. They realized why that were ropes tied along the sidewalks in the shopping area. In the business district, Roger saw a sign on a small building that read: Southern Coal Enterprises, Milo Bartich, Owner. He told Margo he had met that man at an international conference where he had been a speaker a few years previous and suggested they go inside to see if the man remembered him. He was indeed remembered by a middle-aged, haggard-looking man, who rose from one of two desks in a front office. An older woman sat at the other desk. Before the woman was able to ask if she could help them, Milo came from his desk to shake Roger's hand. Margo was introduced, and they were invited to sit in chairs in front of the owner's desk.

Milo's first comment was, "What is a prominent geologist and investor doing in my part of the world?"

"We are visitors in your city," Roger responded. "But I have invested in land in Patagonia, north of *Puerto Natales,* where we are staying."

"Were you here for the big earthquake that even affected us way down here?"

"I was nearly killed in a hotel collapse in *Puerto Montt*," Roger said. "Did the quake damage your mines?"

"Some roof-falls and we were shut-down without power for several days."

"I remember our discussions at the conference in London regarding your brown coal deposits, the subject of my presentation. Do you still have good markets?"

"Not enough. There were times when we produced a half million tons per year. Now, a quarter of that, during good years."

"That massive, nationwide power blackout got me thinking, again, about local, small power-producing plants. My staff and I are working on a proposal for such a plant, a hydroelectric plant in the province to the north of you. Have you thought about such plant, burning your coal?"

"Not since you talked about viable technology at the conference. What is the status of clean-coal technology?"

"The technology that I discussed, fluidized-bed combustion, is even more efficient now and is being accepted by regulatory authorities in many places in the world. South Korea has plans to build a large, 800-megawat plant, using the technology, but those I have invested in are small, under 100 megawatts."

"Would such a plant not be what this city needs?" Milo asked.

"With the coal reserves in this region and your prior production history, a plant as large as 50-megawatts should be considered."

"Would you me interested in working with me to see that such a plant is built?"

"Margo and I came to visit your city, not looking for an investment opportunity," Roger answered. "However, if you would take the lead in finding a plant location and dealing with the government authorities, I will consider such a move. I don't have much information about available equipment with me. I would have to contact the company in Boston with whom I have worked in the past. I do have brochures describing the current technology I could send you."

"Please do that. This is the first time I have been excited about the coal industry of Patagonia in years. My secretary will give you mailing information."

"I will keep in touch," Roger remarked as he and Margo got up to leave. Milo shook their hands, and he did seem very excited.

Back on the windy sidewalk, they started back for the hotel. "That was a fortuitous stop," Margo offered. "His excitement encouraged me," Roger said.

The evening was spent at the hotel. They enjoyed a Croatian meal, love-making and some sound sleep, before beginning the return journey. At the airport where the Beechcraft was being worked-on, they stopped to learn the progress and to retrieve a file on coal-fired plants from a cabinet where Roger kept such data on the plane. They were told the plane would be ready for a check-flight the next day.

Their pilots had been enjoying the life of tourists at the lodge but were very happy to hear the news about the plane and asked if they could take the Range Rover to the airport the next morning. Roger replied, "If you make certain an envelope, I will provide you gets into the mail. What's in the envelope may lead to another international flight for you two, so make certain the plane is air-worthy."

The most exciting thing Roger and Margo learned at dinner that evening was that Doctor Grayson was certain the bone they would free from the quarry wall the next day was another leg bone of a giant ground sloth. In addition, he learned that Rios, Afton, and Derek had collected more seeds from hardwood brush, as well as seeds from broad-leaf plants and tall grass on which rheas feed. Derek reported that he and Alton had concluded that these plants set out and sown in areas of ice retreat would provide for the best expansion of habitat for the wildlife in the region. When asked, Derek said they had determined that the best site for a hydroelectric plant would be on an east-facing slope, adjacent to the retreating Grey Glacier, west of the national park and within the province boundaries.

The following morning, the pilots left for the airport with the envelope addressed to Milo Bartich. All, except Heidi and Harriet, loaded into the cab and onto the flatbed of the truck driven by Raoul headed for the excavation to watch the removal and loading of another mega-fossil. While the loading was taking place, Margo and Afton walked up the ravine along the flowing stream in quite conversation. Afton told Margo how impressed she was with what she had done to become, not just a part of the lives of those with whom they were associated, but an inspiration. Margo thanked her and gave credit to the advice she had offered her in an earlier day they spent together. She expressed hope they could continue to expand their friendship and spend more time with one another because this was her first chance to create a close friendship with a woman her age. They returned to see a jubilant group admiring the fossil on the truck and continued their walking visit back to the lodge.

It was an exceptionally warm, early fall afternoon, with temperature near 70 degrees. The girls had unfolded chairs and tables on the front porch where they served a late lunch, eaten first by those who had been to the ravine and had taken the fossil to the fossil repository created. The pilots returned in time to eat, also, and reported the plane checked out, perfectly. Ned said the plane had been serviced, cleaned, and refueled.

Doctor Gray went below to examine more closely the fossil and Raoul and Luis drove home in the truck after the meal. The others remained on the porch and a discussion was held regarding the future need for aircraft. Ned reported that he had found a small helicopter in a town across the border in Argentina that could be rented, with a pilot. Derek said that his analysis of the hydroelectric project suggested that they would not need such an aircraft. The surveying and aerial mapping company he had contacted had their own aircraft that would be used to provide detailed topography and the amount of overflying, on his and Afton's part, would be minimal. Construction would require a large helicopter. Margo suggested that the small rental airplane she had flown could be used for low altitude reconnaissance. Roger listened to the discussions. He concluded that engineering design was all that would be needed after the work of his staff was completed, and a detailed topographic map was available. The engineering firm he used would be asked to prepare a detailed feasibility study for presentation to the province government. Therefore, he could plan a trip to Boston in the repaired Beechcraft to initiate another small-power project.

The overflying of the project that Derek had mentioned was accomplished with Margo as pilot and Roger, Derek, and Afton onboard the single-engine airplane. It was the first time any of the passengers had flown with Margo. The confidence in her ability that she exhibited from the beginning of the flight was very re-assuring. As directed by Derek, she flew at low altitude to the terminus of Grey Glacier and along the eastern front where evidence of the retreat of the ice was obvious. Making a sweeping turn, she flew the route of the proposed pipeline to the site where Derek thought the generating plant should be located.

Beyond there, Margo had to put the plane into a steep climb and banked hard to avoid crashing into a cliff and steep slope. Possible powerline routes that Derek had plotted on an illustration obtained on the internet were flown. This invigorating, exciting flying took several hours. Upon landing, each of the passengers expressed how comfortable they had been on the flight with Margo at the controls. Roger told her he was overwhelmed by the skills she had acquired in such a short time. The flight was discussed on the drive to the lodge and it was the principal topic at dinner.

The aerial mapping company that Derek had arranged to use flew out of a private airport in the Tubio Valley of Argentina. He drove there with Roger. The layout of the topographic map and the scale required were provided the manager of the company. Three copies, and an electronic version were requested. Roger signed a contract for the work and provided the location of Lautaro Lodge, where the final product was to be delivered. They were told the ground control would be set right away but obtaining the required aerial photographs would have to await a clear day, which was unpredictable.

The coal mines where Roger had been told several men from *Puerto Natales* now work was nearby. They drove by those mines on the way back but did not stop.

The next morning, the issue of restoring the lower part of the ravine where the fossil excavation had begun was discussed by Roger, Derek, and Rios. Derek's suggested that a new water impoundment be created below the mouth of the ravine. A fish-hatchery or fish-farm beyond that were discussed. When asked if he could recommend a contractor to move the remnants of the previous dam and the material being removed from the excavation to build a lower dam and excavate a reservoir, Rios reported he did and was asked to call for a representative of that company to come out and provide a cost estimate. Roger told Rios to meet him and Derek at the site after he made the call.

Derek drove the Range Rover there. He and Roger had just begun walking around the area when Rios arrived with the motor-grader. It was decided that the perimeter of a future reservoir should be marked by a pass of the grader. Slowly, Rios followed Roger and Derek with the grader-blade at an angle to create the limits of a teardrop-shaped feature. The machine was parked and the three of them walked around in the area where the flood from the rupture of the high dam had removed vegetation and much of the soil. As they walked, Derek commented, "Fly-fishing is one of the biggest tourist attractions in the region. There are a several native game-fish species in the rivers and lakes, but those have been augmented by the planting of many, popular fresh-water fish species. A hatchery here could restock streams and lakes on this *estancia* and be sold to owners of others where fishing is an activity for tourists."

"I have carefully analyzed commercial fish-farming at operations on land and I think we should consider that, too," Roger informed his companions. "The environmental challenges are many, but I am aware of some fish-farms that have been established under the tightest regulations and oversight that are profitable. In the best of those operations, there is constant re-circulation of water with the filtering of waste. The waste is used as fertilizer to grow flowers and other plants that are not in the human food-chain in hothouses. Fish food is becoming an issue with some environmental groups. They do not understand that the vast populations of fish in the oceans not now providing food for human consumption can provide feed for fish being raised what humans can eat. There are, also, fish foods being produced from vegetable material to appease critics."

"We could establish such an operation for you," Derek commented.

Roger responded, "Do some research and I will send you my complete file."

A pickup truck arrived at the site as the conversation continued. A large, muscular German man stepped out of the truck, walked to them, and introduced himself as Paul Horst, the owner of Horst and Son Construction. The excavation work planned was explained to him as Roger showed him around the reservoir site and to the previous dam site. Derek and Rios walked down the slope to the highway. Rios suggested that the overflow from the fish operations might be directed to create a swampy area created, with small ponds for flamingos and migratory birds, between the fish-raising area and the highway, saying he could do that with the motor-grader.

Derek agreed. The thought he voiced was that this would be a significant fall and winter project for them both. Roger drove to pick them up after the contractor left. Rios' suggestions were explained to him as they drove back to the lodge. Roger told them that the contractor had promised a cost-estimate the next day and he felt comfortable that it would be a fair price, so they should plan to move forward with the project and develop it as they thought best. The work could begin, he told them, with the clearing and removal of the remaining soil and vegetation with the motor-grader that they had left on the site.

Derek went to his workspace and began a drawing of the project. Roger asked Margo to bring a camera and to hike with him for photographs. They crossed the ravine bridge to the prominent point where many photographs of Rios at work at the reservoir site, as well as those in the fossil excavation, were taken. The two of them sat for a long time on the rock outcrop and discussed all the things in which they had become involved since arriving in Patagonia. They discussed their next move to advance what had been initiated: Meeting with a coal-fired plant designer and builder in Boston, finding financing for a plant at *Punta Arenas*, and obtaining engineering design and a cost estimate for a hydroelectric project.

The weather had cooperated. An overnight delivery-truck had arrived with the topographic map of the hydro-electric site and the CD with the data before they returned to the lodge.

At the dinner table that evening, Doctor Grayson reminded Roger that he had agreed to seasonal work here and had commitments elsewhere, so he would be flying out the next day. He said he would leave the fossils collected where they were and have his helpers store the equipment used at the excavation in the garage. Roger asked the others working for him and living at the lodge to meet with him in the conference room at ten the next morning for a staff meeting.

That meeting began by Roger telling everyone that he hoped to have upscale accommodations and guided tours from the lodge made available to tourists in the spring, so he and Margo would initiate international advertising in the next few months. He appointed Harriett, Manager, and Heidi, Assistant Manager, of what was to be called the Lautaro Lodge, with increases in their wages, and told them to hire additional cooks and others, as needed. He told Rios that in addition to the other duties he was performing, he would be the Tour Director. Each of the ideas that had been mentioned to him for creating trekking and horseback tours, including fishing, wildlife viewing, fossil-hunting, as well as trips to photograph spectacular views and wildflowers were discussed. He suggested Afton and Derek prepare maps and information handouts.

Rios reminded Roger that the hunting season would soon bring poachers that had to be dealt with, telling him that hunting had not been allowed for many years on the *estancia*, so more herds of Red Stag congregated here each fall and hunters had learned that. Roger suggested that permanent signs, declaring that no hunting was allowed, be posted wherever tails and areas of easy access came onto the property and that the government authorities be notified of this action. Further, that patrolling be expanded, even if others had to be employed. Afton reported that she planned to continue what had been started which involved growing plants with the intent to expand wildlife habitat and for land restoration. She said she would like to make another trip to the edge of the retreating ice to broadcast seeds in a test plot.

Roger complimented her for her work and approved any test plots she thought appropriate. Derek suggested that he thought that his additional, available time should be spent during the next few months in determining wildlife and fish populations. Roger agreed, and the meeting ended. The participants expressed feelings that they were pleased with their roles in what was to become the foremost resort and wildlife reserve in the region. Roger shock hands with everyone, expressed his appreciation for their contributions, and gave them envelopes containing checks for their services. In Derek's envelope was a second check intended to cover his expenses in coming to Roger's rescue. Derek found it was more than enough.

Over the next several days, Derek stayed bus driving the Land Rover. He took Doctor Grayson and his luggage to the airport and Raoul and Luis to their homes. In the city, he picked up the cost estimate and contract for the reservoir construction one day and returned the signed contract the next. On that day, he ordered metal signs that had been designed by Roger and went to a bank where he opened an account with his checks and left with Chilean currency. Following emotional farewells, Margo, Roger, and the pilots departed in the company plane after Derek left them and a mound of luggage next to where the plane had been moved from the maintenance hangar.

The trip to the edge of the retreating ice for Afton to create a test plot included a one-night stay at Patagonia Camp for her, Derek, and Rios. Two yurts were rented near each other on a hill with a lake view. Short hikes were taken before and after a dinner was enjoyed in a hotel restaurant. The next day, the trip ended before noon where Rios had previously parked. With packs containing lunch from the restaurant, bottled water, and blended seeds, the three of them hiked to just below the ice front where Afton had collected ancient plants.

There was a stark difference along the edge of the ice. Serac, forming large masses, had accumulated above the site with some blocks of ice extending, vertically, for more than ten feet. As Afton began broadcasting seed by hand, Rios and Derek climbed in opposite directions from her. All at once, a loud crashing-sound was heard. Her companions turned to see Afton struck by a falling block of ice. The blow spun her around. She fell and slide down the slope a few feet. Derek was the first to reach her, finding her unconscious. He straightened out her contorted body, removed her down jacket to allow examination and placed it under her head. Rios got to them. Derek told him that she had a badly broken arm, at least, and had been knocked out.

"We must get her to a hospital," Rios commented as he lifted her into his arms. Derek placed her jacket over her, retrieved her pack, and they started back to the vehicle. Over the steep, wet terrane, Rios carried her without ever stopping. Derek rushed ahead, opened the vehicle doors, lowered the back seats to create a place for her to lie, and started the engine and heater. Gently, Afton was positioned in the space, covered by her jacket and a blanket that was in the vehicle.

Having seen no medical clinic or hospital at Patagonia Camp, it was obvious the hospital in *Puerto Natales* was their next stop. Rios assumed that would take at least two hours. Both were deeply concerned about their associate. As they traveled, Derek and Rios discussed the dangers on and around glaciers, one of which they had learned this unfortunate way. Rios commented that shifting blocks of ice caused nearly as many injuries and deaths as crevasses to hikers on glaciers.

The hospital in *Puerto Natales* was modern and appeared to be well staffed. Once Afton had been moved into the emergency center, Derek and Rios went to a waiting room where they were to stay for many hours before receiving a report on her condition. A young doctor finally came to tell them that Afton's very bruised and broken left arm had been put in a cast, that no other injuries to her body had been found, but she had not regained consciousness. He suggested that a telephone number be left at the reception desk, so they could be notified when she came-to, something that he expected based on her vital signs. Derek went to the reception desk and completed admittance forms and left the number at the lodge. The drive back to the lodge was in silence. Harriett and Heidi were now the only ones there to be told about the accident and Afton's condition. It was a sober, reflective evening as the four of them ate dinner together.

Progress at the reservoir site amazed Rios when he went there after feeding the horses the next day. He began to level the area below the dam that was being formed with the motor-grader were Derek was planning to establish fish-raising operations.

Heidi made Derek aware that an apparently motherless fawn had been seen near the sheep and goat pasture. He found a frail, very young Andean doe lying against the fence. In his arms, he carried the fawn to the unused box-stall in the barn where rescued fox had been kept and a new rescue operation commenced. This time he had to fashion a rubber glove with which to begin feeding goats milk to an abandoned offspring. Knowing Afton would be assisting him, if not for the accident, he began to realize how much he missed her already.

With the fawn fed, probably the first nourishment in days, Derek walked to the reservoir site. Rios climbed down from the machine he was operating and the two of them discussed the size of leveled land needed for a hatchery or fish farm. Derek pointed out that he had been doing some design work, but he was still uncertain about the facility they should construct. Rios told him that he thought the existing game-fish populations should be better understood before a hatchery to restock lakes and rivers was created, saying that although fly-fishing was a popular sport with tourist, he did not think there was too much pressure on those populations, currently.

"What is your opinion about fish-farming?" Derek asked.

He replied, "My country is a leading supplier of salmon to the world, much of it from farming operations which are expanding in the waterways. The land-based system that Roger discussed seemed viable and would probably be viewed more favorably by the government than subsea pen systems."

"I agreed with your assessments. I should initiate the determination of fish and wildlife populations that was the first task assigned to me and do more research of fish farms. With the no hunting signs, we could combine posting them with patrolling for poachers and making counts. While you finish what you have started, I will go to see if the signs are available and check on Afton."

He found the one-hundred metal signs were available, but there was no change in Afton's condition. He was told that he could sit by her side in the hospital room. He sat there for hours, watching her steady breathing without movement of any part of her body. He prayed for her, something that he had not done for a long time.

Chapter Seven
The Wildlife Count

Estimating the wild inhabitants on land and in the waters of the earth is, obviously, a great challenge. Derek had learned the professionally accepted methods for doing that, which involved actual counts in representative habitats, while in university, and he had conducted numerous investigations as a Wildlife Conservation Officer in Africa. However, those previous investigations had been intended as guides for hunting of specific animals, which was not to be a part of what was to be the attraction for people staying at the Lautaro Lodge, so completing his new assignment would be much more different. Locating places where large populations of the unique mammals and flightless birds could be observed was important.

With more than 460 species of birds in Patagonia, bird-watching would be emphasized, particularly because of the wide variety of unusual species. This required a much more comprehensive study on his part, Derek realized. As a fisheries expert, he had been concerned with fish populations to support sports fishing before. In the lakes and streams on *Estancia Margo*, healthy, sustainable populations of native species was desirable, so an understanding of current populations was essential.

The combined efforts of Derek and Rios began each morning for the next few weeks, with them on foot, leading a horse with a pack containing signs. They planned the hikes each day on the large aerial photograph on which the property boundaries had been plotted, the photograph that Roger had brought with him.

Rios carried his rifle over his shoulder. Derek had learned, as a conservation officer who often encountered armed men where they were not allowed, that a firearm could become a necessity, but he had left his guns with his Zulu friend, and had not acquired another.

It took only one day for them to become aware that poaching could become a big problem. Several Red Stags, carrying trophy racks, were seen with large harems of hind, as well as several very large bachelors traveling alone, or in groups. While Rios posted signs, Derek flagged *stands* where observers and photographers could be positioned for a thrill of a lifetime in seeing these animals. Even in Africa, Derek had seen few wild animals he thought matched the grandeur of these deer. The time it took for Derek to photograph, describe, and record sightings of birds and animals meant that only short segments were traversed each day. Rios was not bored. He had lived most of his life on the *estancia,* but he had never spent the time to observe the wide variety of species all around him.

Each evening, they hoped for word from the hospital that Afton was awake. Upon receiving that word from Harriett one evening as they were putting away the horse, they both went to the hospital to visit her without eating the dinner prepared for them. Afton was sitting up in bed when they got to her room. Her face was drawn, and her arm was still in traction, but she smiled and told them how happy she was to see them. Her first question was: "What happened to me?"

"Don't you remember?" Derek asked.

"I remember sleeping in a hut and waking up in this bed," she answered.

"In between those times, you cast seeds at the edge of a glacier, and part of that glacier fell and knocked you down. Our giant of a friend carried you to our vehicle and we brought you here for treatment. Since then, we have worried constantly and prayed for your recovery."

"My nurse told me that a handsome young man spent hours at my bedside. I assume that was one of you two."

"I hope our prayers helped, but we were helpless to do more for you," Derek responded.

"What have the doctors told you?" Rios asked.

"That my arm was a mess, but they think I will have full use of it when the cast has been removed in a few weeks. I suspect I have the two of you to thank for saving my life."

"The God of the Ice saved you." Rios said. "The block of ice that knocked you down was huge and could have taken you rolling down the hill with it. You are a very lucky young lady. There were no closer medical services, so we brought you here. We trust you have been given proper treatment."

"Everyone here has been so kind and thoughtful, and I have confidence in the doctor, so I am certain that I will soon be back at the lodge, fit to help you. What have you been doing in my absence?"

Derek explained the progress made on the reservoir and the work they had been doing. He told her she was needed to help with an orphaned fawn he was trying to keep alive.

A nurse entered the room and told them that visiting hours were over. They each kissed Afton on a check as they left, promising to return each evening. Harriett and Heidi had kept food warm for them and she and Heidi were waiting, very anxious to hear about Afton's condition.

The ensuing routine of Derek and Rios consisted of spending long days in the hills and in the compound caring for the horses and fawn, evenings in Afton's hospital room, and eating a late dinner before going to bed. This continued for several days. One evening, Harriett had a special delivery letter for them to take to Afton. She opened the letter in front of them, saying it was from Margo. With that letter, regular written correspondence began between two woman who had become very good friends that would continue for years. Margo provided general information about where she and Roger were and what they were doing. In her response to that first letter, Afton informed Margo of the happenings at the lodge, not mentioning her accident.

One morning, Paul Horst approached Derek and Rios in front of the barn. He informed them that the reservoir would be finished in a few more days and that they should go there to inspect the work. Both were very pleased with the construction work that they saw when they walked to the site, following behind Mister Horst's pickup. The motor-grader that Rios had left there was being used in the final grading of all surfaces, something that Rios had intended to do. Culverts were in place in the dam for a spillway and the stream had been diverted to the impoundment. When Mister Horst returned the following week, Derek signed the forms presented to him and thanked the contractor, telling him he could pick up the bank draft from Harriett that Roger had left with her.

The field work needed to estimate wildlife populations continued with Derek making observations, taking many photographs in the various habitats, counting dove coos and listening for other bird calls. Rios continued installing signs of the property perimeter, so they were not together much of the time. One day when they were not far apart from each other, that proximity became fortunate. Rios confronted three poachers tracking a Red Stag. They had been drinking and became belligerent, refusing to leave the property when asked. One pointed a rifle at Rios, telling him to "*bug off*" and leave them alone. Rios left his rifle slung over his shoulder and repeated his order for them to leave the property.

Derek had noticed a vehicle in an open area in the brush and photographed it. Hearing voices, he hiked to the confrontation. Repeating Rios' order upon approaching the hunters, he added, "I have pictures of your vehicle and I have called that description, as well as yours, to law enforcement on my satellite telephone. You will be found and prosecuted for any harm done to my friend or me. Should you leave, as we have asked, we will not pursue a case of trespassing against you this time, but we have the legal right to shoot you and we will do that if you trespass again."

Shouting insults, the hunters started back to their vehicle. Derek and Rios watched them until they went into tree cover. Then, they went further up the slope to where Derek had seen their vehicle. They watched as the men shot a guanaco, apparently out of spite, got into the vehicle, without unloading their guns, and departed.

"If those men are representative of the poachers we must face," Derek said, "This is going to be a dangerous hunting season."

Rios replied, "The word will circulate that we are patrolling and posting the property. Maybe, we will face few more like them. Most of the hunting is done by those staying at resorts, with guides. The guides will honor our posting of this *estancia*."

The two of them spent the remainder of the day traveling together, once more. Retracing the route later in the day, they sighted an Andean Condor circling the guanaco that the hunters had killed. They watched for a long time. Derek was in awe of the huge bird he had studied but had not seen before. The wing-span seemed to be more than ten feet.

Back at the lodge, Harriett had things to tell them: Afton was going to be released from the hospital the next morning, and she had received a telephone call from Roger, asking her to go to the bank to sign the forms that would allow her to draw funds from an operating account, as he had authorized by a call to the bank manager.

Derek had seen waterfowl circling the reservoir that evening, so he suggested that Rios and Harriett go into the city the next morning, while he spent the day recording the use of this new, man-made habitat. The trip to the city in the Range Rover began right after breakfast. After feeding the fawn and horses, Derek walked to the reservoir. He carried wooden posts, the ends of which he had chopped into points with an axe, a piece of canvas, the axe and his camera, carried over one shoulder. Near the eventual high-water level of the reservoir, Derek drove the posts into the ground and built a *blind,* the front of which he covered with brush taken from the nearby hillside. His presence caused ducks and geese to fly, but flamingos at the far end of the water did not.

Sitting on the ground behind the cover, Derek waited with his camera and notebook. Within a few minutes, waterfowl began to fly in and land on the slowly expanding water surface. The number and variety of the species Derek recorded that day he found amazing, like everything else in Patagonia.

The return of Afton to the lodge was met with much joy. The resumption of their evening on the porch, even though they now had to wear warm coats, pleased Derek very much. He had missed Afton a great deal, and the first evening he told her so. Her arm cast was in a sling, but she explained it could be removed in a few more days. "In the meantime, I need to make myself useful again," she told him.

Derek responded, "Heidi has helped me feed the fawn at times. You could relieve me of my part of that task. Heidi has wanted to help out more, beyond the kitchen. I suggest you let her help you, by adding hands for your other activities. We will need many more seeds, come spring."

Afton and Heidi became a good team. Their association extended beyond the day that Derek drove Afton to the hospital to have the cast removed. Afton found her assistant was very bright, wrote neatly, and was excited about the work. Soon, Derek had Heidi helping him with charting his findings and organizing his digital photographs, after a printer he order on line arrived. Harriett had begun to plan for visitors to the lodge. Both Afton and Derek started to help the girls prepare meals, and clean up afterwards. A happy group worked, diligently, throughout the early fall at the lodge.

The day a special delivery package arrived from Roger, the work load expanded. He sent detailed drawings of a fish-farming facility with instructions that he wanted such a facility built next to the reservoir. It was a Recirculating Aquaculture System designed by RAS Enterprises to raise Atlantic salmon. Roger's memorandum expressed his thought that, due to the climate, the system should be installed in a building. Derek, Rios, and Afton spent two days studying the drawings. Rios' knowledge of the builders, manufacturers, plumbers, electricians, and other technical people in the region that could be used to complete the task would have to be called upon. He told them that because *Punta Arenas* had an industrial base in that society that included oil production and mining, much of the material and workmen would have to come from there.

A local building contractor he mentioned was one he thought was capable and honest. Rios and Derek considered a fact-finding trip to *Punta Arenas*, but before they left, another memorandum from Roger arrived to inform them that he had signed a turn-key contract with the designer who would have the equipment flown-in and would install the system. He would send a Spanish-speaking expert to handle all the permitting and manage the facility. Those at the lodge would be required to contract for the building, and provide initial ground transportation from the airport, rooms and food for the crew, and make the truck available for moving equipment and supplies from the airport to the site. Greatly relieved by the limit of their assignment, Derek and Rios went to *Puerto Natales* to secure a contract for the construction of the building.

Rios had already leveled a site for the building, so construction began on a steel building within a few days. While the building was going up, Rios continued the grading of small ponds and dikes to create a wetland between the building and the highway, something that Derek thought was even of more importance now. The small discharge from the fish-farm would flow into that area and comingle with the overflow from the reservoir, the source of the recirculating water.

Within a few days after Rios had finished the motor-grade work, the reservoir filled, and water flowed in a channel he had created on one side of the building. The water began to create wetlands. Almost immediately, water-fowl could be seen there, so Derek build another blind of brush to conceal his presence and added to his observations and count of birds.

The next effort undertaken by Derek and Rios was to build more observation *stands* and *blinds* in the areas were Derek had found the birds and mammals were concentrated. That took them, once more, all over the *estancia* on horseback. In doing that, they sketched trail maps for guided and unguided tours. With the help of Heidi, Derek created pamphlets on which the sketches were attached that described the wildlife that might be seen on each trail. Rios recommended that Raoul again be hired in the spring to act as a guide and went to get him, on occasion, to traverse the trails with him, so he would be prepared to guide tourists.

Derek knew hunting was not to be an activity for guests at the lodge, but fishing would be, so he began taking catch and release trips to identify the best fishing areas. The size and number of fish species he caught was unexpected. Of the large fish he caught, three were subspecies of salmon that had been introduced and three were native: *tollo, aplochoton*, and *peladilla*.

Afton continued her work with the moss and lichen she had collected in the area where the ice had retreated, the area where she nearly lost her life. Lateral stems and branches had grown from moss she had set out and there were sprouts in the nutrient-rich soil on which she had placed plant particles. Excited about her discovery, she began to write a professional paper describing the details. Her other big interest became the fawn. It had been released in the area near the sheep and goat pasture where Derek had found it. It stayed in the grassy area behind the apartments.

At first, Afton ground leaves and placed them in a feeder box. Next, she brought branches of the plant they had determined was primary forage for deer from the slope and hung them near the feeder. Almost at once, the fawn began to nibble the leaves. Reporting this to Derek and Rios, Afton expressed her excitement about that experiment, also. She was told that her work with the fawn confirmed that they were on the right track in expanding deer habitat. They promised to supply her branches for the fawn.

The crew that was to install the system for a commercial fish operation, with their luggage, filled the Range Rover. Their flight was late, so Derek had to park the vehicle and wait more than an hour for them, during which he walked through the terminal and studied the many posters advertising resorts that awaited incoming tourists, and he purchased a guidebook at a newsstand to read about those facilities. That made him aware of the competition that Lautaro Lodge faced, and he wonder how the advertising campaign that Roger and Margo planned was going. In his mind, a profitable aquaculture operation might provide a better return on his client's land investment in Patagonia, so the enthusiasm and professionalism displayed by the five men from RAS Enterprises he helped into the vehicle after the plane from Santiago arrived pleased him.

A fine building, with a secure source of fresh water, was in place for them to create their system, the equipment for which, he was told, would arrive the next day on a chartered cargo plane. The man in charge, Henry Watson, informed Derek that they had been served dinner on the plane, but they had been flying for two days, so everyone was anticipating a good night's sleep. Derek commented that they could expect that at the lodge. Harriett and Rios greeted the group as soon as Derek parked in front of the porch. Derek knew the accommodation plans, so he invited Mister Watson to go with him to the rooms that Doctor Grayson had occupied, while his crew was shown to bedrooms in the main building. The first impression of Henry Watson, expressed as Derek escorted him to those rooms, was like that of everyone else who came to the lodge: "What a fine facility."

Derek opened the door and placed the suitcase he had been carrying inside as Henry entered. The breakfast arrangements were explained, and Derek bid him goodnight. Walking to his quarters, he found Afton's door open with her and Rios inside waiting for him to ask about the crew. He entered the room and sat with them at the small table. What he had to tell them about his first impression of these men from Boston was positive, based on his short conversations with them. Headed to their beds, they were hoping for a good outcome from this new venture.

As had become routine, Derek walked around the compound early the next morning. For the past few weeks, the walk had been under a dark sky, with the only illumination from lights at each corner of the buildings, and the cold air required him to wear a heavy coat. The fawn had become a pet and followed him. The sheep and goats paid no attention to him, but the horses appeared very happy to see him. He always fed them in the morning. On his way into the main house, Derek mused that he was experiencing the winter cold and darkness that he had worried about, thankful that the building in which he would be working with the new crew had adequate lighting and propane heaters.

As Derek had expected, a big breakfast had been prepared and there were men already eating and drinking coffee in the dining room when he went to the kitchen. Mister Watson soon arrived, as did Afton and Rios. Derek took the opportunity to introduce everyone, barely remembering the names of the crew, and explained the language situation. That explanation included a statement that Afton was from America and that the girls and Rios understood enough English to provide necessary assistance or services.

At the dining-room table, Derek explained the heated and lighted building in which they would be working. He said that the building was within walking distance, but the truck to be assigned to them would be brought to the front of the building. Mister Watson said they would start by laying out where the components would be placed in the building and that a man with an international driver's license would begin hauling equipment, as soon as he received word on his satellite phone that the cargo plane had arrived.

Discussing their feelings that this was a well-organized group, Derek and Rios moved the truck and Range Rover to the front of the house. The plan was to have the truck follow them to the facility this first morning. Rios left the truck running, with the heater on, and joined Derek in the Range Rover. They did not have long to wait before the truck, with the crew and some tools, was ready to leave. Parked near a side door to the building, Rios went inside and turned on the lights and heaters. The crew expressed their pleasure with the features of the building when they entered, mentioning how the extensive use of sky lights and windows were going to prove very beneficial during the installation and the operation of the system.

Derek was happy that he had insisted on those features. Immediately, drawings were made on the concrete floor, with colored chalk. The place where each component was to be placed was marked. Derek and Rios watched for a few minutes before returning to the compound where they found Afton waiting for them at the doorway to her workspace. She had something to discuss with them.

"I was told that the fish facility would be filtering out waste, a good fertilizer," she said. "And that the plan calls for an associated hothouse where that material could be used in growing plants. I suggest that the facility is close enough to our existing hothouse that we could have the filtered material moved there. I have thought a great deal about the size the deer forage-plants should be when they are set out. For them not to be pulled out of the ground, they need to be quite large, with a good root system tightly compacted in the soil. That means they should stay in the hothouse, in plastic containers, for quite some time, possible as much as a year. The fish fertilizer should enhance the growth and shorten the time, but I think a hothouse expansion will be needed for us to grow a significant number of these bushes for deer feed."

"That makes good sense," Derek commented. "We have been authorized to do what we think necessary in that regard. With the truck in use, we will have to have the building supply store deliver the material we will need for a hothouse expansion. Let's make an order list."

The needed building materials increased greatly when another request was received. That request came in a letter to Afton. "I will read a portion of my letter from Margo to you," Afton told Derek and Rios, one afternoon:

'Roger would like an addition to the main house built to match, exactly, the wing of apartments. That will require rebuilding the garage in another place. In that new wing, he would like a master suite where he and I will stay.

All of the main house bedrooms will then be available for guests.'

Derek observed, "That implies they are finding many interested in staying at the lodge. That would be great."

"This will be a huge undertaking," was Rios' first reaction. "The stonemason who worked on the original buildings is dead, but I think his sons still do such work. The stone quarry is overgrown, but there is still a large amount of stone remaining from the last blasting."

"I hope the contractor who did such a good job in constructing the steel building works with other building materials. That building is superb," Derek said.

"He does." Rios responded. "We should go talk with him."

They found that the contractor, Herman Wilson, was very receptive to such a large, new project on the *estancia* and that he had engaged, several times, the young stonemasons who had worked there before with their father. He discussed the fact that if the work was started right away, as many as ten days of work in some months might be impossible due to rain and snow, and floodlights would be required to assure effective work periods each day. A time was set for Mister Wilson to come to the lodge to study the project for the development of a cost estimate.

On the way back to the lodge, Derek and Rios stopped to determine the availability of Raoul and Luis and if they could find the use of a vehicle to commute. They learned that Raoul had purchased a pickup truck and that he and Luis were anxious for more work.

While Derek observed the work at the fish facility, work that involved putting elements in place as they arrived from the airport on the truck, Rios took Raoul and Luis with him to remove the vegetation that had grown in the stone quarry. That completed, they disassembled the wooden structure that served as a garage, stacking the lumber near a new location that Rios and Derek had marked out, at a right-angle to the existing location, extending to the above-ground steel tank where diesel fuel was stored. When Mister Wilson arrived a few days later, Rios escorted him through the existing apartment wing and helped him stake out a duplicate wing. He was shown the new garage location and the stone quarry. The next day the builder returned with a contract covering the building of the residential extension and rebuilding the garage. That was forwarded to Roger's office in London, electronically.

While the hothouse extension was being erected, Afton was transplanting into plastic containers the small plants that had grown from the seeds she had planted. She also planted starts of the flowering vines that formed the beautiful cover along the walkway in front of the apartments, so it, too, could be duplicated.

The installation of equipment at the fish facility went smoothly. Removable panels that Derek had designed during construction of the building were where the water intake and discharge pipes were installed. The crew working there had installed several other systems, but never, Henry Watson told Derek, where his crew had been housed and fed in such style. The liquor had been returned from Derek's closet to the cabinet in the living rooms, so the crew even had access to drinks after work.

The area around the lodge became a major construction zone after the signed contact with Herman was returned. His crews and equipment moved in and a subcontractor began moving stone from the quarry. As soon as footings were installed and the concrete dried, the two young stonemasons began building the walls. That created an interesting situation. Harriett had formed strong feelings for the boys when they worked with their father on the other apartment portion of the lodge and their living quarters in the back. The boys did not have to bring lunches, for the girls spent time with them while eating the lunches they had prepared.

The relocated garage was erected in a few days by two carpenters and a helper. Rios and his crew moved the water line to a new wash-rack area. The motor-grader and Range Rover were parked inside. The fossil excavating equipment and other items were relocated inside, as well.

The morning, at breakfast, when Mister Watson announced the facility would be finished that day and his crew would be leaving, he reported that a man who spoke Spanish would soon arrive who Roger had hired to obtain operating permits, stock the tanks, and supervise the operations of the facility.

He spent several minutes expressing his appreciation to those at the lodge for the most enjoyable job he and his crew ever had. The same feelings were expressed by each crew member as they left the lodge, with their luggage, for Derek to take them to the airport later that day.

Upon his return, those who had served the crew and had been associated with them during their stay asked Derek to give them a tour of the facility and explain the system. They walked there together. The six round, aluminum tanks glistening with fresh, clear water and the brightly painted equipment amazed all.

Derek discussed the system: "It will start with Atlantic salmon smolts weighing about 100 grams being placed in the tanks full of water that flows by gravity from the reservoir and is disinfected using ultraviolet light. The feed will be spread, automatically, on the surface water in each tank. Drum filters will screen out the waste. The carbon dioxide given-off by the fish will be removed by blowing air through the re-circulating water and vented outside. The harmful ammonia is to be removed by biofilters, which consist of large colonies of two bacteria on grains of sand suspended in the water, and the safe nitrate also vented outside. A small amount of fresh water is added each cycle and the same amount discharged to the swampy area that Rios created. Oxygen is added to the water just before it reaches the tanks."

Afton asked, "How many adult fish will be produced?"

"The fish density will have to be determined by the expert who is coming, but the facility is intended to be commercial," Derek answered. "I think Roger's plan is to sell live fish to the existing processing plants in *Puerto Natales*."

The expert who arrived a few days later was named, Miguel Cabrera. The rooms next to Afton's were assigned to him. He was of middle-age. The personality he displayed from the first day was much more congenial than Doctor Grayson, who had spent time in that unit. He told the others that he had managed a fish farm in central Chile. His transportation was a second rented vehicle, a pick-up truck, so he was able to undertake his assignment with little assistance.

There were signs of spring approaching when the exterior of the stone addition and roof were completed. With the help of Afton, Harriett, and Heidi, began design work on the interior. When the suite for the owners was complete, there was enough floor-space left for two other living units. A door from the walkway to the lower level of the main building was created, like the one from the other wing, and Afton planted vines along the walkway.

Before the young stonemasons departed, after completing beautiful work, Harriett and Heidi prepared a special late lunch for them. The four youngest of those who had an association with Lautaro Lodge enjoyed a well-deserved afternoon together.

In letters between Afton and Margo, the decision was made that the furnishing of the new units would be left up to Afton and the girls. That required several trips to stores in the city, but the results were deemed fitting for the lodge by everyone to which the units were shown.

When spring weather arrived, the fish facility was in full operation, many more plants were growing in the expanded hothouse, and the new wing and the bedrooms in the main building were ready for occupants. Rios had sheared the sheep. Before completing their latest work period, Raoul and Luis had shod the horses, and groomed them. Each had been ridden several times, so they were again quite gentle.

Chapter Eight
The First Guests

Correspondence between Margo and Afton provided information regarding the attempts being made to create clientele for the Lautaro Lodge. Roger had formed an opinion that personal contact with associates and friends in London would result in initial interest, and those who took advantage of the opportunity to stay at the lodge would spread a favorable report to others upon returning. The thought was to make it an exclusive *get away* for wealthy and famous people. Those who decided to spend time there would be made aware that they would enjoy a high degree of privacy by flying into the Gallardo Airport where lodge personnel would be met and transport them directly to the lodge.

The standards required to satisfy those who would come later were established during the visit of the first party, Lord Edward Pennington, his wife Mabel, and two teenage boys, Howard and Horace. A telephone call from Roger, taken by Harriett, explained that Lord Pennington was related to the English royal family and that his report of a pleasant stay to his many friends, associates in government, and family members would launch the lodge operations. From the time Derek picked them up at the airport, the couple was very demanding, and the boys were often rude and unruly. The lord and lady were interested in relaxing in the lodge and having every request for food, tea, and liquor complied with, without delay. They had brought books to read.

None on the *estancia* had experience with catering to spoiled teenagers. However, the Pennington boys appeared in awe of Rios, if not afraid on him, so he was able to show them around the area without confrontations. They both rode, so a trail ride was organized for their initial tour of the area. That turned out to be an all-day event that included lunch by the lake, surrounded by guanaco and rheas. They also saw a herd with a huge Red Stag when crossing the ridgeline, a female puma with two young, and a circling condor. The excitement exhibited by the boys during that first trip was obvious to Rios. It was voiced, loudly, to their parents back at the lodge. The boys asked Harriett, who was acting in her role as manager and had been taught some English by Afton, to arrange for another ride the next day.

To assure privacy for guests, a table and chairs had been set up in the lower-level conference room where Afton, Rios, Derek, and Miguel were served their meals by Heidi, who served the guests in the dining room. At dinner the evening after the first trail ride with the Pennington boys, Rios conveyed his belief that the boys had seen a part of the world they never dreamed existed. That world was expanded the next day. They were awake long before their parents and followed Heidi to watch her milk the goats. Although it was a very chilly morning, they romped with the fawn and walked with Derek to feed the horses.

The boys ate breakfast alone. When they had finished, Harriett informed them that Rios would have the horses ready for another trail ride. That day, they saw the majesty of the high mountains and the ice fields from the ridge where they ate lunch, and saw herds of Andean deer, many birds, as well as a large puma chasing and a fawn into dense brush. As on the previous day, the chatter between the two of them was nearly constant. They had no camera. When Derek learned that, he put together a portfolio of photographs and presented it to them after their second ride. Rushing to their parents, they showed them beautiful 8-inch by 10-inch photos of essentially everything they had seen on the *estancia*.

Their continued excitement was conveyed to all, and Derek spent the following day with them. He took them on a tour of the fish operation. That seemed to fascinate them, too. They then were taken to observe the waterfowl in the nearby wetlands. While sitting on a bench that had been installed in a blind, they watched a flock of flamingo land, and nearly constant flights of many ducks and geese. On a hike up the ravine, they climbed to the fossil excavation. Derek discussed the fossil-bed exposed there, told them where they could see bones of a giant animal that had been removed, and showed them the continuation of that strata as they hiked up the ravine.

From near the head of the ravine, Derek took them on the well-used trail back to the lodge, stopping to eat lunch in a grove of trees inhabited by owls that made their presence known by loud hoots. Back at the lodge, the boys visited the lower level where they viewed the fossils and spent time with Afton, watching her press new flowers.

It was a family outing the next day. The entire family rode with Derek in the Range Rover to Patagonia Camp, where they were treated to a fine lunch, and to *Torres del Paine* National Park. In the park, Lord and Lady Pennington sat in the vehicle for more than an hour as their sons hiked a trail with Derek. Returning, the boys expressed their feelings of more excitement about what they had seen.

The day after the family trip, the Pennington's left the lodge. Each expressed to Harriett, Heidi, and Rios their appreciation for what Mabel referred to as a marvelous stay, as they helped them with their luggage. Derek was thanked when he left them at the airport.

Back in the dining room for dinner, everyone voiced a sense of relief that the first group of guests at Lautaro Lodge had left, seemingly with good feelings about their stay. Rios commented that the boys had experiences things that they would never forget.

For the next two weeks, activities at the lodge continued without a word about additional guests having been scheduled. Then, an express letter arrived from Margo in which she explained what had happened when the Pennington's returned to London: As hoped, the family told everyone who asked about the great accommodations, friendly staff, and experienced guides at Lautaro Lodge in Patagonia. Based on their recommendations, two couples known well by the Pennington's booked a week at the lodge. They were to arrive at the end of that week, according to a flight scheduled Margo provided.

Derek was at the airport waiting when that flight arrived. The two English couples were easy for him to identify among a small group that left the plane. They were well-dressed in fashionable wool clothes, appropriate for the weather they expected. Their ages seemed a few years younger than that of Lord and Lady Pennington, and they were congenial from the time Derek approached them and introduced himself as a member of the Lautaro Lodge staff. The names they provided were Royce and Alice Wendel and Ronald and Nancy Morrison.

Derek escorted them to the Range Rover where they waited while he went for the luggage described to him. Leaving the airport, Mister Wendel asked if they could be shown *Puerto Natales* before going to the lodge, saying he had read a lot about the city, and he liked to see the area around where they stayed.

Missus Wendel added, "He also wants to make sure there is a hospital in case my palpitating heart acts up."

As he drove them through the city, Derek pointed to the hospital and made them aware of the great care that one of his associates at the lodge, Afton Atkins, had received there for a badly broken arm. Noticing the café at the edge of town that had become a favorite of those working at the lodge, Nancy Morrison asked if they could stop for tea because that served on the airplane was not very good. Derek explained that the café was very clean, and the servers were friends of lodge personnel, but the population in the area included few tea drinkers, so he could not vouch for quality.

Upon recognizing Derek, the group was welcomed and taken to a large table. Others in the room acknowledged them as they passed by their tables. In a friendly atmosphere, the couples became aware of the nature of the native population of Patagonia and were served tea, reported to have been grown in Chile, that was declared excellent. Derek asked for, and was provided, a tin of tea leaves to take to Harriett, in case she had not stocked that brand. Leaving he paid the bill and left a substantial gratuity.

Not wanting to create any type of friction, Harriett had planned to have these guests occupy adjacent, smaller rooms, instead of one couple staying in the master bedroom. The rooms were just as well-furnished as the larger bedroom, and both couples expressed their pleasure with the accommodations when escorted there by Harriett and Rios.

The congeniality that Derek detected became obvious to all at the lodge, beginning that first evening. Touring the entire main building when they came from the bedrooms, the new guests shook hands and spoke with everyone they encountered, even though the language situation had been explained to them on the way to the lodge and they spoke only English. Missus Wendel even asked Afton how her arm was doing.

Pre-dinner cocktails were prepared by Mister Wendel. While sipping a drink, Missus Morrison visited with Harriett in the kitchen. Seeing only four place-settings on the dining room table, she asked where the other ate their meals. When told the staff and guests ate at separate tables, Missus Morrison insisted that they all eat together, so they could get to know each other. That pleased everyone, particularly Heidi, whose serving duties were greatly reduced.

It was obvious from the discussions at dinner that the Pennington's had not told their friends much about the features and activities on the *estancia*. Afton asked if they had spoken with the Pennington sons about their stay. Nancy responded, "I think, by that question, that we should have done so. I suspected that the Lord and his Lady spent most of their time in this magnificent home."

"They did ride in the Range Rover with me to see some of the spectacular scenery one day," Derek said. "But the boys took advantage of seeing a lot from horseback and hiking."

"We ladies are not horsewomen, but we love to hike," Nancy said. "However, our dear husbands think fly-fishing is the ultimate sport. They would walk or ride miles to a good trout stream."

"Knowing that, Rios, our Tour Manager, can begin to plan activities for you," Derek said. "Do you want to begin as early as tomorrow?" The answer was, "Of course we do."

Meeting in Afton's quarters after dinner, Derek told her and Rios that he had learned Missus Wendel had some sort of heart problem. "I didn't know how to ask if that would restrict the hiking the ladies love to do," he added.

"Let me start with them on a hike to observe the wildflowers not far from the road," Afton suggested. "I will ask about any limits to hiking into the higher terrain."

"Good idea," Derek said. "I promised to help Miguel tomorrow. Could you take the men, on horseback, to the stream feeding our lake, Rios? There, they should catch fish they could only dream about in the United Kingdom."

The first day with these English guests turned out to be exceptional. The weather cleared, and the breeze was light. With breakfast finished, Alice and Nancy changed into warm clothes and hiking boots and joined Afton, who was carrying a lunch, bottled water, and her camera in a backpack. They walked down the road and turned in to the lower part of the basin that Margo had found so delightful. The spring flowers had just started to bloom. Patches of them among ferns and budding trees created a beautiful setting. The pace maintained convinced Afton that the ladies had done a great deal of strenuous hiking.

Stopping for lunch, Afton asked, casually, if they were up to more difficult climbs. Alice mentioned that a heart murmur and slight palpitations were detected during her last physical examination, but she felt good and did not worry. Her husband worried enough for them both, she said. Afton, then, led them through the basin and to the ridgeline where the majestic high mountains and ice fields were visible, before they hiked back to the lodge in time for afternoon tea.

As Derek had predicted, the male guests experienced the best fly-fishing of their lives. In a segment of the stream were Rios took them, they caught and released dozens of large trout. Rios tended the horses and watched from a hill. Rejoining them, he helped release from their hooks six large salmon that he cleaned, wrapped, and placed in the backpack in which he had brought lunch, a thermos of tea, and bottles of water, trying to explain that he had promised Harriett fish for dinner.

It was hard to tell who was the most excited at dinner that night, the fishermen, or the hikers. Dinner was prepared and served by Harriett and Heidi, who considered broiled, salmon-filets the best dish they had to offer, with a sauce they learned how to prepare from their mother. Compliments were expressed by everyone at the table.

A call was taken by Harriett when she was helping prepare breakfast that would clearly establish her authority as lodge-manager. The provincial-government man with whom she had spent time, Juan Ledesma, informed her that his brother Tomas, his wife Mary, and son Marco were arriving from Santiago that day and he wanted them to spend some time at the lodge. His brother, Juan told her, was Chief of Staff to the President of Chile. Knowing she must accept these additional guests, without regard to the added efforts that would be required to accommodate them, she told Mister Ledesma they would be considered honored guests. Juan commented that he would bring them to the lodge by dinnertime.

When she discussed this with Rios when he came to the kitchen, she was told that she had done the right thing, but that the staff would have to be expanded. His recommendation for such expansion was to have Raoul and his sister, Rosanne, move into the new quarters. Harriett knew them both, of course, and was aware that Rosanne had once worked as a cook. She made the call and later prepared the two new, smaller units for them. This development was exciting for Heidi, not only because she would have help, but because she had strong feelings for Raoul.

The lady hikers wanted to go beyond the ridge to the grasslands they had seen and suggested they could go without Afton if she had other things to do. Afton had other things to do, but she felt uneasy about them going so far without a guide, so she told them that she needed to check for a special spring-blooming flower in the grasslands. As the day before, the trio embarked on a day-long hike, during which herds of guanaco, many rheas, and carpets of new grasses and flowers were seen.

Afton found, unexpectedly, a few plants new to her and added them to her collection. Derek accepted the challenge of taking Royce and Ronald where they could observe Red Stag, an animal that they told him they had hunted in Europe. From a *stand*, in a rock outcrop in a wooded area above the large ravine, they watched and took photographs of the largest deer either of them had ever seen, with a harem of seven. Both expressed a feeling that this experience was better than hiking through a forest to kill one. After lunch and tea, the men continued to hike to the ridgeline and back to the lodge on a different trail, observing other Red Stag, a small Andean deer herd, and a multitude of birds, including large coveys of quail and flights of dove.

The English couples were back at the lodge, enjoying sherry in the living room that Harriett had ordered as part of her weekly supply of food and beverages, when Juan Ledesma arrived with his brother and family. They were greeted by Harriett and Rios on the porch. Tomas, Mary, and Marco were escorted to the master bedroom and an adjoining room, with Rios carrying all the luggage. Juan introduced himself to the others and was offered a glass of sherry, which he accepted out of courtesy, never having tasted that wine. Tomas and Mary joined them and, they too, accepted a glass of sherry. At once, the group became involved in discussion, mostly about Patagonia. They all spoke English. Tomas explained that he had studied government affairs at a university in London, so he also wanted to discuss the United Kingdom.

Rios had stayed with Marco. He told Rios that he had trekked in the northern ice fields and wanted to know if it would be possible to cross a part of the southern ice fields from here. He was informed that was possible and that Rios had done that many times. Marco showed Rios the spiked hiking shoes he had brought to do that. Leaving him, Rios told Marco he would arrange for the two of them to make the trek, realizing that his arranging of tours for guests had become a challenge. He discussed that with Derek and Afton after dinner.

All chairs at the dining-room table were occupied that evening. Juan Ledesma had accepted an invitation to stay. Not knowing whether, or not, the guests would all be assembled by dinnertime, Heidi had prepared a large pot of lamb stew and baked six loaves of bread. The meal was enjoyed by everyone. The conversation was wide-ranging at the table, and afterwards in the living room. When Juan left, he told his brother that he would pick up him and his family in two days.

The discussion held by Harriet, Afton, Derek, and Rios, later, was a planning session concerning the next-day activities. Derek said he had been told in private conversation with the Ledesma brothers that Tomas wanted to tour the fish operations and be explained the hydropower project that Juan had told him about. Fortunately, the engineering report covering the hydro-project had been received, Derek reported, so he would tack a copy of the detailed map on a wall in the conference room, with photographs of the site to show Tomas. Rios told them of his promise to the boy, Marco. Harriett suggested it would be a good day for a sightseeing tour that the English couples had requested, and that Raoul, whom she had asked to come the next morning, could drive them in the Range Rover if Rios and the boy took the truck. Afton offered to entertain Missus Ledesma.

Raoul and Rosanne arrived very early. Harriett and Rios came to the porch to meet them and helped them get settled into quarters not previously occupied, to their amazement. Raoul parked his truck in the garage and brought the Range Rover to the front of the porch. Rosanne went right to work, helping Heidi prepare breakfast, a meal that she served, first to the staff, and then to the guests as they came from their rooms.

The day started out as planned, except Missus Ledesma wanted to accompany her husband, so Afton decided to go with Rios and Marco on what would be her first experience hiking on an ice flow. They left the lodge, headed to a trailhead that Rios preferred as access to the main southern ice sheet. Raoul departed soon thereafter, guiding his first sightseeing trip in a vehicle.

Miguel and Derek led the Ledesma's on a walk to the fish-raising facility. The sincere interest of the couple was deserving of a detailed explanation of each phase of the operation. That took more than two hours, with long stops to watch the hundreds of sizeable fish swimming in the six tanks. The next part of the tour was the nursery in which the fish waste was being used to grow a variety of plants. There, Derek explained the concept that they had developed for the expansion of habitat for endangered deer with the forage being grown. The thoughts that he and Afton had about creating wildlife habitat, or renewed grazing for domestic animals, on the areas becoming exposed again by the retreating ice were also mentioned.

The concept of generating power for isolated and widely separated communities, using water from melting ice and the steep slopes in mountainous terrain, was of special interest to Tomas. He carefully studied the maps and photographs that Derek had on display and the financial projections prepared by the engineering company that Roger had engaged. Derek explained that the owner of the *estancia*, Roger Richardson, who was also his, Miguel's, and Afton's client, had made a commitment to provide the *Ultima Esperanza* Province officials with a feasibility study that would include everything he was showing them. He also repeated the presentation he had given to those officials earlier concerning the establishment of such facilities around the world. A late lunch was available when Tomas and Mary returned to the lodge. They thanked Derek for his time and said they would like to look around the compound after lunch.

On the way to the parking lot at the trailhead, Rios stopped at a store that catered to those trekking in the region for Afton to purchase an attachment with spikes for her boots, and a rolled length of rope that he always carried over his shoulder traversing the ice field in case someone fell into a crevasse, something he was worried about because of the snow that must have accumulated over the winter. That precaution proved wise. After hours of hiking in unusually pleasant weather, a bridge over a crevasse broke away as Marco was crossing. A large block of ice and snow fell tens of feet into a hidden crevasse with Marco falling on top of the block.

Fortunately, the mass formed another bridge that prevented Marco from falling even further. Calls from Rios and Afton received no response from him. They speculated that he may have been knocked unconscious, but the sunlight on his body showed it was not contorted, so they hoped that the fall had not broken bones. The two of them discussed the dilemma they faced. Rios clearly had the strength to lift him up, if the rope was over a shoulder, but unless he came-to to secure the rope, Afton would have to go down and she feared reinjuring her arm. The solution Rios devised was to form a sling from pieces of rope he cut with his pocketknife for Afton to sit in while he lowered her, and for her to ascent, after Marco was raised. He explained that she should hold the rope with her uninjured arm and push away from the crevasse walls with her feet.

Rios firmly planted his feet in the ice and lowered Afton, slowly. Next to Marco, she untied the rope-sling and examined the young man. He did not seem to have broken limbs. With snow on her gloves, Afton began patting his face, gently. His eyes opened. He sat up and stared at her and at the walls of ice. Telling him that Rios would raise him, she tied a loop of rope over his head and under one arm. When she called to Rios, Marco began his ascent. The movements and weight of the two of them on the bridge of ice and snow caused it to begin to shift.

Afton repositioned herself in the rope-sling and prayed for the return of the rope before the bridge failed. No sooner than the returning end of the rope reached her, and Afton had tied it to the sling, the second bridge collapsed. During her ascent, she could see further down the crevasse for what appeared to be hundreds of feet. Marco, lying on his stomach at the feet of Rios, looking down, saw that happen and reported it. Rios commented, "Once more, the God of the Ice saved that pretty young woman."

Not knowing what Rios meant, Marco said, "That pretty young woman and you saved my life. That I will never forget!"

Back together, the three embraced, sat on the ice, and recounted the near disaster. They ate a lunch that Rosanne had prepared for them which helped to calm them. Amazingly, there had been no serious injuries resulting from an event dreaded by those trekking an ice sheet where several lives had been lost over the years. Thankfully, the trip back to the truck was uneventful. Marco asked, on the drive to the lodge, that he be allowed to tell his parents about what had happened in his own way, at an appropriate time, because only recently had his father allowed him to do things without him.

Only positive things about the trek on the ice were offered at the dinner table. The trip made to the national park and Patagonia Camp with Raoul was explained with a sense of wonderment. The guides, Raoul, Rios, and Afton sat, quietly.

The Ledesma family left the lodge with Juan the next morning. They could not have been more complimentary to everyone who had served them and had reported the activities taking place on *Estancia Margo* to them. Several of those comments were quoted in a letter written to Margo by Afton in which she mentioned the activities of the last few days with a nearly full lodge. The English couples spent one more day relaxing at the lodge and taking short walks together. They, too, were full of compliments and expressed many words of thanks when Derek took them to the airport, saying their return should be expected.

It was necessary for Afton to report again to Margo regarding activities with the lodge overflowing with guests when next she wrote. Harriett received a letter from the headmaster at the school where the Pennington boys attended, John Bickford, informing her that he wanted to bring an entire class to the lodge, ten boys, including Howard and Horace Pennington. He suggested a dormitory arrangement be considered because the boys would each have a sleeping bag and a seaman's bag of clothes, as they did when he took them camping. A telephone number was provided for Harriett to acknowledge that the lodge could accommodate the headmaster and the boys.

Once again, Harriett was compelled to respond in a positive way and undertake the necessary adjustments and arrangements. Furniture was moved from the conference room to other rooms on the lower level. Rios was sent to the city to purchase folding cots that were arranged there. The table where staff had eaten at that level was moved to the kitchen next to the smaller one. In discussing tours for the group, Rios decided a division of the group would be required. One half would hike, and one half would go on horseback each day. He and Raoul would lead the tours. Transportation to and from the airport would involve the Range Rover and the truck.

Because of the way the Pennington boys had acted some of the time on their previous visit, the staff was very nervous about the five days they would be spending with English lads. They need not have worried. The headmaster was a disciplinarian. The group acted like a military cadet-unit, obeying Mister Bickford's directions, always. He said it was intended to be a learning experience for the boys, and it was. Each boy made an entry in a journal every day, describing what they had seen. When John learned that Afton and Derek were trained professionals in their chosen scientific fields, he asked them to give lectures in the living room in the evenings, with the boys sitting, quietly, on the floor. The German language was taught at the school, so conversation in that language with staff members, and Derek, was also a learning experience for some of the boys.

What was experienced under the guidance of Rios and Raoul throughout the *estancia* would never be forgotten, and, probably, never equaled, during the lifetime of many. The stay by the boys from Hargrove School, and their headmaster, at Lautaro Lodge, proved to be pleasant for all involved.

Chapter Nine
Retreating Ice

Harriett located Derek working with Afton in the hothouse when she went looking for him to tell him of the call she had received from Roger, asking that he and Margo be picked up at the airport. Their pending arrival was a surprise. Afton commented that she had recently received a letter from Margo in which there was no mention of a trip planned, and Harriett said she had received no notification of them, or others, who would be arriving. Nevertheless, each voiced their thoughts that this was good news for they felt a need for directions.

There was another couple waiting at the curb with the Richardson's when Derek arrived at the terminal. Margo embraced him, and Roger shock his hand before he was introduced to Austin and Faye Merrill. Derek loaded the luggage and held doors of the Range Rover for them. On the way to the lodge, Margo explained to Derek that their companions were parents of one of boys from Hargrove School who had stayed at the lodge, earlier, however, they had not known each other until boarding the same plane in Santiago.

Missus Merrill commented: "We had to come see for ourselves what Jon had experienced. He said Lautaro Lodge was the most fabulous place on earth."

Derek responded: "Those of us working here believe that is true and we will do all we can to make sure you have an enjoyable stay."

Roger explained the location and setting. Margo, sitting in front next to Derek, asked about the staff.

As was the custom, Harriett and Rios were waiting on the porch. After introductions, the baggage ownership was explained to Rios, and he took the Merrill's luggage to the master bedroom. Margo embraced Harriett, then, held her at arm's length, saying: "Just look at our manager, Roger. In that tight skirt, lace-trimmed blouse, and lovely, woven vest, Harriet looks as if she could be a receptionist at the Ritz." Blushing, Harriett said that she made her own clothes and escorted the Merrill's inside.

"Our manager is a very pretty, talented young lady, Margo," Roger commented. "She looks mature and very sophisticated."

"You can be proud of her role as manager under some trying and unusual conditions," Derek offered.

For the first time, Roger commented about the new appearance of the lodge when he stepped away from the vehicle. He said, "The addition is better than I could have ever imagined. It appears as if the entire facility has looked like this for decades, including the vine-covered walkways."

"Let me show you to your new quarters," Derek suggested, as he picked up the other suitcases. "I think you will like them."

"Very impressive!" was Roger's comment when he followed Derek and Margo inside the unit.

"The rock fireplace and the furnishings make this a place I can call home," Margo announced.

"I have so many questions and information for you running through my head, Derek," Roger said. "But we have been on the go for days, so we will just relax and enjoy our new place for a time."

"Can I have something brought to you?"

"Tea would be very nice," Margo replied, gratefully. "Roger can build up a fire in front of which we will unwind."

When Derek went to ask Heidi to provide tea, the Merrill's were enjoying cups of Chilean tea in the living room. Derek took the opportunity to ask them about their main interests. Faye answered: "I am an avid bird-watcher and Austin thinks fly-fishing is the ultimate pastime. Would there be a way we could combine those things?"

"Many ways," Derek answered. "If you ride, there is a trip you could make during which you would see many birds, even magnificent flightless birds, and both catch large salmon."

Austin responded, "We do ride, and I have wanted to teach Faye to fish for years."

"Rios will arrange such a trip at your convenience," Derek commented as he went to move the vehicle to the garage.

Roger built a fire in the fireplace and added split-logs from a pile on the hearth before settling into a reclining chair in front of the fire. Within minutes, he was asleep. Margo chose not to stay next to him. She rushed to the other wing to find Afton. Returning from the garage, Derek stopped at Rios' unit to tell him what the guests wanted to do, then went to his quarters. There, he could hear voices and laughter coming from a joyous reunion of friends in Afton's rooms.

Harriett spent the afternoon with the guests, answering their questions, including some about how their son and his classmates had acted. Rosanne and Raoul were working on an as-needed basis, so Heidi was alone in the kitchen. As was the situation on previous days, Heidi was uncertain when everyone would come to dinner, so she prepared what had become a very popular lamb stew and left it simmering on the stove. She made a large salad and fresh bread to go with the stew.

Dinner was eaten in relays, as Heidi had expected. By the time that Roger and Margo came to the dinner room, the Merrill's had retired. Rios was with Harriett in the living room, discussing guest activities. Derek and Afton were at their favorite place, sitting together on a porch swing. They spoke to Roger and Margo as they walked by.

It was a case of getting down to business the next morning. After breakfast, Roger asked Afton and Derek to meet him in the conference room. Rios was prepared to take the guests on a long ride, beyond the lake, and Harriett asked Margo to go over the accounting system she had set up.

The first item that Roger wanted to discuss was the feasibility study for a hydroelectric power plant. He was told, by Derek, that the study had already been presented to Juan Ledesma and his brother, Tomas, the Chief of Staff of the nation's President, and that it was ready for formal presentation to the provincial government. Roger commented, "Margo informed me of the chance opportunity you had to make the presentation. That will, surely, mean much in our future relationship with the country. I could not be more pleased. Now, it is my turn. I will take the study to the province offices, today. I have a report on my studies of the other opportunities resulting from ice retreat which I will leave with you two to study. This evening I will explain a specific plan on which I want your input."

While Roger went to *Puerto Natales,* Afton and Derek studied the information that was left for them. They were amazed by the detail. Included were many satellite images showing, in detail, the glaciers and ice field on which Roger had marked his interpretations and those of others. Maps were included in the package, with notations and outlines, that also represented a very extensive study by Roger, an experienced geologist. They voiced doubt that any other professional had done more work on the retreating ice in the region.

The presentation Roger offered that evening confirmed that his work was a part of an evaluation of the economic opportunities being created which he had discussed with them, previously. He explained that the retreating glaciers were expanding the surface water impounded in the lake in the canyons that enclosed the termination of the flowing ice, but the landform exposed in those canyons was filled with shattered rock and little useable land. Moreover, moraines, both lateral and terminal, greatly affected future use of exposed land, he told them, and added, "However, in the side canyons draining into the glacier-filled canyons and on parallel ridges new vegetation is springing up, as the total ice sheet retreats. Look at that situation on this image of an unnamed glacier that has lost about half of its length over the past thirty years. The newly exposed acreage is very significant."

Roger pointed out what he had mentioned and his notation regarding the approximate, now useable, acreage on a satellite image. Then, he discussed the economic element of his specific plan: "The land value of this acreage is very low, and I have learned a large block in the area is for sale, on which Angora goats are raised. If we can expand the forage for goats, as you are attempting to do with deer habitat, the existing herd could be greatly expanded, and mohair remains in high demand."

Afton made the first comment from the listeners: "Goat are browsers, like deer, but they are not so particular about what they eat."

"That is true," Roger said. "But the nutrient intake for an Angora to produce a valuable fleece has to be very large due to the rate of hair growth. You should initiate a study, Afton, to determine the best plants for them to eat. Also, they are not a hardy animal. Cold weather is not very conducive to large herds without sheds, but there are many raised in southern Chile, and Argentina is a major producing country. I would like us to conduct a study that considers all the economic factors. If a viable project can be generated, that would be another way for us to prove the value of our group to the governmental bodies that control everything that happens in Chile."

"This is a fascinating concept," Derek said. Afton concurred.

"Juan Ledesma wants you to show him the hydro-site tomorrow, Derek. Afton, Margo, and I will take the first trip to a goat pasture. Your time will come."

Heidi had the opportunity to again prepare her best meal with filets of salmon that evening. As always, those dining, complimented her. Discussions at the table were dominated by Faye telling of the exciting events of her day. She revealed that before today she thought that Austin's time fishing was a waste, but she now understood the thrill of landing a big fish. The sightings of birds, she raved about, included many rheas and a circling condor. A plan to ride through a different part of the *estancia* the next day was made.

The trip to the Andoni Goat Farm was quite long and the roads very poorly-maintained, but Roger, Margo, and Afton arrived without incident. Rolando Sotillo, a Basque herder, greeted them, coming from a shed. The landowner with whom Roger had made contact in *Puerto Natales* had told him about Rolando. He introduced himself to the visitors.

The visitors soon learned that Rolando took good care of the herd. They were shown more than fifty recently sheared adult Angoras and dozens of kids held in a pasture with good fencing and an adequate shelter. A long shed had overhead propane-fired heaters, and clean, straw-bedding. When Roger asked, he was told that during daylight hours, with no rain or snow, Rolando went with the herd and his four dogs into the adjacent hills. Roger said they wanted to hike into those hills. Without responding, the herder waved his arm, suggesting his approval.

Afton carefully examined the vegetation as they walked and commented that the herder didn't allow the stripping of too much brush or overgrazing in any area they traversed. The absence of brush marked the area once covered with ice. That area was bounded by an area of sparse vegetation. There, Afton knelt and studied the ancient plants that were much like those in the other area she had studied, thankful there was no overhanging blocks of ice. The moss and lichen offered no feed for goats but were adequate to limit the erosion of the soil profile, she commented. Many rocks were scattered where the ice had retreated.

Margo asked, "Beyond the land-holdings owned by Rolando's boss, who owns the land?"

"I suspect that will be debated for decades," Roger replied. "It has not been bare land, for many centuries. One governmental agency or another will claim it, but I wouldn't expect anyone to require termination of grazing on introduced plants. At least, that would be my hope, if we buy the property to expand and improve the herd."

"I would recommend that the improvement of forage be accomplished by broadcasting a seed mix of wide-leafed forbs and clover over the entire area," Afton commented as they walked back to the shed. "I have started research to determine the best mix."

Rolando was waiting for them, surrounded by his border collies. Afton asked him about where he lived. He answered: "A stone cottage in the adjacent woods has been my home since I came here from northeastern Spain. It was built for the family I was to work for, but the land was sold to Herman Borsch, who lives in the city, before the cottage was occupied."

"You live alone?" Afton asked.

"Since my wife and son died of a fever many years ago. I'll show you, if you want."

"That would be grand," Afton replied.

They were taken along a pathway leading into dense trees not far from the shed. The cottage they were shown was a complete surprise. It was made of stone, with a wide, wooden porch in the front on which several cords of spilt wood were neatly stacked. The interior consisted of a combination kitchen and living room in front, two small bedrooms and a bathroom along a hallway, and a large bedroom at the end of the hall. There was a fireplace in each room, a wood-stove, sink, and refrigerator in the kitchen area. Each room was furnished with old, but well-built furniture. Everything was clean and well-organized, which Afton commended about.

"Mister Borsch sends a woman with food and supplies for me each week," Rolando said. "While here, she cleans. I am paid little as a herder, but I am satisfied with living here with the goats, my dogs, and memories." Later they were to learn that the farm had been named after his son, Andoni, who had helped his father for nearly ten years before he died.

On the drive back to the lodge, Margo asked to be told those things Rolando had said that she did not understand, and she made the commitment to more rapidly learn the Spanish language. Roger and Afton discussed the possibilities they saw. Roger expressed his thoughts that the goat herd could be enlarged somewhat now and greatly increased with an improvement and expansion of the forage. Afton cautioned that supplemental feed might always be needed. She expressed her thoughts that the shelter would need to be expanded for kidding, as the herd grew, a regular supply of straw would need to be secured, and a shearing shed built.

"This access road needs to be improved for regular use and to support trucks hauling animals, feed, and straw in and fleece out," Roger added. "Rolando would need help, but that fine cottage and the existing supply of groceries will accommodate such help."

"It would not be the normal herding job," Margo offered.

"Associates at the lodge may be of assistance," Afton said. "Rios is a very good motor-grader operator. If the machine at the lodge was moved on a truck-trailer to this road, Rios would have a good road graded in short order. Also, Raoul told me once that his family was engaged in tending sheep for generations and he favored such work."

Derek had returned from the trip with Juan Ledesma when they drove into the compound, and he was feeding the horses. Anxious to explain the goat farm, Afton joined Derek. Leaving the vehicle in front of their unit, Roger took Margo by the hand and they went inside.

Before the horses were all feed from the loft of the barn, the trail-riders returned. Climbing from the loft, Afton greeted the Merrill's and Derek helped Rios unsaddle the horses, remove the tack, and turn them into the corral.

Once again, Faye appeared overwhelmed as she, excitedly, recalled some of the multitude of birds and animals they had seen. She said that so many different birds, of all sizes and colorations, were something that she had never expect to see in one place. Austin commented that on the *estancia*, Faye had learned to fish, and he had become an avid bird-watcher. He also called the Red Stags they had seen "awesome."

During dinner, Roger mentioned the goat farm they had visited, and it was discussed. Hearing the discussion as she served, Heidi asked how many goats were on the farm. Roger reported his estimate of the number of adults and dozens of young. Heidi responded, "I love our goats. Seeing that many would be a great treat for me." Having determined, by her actions, that Heidi may be in love with Raoul, Afton said to herself: *I can see Heidi and Raoul living in the stone cottage on the Andoni Goat Farm.*

The ownership of the farm changed the next day. Roger and Margo drove to the city, took Herman Borsch to the bank, and the ownership was transferred to them, jointly. The three of them then went to the home of Mazie Swanson and arrangements were made for her to continue her services to the farm. Mister Borsch insisted that he treat Mazie and the Richardson's to lunch at his favorite German restaurant. He seemed pleased by the transaction, one he said he had contemplated for years, and told them that a trip to Germany to visit relatives would now be possible.

Planning regarding the goat farm began on the ride to the lodge. Margo made a 'to-do' list that included: finding new goats that could be purchased; Afton completing her studies and spreading proper seeds; assigning the truck at the lodge to the farm and leasing a replacement; finding a truck with a low-deck trailer to move their motor-grader; and interviewing Raoul to determine his interest in a new, permanent job. Margo mentioned that the first thing they should do was notify Rolando.

"Let's see if Raoul has an interest in working there and take him with us, if he does," Roger suggested.

That evening, after dinner in which another exciting day with Rios was discussed by the Merrill's, Roger requested that Harriett call Raoul and ask him to come to the lodge to meet with them. Raoul arrived early and after a short discussion on the porch with Margo and Roger, he committed to the new assignment. Finding that Afton had volunteered to take the guests hiking that day and Margo wanted to go with them, Roger asked Rios to accompany him and Raoul to the farm.

Upon learning that he was expected to improve the access road, Rios asked for several stops, so he could examine the road condition and the drainages that needed culverts. He reported that it would require a few days for him to make proper improvements.

Rolando had been told of the sale during a telephone call. His response was muted when he greeted the new owner, as he left the vehicle. That turned to an expression of pleasure when Roger explained his plans to expand the herd, and he introduced those with him as men who would assist in accomplishing that. Once more, Rolando described the operation while they walked through the herd. Raoul asked pertinent questions, but explained that his experience had been with sheep, not goats. The vast difference in the raising of the two breeds was explained by Rolando. Catching a goat by a horn, Rolando pointed out the new hair, telling them that the growth rate was about three-quarters of an inch a month and that shearing was done twice a year when the hair was nearly six-inches long.

Roger explained that he had arranged for Mazie to continue her services to the farm. Raoul told Rolando that he had accepted Roger's offer of a job and asked to be shown where he would live. While the two of them walked to the cottage, Roger and Rios examined an area where the shed could be extended, and a shearing shed built. They discussed what they were doing when Rolando and Raoul returned. The plans and the good feelings he had developed, already, for his assistant, convinced Rolando that the new ownership was going to prove good for him. He told the others that.

"Living on the farm will be a big improvement over where I live now," Raoul commented on the ride back to the lodge. "The job will be a challenge, but I'm sure I can learn to care for goats, after four generations of my family working with sheep. Many things will be different, but I will learn."

Roger invited Raoul to stay at the lodge for dinner. Upon arrival there, he greeted Margo and the lodge guests in the living room and went to the kitchen to inform Heidi. That pleased her greatly. She told him the meal would be ready in an hour. Back in the living room, Raoul listened, with the others, to the description of the hike and joined the others in drinking tea.

Rios escorted Raoul to the lower level of the main building where they found Afton in her work space. She welcomed them and asked what they thought about the farm, receiving favorable comments. Explaining that she had obtained, from the internet, a report prepared by an agriculture extension at her university that described the raising of Angora, she asked Raoul to sit and listen to a summary. Included in the presentation that Afton read from her notes were the following comments:

Angora goats are the most efficient producer of fiber on earth.

They are generally relaxed, docile, and somewhat delicate.

Fleeces grow year-around, causing strain and lack of hardiness.

An adult should produce 8 to 16 pounds of mohair per year.

High-nutrient feed is most important; Browse supplements are recommended.

Shearing should be done twice a year, before breeding and before kidding.

Care should be given to keep mohair clean and free of contaminants.

Animals with long, straight, hollow, and brittle hair should be culled.

Bucks should be chosen for body conformation, fine hair, and open faces.

Does are seasonally in estrus; Bucks should be left with does for six weeks.

The gestation period is about 150 days but can vary significantly.

Twins can account for 40 percent of births; Triplets are common.

Does and kids should be left undisturbed for several weeks.

Twins and triplets should not be left with singles.

Vaccination are important; Navels should be treated, and antitoxins given.

Sharp points on horns may be clipped for the safety of animals and handlers.

Raoul responded that from his short visit with Rolando it appeared as if many, but not all, of the procedures that were part of what Afton had outlined were a part of the operations at the farm. He said he was not sure if someone new, like him, would be able to instigate any changes, but he asked for a copy of the list. She offered to write one in Spanish for him.

Derek had fed the horses. Joining the others, he asked for their impressions about Roger's new venture. Afton was the first to reply, "It will be a challenge to expand the forage to enlarge the herd, but I think we can do that. The concept of using land exposed by ice retreats for production of fiber, if we can prove it is viable, could have far-reaching impacts in many parts of the world, and could be readily applied to the production of food and fiber." Rios remarked that the road improvement was needed and the expansion of structures that Roger had discussed with him was doable. Raoul commented, "I had no idea of the potential of Angora herds until today. Raising them is, clearly, much more difficult than raising sheep, the animal that provided a way of living for my ancestors."

Once again, the discussion at dinner centered around the activity of the guests and the hike they took with Margo. There was little discussion about the goat farm. After dinner, Raoul spent time in the kitchen with Heidi discussing the goats while he helped her clean up. She voiced to him her feelings about goats, particularly those she had raised. They embraced as he left to drive home.

Roger displayed quick actions the next day, as he had always done on the estancia. It was the end of the Merrill's stay. He bid them farewell with Margo by his side, while Derek prepared to take them to the airport. He asked Derek to locate a truck and trailer to move the motor-grader when he finished the airport run. Rios was asked to take their truck to the supply store for the culverts he needed for the road improvements and to return with Raoul, packed for a move to his new quarters.

Before Rios left, Harriett approached Roger with a request. She said that reservations had been received that would soon fill the lodge with guests, so she wanted to have Rosanne, Raoul's sister, come to help her and Heidi. Roger readily agreed. The next stop for Roger was to talk with Afton. He was pleasantly surprised to learn that she had found a supplier of seed for Angora forage in Texas. He authorized her to order the amount needed to seed five thousand acres, telling her that was more than was needed right now, but they could store it until it was needed. Afton explained that until a dense crop of new forage was well established, the small herd would have to browse in the wooded areas near the pastures and be fed supplemental food. Expansion of the herd through the purchase of adult goats would have to be delayed for some time. His response was: "We may have to find other favorable areas."

Witnessing her husbands frenzied activity, Margo insisted that he take a break and go with her to paint. They walked to the wildflower area where Margo and Afton had spent pleasant hours. While Roger watched and napped, Margo began a painting for which she would receive high praise.

Rios returned with only Rosanne as a passenger. Raoul arrived in his own pickup. Not wanting to bother Roger again about the added help, Harriett asked Margo to review the sleeping arrangements with her that she planned. She explained that although Rosanne had stayed in a new apartment unit before, those two units would be needed for others because Luis would be needed as a guide again, and she understood that Doctor Grayson would be returning, so she suggested that a bed from the unit where Rosanne had stayed before could be moved to the rooms she and Heidi could share, and another bed purchased.

Margo asked, "Is there room for three in the girl's portion of the lodge?"

"Come and see," Harriett suggested. For the first time, Margo went to the rear section of the main building. She was amazed by the lovely arrangements. There were two large bedrooms, a dressing room, a bathroom, and a fully-equipped sewing, carding, and weaving room. "Heidi and I grew up sleeping in the same room before we lost Mother," Harriett said. "Heidi said she would be very comfortable sharing that room with Rosanne."

Margo knew that Roger would approve of any arrangements that she and Harriett made, but she took the opportunity to tell him about this one, as Rios and Raoul were seen moving a bed, because she was so impressed with where the girl's lived and their other activities. She told him, "Our girls are simply

116

amazing, my Dear. In addition to managing and cleaning the lodge and feeding the quests, they card wool, weave, and sew clothes."

"Don't forget milking goats and caring for them and the sheep," Roger added. "We are so fortunate to have many fine people associated with us. Our ventures in Chile have to be successful."

As Rios suggested, Raoul was to spend some time in the unit where he had stayed once before, until the two of them started work on the access road to the farm. Derek informed them a truck and trailer would arrive a few days later to move the motor-grader. Rios and Raoul made plans to lead the transport-truck in the lodge truck, loaded with culverts.

The work on the access road took several days. Rios and Raoul had taken clothes with them and they stayed at night with Rolando. A lasting, mutually-beneficial relationship developed between Rolando and Raoul while discussing the planned enlargement of the goat herd in the evenings and working together when Raoul was not needed to help Rios. One day, a surprised visit was made. Derek drove to the farm in Raoul's pickup, with the remainder of his belongings, followed by Roger and Heidi in the Range Rover. It was the first visit by Derek and Heidi. Raoul showed them around. Roger met with Rolando to discuss several business matters, including the arrangements for the fall shearing and the sale of the mohair.

Heidi had asked to be included in the trip, telling Roger of her affection for goats and her thoughts that Raoul could use her help in getting settled in a new home. Her affection for the animals was manifest as she moved through the herd, stroking the hair on several adults and kneeling to pet kids. She helped move Raoul's things into the bedroom in the cottage where he was staying and prepared lunch for him and the others. She wanted to hug Raoul as she, Derek, Rios, and Roger left but refrained from doing so. Sitting in the vehicle while the others walked along the road with Rios, inspecting the improvement work, she thought about a life with Raoul and a large herd of goats.

Chapter Ten
The High Mountains

Roger and Margo made reservations to fly home to London on commercial airlines, with a stop in *Punta Arenas* to discuss the progress in securing the financing of a coal-fired power plant with Milo Bartich. They scheduled their departure to be near the time of the anticipated arrival of the next group of guests, to save Derek a trip to the airport. Before leaving, they met with the entire staff, including Luis whom Derek had brought from his home to, once again, provide guide services. Their gratitude for all the work that had been done to advance the Chilean projects was expressed. The future activities planned were discussed. Margo announced that she had created a web page on the Internet so hopefully, the lodge would continue to become more and more popular, and be full of guests much of the time.

The plane with the Richardson's onboard left for *Punta Arenas* more than an hour before one from Santiago arrived. Derek spent that time with several from other resorts waiting for guests, as well. Each of them had a sign with the name of the resort for whom they worked. Derek assumed those who he had come to pick up would know him by a lack of a sign. That proved to be the case. The first two couples leaving the terminal paused to look at all the signs and headed directly toward him, carrying their luggage.

Derek rushed to help them and introduced himself as a representative of Lautaro Lodge. Each of these guests appeared to be in their late fifties or early sixties. They spoke German, seemed happy to be there, and appeared very friendly, joking with Derek about the array of others waiting for passengers to depart planes. He spoke with them in their native language.

It had become customary for Derek to discuss the region on the drive to the lodge with guests. He did so this day and answered many questions, some about German emigrants they had been told about. He informed them that the original lodge where they would be staying had been built by one of those emigrants. Smelling beer, he hoped that Harriett had stocked up on that beverage for these guests. It turned out that Derek need not have been concerned about the beer supply. Harriett had ordered several cases bottled by a local German microbrewery. After the guests had been escorted into the lodge, Derek parked the vehicle in the garage. Returning, he found the men enjoying the local brand of beer and the women sipping Chilean red wine in the living room.

It was anticipated that nearly every chair in the dining room would be occupied by guests within a few days, so a second table was being set up in the conference room for staff members. Derek went to help Heidi and Rosanne do that. In the adjoining room, Rios and Luis were discussing tours. It had been decided by Rios and Harriett, that times of guided tours would be scheduled and announced to the guests. Those taking un-guided tours would be provided trail maps and brochures and be asked to sign out before leaving the lodge. Derek informed the others that he had been told what the guests upstairs wanted first; to tour the fjords, which meant he would have to go to *Puerto Natales* early in the morning to arrange for a boat.

Soon after daylight the next morning, Derek approached the boat of Juan Aparicio. He was recognized from the frantic trip the two of them had made to *Puerto Montt*. Juan was happy to have a local charter. Derek expressed his positive feelings about a voyage he was looking forward to making. He said he would provide a narrative in the language of the tourists, regarding the sea life and answer those questions he could.

Derek hurried back for the guests, arriving at the lodge as breakfast was just finished. Heidi had prepared a large basket with food and drinks for lunch. Handing the basket to Derek, she also gave him a mug of coffee and bacon sandwiches. The guests were cautioned to wear heavy clothes because the cold winds were often fierce in the fjords.

Juan welcomed them aboard his boat, on which he had hosted many tourists. When asked which way they wanted to go, Derek replied that he had been told by the guests that they wanted to see the high mountains. Heading northwest, the overcast skies began to clear. Heavy winds persisted, but the sun began to shine. Soon, the high mountains and the surrounding ice field became visible.

In an eastern branch of the fjord, they reached a place where *calving* of huge blocks of ice from the Balmaceda Glacier into a waterway could be seen. They remained there for several minutes. Then, the boat was turned around and the tour went into the waters southwest of *Puerto Natales,* where they began to see abundant sea life. Derek pointed out Magellan penguins, sea lions, and elephant seals on the beach, streamer ducks racing along the top of the water, red-legged cormorants and other birds in the sky and perched on cliffs. Huddled out of the wind, the beer and wine were drunk, and the sandwiches eaten.

Back at Juan's berth, they all thanked him for the tour. Once warmed by the heater in the vehicle, one of the men suggested more beer. Derek had been told the microbrewery had a tasting room, so he drove them there. While more of his beer was drunk, the owner provided them with a history of German and other European emigration to the area. Derek refrained from drinking, so a safe, uneventful trip back to the lodge followed in the early evening. The traditional lamb stew, simmering on the stove, a salad and fresh bread, awaited them at the lodge. The meal was eaten with more beer.

The German guests chose to take short, unguided hikes on trails near the lodge each day, when not conversing and drinking in the living room. The next group of guests could not have been more different. Derek returned from the airport two days later with an anthropologist, Doctor Roderic Sanchez, his wife, and two teenage daughters from Madrid. Doctor Sanchez planned to spend his time at the lodge completing a paper of early inhabitants of Patagonia and he wanted his wife and daughters to see a southern portion of the region where the people he was writing about had lived.

Finding descendants of ancient people living and working at the lodge was not expected. Doctor Sanchez took advantage of the additional research that was offered. Harriett had a sincere interest in her ancestry and had learned a great deal from her mother and grandmother. Rios and Luis were of different tribal groups, but Luis was Mapuche, like Harriett. That tribe was the subject of the Doctor's paper. The natives spent hours each evening with Doctor Sanchez. Because of his size, Rios' family history was of interest, even though he was of the Tehuelche tribe.

The Sanchez women were experienced horsewomen, so they took advantage of guided rides with Luis that were offered daily. One day, Luis took them to a location that oral history suggested was a site of an early native settlement. The site seemed the best for such a settlement that he had ever seen, Luis explained. He suggested that the flat terrain adjacent to a wooded area could have grown food, a rock outcrop provided a buffer from strong winds, and there were several springs. Hearing about the site from his family, Roderic joined them on a return trip and spent the entire day with them in careful examination of the site. No artifacts were found or evidence of dwellings. However, he concluded that it was a potential settlement site that should be excavated.

The two men for whom the other lodge bedroom was being held arrived in a rental car the next day. They were young Italians. It was to be learned that they lived near the Switzerland border. They spoke German and Spanish, as well as Italian. In the first meeting with staff members, they referred to themselves as experienced mountain climbers. When Derek informed them that many resorts in the region provided very good guide services for climbers, but not Lautaro Lodge, he was told they did not need a guide. Realizing it would mean loss of revenue to his client if these men went to another resort, Derek, nevertheless, pointed out to them that the high mountains of Patagonia presented challenges to hikers not found in other regions of the world, so they should engage a guide. He felt a responsibility to do that.

Also, establishing a base so far from the mountains made no sense to him, and he had a feeling that problems were ahead if they became guests. Derek's arguments were ignored. Food for a two-day hike, to be placed in packs they left with Harriett, was requested when she showed them to their room. She was told they had eaten dinner, but they expected breakfast at six in the morning. Harriett started to explain the meal schedule but decided to accommodate them.

The hikers ate a hardy breakfast, took the packs that Heidi and Rosanne had filled with pre-cooked meats, bread, crackers, cans of soup, fruit, and vegetables, and departed the lodge. Derek was on his morning walk around the compound. He met them at their vehicle and gave them the number of his satellite telephone. Learning they carried such a telephone, he told them to call him if they got into trouble, a gesture that would prove to deeply involve him in their troubles.

The activities of the staff and the other guests continued that day. Derek and Rios worked in the hothouse and with Miguel at the fish operation. Afton finalized her order for goat-forage seed and forwarded the order. It wasn't until mid-morning the next day that the hikers staying at the lodge, Roberto Boitano and Georgio Oneto, were heard from. The one calling reported that they parked their car at the *Los Torres* campground, hiked up the north-facing slope of the mountain to take photographs of the three towers, the central one of which they planned to climb later. Heading back down the mountain, they became disoriented and instead of finding the trail to the campground, they became lost in dense woods. The caller added, "My friend slipped from a fallen tree trunk and wedged his leg between that log and another. With much difficulty, I freed him, but I fear his leg is badly broken. Yours is the only contact number we have, my SOS calls go unanswered, and the canopy of trees is too dense for us to be seem or rescued from the air. We need you to come into the woods and rescue us."

"That is a nearly an impossible request. How would we be able to locate two lone men in dense woods?" Derek told the caller.

The final words spoken on that call where, "You must try."

Derek explained the situation of Rios. They took their packs to the girls for food, changed into heavy clothing and hiking boots, then loaded sleeping bags and a first-aid locker into the Land Rover. Within a half-hour, they were on the road to the national park on what they both considered a very difficult mission.

During the hour and a half drive to the national park, they received calls from the same caller, who now identified himself as Roberto, about their progress. Derek told them they would begin searching as soon as possible and cautioned him about using up battery-life on the phone that would be needed to find them. A stop was made at park headquarters to report the situation. Unfortunately, there was no park service help available. An avalanche had trapped hikers and their rescue teams were involved with that incident. They found the rental car of the Italians and parked next to it in the campground.

Rios suggested their best approach would be to hike along the tree-line and look for a trail trending down the slope that the hikers may have taken, hoping to intersect a trail to the campground. They tied sleeping bags to their packs and Rios took the first-aid locker. They started the trek and found several trails which they traversed down for some distance. The tree-line route was followed until long after dark, in the hopes they could see light from a fire. Completely exhausted, they found a place protected from the wind to sleep for a few hours, ate, and drink tea from the thermos. At daylight, they continued. Finally, a thin column of smoke was sighted. Derek called the Italians satellite phone, but there was only silence. "Probably, a dead battery," he surmised.

Rushing down toward the smoke, they came across a place where fallen trees blocked the trail. Climbing over the trees, they discussed the fact that this must have been were the accident happened. Just beyond, they found that the hikers had fallen asleep and let the fire die-down. Derek built up the fire, woke Roberto, and tested the phone next to him, finding the battery was indeed dead. Rios looked at the other man's twisted leg, telling himself: *This man's hiking days are over. He may walk again if we can get him to a hospital, but it has been so long since the break that there is not anything that we can do for him here.* The last part of those thoughts he voiced to the others.

Rios and Derek decided the best way back to the vehicles was the way they came. A stretcher was created by affixing packs between two limbs. Georgio was laid on it and Rios and Derek struggled back up to the tree-line. There, Rios fashioned a way to carry the injured man on his back. The hike to the campground was difficult for all, and excruciating for Rios, but they made no stops. The back seats in the Range Rover were lowered and the injured man laid there. Derek told Roberto to follow them, saying they were going to rush his friend to the nearest hospital. The pain in his leg soon caused the injured man to drift into unconsciousness. Rios and Derek discussed the severity of the injury.

The nurses at the hospital remembered Rios and Derek from a similar mercy mission when the vehicle was backed to the emergency entrance of the hospital in *Puerto Natales*. Roberto parked the rental vehicle and joined them. Derek suggested that he register his friend, stay with him to learn what could be done for him, and return to his room in the lodge for rest. Leaving the hospital, Rios and Derek discussed the fact that they had done everything they thought possible for these guests. They voiced deep concerned about the injury.

The German couples had left the lodge earlier that day for home and the others had eaten dinner when Rios and Derek arrived at the lodge. Harriett explained that she had called for a van-for-hire to take the couples to the airport. Thankful that food had been saved for them, the rescuers ate and went to bed.

Another trip to the mountains was requested the next morning. Doctor Sanchez asked if his family could be taken there by Luis and Harriett, after they toured the area to the east that had been part of the Mapuche Kingdom, explaining that the kingdom, under a French king, once stretched from the Araucania Region to the Strait of Magellan. He added: "My work has been with people living to the north, and I don't expect to find ancient dwellings near here, but Harriett has told be about her grandparents and has memories of where they lived. She showed me unique craft-work created by her grandmother." Rios and Derek had no objections, they thought they deserved a day of rest. Rather, they helped the others engaged in their assigned activities.

Roberto returned in early afternoon. His report on his friend's condition was much as Rios had expected. He would walk again, with the aid of a cane, but would need to be hospitalized for a least a week and undergo extensive physical therapy for months. Roberto requested that he be allowed to stay at the lodge until he could escort his friend home. Both Derek and Rios expressed sympathy and Derek told him he would be welcome to stay at the lodge for as long as he wished. Derek offered to secure a guide for him if he still wanted to hike the high country and suggested some possible hikes in the Dorotea Range, to the east of the lodge, telling him that the range was not high, but that vertical cliffs along an escarpment were popular with mountain climbers. Roberto thanked Derek, saying local hikes appealed to him, but now he needed undisturbed sleep. As he went into the lodge, Derek suggested he charge his phone-battery as he slept.

Only Rios and Derek had spent any time with the Italians since they checked-into the lodge, so the absence of one of them at dinner was not noticed at first by the others. Derek provided a brief explanation of his injury while hiking, expecting Roberto to elaborate, but he didn't. The Sanchez family reported on a pleasant trip. The Doctor's only comment about the Mapuche Kingdom was that the site of the village, where Harriett thought her grandmother once lived, gave him two locations to describe in his paper of possible villages in the region. Roberto did spend time describing his experiences in climbing mountains in the Alps and elsewhere. The older of the Sanchez girls, Valeria, showed an interest in those experiences, and in him. She was only a year or two younger and appeared enamored with this dashing, handsome Italian. She continued to question him about hiking, sitting in the living room after dinner, while her sister, Camila, read. Their parents went to their bedroom early.

The next morning, Valeria told her parents that she had been invited to go with Roberto to a popular climbing area nearby, where he would teach her the basic elements of climbing. That was not well received by her mother, but when Roberto promised the climb was short and she would be safe, the parents agreed. Before the couple left the lodge, Roberto told Derek about the pending lesson and asked for directions to the trailhead leading to the base of the escapement he had mentioned in the Dorotea Range. Derek provided a map and several photographs he had taken on the morning he arrived at the lodge. He also suggested they ask for lunch and bottled water to take with them and reminded them to dress in warm clothes. At mid-morning, the couple left in the rental car.

In mid-afternoon, Derek received another frantic call from Roberto. He reported that Valeria had fallen, that he didn't think she had broken a bone, but she would not be able to walk back to the car. Learning from him their location, Derek told them that he and Rios would be there, as soon as possible. Finding Rios in the barn, what now appeared to be the lodge rescue team, left in the Range Rover. The hike from the trailhead was short. Valeria and Roberto where located within an hour. Rios examined the girl's leg and declared no bones were broken. The injury appeared to be a sprained ankle. Taking elastic tape from the first-aid locker he had brought, Rios wrapped the swollen ankle tightly, while Roberto showed Derek where the rock-face they were climbing had given-way and released the rope that was supporting Valeria. Derek realized that an experience climber should not have expected conglomerate strata to hold their weight, but he made no comment. The short distance of the fall, he thought, was very fortunate.

Rios raised the girl to her feet. She wrapped an arm around Roberto and hobbled next to him down the trail. Rios smiled at Derek and said: "This time the hospital staff is not needed."

The accident was explained to Camila, the girl's parents, and others back at the lodge. Harriett provided a bucket of ice water in which she placed the ankle and confirmed Rios' opinion regarding a sprain, predicting that when the swelling went down, the pain would be less, and Valeria would be able to walk, normally. Camila whispered to Derek that her sister was such a baby.

The parents accepted the extent of the injury explained to them. Roberto was still concerned that the young woman for whom he was developing strong feelings could have a more serious injury, and insisted he take her to the hospital for an X-ray when he went to see his friend the next day. Visiting hours at the hospital had not commenced when they arrived at the hospital. By the time they were allowed in Georgio's room, Valeria had been registered, and the X-ray procedure completed. The patient was asleep, so they sat, quietly, in chairs at the foot of his bed until he woke. Georgio's first comments were, "Falling-off a log. What a way to end my climbing, something I have enjoyed doing with you, Roberto. What will our families and friends at home say about this?"

"No one will hear from me anything about what happened," was the response to that question. "The important thing is that the leg heals properly and your work hard at therapy, so all other activities will not be seriously affected. I feel like I carry bad luck with me. My new friend here, Valeria Sanchez, fell while I was teaching her to climb. Her ankle injury does not appear serious, but an X-ray was taken here to make certain."

"Are you staying at the lodge where we stayed, Valeria?" Georgio asked.

Roberto answered for her, "She is, and I will be staying there and visiting you each day until we can go home."

"You are a pretty woman, Valeria," Georgio said and added jokingly, "Do you have a sister?"

"I do have a younger sister, Camila. She and my parents will be at the lodge for a few more days."

"I will miss meeting them, but I appreciate your visit, today. Try to keep unlucky Roberto out of trouble."

After the hospital visit, Roberto took Valeria to lunch at a waterfront restaurant. Walking up a ramp and to a table by the window, Valeria hardly limped. Much of the afternoon was spent there, eating and drinking wine. Their conversation became personal and they exchanged home addresses, pledging to see each other again in Europe. They enjoyed each other's company during the trip back to the lodge.

The next travel into the mountains involved Afton and Rios for the purpose of determining if the seeds Afton had sewn next to the ice sheet had germinated. As before, they spent a night at Patagonia Camp, parked near the ice sheet, and climbed to Afton's test plot. Rios walked to the lateral termination of the ice to check for loose blocks like the one that had injured Afton. Finding none, he hiked to where Afton was examining tiny plants and reported that to her. Excitedly, she told him the wildlife forage was growing.

After marking the corners of a one-meter square with piles of small stones. She counted the individual plants within the square and photographed the site.

"We should hike in both directions from here, along the newly exposed land to determine how much new wildlife habitat such re-seeding could establish," Afton suggested. They did that, together, until late afternoon. Afton explained to Rios that one of the factors in good deer habitat was continuous woodlands that provided cover through which the animals could move from one browsing area to another, and she made sketches of the tree-line as they hiked. Deciding it would be late before they got back to the lodge, they registered, once again, for two yurts upon returning to Patagonia Camp. They went to a restaurant for dinner, their first meal since breakfast at that same place.

A young man sitting at an adjacent table apparently heard them discussing the ice field. He asked to join them, telling them he, too, was studying the ice. Pedro Rodrigues was the name he provided when they welcomed him and stood to shake his hand. He reported that he worked for a governmental agency that was documenting the retreat of ice and discussed his specific assignment: "The entire ice front is being mapped with aerial photography. From survey points set many years ago, I am recording very accurate measurements from those points to the ice front, to augment measurements on the maps made from the aerial photographs."

"You shouldn't be working alone," Afton told him. "I was once injured by a falling block of ice, and I am here to tell you about it only because of the men with me at the time, including my friend with me now."

"My assistant was very tired, so he has gone to bed, early. What are you and your friends studying?"

Not wanting to divulge her discovery of ancient plants, the subject of the professional paper she was writing, Afton described only part of the work they had been doing, saying, "I am a botanist. Today, we mapped the trees downslope from the ice front. What your group is doing would aid our work greatly. Do you think I could be given a copy of the map being created of this area?"

Pedro replied, "The mapping will be made public, so I'm sure that would be possible."

Addresses where exchanged and the three of them discussed the ice retreat throughout dinner. Afton insisted on putting the charges for the meals and wine on her credit card. They parted in front of the restaurant with comments that they hoped to meet again.

Afton and Rios retired to their yurts. Pedro walked to the hotel.

After a light breakfast, the trip back to the lodge began at sunrise. Arriving there, it was learned that the Sanchez family had left, and Roberto had decided to trek, alone, on the ice field, against Derek's advice. Learning of that Rios commented, "I hope we will not have to rescue that unwise Italian, again."

Afton was anxious to tell Derek about the germination of the seeds they had collected and prepared for planting. At her computer, she printed the photographs she had taken. His comment was, "There are some great shots for inclusion in your paper. I see much professional admiration for you ahead and value in your discovery." She explained the map she had requested of the area where her test plot was located. Derek suggested they work together on another paper discussing the improvement of deer habitat and submit it to the management of the National System of Protected Wildlife Areas, in Santiago.

Chapter Eleven
Vegetative Cover

The seed that Afton had ordered arrived, in an amount less than Roger authorized, for improving goat forage. She had also been authorized to spread the seed from an aircraft. However, a storm-front had moved-in that would prevent that. Knowing that having the seed sown right away so that the pending rain would assist early germination, Afton discussed spreading the seed by hand with Derek and Rios. Rios told her that he had seen larger spreaders at the supply store, with straps and a crank, that a person could carry to distribute seed at a set rate. It was Derek's opinion that, although the terrain was very rocky, there were enough of them to do the job with hand spreaders.

The only guest now at the lodge was Roberto Boitano, who continued his activities without guide service, so a crew of Luis, Rios, and Derek were going to join, Raoul on the farm to spread seed, under the direction of Afton. The truck that was to be assigned to the farm was loader with the seed and driven by Rios to acquire four of the spreaders he had seen. He was to meet the others at the farm. Before the others departed in the Range Rover, Harriett asked if Luis would be able to stay at the farm with Raoul, so his room would be available for use by one of the couples due to arrive for a medical conference. Luis said he would be happy to do that and put his clothes in the vehicle. Harriett added bedding and told Derek that she now had an arrangement with a service at the airport to transport guests to the lodge. Therefore, he no longer was needed to do that.

Rolando and Raoul where repairing a section of fence when the Range Rover arrived. Rolando was overwhelmed by the magnitude of the planned expansion of the goat range when it was described by Afton. She took the opportunity to explain to him that while the new forage plants were becoming established the goat herd would have to be confined to the woodlands area and fed supplements, as required. The two of them walked through the wooded area looking at the plants and leaves the goats would eat. Derek helped Raoul with the fence repair and Luis got settled in the cottage. Rolando asked Raoul to walk the perimeter of the woods to estimate the fencing required to enclose that area and told Afton the material needed for such a fence would have to be purchased in the city. She told him that she had discussed that requirement with Roger.

Rios arrived. The truck was unloaded. The sacks and spreaders were covered with canvas because heavy rain began to fall. It had been expected that the workers would require rain gear, but such periods of heavy rain should be avoided. Rios and Derek drove back to the city for the supplies needed to enclose the woods. The others waited in front of a fire Rolando built in his living room fireplace for the rain to let up.

When the rainfall became lighter, the seeding began with Luis and Raoul wearing raincoats and a piece of canvas held over the spreaders they carried. Afton and Rolando, also wearing raincoats, walked along with them, providing guidance so the area being covered was proper. Afton explained why the temporary restriction to the wooded area was required to give the new plants time to develop. The seeding crew was expanded when Rios and Derek returned. Before nightfall, a large part of the area that had supported the herd was reseeded. Rolando, Luis, and Raoul went to the cottage where the young men prepared dinner.

On the way back to the lodge with Derek and Rios, Afton voiced her pleasure about the work accomplished on the first day. They anticipated the type of evening meal that the girls always prepared for them. They had not eaten since breakfast. The meal did not disappoint them. Slogging through the wet grass and mud had been very tiresome, so they were in bed early.

The second day of seeding goat forage resulted in seed coverage of the entire property that Roger had purchased. The work was less difficult because the rain fell only occasionally and was light. Those from the lodge had brought a large lunch. The mid-day break taken to eat the lunch in the cottage provided an opportunity for everyone to become better acquainted with Rolando. He spent time telling them about his years tending the herd, about his home in Europe, and his family.

At the lodge, the guests that were to attend the small medical conference had begun to arrive. The staff members who returned from the goat farm were served dinner at tables in the kitchen. The conference room had been organized for conference use. Harriett told them that Roberto had moved to a hotel in *Puerto Natales* to be nearer his friend in the hospital, so the seven doctors and their wives scheduled to attend the conference would all be provided accommodations.

The seeding continued during the succeeding week. The rain had stopped, but the rocky terrain slowed the traverses with the spreaders. Care had to be taken to prevent the turning of ankles, or worse injuries. This new area for the goats to eventually browse had not been explained to Rolando. He voiced his concern about that being allowed by the government. Afton explained that Roger considered this a test with the hope it would not only be allowed here, but others raising animals in similar areas would be encouraged by the government to expand their land use, also. The work continued until all the seed that Afton had purchased was broadcast, at the rates she had determined optimal.

The area covered was less than the acreage that her client had wanted, but she was convinced that when the plants were established, the area planted would support a large herd of goats, possibly as many as 500, nearly a ten-fold increase. Rolando was overwhelmed with that projection. He and Afton walked a long distance beyond the seeded area. They became convinced that more ice-free land could provide additional browsing or grazing for domestic herds, if reseeded or natural regrowth proved adequate. The spreaders were cleaned and loaded in the Range Rover. Afton assumed they would be needed to plant wildlife forage beyond her test plot, so they were placed in the garage at the lodge compound.

In subsequent days, the crew working on the farm was divided. Raoul and Luis helped Rolando build a four-foot-high fence, with tightly woven wire, around the wooded area. Rios and Derek began the job of hauling supplemental feed and bedding-straw in the truck. They also hauled wood used to build feeders. The wooded area was made ready to retain the herd while new plants became established. Raoul stayed to build feeders and to assist Rolando with the herd. The truck was left for their use. The remainder of the crew returned to begin transplanting deer forage starts in the hothouse to areas on *Estancia Margo.* The doctors had departed, so the quarters where Luis had stayed before were ready for him.

Less than a fulltime crew was available for this new seeding effort. Vacationers were again staying in the lodge, so a schedule of horse-back and hiking guided tours had to be re-established. That required Luis and Rios as tour guides part of each day. Transporting the plants into the hill country became a problem to be solved by Derek and Afton. A trailer for Rios' ATV was found behind the barn that needed repair work to the flat-bed, which Derek did and added side-boards. He and Afton spent each morning loading the trailer with plants in plastic containers, mostly of a five-gallon size, each with a hardy plant growing in improved soil.

During the day, when he was not guiding guests, Rios drove his ATV into the hills and walked back, returning in the evening to drive the ATV back for another load. Derek and Afton spent long hours digging holes and placing the plant roots and soil into those holes, then compacting the soil. Care was taken in selecting where the new plants were added to the existing brush cover. The intent was to increase the density of forage and to let the existing plants shield the new plants to prevent denuding and to reduce the risk of them being pulled from the ground. They walked back and forth to the job and ate a lunch the girls prepared at the site.

The planting of brush starts was a difficult job, requiring working on hands and knees a lot of the time. It proved to be dangerous, too. One morning, Derek was carrying containers toward where Afton was kneeling, digging holes with a short-handled shovel, when he saw a frightening scene. A crouched puma was creeping toward Afton, by then only a few feet away from her. He dropped the containers, raised his hands, and shouted as loud as he could. The cat sprung, but rather than landing on Afton, it came down beyond her and ran down the hill. Derek rushed to her side and embraced her as she stood. Sitting on a nearby rock outcrop, Derek held her tightly until her shaking stopped, and she was able to speak.

"That was a close-call," she said.

Derek responded, "That it was. You were under attack by the largest cat I have seen beyond Africa. Rios warned us about the danger of puma. Even with all the natural food that deer and large rodents provide, he thinks that the animal does attack with no reason, at times. Even with a rifle in my hands, I could have done little to save you from serious injury, or death, if the cat had landed on you. We must heed the warning and always be on alert. I will carry

Rios' rifle from now on and fire at any other puma we see, to keep them away from our work."

The work by the two of them continued for many days. Fortunately, there were no other sightings of a puma, but the long days took a toll. By evening, they were very tired and did little except eat and sleep when not in the hills. They were happy when the guests left the lodge and Rios and Luis were able to spend the daylight hours helping with their effort. Finally, all the plants from the nursery had been set out. Afton prepared a portfolio with photographs of what had been accomplished.

The next Sunday afternoon, Raoul came to pick up Heidi for a picnic they had arranged by telephone. Excitedly, she had prepared special food and had been looking forward to seeing him again. Knowing that seeing the goat herd would please her, he drove her to a beautiful site for a picnic on a hillside with many blooming flowers he had seen adjacent to the farm. Sitting among the flowers, they discussed their work and their feelings for each other. Packing the picnic basket after a couple of hours, they embraced and kissed, passionately.

At the farm, they walked through the goat herd, still in the fenced pasture with the adjacent shed. Raoul pointed out some of the changes he had convinced Rolando to instigate, including new fencing to separate does with single kids, from those with multiple young. All the animals appeared very healthy to Heidi, which Raoul attributed to the supplemental feed he worked hard to provide. The couple returned to the lodge at dinner time. Harriett insisted they eat the evening meal that she and Rosanne had prepared.

During the meal, Miguel notified the others that he would need help the next day. A tanker truck was scheduled to take the adult salmon, alive, to a processing plant in *Puerto Natales*. Harriett also had an announcement to make: "The lodge has been reserved next weekend for the wedding and a reception for the daughter of Juan Ledesma, the provincial government official who had been to the lodge before. We are to be provided with a list of the things requested of us for that a special event."

Afton had kept Margo informed of the activities of the staff in her regular letters, one of which she had placed in the mail box a few days earlier. These developments called for another letter, she decided, which was written that night.

The fish transfer truck was equipped with a telescoping arm and a large net to gather the salmon from the tanks where they had grown from smolt and dumped them into the truck tank. It was a very modern, well designed system. Rios and Derek were needed to net a small percentage of fish missed by the automated equipment and to carry them in large buckets to the tanker truck. Thousands of salmon ready for processing were loaded in a few hours and the truck departed for the processing plant. Miquel said it would take a few days of circulating fresh water before the next generation was placed into the system. Afton photographed the entire operation.

The requests made of the staff for the wedding ceremony and reception were not unreasonable and easily accomplished. An archway made of willow branches, decorated by wildflowers from the nursery, was erected on the porch. The conference room was cleared for dancing and a small bandstand built at the far end. The food and drink requested for the reception was extensive, but the other meal menus where left up to Heidi and Rosanne.

Learning that Tomas, Mary, and Marco Ledesma would be in attendance, Afton and Derek discussed how the work they had been doing could be properly presented to the President's Chief of Staff. They knew their client would want that done. As it turned out, that could not have been done more easily. The Tomas Ledesma family arrived a day early in a government car. Once settled into the master suite and adjoining room where they had stayed before, Tomas and Mary came back downstairs and asked to meet with the staff.

Their first words were those of sincere thanks to Afton and Rios for saving Marco on the ice fields. Mary said their son had told them about the incident when they returned home from that previous trip to the lodge. Then, Tomas questioned Afton, Derek, Rios, and Miguel about their activities, saying he thought those activities would all prove important to his country. He was aware that the feasibility study prepared for a hydroelectric project had been delivered. He knew of the success of the land-based fish farm, and about the experiments with improving habitat for a rare deer species. He was told about land-uses in areas emerging from the ice for the first time. That was of special interest to him and the President, he told them.

Afton made an amazing, concise presentation covering the goat pasture expansion and her experiment directed toward establishing plant regrowth for wildlife forage in another ice-free area. Derek mentioned the letter he had written to the management of the National System of Protected Wildlife Areas, regarding Afton's experimental test plot and a possible expansion thereof.

Harriett interrupted to say that dinner was being served. They moved into the dining room. Marco joined them. Afton and Rios welcomed Marco with embraces. The discussions continued and many questions from Tomas were answered. Mary and Marco were active participants in those discussions.

The evening was discussed by Afton, Derek, Rios, and Miguel walking to their quarters. Each expressed their feelings that it had been the best forum possible to inform the government about what Roger had asked them to accomplish for him and his company. Afton said that another letter to Margo was in order.

The weekend wedding event took place as planned. Catarina Ledesma married Hector Foerster in a simple ceremony under the arch of wildflowers on the porch of the lodge. It was an unusually warm and sunny afternoon. Nearly two dozen close friends and family witnessed the ceremony, sitting on folding chairs moved there from the conference room, where dancing until a late hour ended the day. The reception after the wedding and the dancing were attended by more than fifty. A local band played during the reception and for the dancing. French and German pastries, prepared by Heidi and Rosanne, and French champagne were served at the reception by the three young woman on the staff.

The other staff members spent the day and evening in their quarters. Marco Ledesma became bored with the wedding events, so he joined Rios. They discussed Patagonia, the portion of the country that Marco had found offered so many exciting things for him to do. One of those things was kayaking in fjords. Rios had never done that, but he promised to take Marco if he was able to get his parent's permission.

Marco's parents spent the next day with Tomas's brother Juan's family in *Puerto Natales*. They authorized Marco to go with Rios on another adventure, feeling he would be safe with this giant of a man who had saved his life before. Rios picked Marco up in the Range Rover in early afternoon at the address he obtained from Harriett. At a kayak rental facility on the waterfront, it was learned that Rios was not comfortable squeezed into a kayak, so he rented a canoe, knowing that he would not be able to keep up with Marco in a sleek kayak. He had, however, experience traveling by canoe as a boy. He and Marco established rules for their trip up the sound. Marco was to be free to travel at his own speed but was to keep Rios within view as he paddled near the shore.

With great force, two elephant seals that Rios startled slide down the bank as he paddled past, overturning the canoe. It was Marco's turn to assist Rios. He raced from the middle of the sound to help right the canoe. The incident became something they both laughed about, as Rios climbed back into the canoe and the seals barked at them. Rios' cold, wet clothes were not comical. He paddled back to the rental facility as fast as he could, with Marco paddling the kayak by his side. Leaving Marco to check-in the kayak and canoe, Rios rushed to the vehicle, found a towel left by someone else and slid into the driver's seat with the towel wrapped around him. The heater was set on high.

Marco joined him and again the two, who were becoming very good friends, laughed at the situation. Parting at the Juan Ledesma home, they vowed to try the activity together at a future time at this place or somewhere else. Rios said he would find a large kayak to purchase. At the lodge, Rios was able to get to his quarters for dry clothes without anyone knowing about him being dumped into the sound.

A copy of the map of the area of Afton's vegetative test plot arrived. The encouragement she had received from Tomas Ledesma regarding the extension of the test area, with the seeds she had collected and prepared for planting, was enough for her to plan such an expansion. The area she had seeds to cover, at the rate she though best, was too small to consider aerial distribution, she decided after studying the map. Once again, the hand spreaders would be needed. There was enough time, she thought, before the next group of lodge guest arrived, for Rios and Luis to help her and Derek do the work. They drove to the site with food and water for three days, a tent she had ordered, and sleeping bags. She had no concerns about sleeping in the same tent with her male associates.

As she had done when seed was spread before, Afton walked adjacent to where the seed was falling and directed changes in the setting on the spreaders and the distance between those carrying them. The sacks of seeds had been carried and left at intervals along the steep slope of ice-free terrain. Mud and rounded rocks of all sizes made it difficult to walk along the slope and stands of trees had to be avoided. Overall, the job was much more difficult than any of them had imagined when they studied the map.

The two nights in camp proved to be a pleasant experience. The surrounding scenery was spectacular. No rain fell. The nights were very cold, but the sleeping bags were rated for such low temperatures. They carried dry wood from the forested areas to the campsite each day, so a fire was kept burning in front of the tent much of the time. A small, propane-fired stove in the tent was used to prepare meals. Luis proved to be the best cook. Evenings were spent telling stories of other camping trips each had made. The experiences of Derek on safari in Africa were of great interest to the others.

The time allotted for the work was adequate. As the camp was disassembled and packing completed on the third day, Afton commented that she was convinced that this experimental site would become the basis for the government taking seriously the expanding of wildlife habitat being created by retreating ice and she was very pleased about what they had accomplished. Derek drove them to a restaurant at Patagonia Camp where they enjoyed an expensive meal, with wine and beer, before returning to Lautaro Lodge.

Harriett had been anxiously waiting for their return and came to where they were unloading the seed spreaders in the garage to tell them about new guests that Roger had called to inform her about. She had been told that a single man, named Josh Wright, was to be assigned the master suite, two other men would be accompanying him, but no other guests were to be allowed, and Derek was to call him after noon, London time, to discuss these guests. It was explained to Harriett that they had eaten dinner on the way back and Derek offered to share what he would learn from the call with them at breakfast.

Derek was up early to make the call. What he learned was to have a grave effect on those at the lodge: A good friend of Roger's would arrive at the airport later that day, accompanied by two bodyguards. The friend, Josh Wright, had taken a job as Operations Manager with an oil company in Trinidad—Tobago. Because Roger had faith in the man's ability, he had invested in the company for whom he worked. Fraudulent actions that involved millions of pounds were discovered by the friend and his administrative assistant, Jenifer Arata. They reported the fraud to government authorities, who arrested the President of the company and the comptroller, the perpetrators. Both Josh and Jenifer, then, received death threats to prevent them from testifying in court, and the protection provided by island officials they deemed totally inadequate, so Roger was called for help. Roger devised a plan that should allow them to remain safe until the court date. It involved his plane flying them out of the country, Miss Arata to friends in Brazil and Josh to the Lautaro Lodge, with two bodyguards who had worked for Roger before.

"What do you want me to do?" Derek asked.

"I suggest you contact someone you can trust to meet the company plane and take Josh and my men to a hotel in *Puerto Natales,* as a diversion. You should meet them and take them to the lodge. Their presence at the lodge must be kept a secret until you are notified of the return of our plane. Then, make sure they get back on the plane, safely. Our pilots will make the return flight to Port-of-Spain with Josh and his associate to testify."

"You can count on me," Derek replied, accepting another assignment far-removed from his consulting contract.

Uncertain what to tell the others about the call, Derek went to breakfast. He knew he must tell them about the need to keep the stay of the next guests a secret, but decided not to tell them the reason, or divulge the fact that two of them were bodyguards for the third. He did explain they were friends and associates of Roger.

In private, Derek asked Harriett if the driver who now provided transportation to and from the airport was trustworthy and found that she thought him honest and willing to do everything asked. Therefore, he called the number Harriet had given him when he received a call that established the planned arrival of Roger's plane. That part of Roger's plan was implemented. Derek meet them at the parking lot of a hotel, introduced himself, and escorted them to the Range Rover, after the other driver had left. On the drive to the lodge, Derek learned that Josh and Roger had studied geology together at university and had remained close friends ever since. The other two men were former law enforcement officers who had worked for Roger on several occasions. All of them where near middle-age, spoke with a strong British accent, and appeared to be in good physical condition.

It was dinner-time when they reached the lodge, so after they were settled into rooms, the entire staff were able to meet them as they entered the dining room, where another fine meal was served. None of the guests had ever been to Patagonia. That meant a lot of questions needed to be answered as they ate. The guests went to the living room for after-dinner drinks and the others to their quarters.

A few days later, concern about these guests surfaced when the girls reported seeing hand guns in two of the rooms while cleaning those rooms. To the others, individually, Derek explained that two of the men were bodyguards but still didn't reveal why Josh needed protection. It was assumed the men carried guns as they strolled around the compound or spent hours reading in the living room.

Josh began to spend time with Derek and Afton in discussions about each-others' professional work. Josh used a computer that Afton offered. He told them he had been keeping up with the growing world-wide interest in oil-shale development, but his experience as a petroleum geologist had been in producing liquid and gaseous hydrocarbons from conventional sources. However, he saw his stay in Chile as a chance to study the potential reserves in the country. Days later, he finished a report, with Afton and Derek's help, that defined potential areas of oil production from shale in the southern part of the nation.

Josh reported that he intended to leave a copy of the report for Roger to study, knowing his friend was interested in Chilean natural resource investments. Derek pointed out that investments in natural resources, particularly lithium, was his client's principal interest, so he would appreciate the report. Roger's reasoning for his other investments—to prove to the government that his organization was an exceptionally good steward of the land in order to receive fair consideration in the granting of concessions for natural resource development when in competition with the major companies—was explained by Derek. Josh expressed his belief that, based on his experience in such matters, the approach was sound, and asked about the projects. Those projects to prove viable land use in areas being exposed by retreating ice, Josh found most exciting.

One morning, Afton suggested it was time to inspect the seeding they had done on the goat farm, so she, Derek, and Rios spent a day there. They found that Rolando and Raoul had started the construction of a shearing shed and while Afton walked through the seeded area, Derek and Rios helped with the construction.

Afton was pleasantly surprised by the plant germination. With a measuring tape she carried in a pack, one-square meter sites were again marked at several places. Within those boundaries, the number of emerged plants were counted, recorded in a notebook, and the sites were photographed. Back with the others, Afton reported that it was time to move the goats into the wooded area. "But first," she added, "Let's eat the enormous lunch that Heidi prepared for all of us."

Canvas was spread in the woods for a picnic. Afton enjoyed some of the food and fruit juice with the others, but she also documented the wide-leaf plants and trees with leaves hanging low enough for the goats to reach, standing on their hind legs. These data would help determine the amount of supplemental feed that would need to be purchased during the time the goats remained in the woods.

Once the picnic was finished and the basket and canvas removed, the gate into the woods was opened. Herding was not necessary. The goats rushed in to eat the fresh, green vegetation. They had surrounded Afton before she had finished her estimate of the amount of such vegetation now available to them. She spent the afternoon observing the browsing animals, in awe of their reach.

The shearing shed was completed by early evening. Those returning to the lodge were satisfied with what they had accomplished at the Andoni Goat Farm. They had no idea of the turmoil to be faced at the lodge in subsequent days.

Chapter Twelve
Abduction

The men determined to prevent Josh and his former assistant from testifying didn't give up looking for them. Through interviews and bribes, they eventually learned they had left Port-of-Spain in a private plane registered to Roger Richardson, the owner of a lodge in Patagonia that was a destination resort advertised on the internet. Two men were dispatched to the lodge. With a rental car obtained at the airport and directions to the lodge, those men followed the highway to a place below the lodge property. There, the car was driven into an area of dense brush where it could not be seen. They hiked to the compound and hid in the garage until late afternoon, noting keys left in a parked ATV.

Moving into shrubs and vines adjacent to the porch of the main building, they stayed hidden, except when venturing to peer through the window into the living room where they periodically saw the man they were after and two other men. That continued until those men were seen going upstairs. Opening the door quietly and creeping inside, the intruders saw no one, but they heard women's voices in the back. From there, they moved, undetected, into the upstairs hallway. Choosing a room at the far end of the hallway with an open door, they waited with the door ajar. Taking turns, they watched for movement from other rooms. A call came, announcing dinner was ready and Josh and his bodyguards left their rooms. The intruders moved into the room that Josh left where they awaited his return.

Upon his return a few hours later, Josh was attacked. A gag was tied across his mouth and his hands tied behind his back with rope. Not a word was spoken as the captors paced the room and sat staring at their captive. In the middle of the night, Josh was forced to walk from the room, down the stairs, and onto the porch. He was held on the porch steps by one of the men while the other one went to get the ATV they had seen. After loading Josh into the vehicle and tying him with more rope, the men separated. One ran back toward where the rental car had been left. The other one drove-off in the ATV.

Derek was awakened by the sound of the ATV and went to the walkway in front of his quarters. In the light cast by the floodlight at the corner of the row of residential units, he saw Josh being taken away. He presumed the vehicle was headed up the slope to the nearest site viable for a helicopter-landing beyond the compound. Without regard for the time, Derek rushed back inside and called to report his sighting to Roger on his satellite telephone.

Roger answered the call. His response was: "I'm a day late. Our plane, with me onboard, is *en route* to pick up Josh. His assistant is onboard. I decided to pick her up, first, so we could talk about the evidence against the men who defrauded the company. You must try to free Josh. He will not be killed right away. The bad guys know that both he and Miss Arata must be silenced, so they will torture him, hoping to locate her and the files she has copied. What do you think is their plan?"

Derek replied, "My guess is that a helicopter is going to land on the ridge at daybreak and whisk Josh away to where he can be questioned."

"Can you intercept the abductor before that happens?"

"We will try our best."

"If you can free Josh, take him directly to the airport and wait in the hangar near where we have parked our plane in the past until we get there. The man who has Josh, as I'm sure you are aware, works for those who are desperate. They are very dangerous. You will be risking your life, I know. Don't take unnecessary chances."

Derek terminated the call and pounded on the door to Rios's quarters. The pounding brought both Rios and Afton to the walkway. He explained the situation and his call to Roger.

Rios offered, "We should ride horses to the ridge. I'll dress and meet you at the stable." When told that Derek knew nothing about the abduction, Afton said she would dress and find out what had happened in the lodge.

Derek had bridled two horses when Rios joined him at the stable. Rios carried his rifle over his shoulder. The two of them rode-off, bareback, at a gallop, headed to the easternmost trail to the ridge. In the lodge, Afton learned that no one was aware of what had happened when she woke the staff and the bodyguards. Not believing the abduction could have happened while they slept, the bodyguards checked Josh's room, finding no sign of a struggle. They assumed that it would have taken more than one man to subdue Josh without him fighting-back. Reporting that to Afton, they were told that Derek saw only one man on the ATV with Josh, and she suggested they search the compound for others. At daylight, the search was made by the armed bodyguards, to no avail.

Seeing the ATV parked with Josh still in it and a man spraying white paint on nearly bare ground when they reached the ridge, Derek and Rios dismounted and tied their horses. Creeping closer, they positioned themselves with dense brush obscuring them from the man's view. Derek shouted for the man to throw-down the pistol in his belt. Instead of complying, the man pulled the pistol and began shooting toward the voice. Rios raised up and fired one round from his rifle. The man fell into the triangle markings he had been making to guide a helicopter, the rotors of which could be heard in the distance.

"You start back with Josh," Derek said. I'll follow with the horses. The helicopter crew can have the downed man."

The rescuers rushed into the cover of dense trees where they could not be seen from the air before regrouping. Josh was cut loose from the multiple bindings and gag. Derek explained to him what he had learned from Roger. They watched as the helicopter descended. The man in the landing site was taken onboard, and the craft flew away. The thought that the helicopter would be seen again was on each man's mind as they returned to the lodge.

With Harriet's permission, the bodyguards had taken the Range Rover to search for evidence of any participants in the abduction. When everyone involved in the incident was safely back in the lodge, they reported finding where a car had been parked off the highway in dense brush. The bodyguards suggested that scratches must have been created by driving into and backing out of that spot which should allow for identification of the vehicle. Derek told everyone that finding other perpetrators would have to wait, because his instructions were to get Josh and his men to the airport, immediately, and wait in a hangar for Roger's plane. Packing and loading the Range Rover were accomplished quickly and Derek followed those instructions.

No problems were encountered getting onto the airport grounds when Derek explained he was delivering passengers to catch a private plane. The wait at the hangar where Margo had taken flying lessons was not long. When Roger emerged from the plane with Miss Arata by his side, he explained the stop would be only for as long as it took to refuel and urged the passengers to hurry onboard when that was completed. There was time for Josh to embrace his assistant, a pretty, trim young woman with light-black skin, introduce her to Derek, and to give her and Roger a brief summary of his ordeal. Roger thanked Derek for his efforts before re-boarding. The plane was soon airborne.

Leaving the runway, Derek parked in front of the terminal and went to inquire about the return of an extensively scratched rental car. He learned that such a vehicle had been returned by one man, who refused to pay for the damages, and that the man had left on a flight to Santiago. Assuming this bizarre incident had ended, Derek returned to the lodge. At dinner, the entire staff was briefed about what had transpired, and why Josh Wright had been a guest.

On the plane, the bodyguards voiced remorse for failing to protect Josh. Roger informed all on board that they were cutting it as close as possible on the return to Port-of-Spain for the trial, but the bodyguards would be needed for the protection of Josh and Jenifer for one night in hotel rooms before they were due in court. Roger was told that the bodyguards would spend that night sitting in front of the hotel rooms.

The court action moved along in a straight-forward manner. The prosecutor introduced Roger as an investor who had been asked to be in attendance by the Board of Directors of the damaged corporation, solicited the testimony of Josh and Jenifer, and presented the supporting documentation to the judge. The case against the defendants was overwhelming. They were ordered to provide restitution for the money they took and sentenced to twenty years in prison.

Still concerned for the safety of a friend and his associate, Roger insisted they return to his plane immediately after the trail, with no plan regarding the future. A van was hailed to take them the 19 miles to Piarco International Airport. The five of them walked to where the plane was parked near the South Terminal. Roger served the passengers wine when all were settled in the plane and told Josh and Jenifer about an offer that the board of the oil company had asked him to make: the positions of President and Treasurer of the corporation were available to them. Practically in unison, they replied that they were not interested. Jenifer explained that in her nearly five years on the island of Trinidad, she had never felt truly safe, and she was certain that the friends of the convicted would seek revenge.

"Then, we should go to London and regroup," Roger suggested. He walked to the cockpit to tell the pilots of that decision.

An attempt at revenge was soon manifest. During the pre-flight check, the pilot, Ned Willis, found a bomb had been placed in a wheel-well. Rushing back into the plane, he ordered everyone to de-plane and to run as far away as possible before a bomb exploded. He and his copilot followed the others. Everyone ran until reaching the South Terminal building. Roger reported the bomb to the first policeman he saw and was told the Transit Police Unit of the Minister of National Security would be called. The officer directed Roger and his party into a special lounge where they could wait.

The lounge had a view of the plane through a large window. The flight crew and Roger paced in front of the window, expecting to see an explosion at any time. Josh and Jenifer took seats and discussed the problems that their good deed for a company who had hired them had caused. Jenifer asked about where Josh had stayed while she was with family members. He described Lautaro Lodge and the staff, promising to take her there some day.

It seemed like a long time before an armored vehicle was seen arriving at the plane. Men in body armor, presumably a bomb squad, could be seen examining the exterior of the aircraft. Everyone watching hoped the men were experienced and had proper disposal equipment.

The police officer returned to the lounge with an older man in civilian clothes. He said the man with him was from the office of the Minister of National Security. When that man asked about the bomb, Ned explained where he had seen it. On a hand-held radio unit, that fact was reported. Nervously, all watched as a man spent time near the wheel-well. With the bomb removed, examined, and placed in a sealed container, it was reported that the bomb was designed to explode when the wheel was retracted. The man from the Minister's office asked that the owner of the plane stay for an interview and to fill out a report, saying the others could return to the plane. Roger had to provide a complete explanation of why his plane had been a target, which he did as he watched the others walking back to the plane. The interviewer mentioned how fortunate Roger was to have such a cautious pilot, something that had been proven many times over the years.

Another pre-flight check had been completed when Roger reached the plane. Soon, the plane was safely airborne, and the beautiful Caribbean Sea could be seen from all windows. At cruising altitude, the copilot, Ted Benson, came back to help Roger prepare a meal for everyone. The passengers ate, conversing about the entire ordeal. Josh expressed his sincere appreciation for the help of everyone and expressed his hope that the incident was now behind them. With the galley dishes and cups back in cabinets, thanks to Jenifer, all onboard relaxed. After a couple of hours, the passengers were asleep.

Before the descent to Gatwick Airport began, Roger and Josh were awake, talking about the future. Josh had taken from his suitcase his copy of the report on Chilean oil shale he had prepared and left for Roger at Lautaro Lodge. Roger studied the report and a long discussion ensued between them about the economic potential of the expanding exploitation of this non-conventional fuel source. Roger suggested that Josh spend some time in his London office conducting economic analyses.

The flight crew had left a car at the airport and offered to take the bodyguards with them into the city. Margo was at the company hangar with her car. She greeted Roger with a tight embrace and kiss. She informed Josh and Jenifer that she expected them to say at their home. She had not met them until then, but she knew Roger would want that. With the luggage in her Mercedes, Margo drove them to a magnificent home between the airport and downtown London.

During the next week, Josh went with Roger to his office and studied the available data he could find on the economics of oil-shale production. Roger spent his days in and out of the office, working with financial institutions and tending to the affairs of a growing investment company. Jenifer was thrilled with her time with Margo. She was given tours of a city she had longed to visit during much of her life. An early highlight was a trip to a gallery of paintings with subjects related to the natural environment. To her surprise, scenes painted by Margo were featured. Many, Margo told her, were of scenes in Patagonia near Lautaro Lodge. More than ever Jenifer hoped Josh would keep his promise to take her there.

The prelude to a most significant highlight for Jenifer occurred one evening when she and Josh were alone. Margo and Roger had left them in their home to attend a political gathering. The housekeeper/cook prepared a fine evening meal before she went to spend time with her parents. After dinner, enjoying wine, Josh asked Jenifer to marry him. They had grown close over the short time they had known each other, and Jenifer had thought her feelings for him were true love, but there had been little to suggest that Josh felt the same way about her. She stammered with words of excitement, when he placed a diamond ring on her finger. They kissed with great pent-up emotion, both having a desire to go to bed together. However, that opportunity ended when Margo and Roger returned.

The announcement was not a big surprise to their host and hostess. Both had detected mutual, loving feelings between their house guests and had discussed that fact. Roger opened a bottle of champagne to celebrate the occasion and plans for a wedding commenced. Margo was quick to recommend events like the ones in which she and Roger were married: a simple ceremony in the local Anglican Church, a home reception, and a long honeymoon, all of which pleased the couple. Jenifer asked if a honeymoon at Lautaro Lodge would be possible. That idea thrilled them all, Margo and Roger because they were very proud of the lodge in which they had invested so much time and money, and Josh because he had hoped to take Jenifer there for them to enjoy what he had missed, earlier.

The English wedding and reception were lovely. There were only a few guests at the reception, those that Josh had met in Roger's office, those who had flown with the couple, and those from the church. The decorations, food, and wine were superb. The home was vacated for the wedding night. Marco and Roger spent that night at the Ritz Hotel in the city.

During the next two days, the newlyweds flew on commercial airlines to *Puerto Natales*. Margo had made certain that their arrival was anticipated. Derek picked them up at the airport. Afton had decorated the master suite with bouquets of wild flowers, and a second reception was organized. Doctor Grayson had returned for a few more weeks of work in the fossil excavation and there were four guests from Japan in the middle of a one-week stay. All staying on the property were invited to join in the celebration. It was a grand affair. Heidi and Rosanne had prepared a feast and Derek had chosen local wines and beer to be served. Jenifer and Josh could not have been happier.

The main work activities on the *estancia* during the next week were the expansion of the fossil excavation by Doctor Grayson, and Luis and a second, seasonal, gathering of seeds for the enhancement of deer browse by Afton, Derek, and Rios. The Japanese guests were picked up to be taken to the airport. Josh asked for use of the Range Rover, so he and Jenifer could tour the area. He was informed by Derek that the vehicle was for everyone to use. The two of them also spent many hours hiking the property. Then, Josh went back to work with Jenifer helping him.

A large package containing topographic maps and aerial photographs arrived from the office in London, addressed to Josh. The items were what he had ordered while he worked in that office. Organizing these in the conference room, he explained to Afton and Derek that their use would be in mapping the portion of the Magellan Basin extending south to *Punta Arenas*, an area that his research indicated had the potential for the production of non-conventional oil and gas—from oil shale and sandstone with low permeability—in addition to the lignite and sub-bituminous coal now being mined. He told them he was going to develop a plan to undertake the field work, recognizing there was only a few weeks of the summer season remaining. His need for a mapping assistant was discussed. Afton suggested he interview Luis' younger brother, Ramon, for that job, saying she had met him when he came to visit his brother, and she was impressed by him. Derek added, "If he is as conscientious as Luis, he will be a good assistant."

That evening at dinner, Josh asked Luis if his younger brother would consider working for him in field mapping in the hills and along the waterways. Luis replied, "Ramon worked as a horse wrangler for a resort until horseback riding there was discontinued. He now seeks a new job. The two of us have hiked a lot, he has experience with a canoe, and he knows how to survive in the wilds. I know he would serve you well."

"Would it be possible for you to go with me to meet Ramon in the morning?" Josh asked.

"If we go very early, so I will be back in time to begin work with Doctor Grayson."

"We can do that. Let's leave at sun-up."

Before he went to meet Luis at the vehicle the next morning, Josh called Roger. He explained his plan to hire a field assistant and to begin the field mapping they had discussed. That was approved, and Roger told him that arrangements had been made for him to lease another field vehicle of his choosing, and he should charge whatever equipment, supplies, and food he would need at the stores where Harriett maintained accounts. Luis was in the vehicle when Josh arrived.

Ramon and their mother, Rosa, were ready to receive them when they drove to the family home. Rosa had prepared coffee and a large breakfast. After a short discussion, Josh was convinced that he and Ramon would make a good team, and that Ramon had the experience in the region that would be most helpful. After breakfast, Ramon showed Josh a storage room where he kept a great deal of camping equipment that he said would be available for their use.

Returning to the table where Luis was still sitting with their mother, Josh suggested that Ramon go with them to the vehicle-leasing company to pick out a vehicle for their use. There, a new hard-top Jeep was chosen. Josh and Ramon signed as drivers. Knowing that Luis was concerned about getting to his job on time, Josh suggested he head back in the Range Rover, which he did. Josh and Ramon went to the supply store where Ramon was asked to pick out what would be needed to supplement his equipment, while Josh had the store manager call Harriett for authorization to add the costs to the lodge account. What was chosen was loaded in the Jeep.

Josh asked about a large canoe in which the two of them could travel with camping equipment, mapping equipment, food, and rock samples. Ramon suggested a local builder of canoes that were very sturdy. Returning to the lodge, a canoe was secured on the roof of the Jeep. Josh backed the vehicle into the garage and the canoe was hung from the rafters. Arrangements were made for Ramon to take the Jeep home, organize the loading, and to come back for Josh the next morning to begin the work. Josh made Ramon aware that the first few days would involve examining, sampling and measuring the strata to east of the lodge, an area close-by that was frequented by rock-climbers, so they would not need to camp.

At the end of the first day, during which Ramon walked along the top of the cliffs with one end of a 300-foot measuring tape and Josh worked below him, a routine was established that provided measurements of the various, exposed strata in the region, and detailed descriptions. Samples of each rock type were placed in small bags on which identifying numbers were written and recorded in a notebook.

That evening, Ramon was asked to join Josh and the others for the evening meal at the lodge, as Harriett had suggested, but he said he thought he should spend the evenings with his mother, whenever possible, so he left Josh at dusk.

The first phase of the work took four days to complete. The next phase consisted of traversing the hills and mountain slopes south of *Puerto Natales* where shorter segments of exposed strata were marked on a topographic map from coordinates obtained from global-positioning equipment, the thicknesses measured, and the outcrops sampled. A campsite was set up in a beautiful, wooded area. It included Ramon's tent and camping equipment. Work progressed from that campsite, driving the Jeep wherever possible and hiking with backpacks where required. At the end of five days, the camp was disassembled with the intent of moving further south after a two-day break. Ramon spent the break with his mother and Josh with his new wife and the staff at the lodge. The schedule of work weeks, breaks, and the southward movement of the camp continued for a month.

Margo continued to write and call Afton regularly. In a call soon after Josh and Jenifer arrived, she asked that Jenifer be provided companionship while her husband was not with her and that she be given something to keep her busy, if that was possible. That should not have been a concern. Jenifer helped everyone at the lodge, from meal preparation and housekeeping to acting as an assistant to the professionals. She also helped her husband by locating a laboratory on the internet to conduct analyses of the samples he collected, forwarding the samples to the lab, and filing the data received.

During any leisure time, she asked to be shown the areas that Margo had painted. At the site where Margo first painted abundant wildflowers, Afton and Jenifer spent an entire afternoon engaged in discussing personal matters. The strong bond of friendship that had developed between Margo and Afton was explained. Jenifer mentioned that she, too, considered Margo a friend, although they had not spent much time together. Jenifer asked about the attitude of the local citizens toward people of mixed-color and was told that Afton had not met any since arriving and that she had been told the entire population of negroes and those with negro blood in Chile was very small. She expressed her opinion that it should not be a problem for her, because the natives and mestizo were part of the existing society.

The work required to examining the strata and other geologic features exposed on the slopes and in the cliffs bounding the fjords and narrow waterways was much more challenging for Josh and Ramon. Two days were spent paddling the canoe from the dock at *Puerto Natales* and returning there. After that, the boat of Juan Aparicio had to be rented to take the canoe to places further to the southwest. Each day thereafter, the team lowered the canoe from the boat, paddled during daylight hours to extend the study, and returned to the boat to spend the night.

On those days, the canoe was beached wherever possible, near rock exposures that Josh had studied with binoculars. Only occasionally did the enclosing terrain allow for measurements of the strata thickness, but samples of each rock type that was accessible from outcrops were collected. Both from the beaches and the boat, photographs were taken by Josh using a digital camera with a long lens. During this later phase, Jenifer went with them to help Juan prepare meals and Derek joined them to study the enormous number of seabirds and sea mammals he knew they would encounter.

The experience was one that Jenifer would never forget, particularly the sight of birds in flight, so numerous that the sun rays were blocked, and birds on nest, tightly packed in the cliffs. The bird droppings totally obscured the strata of rock in some areas. Even Derek did not expect some of the sightings. He took many photographs of penguin and flying-bird colonies, sea mammals on the shore, and breaching whales.

One evening, Jenifer brought up the issue of race with Juan and asked if she should expect discrimination in the region because of her mixed blood. She informed him that she grew up in Brazil where no one was totally of European ancestry, but she had been told that elsewhere in South America those with mixed heritage suffered discrimination. Juan told her his father was born in Italy, came to Chile on a sailing ship as a crew member, and married his native mother, of the Mapuche tribe, and although he was not accepted in the society of pure Europeans, he had not suffered much discrimination. That gave Jenifer some degree of comfort.

The extra help was appreciated and became a necessity. Climbing a cliff with one end of the measuring tape, Ramon fell. Josh rushed to him. Helping him to his feet, they determined that he had sprained an ankle. The pain was severe when he put weight on his right leg. With help, he limped to the canoe. After Josh loaded their equipment, they paddled back to the boat.

Reporting the accident to those on board, Juan threw a rope to Josh to place over Ramon's upper body, so he and Derek could assist him in re-boarding.

At dinner that evening, Josh explained that the geologic formation he had been mapping was thin in this region, so he felt a few more days was all that would be needed to complete his work. Derek replaced Ramon to complete the work. On the way back to the dock, Juan guided his boat into waterways to the north where glaciers and the ice sheet could be seen, something that Jenifer and Josh greatly appreciated.

Ramon chose not to go to the hospital when they arrived back at *Puerto Natales*, telling the other that he was certain the sprained ankle would get better, tightly wrapped the way Derek had treated it, and the pain was easing. He was dropped at his mother's home and Josh drove on to the lodge.

Now began the job of preparing a geologic map that incorporated the data gathered during the field work and studying the analyses of the samples collected. Derek offered Josh the use of a drafting table, equipment, and heavy gauge drafting paper. He and Jenifer created work space at one end of the conference room and added desks and filing cabinets. Data from previous exploratory drilling for oil, gas, and coal that Jennifer had requested from agencies in Santiago arrived. Subsurface data from those drill holes were used to create three dimensional models and related cross section displays. Within a few weeks, Josh had defined prospects for additional exploration drilling.

Jenifer had experience working for the company on Trinidad that was related to the securing of permission from landowners to conduct drilling. She spent many long hours in the province offices to determine ownerships in the areas that Josh had determined to have the greatest potential for commercial production, given developing technologies for fracturing of strata to release contained hydrocarbons. She solicited the help of Ramon to visit landowners and their representative to obtain permission to explore for, and produce, oil and gas from the surface land overlying those areas.

In several binders, the results of all this work was placed in boxes to be forward to Roger for his review. Roger considered the information so valuable that he sent his company plane to pick up the boxes, as well as Josh and Jenifer. The couple was very proud of what had been accomplished since their ill-fated experiences. Derek took them to meet the plane, after they said goodbye and thanked the lodge staff. Josh voiced his opinion that they would be returning to participate in the discovery of oil and gas in Patagonia.

Chapter Thirteen
Mapuche Homelands

Doctor Grayson had found, cleaned, and had moved to the lower level of the lodge, a lower jaw of a giant sloth and was anxious to continue his excavation to a level that appeared particularly promising for more fossil recovery, strata that was exposed on the rim of the ravine. However, his season at the site on *Estancia Margo* was to be limited because he planned to visit a site of new dinosaur discoveries in the Araucania Region before returning to the United States, so he requested someone else to help him and Luis. Derek suggested Ramon, who had reported his sprained ankle had healed. Ramon joined the paleontology team. Another bed was added to Luis' quarters and the brothers both became full-time workers at the lodge. Derek helped Rios with the guide services for guests and Afton continued the seed preparation and hothouse plantings. Afton also took regular trips to the goat farm to examine the new growth of forage.

As the time of the doctor's departure approached, he devised a plan that involved driving the nearly 900 miles to the area of dinosaur finds, accompanied by his helpers. He explained at dinner one evening: "With my helpers, the excavating tools and equipment we have been using, and a rented vehicle, we could initiate an excavation at a site east of *Temuco* where an unusual dinosaur bone was found by a boy and it was reported to my university by a previous investigator."

Rios' response was, "You have no idea about the difficulty of such a trip and you would be in the homeland of the "People of the Land" where you would need to interact with the indigenous population. Luis and Ramon are descendants of a Mapuche *lonko,* chief, so you would have help if your team got there. However, there are conflicts between the Mapuche and the government. They also resent outsiders."

Derek added, "I think you would need Roger's permission in addition to agreements with our friends and associates."

"We have discussed, between ourselves and Mother, visiting the lands of our people many times," Luis commented. "I would consider such a job a great opportunity."

"I would too," Ramon said. "My camping equipment would be made available for the trip. The Jeep we used for the geologic mapping would be the proper vehicle to drive, but we would need to pull a trailer. Rios is right. The journey will be challenging."

When Doctor Grayson called Roger, he agreed that the Vergara brothers could accompany him on his planned trip, after learning that Ramon had been hired fulltime, but Roger insisted that Afton go along as well. Roger asked that Bob have Afton call him. In her conversation with her client, Afton found that Roger had agreed to the doctor's plan and that he offered to pay expenses with the proviso that she be in-charge of the expedition. He explained that he had two reasons for her going: the native people needed to be made aware of the value of land from which the ice sheets were retreating; and he wanted her to learn the details of the conflict caused by the destruction of the *Valdivia* rainforest through the planting of economic tree species on tree plantations. Her participation in the venture was exciting to Afton.

With the concurrence of Harriett and Derek, Ramon drove the Rand Rover, with Bob sitting next to him, into the city. The Jeep used before and a small trailer were rented. Ramon drove the Jeep to his home to load his equipment, while Bob took the Range Rover to purchased food, supplies, and a second tent for Afton to use, all charged to lodge accounts. When the pending trip was explained to Ramon's mother, she provided him with names of tribal members she could remember before his father brought them south and took a job on a sheep ranch.

In anticipation of the needs on the journey, the kitchen staff had prepared a large amount of food, which was packed in canvas bags. Many cuts of cooked meat and dried fish were placed in chests. All of this, extra warm clothes, and bedding were packed by Ramon in the trailer with his belongings, and those of the others. The long road trip began at sunrise on a clear morning. The brothers planned to share the driving and sat in the front seat, with Bob and Afton on the rear bench-seat. The drive to *Coyhaique* took 17 hours. The scenery, much of which was familiar to everyone except Doctor Grayson, was spectacular.

High snow-capped mountains, glaciers, and the southern ice sheet dominated the views. The road skirted Bernardo O'Higgins National Park, an area new to Afton, some 30 miles from the lodge. They stopped for short periods of time for photographs and ate lunch at one stop. Discussions among the travelers included the subject of ice retreat due to climate change. Afton explained how the staff at the lodge was attempting to prove some positive aspects of the change that involved use of land exposed for the first time in hundreds of years.

It was dark when they reached *Coyhaique*, a significant city. Three rooms were secured at a hotel, using Doctor Grayson's credit card. Bob and Afton took adjacent rooms, Ramon and Luis went to a room on the same floor, after parking and locking the Jeep and trailer. Dinner and breakfast were eaten in a hotel restaurant.

The second-day drive included views of extensive farmland during the first few hours. Higher elevations were crossed to *Puerto Aisen* where lake country began. For the remainder of the day, they traveled through varied terrain and around several lakes. Realizing it would take a very long day to reach *Temuco,* the decision was made to make an overnight camp near *Vincente Perez Rosales* National Park. Ramon, Luis, and Afton were experienced campers, so two tents, a fire ring, and logs for benches were soon in place in a grassy area a mile from the road. Air mattresses, bedrolls and lanterns where placed in the tents by Luis and Afton, while Ramon warmed small steaks, and boiled rice and beans.

Doctor Grayson explored the area until called to dinner. The evening was cold, but the sky clear. The travelers spent a pleasant evening, eating and in conversation, sitting around a large fire. Ramon and Luis were asked about their people, the Mapuche. They relayed what their mother had told them about their heritage and the turbulent history of the tribe, who now represented more than 80 percent of the native people of the country. Retiring to the tents, everyone slept well.

The next day, wet flatlands were encountered and then extensive farmland, as they approached *Temuco*, a city divided by *Rio Cautin*. Crossing a bridge to the northern section of the city, they took rooms in the *Tierra del Sur* Hotel. From the first night in the hotel dining room, Doctor Grayson began to meet fellow paleontologists. Many dinosaur bones had been found in the region recently, including those thought to belong to the largest dinosaur ever found, so many professional and amateur paleontologists had come to investigate.

Bob soon became involved in discussions and trips to excavations with other professionals, suggesting the others who came with him enjoy themselves in the city for a few days before they headed to the site he came to investigate.

Afton took this opportunity to study a part of the *Valdivia* rainforest, accompanied by the brothers. They kept their hotel rooms and ate breakfasts in the hotel dining room, but made trips into forested areas, often eating lunch and dinner from the food supplied by the lodge and returning long after dark. The temperate rainforest was the most fascinating ecosystem that Afton had ever visited. Closely-spaced trees with slender trunks grew to heights above one hundred feet. The dense understory consisted of a wide variety of broad-leaf plants and a profusion of multi-colored flowers. It was no wonder, she told the young men with her, that their people were attempting to save this habitat.

While Afton spent time studying the flora in detail at one stop, recording her findings and taking photographs, Luis and Ramon hiked a narrow trail. Upon their return, Afton was told that they had seen a pudu, one of the world's smallest deer species. She asked that she be taken to try to photograph the deer, saying that Derek would also be very interested. They hiked, cautiously, to the site and spent a long time watching for movement in the dense broadleaf plants and bamboo thicket. Finally, a chestnut-brown animal, with a tuft of hair nearly hiding tiny antlers, moved onto a narrow path. Afton began taking photographs. They obviously had not been seen or heard. The tiny deer stayed in view for several minutes and began grazing on succulent, low-growing plants. When alerted by a sound from somewhere, it made a barking sound and bolted into the vegetative cover.

"That animal was little more than a foot tall," Afton remarked.

"A southern pudu," Luis said. "Those in the Andes, where they are sometimes called Mountain Goats, are somewhat taller and more numerous. We chased after them as young children."

From that place at the edge of the rainforest, Afton began to examine adjacent areas where de-forestation had involved burning. Her primary interest was in regrowth. She found that numerous plants species were recovering. She studied areas where the perimeter of the habitat was expanding, naturally. There, too, many new shrubs, trees, and flowers were observed.

Finding that Doctor Grayson had not returned to the hotel after several days, Afton decided they would spend time reviewing the development of tree farms in the area. At the first farm they visited, they met a representative of a

Chilean timber company. Finding that Afton was a professional botanist with a keen interest, the man offered to show them the farm he managed and got in the Jeep with them. They drove on narrow roads around blocks of Monterey pine, Douglas fir, and Eucalyptus trees. Their guide told them that timber interests had planted hundreds of thousands of acres of such trees, only a small percentage of which was where the rainforest had been removed. He added, "Nonetheless, protests driven by exaggerations are beginning to affect the lumber business. Some U.S. companies with chain-store distribution have cut back on purchases, thinking they are helping the environment."

Afton responded, "The carbon-dioxide 'sinks' created by extensive tree plantations, with continuous production, as well as the reduction of the pressure on native forests for wood and fiber needed by mankind, are positive environmental elements often not considered by protestors." The guide agreed, and Afton explained her meanings to her companions.

On the way back to the city, Afton explained to Luis and Ramon the opinion she had developed regarding one of the conflicts between their people and lumber interests. It was her belief that the preservation of the vast rainforest would be possible while continuing to expand the harvesting of lumber from tree plantations because there remained many acres of rugged terrain that was not suitable for leveling to plant commercial trees, into which the native habitat would expand, naturally. Also, she told them, such expansion could be aided by transplantation efforts by concerned parties. As to the desire of their people for autonomy and the settlement of territorial claims, those were other matters, she said, that she knew little about.

When Afton asked again at the reception desk at the hotel if Robert Grayson had returned, she was told he had not, but there was an officer of the *Carabineros de Chile*, the national police, who wanted to talk to her about him. She called the number given her and was asked to wait in the lobby for the officer. She ordered tea and waited. What Officer Jorge Alvarado had to tell Afton when he arrived was a shock: "Your associate and another well-known paleontologist have been captured by guerillas and are being held for ransom. My office was informed, by telephone, that they are being held where they cannot be found and will starve to death unless two hundred thousand American dollars are left in an abandoned farmhouse that the caller described."

"When did this happen?" Afton asked.

"The call came-in last evening. My staff considers this the most unusual ransom attempt they have witnessed. There is no way to negotiate an exchange, and there is no assurance that the men will live, even if the money is given to their captors."

Afton responded, "There is no ready source of the ransom money, either. Doctor Grayson is no longer associated with a university that might pay to have him returned. He is a consultant from the United States. That may be true of the other man, too. Furthermore, Bob has not been back to the hotel for several days. A starvation period could have started some time ago. Has a search been initiated?"

"It has, but we have no idea where they were taken. The excavations underway that we understand they were going to visit are widespread in the province, and the native population in many areas is less than cooperative."

"I'm traveling with two associates who were raised in the province and speak the Mapuche language." Afton said. "We will join the search."

"That could prove valuable. Please keep my department appraised of your efforts," the officer said as he left.

In her room, Afton called Roger on the satellite telephone that Derek had loaned her to report the incident. He reported that he would make some calls to raise the ransom money, but he agreed with the officer's assessment that paying the money would probably not secure the release of the men.

The captured men had been in a shallow cave for more than 48 hours, having been stopped in a road block by armed men and taken there without a word being spoken by those men. Using a tree-harvesting machine, large logs were leaned against the opening of the cave to close it. The logs were so close together had only thin beams of light penetrated inside. There were seeps of water on the cave walls and the temperature was moderate, but the men realized the starvation they were facing. Neither understood the reason they were captured.

At daylight, the Lautaro Lodge crew was on the road, beginning a search with little guidance. Afton had spoken with others aware of the dinosaur digs in the region and found there were several. One man marked some of those sites on a map of the province for her, but no one she spoke with knew where Doctor Grayson might have gone with another professional, Doctor Walter Kerry. Several roads led to sites shown on the map. At Afton's suggestion, they started their search in the most heavily wooded areas, reasoning that aerial searches had begun.

Everyone on the road and those in the scattered homes that they passed were questioned in Spanish or the language of the Mapuche. Most refused to answer their questions. Finally, one man reported that he had been stopped by a road block on his way to work at a fossil excavation three days earlier, and he described the site. Now, they had a promising place to start a detailed search, but it was late in the afternoon. By the time, they reach a site where there were many tire tracks and footprints, suggesting it was where the roadblock was set up, it was nearly dark. They decided to make camp a few hundred yards off the road in a secluded area, among dense trees.

Afton suggested that if they were harassed, Luis and Ramon should say they were from the area, working with a botanist they had hired. A simple meal was prepared on a small fire and eaten in their tents. Throughout a restless night for each of them, they contemplated what might be found the next day. Before morning, it rained very hard for a few minutes.

Hiking some distance apart, through wet undergrowth, they hoped to find evidence of recent activity, even after the rain had obliviated tracks. After a mile or so, they came upon a place where trees had been selectively cut. No one was working there, but a piece of equipment used to grasp tree-trunks, as they were cut, was parked in an opening and there was a large pile of logs ready for loading onto trucks, nearby. Hiking became easier, so they made good time for another two hours, but no place where captives could be held were found. They ate a late lunch and started back to camp. This time, they moved into the dense forest bounded by a hill with many rock-strata exposures.

Ramon was the first to see a very unusual stacking of large logs, in a near vertical position, leaning against a rock outcrop. He pointed it out and the three of them went there. Not really expecting an answer, Afton asked if there was anyone around. A weak voice answered from behind the logs. Peeking between the logs from where the voice came, she saw movement.

"Are you there, Doctor Grayson?" she called.

The response was, "We have been left in a cave behind those large logs, without food. We are nearly starved."

"We will get you out," Afton said, without knowing how they could do that. She turned to see Luis racing through the forest.

"He will bring the machine the captors must have used to stack the logs," Ramon said.

"Does he know how to operate the machine?" Afton asked.

Ramon replied, "If the keys are in the ignition, he will soon learn how. He is good with heavy equipment."

"Maybe, you should bring our Jeep and trailer here, following the logging roads," Afton suggested. Ramon ran toward the camp.

Back at a space between logs, Afton asked if the men were unharmed, only very hungry.

"There is water seeping from the rocks, thank God. The men who put us in here only left us with a few bruises," Doctor Grayson told her. "Do you know why they captured us?"

"A ransom of two hundred dollars was their demand, before you were to be given anything to eat."

"Who did they think would pay to save us?" Doctor Kerry asked.

"Roger Richardson is raising the money," Afton answered. "I should call him to tell him that will not be necessary."

Afton stepped away from the hill. First, she called the number that Officer Alvarado had given her, and, then, Roger to whom she conveyed their apparent success, knowing the men were far from free. She told him that she had explained to a police officer their location and was expecting help from his department. As she finished the calls, she heard the machine.

It took Luis less than a minute to lay-back two logs from the cave entrance. The men walked into the afternoon sunshine. Afton suggested they sit on the removed logs until Ramon got there with food. In anticipation of that, Luis built a fire. Presently, Ramon arrived. Knowing the men should eat sparingly for a time, Afton made a stew with the meat still in a cooler, dried beans, and onions. She put the pot on the fire and gave them slices of Heidi's bread, which were devoured.

Doctor Kelly commented that he assumed their capture was part of some protest. Luis informed him that it probably was, but he thought they would be allowed to die in that cave, if the ransom was not paid. He also made the comment that they were all now in danger.

"We can only hope that the national police arrive soon," Afton said. "We are unarmed." As soon as she said that, voices were heard.

"Quickly, we should all get into the cave." Luis said. "If those coming were police, they would be in vehicles."

As Afton followed the others into the cave, she took the pot from the fire and the two bowls she had found in which to serve it.

Four men approached. Seeing the cave blockage had been disrupted, they began to speak to each other in the Mapuche language. One man climbed onto the machine, obviously intent on repositioning the two logs. Another man stood with a rifle pointed at the opening.

"They plan to lock us all in here, now," Doctor Kelly stated the obvious.

"I will talk with them," Luis said as he stepped out.

Ramon was the only one in the cave who understood what was being said outside. What he translated for the others was not good, "They plan to shoot my brother and close the opening," Ramon said and started out to try to help Luis. Afton restrained him, saying they would shoot him, too.

Before a shot was fired, the loud sound of sirens could be heard. The man on the machine jumped down and the four of them ran. Greatly relieved, Afton and Ramon joined Luis. The starving men stayed in the cave long enough to eat the partially cooked stew.

Officer Alvarado was the first to step from a police car. "The perpetrators went that way," Afton said as she pointed.

He replied, "They will not get away. I left men at their vehicle and others following their tracks in the mud. Is everyone all right here?"

"We are!" Luis replied.

"Did they get the money?" Afton said.

The officer replied, "We fooled them. Instead of money, the bag left at the farmhouse contained a note saying the men had been rescued. We tried to follow the man who came to the farmhouse, but we lost him. Obviously, he got word to the others and they came to find out if the captives had been released."

The captives emerged from the cave. Doctor Kelly's first words were, "That young man risked his life in front of a rifle barrel."

"I hoped to convince them that they were not helping any cause," Luis responded.

"If it was for a cause instead of money, they got a lot of publicity," the officer said. "The abduction is worldwide news. I need the captured men to ride to the city with me. I want statements from them."

"We will follow," Afton commented. "But we need to disassemble a camp."

Officer Alvarado responded, "We saw your camp. Your crew is very resourceful, as well as brave."

Doctor Grayson had provided a statement to the police and was in this hotel room when the others in his party arrived. Hearing Afton in the adjoining room, he called her on the house phone to inform her that he had been mobbed by reporters when he arrived, so he was going to eat dinner in his room and continue to avoid making any statement to reporters. When asked his plans, he told her he was obligated to examine the site he had come there to see, that was less than a two-hour drive away. He said he wanted to go to *Puco*, situated on the shore of Lake *Villarrico*, for a couple of days and, then be taken to the airport near *Temuco*, so he could fly home. "I want to leave before sun-up to avoid the reporters," he added.

It seemed obvious that the reporters had not yet connected Afton, Luis, and Ramon to the abduction. Afton knew they would, so she invited the brothers to her room for a room-service meal and to discuss Bob's plans. They had a lot to discuss that evening. As requested, the others were waiting for the doctor in the parking lot and were on the highway to *Puco* when the sun rose. They secured rooms in a waterfront hotel. Before she had settled into her room, Afton received a call from Bob to informer her that he had arranged to meet Pedro Otero, the boy who had reported finding a dinosaur, and his mother, right away, so the party left the hotel.

Doctor Grayson directed them into a wooded area between the town and on the flank of a massive volcano. The instructions he had received led them to a small, frame house. Pedro, who was about ten years old, and his mother greeted them. The mother had discouraging news, interpreted by Luis: a *Machi,* shaman, had visited the site of Pedro's discovery and found sacred stones she said were part of a stairway for spirits to another world, *Menu Mapu.* That meant that digging in that area would upset the gods. The doctor asked to speak with the shaman and was informed her hut was within walking distance. He asked Luis and Afton to walk there with him, Missus Otero and Pedro. Ramon stayed with the vehicle, sitting behind the steering wheel.

A young, native woman came from the house and approached Ramon. He thought she was very attractive, with a slim figure, long dark hair, and reflective brown eyes that seemed to express friendliness as she smiled at him.

She introduced herself as Rosita Carrasco and asked if the vehicle could be hired. Tongue-tied, due to the sudden appearance of such a beautiful woman of his age, Ramon took some time to respond, but was, finally, able to tell her that he, his brother, and a friend were working for the man who had just left with the Otero's. He asked why she needed the vehicle and invited her to come sit in the seat next to him. As she did that, he noticed her shapely legs beneath a colorful, woolen skirt and a woven poncho.

"I need to take food and medicinal supplies to my grandmother who lives high on the mountain where my grandfather's family grazed goats for generations. When grandfather died, I tried, unsuccessfully, to convince her to move."

Ramon asked, "Do you live with her?"

"I do now. Before grandfather died, I was at university in *Coyhaique*, but now Grandmother has only me to take care of her. My parents were killed in a bus accident crossing the Andres after visiting friends in Argentina. My mother was her only child."

"I see no other vehicle," Ramon said. "How do you get around?"

"When I arrived in *Puco*, I purchased a mountain bike. With that, I can carry little."

Ramon had developed an idea, which he mentioned, "Those with me from Patagonia might agree to me helping you, hauling supplies, while Doctor Grayson and my brother, Luis, dig for bones, as they do down south." He certainly hoped they would, because he was enamored by this young woman and wanted to get to know her. They talked for more than an hour, waiting for the others, often about personal matters.

They got out of the Jeep and walked toward those returning from a meeting with the shaman. The expressions of gloom on their faces suggested the meeting had not gone well. "Let's get out of here," Bob said.

Afton told Ramon that the doctor had decided he wanted no more confrontations with the Mapuche and wanted to be taken to the airport. Ramon introduced Rosita and explained her request. Afton and Luis agreed to help her.

"You can all stay in the town while I take the doctor to the airport," Luis offered. "We can help Rosita tomorrow before heading south." He, too, was enchanted by the young woman's looks.

"Do you have a way into town?" Afton asked. "You can spend the night in the hotel room with me where I left my things and we can help you with what you need to do in the morning."

The reply was, "I will ride my bike." Afton gave Rosita the name of the hotel and the number of her room. Bob began to honk the Jeep horn.

At the hotel, Doctor Grayson argued that he should not pay for a room in which he never slept, gathered his belongings, and returned to the Jeep. Luis started to the airport with him. Afton and Ramon discussed the fact that the doctor had not once thanked any of them for their assistance or for saving his life. Afton offered her credit card to pay for rooms and meals. She and Ramon sat on a bench in front of the hotel, with a view of a magnificent lake, and waited for Rosita. Ramon told Afton what he had learned about this new acquaintance.

Seeing Rosita, they joined her at a bike rack and escorted her to Afton's room. She carried a back pack containing extra cloths and toiletries. Immediately, the two young women bonded. Rosita spoke her native language, Spanish, and English, she told them. Ramon said he was more comfortable speaking Spanish, so the three of them conversed in that language, as they spent the afternoon walking the shore of the lake and in the hotel lounge. Luis returned in time to have dinner with them in the hotel dining room.

"The doctor did not escape the reporters," Luis told them. "Two were waiting for him at the airport." That comment required an explanation for Rosita. The remainder of the dinner conversation was centered on Rosita. She was straightforward about her plans to stay with her grandmother during the few years of life left for her.

Early the next morning, Afton and Rosita found Luis at a large table in the dining room, surrounded by distinguished older men. When they joined them, Luis said he had been asked to explain what he was doing in Patagonia. Ramon came to the table. Discussion continued in the language of the Mapuche. Only Afton knew nothing about what was being said, but she felt certain that the second objective of the trip, voiced by her client, was being met. She was also happy that Rosita was learning about their jobs.

After breakfast, Rosita's bike was secured to the rear door of the Jeep and the others helped her shop for the needs of her and her grandmother in the coming months. Afton tried to pay for some of that, but Rosita refused that type of help.

The roadway above the home of the Otero family was steep and very rough. It seemed too difficult for Rosita to traverse on her bike, but they knew she did. The dwelling Rosita shared with her grandmother was situated near the tree-line. The volcano, sparsely covered with grass, loomed above a narrow terrace. The dwelling was circular in shape, made of tree limbs and thatch. Luis commented it was like those dwellings he remembered from his youth.

Although the grandmother appeared to be in her seventies, she was still pretty and spry. She greeted Rosita and the others, dressed in bright-colored, weaved clothes, and invited them into her home, where she served them tea. Luis and Afton sat with her, after finishing the tea. With Luis interpreting for Afton, they learned a lot of family history, which included stories of generations who grazed goats on the slopes of the volcano and many volcanic eruptions. Ramon helped Rosita store what they had brought in a shed behind the dwelling.

As the visitors departed, Rosita embraced each of them and kissed Ramon on a check. The grandmother presented Afton with a beautiful poncho. Rosita and her grandmother thanked them and invited them to return. In near silence, Luis drove them down the mountain, each one contemplating the experience. They spent another pleasant night in the hotel by the lake, before starting for Lautaro Lodge.

The route was as before, but the days of travel were scheduled so they spent each night in rooms in one of the resorts or a hotel in a small town. As they traveled, Afton and Luis spent hours discussing the future of his people. Ramon paid little attention to those discussions. Day and night, he thought only of Rosita.

Things went very well until they passed Patagonia Camp. On a steep part of the highway, a tire on the trailer blew out while Ramon was driving. At the side of the road, he stopped. Luis got out and placed rocks behind the Jeep tires to prevent the vehicle from moving while the tire was changed. Before starting again, Luis and Afton removed the rocks behind the tires. On the highway side, Luis threw one of the rocks, intending for it to land on the slope on the opposite side of the road. He did that without looking for anyone.

Unfortunately, a man on a bicycle was passing them. The rock struck his front wheel and forced the bike down the slope, with him tumbling down it. Luis rushed to him and helped him to a sitting position, asking if he was all right. He replied that he was not hurt. Afton slid down, stopping next to them.

She asked, "Are you sure you are not hurt?" To her question, the man answered, "I should know. I am a medical doctor, an orthopedic surgeon."

Luis helped the man to the Jeep. Ramon took the bike from Afton as she brought it up the slope and tied what was left of it where they had carried Rosita's. The man introduced himself as John Hutchins, as he was helped into a back seat in the Jeep. Afton told him the lodge where they worked would be reached soon and he was welcomed to stay there while his bicycle was repaired. He voiced his desire to have it repaired or to buy a new one, because he hoped to complete his trip to *Punta Arenas*.

Chapter Fourteen
New Beginnings

The arrival at the lodge was in late afternoon. Ramon parked in front of the porch. Harriett and Rios came to greet them and were introduced to John. The circumstance of John being with them was explained by Afton. Rios helped him remove the twin packs from the damaged bicycle, commenting that he should seek repairs, because the replacement of such a fine bike would not be possible in the area. Carrying the bags to a room that Harriett had assigned to John, Rios informed him that he had time to shower, change, and enjoy a drink downstairs before dinner.

When John came downstairs, Georgio Oneto was in the living room, sipping a glass of wine. He had returned to the lodge to enjoy the accommodations and activities he had missed the last time, due to the unfortunate accident that required Derek and Rias to rescue him and his friend Roberto Boitano. He had spent weeks in the local a hospital, and months undergoing physical therapy. John poured himself a glass of wine and the two conversed.

John explained he was taking a long bicycle ride through Patagonia and Georgio told him about his life in northern Italy and about his accident the last time he checked into the lodge. They were called to dinner by Harriett. Georgio rose, took his cane, and led John to the dining room. John's experience with limb injuries caused him to watch the movement of Georgio carefully.

The absence of Heidi was noticed by the staff that had returned when they came to dinner. Harriett explained that she had gone with Raoul and Rolando to Argentina to buy goats. The staff and the two guests ate a meal prepared without the help of Heidi. Afton asked Georgio about the activities in which he was engaged. He replied that although he could not climb mountains, he was able to hike the trails behind the lodge, and Rios had taken him on very enjoyable horseback rides, adding that he was very happy he had returned.

Sipping after-dinner drinks, Doctor Hutchins told Georgio about his profession: "I am an orthopedic surgeon. At my clinic in San Antonio, Texas, I have repaired many legs seriously injured in war, and elsewhere. I can see you get along quite well with the use of a cane, and if you can hike, it is possible I could perform corrective surgery to give you much more leg movement."

"My first love is mountain climbing. Should I be able to make even simple climbs again, I would be a happy man," was the reply.

"Where were you initially treated," John asked.

"At a hospital in *Puerto Natales*," Georgio said.

"When I take my bike to the city for repairs, I will ask to look at X-rays and tell you what I can determine from them," John said.

John was asked about the long journey he was taking alone. Answering he said that he had lost his wife to cancer and had decided to make a trip with only her memory.

While that conversation was developing in the living room, the staff had gathered in the conference room. Each participant provided input to a description of an eventful trip to the Araucania Region. Many questions were asked and answered. Derek explained to Afton that in her absence, he had gone to the goat farm, reviewed the new forage growth, and conferred with Rolando about adding to the herd. It was decided that the original fenced pasture would support a larger herd with minimal supplementary feed, and that an expansion before the second shearing would increase the revenue from mohair significantly, so the gate to the pasture was to be left opened. A friend of Rolando's agreed to watch the herd while he and Raoul went on a buying trip. Harriett had provided a bank draft and Heidi insisted on going with them in the farm truck. Derek added that he had obtained approval for these actions in a telephone call to Roger.

The gathering broke up. In her room, Afton found two letters from Margo that she was anxious to read. Her reply to those letters took a long time and required many sheets of paper.

After breakfast the next morning, two vehicles left the lodge. John went with Luis and Ramon to a bicycle repair shop recommended by Rios. Finding his bike could be repaired, John left the shop with Derek, who had followed them there in the Range Rover, and asked to be taken to the hospital. The brothers unloaded Ramon's equipment and discussed what they had learned about her homeland with their mother, before returning the Jeep and trailer.

Derek sat in the waiting area of the hospital while John presented his credentials and asked to see the X-rays of a previous patient. He asked that copies be forwarded to his office. Luis and Ramon were waiting for them at the rental yard. John was taken on a tour of the city, with a stop on the waterfront for lunch.

John had encouraging news when he got back to the lodge. He told Georgio that he thought that an operation he could perform, if Georgio was able to come to his office, would make his leg nearly as good as new. A promise was made to get to that office, somehow. More good news resulted from the arrival of Roberto Boitano. Harriett had kept the reservation for Roberto and his wife a secret, as a surprise. The arrival was a real surprise. Georgio did not even know that his friend had married. The bride was Valerie Sanchez, the young woman Roberto had met on their first trip to Lautaro Lodge.

This time, Roberto had contacted a professional guide to escort them on a climb that he believed that Valerie was now qualified to make. Arrangements were made for Georgio to witness part of the climb from a helicopter.

There were more surprises for the lodge staff when those who had gone to buy goats arrived. Heidi announced that she and Raoul had been married in a simple church ceremony, with Raoul's mother and Rolando as witnesses. That was not totally unexpected. Most had been aware of Heidi's feelings for Raoul for some time. The bigger shock was that Rolando was going to retire and turn the goat-farm management over to the newlyweds. Harriett offered to organize a wedding reception and retirement party. Neither were wanted. Rolando said a livestock truck was close behind them. As they drove off in the farm truck, Afton rushed to her quarters to compose another letter to Margo.

When they went to the farm a few days later, Derek and Afton found that an additional fifty goats had arrived, Raoul and Heidi were settled in the farmhouse, and Rolando and his friend were taking a much deserved, leisurely trip. It was obvious to Afton that the new forage in the pasture was adequate for the larger herd. The wooded area had been stripped of vegetation to the highest tree branches the goats could reach, but re-growth had started. She knew the plants would eventually grow back and, that with herding, the animals could be allowed into the planted area beyond the pastures if that became necessary. Raoul informed them that the shearing-crew had been scheduled and requested the help of Luis to haul the full sacks to fleece to a buyer when the shearing began. Heidi was with them throughout their stay. She seemed as happy as anyone could be.

Following the departure of Doctor Hutchins, on a repaired bicycle, the two Italian friends and a new Spanish wife, a large group of tourists from the United States arrived at the lodge. The new group consisted of three middle-aged couples and five teenagers. The guide services became taxed, because varied interests were expressed by members of the group. Fly-fishing became very popular after the two boys that Derek took to the river came back with large salmon. He made several more trips with those boys and the three fathers. The three girls found spending time with Afton hiking the trails to observe wildlife and blooming flowers enjoyable. The mothers all rode, so Rios and Luis took them on long trips. Riding into the grasslands, where guanaco herds were numerous became something everyone wanted to do, so over a few days each of the guests took such a horseback trip.

The men all worked for an investment banking company in Denver and the trip had been sponsored by that company. The questions asked of the professionals and staff led to evening seasons that Harriett thought too business-like for a resort, so she decided it was a good time to instigate a new regular activity that she had thought about a great deal. She hired a band, had the conference room cleared, and offered dancing and refreshments after dinner. That became a highlight for all. The staff joined the guests for exhilarating evenings. Dancing partners were changed regularly. Rios, of course, danced with girls and woman much shorter than himself. Because of the uniqueness of that, Rios soon became a partner who was sought after. Derek and Afton danced together many times and were told they made a handsome couple. Business matters were no longer discussed.

One evening, Ramon came to the dance and told Harriett he had something very serious to talk to his brother and Derek about. Derek led them to his quarters where Ramon informed them that there had been a massive eruption of the *Villarrico* Volcano. Luis knew what that meant and explained to Derek where their new friend and her grandmother lived. Ramon said, "We must go to see if we can help. I borrowed a car to come get you, Luis, which I will leave at the airport. Mother and I scraper-together air fare, and there is a flight to *Temuco* leaving in two hours."

170

"You are needed here now, Luis, and they expect your help at the goat farm when shearing begins," Derek said. "I will go. You keep the money, Ramon. I'll charge the tickets on my credit card. Wait a minute for me to pack a few things."

Derek put extra clothes, other necessities, some gold coins, and his satellite phone in a backpack. Grabbing a heavy coat and hat from a rack, he went to the borrowed car. Luis wished them luck, as Ramon drove off.

The car was left in the long-term parking lot, with the keys hidden beneath the seat. Derek purchased two round-trip tickets, obtained boarding passes, and met Ramon at the appropriate gate. While they waited for the flight to be called, Ramon told Derek about his feelings for Rosita, "I don't know how it could have happened in such a short time, but I have fallen deeply in love with a young woman who is in big trouble."

"Love emerges, it seems, in many ways," Derek said. "I think it hit me this evening while dancing with a woman I have known for some time."

The two of them, then, sat quietly until the flight was announced. Sitting next to each other during the flight, they tried to develop a plan. Ramon explained the distances and the problems that would be encountered.

The airport terminal at *Temuco* was full of people trying to leave the region. Fortunately, there was a small, four-wheel-drive pickup still at a rental facility near the airport. With their packs in the back of that truck and Ramon driving, they took the highway to *Puco*. A steady stream of cars was leaving the area. A few miles below the town, a roadblock had been created to prevent anyone from going into the danger zone surrounding the volcano. Ramon got out and pleaded with the police officer in charge to let them try to rescue friends, telling the officer that they were living too close to the eruption to be rescued from the air. It took several minutes of debate, but the officer, finally, pulled back a section of the barrier to allow the truck to cross. Derek slid behind the steering wheel and drove through. Ramon jumped in and directed Derek to and through *Puco,* a town that seemed totally evacuated, and on the road to the Otero home. It too was abandoned.

There was mud and debris flowing down the roadway above there, so the truck was parked. After moving their packs to the front seat, the truck was locked, and they started a treacherous hike up the road. A glimmer of sunlight was penetrating the falling ash. The roadway was clogged, so they hiked along a berm bounding it. Neither of them had ever hiked in such conditions.

It took them more than an hour to reach the terrace on which the dwelling was situated. A flow of mud and ice, called a *lahar,* had reached the structure. Thick flow-material was engulfing it. Rosita was sitting in front of the entrance, holding her grandmother. Ramon rushed to them and was told the grandmother was dead. "Fright caused her heart to stop beating," Rosita told him.

"Come! We must get out of here," Ramon commanded.

Rosita replied, "Not until she is buried where she lived so long in happiness."

They realized that they would all be buried by mud and ice very soon, but Ramon and Derek understood Rosita's feelings. Derek searched around, found a shovel, and began to dig a grave in a flower garden on the far side to the terrace. Rosita and Ramon carried the body there. While Derek and Ramon took turns digging, Rosita wrapped her grandmother in a woven, wool blanket. Knowing that if the speed of the flow-advance increased, they would be trapped, the digging became frantic. Rosita watched as everything she owned, except the shoes, clothes, and poncho she wore, were lost. She knelt as the last of her family was laid to eternal rest and covered with soil. She whispered a loving farewell.

Ramon helped Rosita to her feet, took her hand, and the three of them ran through a wooded area to the roadway. The debris in the road was thicker and moving rapidly, causing fear that the truck might be buried. It was not, but it was going to be difficult to move it. The doors were opened, packs stuffed behind the seat, and Rosita helped in. Ramon sat next to her and Derek got behind the steering wheel. The tires spun in the mud and the movement down the road was sporadic, but they made it to the highway near *Puco,* where they saw a few people on foot. Some appeared badly hurt. Rosita asked to be let out to see to them, divulging for the first time that she had been to nursing school and was taking classes to qualify her for medical school when she had to leave university to assist her grandmother. "I could provide help if I had supplies," she said. Derek and Ramon helped the people into the bed of the truck. "Let's get them to help," Derek said.

At the roadblock, there were many others waiting to be moved to already overwhelmed medical facilities in *Temuco.* Those injured were moved from the truck to a grassy area beneath overhang of trees. Ash was falling, but it had cooled.

Rosita and her rescuers spoke with the officer in charge. They were told that a request for ambulance service had been transmitted hours before. They asked if there was not a way to obtain medical supplies to help the people where they lay. The thought of breaking into a store in *Puco* was being discussed when a store owner approached the group. He said he had returned, hoping to see if there was anything left of his business. He offered to go back and provide anything that was left that would help these people. Derek offered to take him.

Driving back, lava flows and ejecta were visible at the top of the volcano, indicating the disaster was not over. However, the main *lahar* seemed to be moving around the center of the town and into the lake. Pushing through mud and debris, Derek was able to follow his passenger's directions to his store. It was still intact. The two of them loaded in to the pickup all the first-aid kits in the store, a roll of canvas, rope, cots, blankets, bottled water, and some hand tools. Getting back in the truck, Derek took one-ounce gold coins from his pack and handed them to the store owner, who didn't know what to say. Derek said, "You should not have to bear all of the costs for helping those who have been injured by nature."

The officer at the roadblock was surprised to see the truck return so soon. Ramon and Rosita were not. They had developed confidence in Derek. The store owner left in his car to tell his family they still had a business.

As Rosita opened first-aid kits and began to treat the injured, Derek and Ramon cut tree limbs, tied them to strips of canvas, and formed a long lean-to. They helped those hurt to cots or onto strips of canvas beneath the cover that was now catching the falling ash. They distributed blankets and bottled water. Rosita moved among the group, continuing to do what she could to relieve pain and to treat wounds and burns. Eventually, ambulances began to arrive. The most seriously injured were moved first. Others were moved into vans that arrived. Officer Alvarado of the national police arrived. Recognizing Ramon from the abduction incident, he walked to the backshift medical facility and was introduced to Rosita and Derek. When asked, Ramon told him that he was back in Patagonia when he learned of the eruption and that he and his associate, Derek, had returned to help a friend. Not understanding the explanation completely Officer Alvarado complimented them for their service and went to talk with the officer in charge.

All the injured in that area were, finally, moved to proper facilities. Exhausted, Rosita sat on one of the cots, worrying about what she could do to help herself. Ramon sat next to her and put an arm around her. "What will happen to me now, I do not now," she said.

"You have no one here," Ramon said. "You must come with Derek and me. He lives and works at a lodge where you can stay until you figure that out. My brother and I work for the lodge, also. You will like it there."

Derek heard the conversation. He confirmed that he was certain that Rosita would be welcomed at Lautaro Lodge.

As they prepared to leave, the officers told them that the police department would disassemble the facility they had created. The officer in charge recorded their names and the address of the lodge. He told them they would receive commendations for their humanitarian work from the government. A news reporter arrived on the scene, but the good Samaritans left before he could interview them.

It was long after dark by the time the rented truck had been returned. Certain that all the available beds in *Temuco* were occupied by evacuees, they went to the airport terminal and found places to relax in a lounge. Derek purchased a ticket for Rosita and obtained boarding passes for a flight leaving mid-day. Rejoining his companions, Derek found them asleep on a couch, with Rosita's head on Ramon's shoulder. He sat in a chair next to them, and he was soon asleep.

It was daylight when they were all awake. Food was now important, for none of them had eaten since the volcanic activity. Derek lead them to a restaurant he had seen when purchasing the tickets. Breakfast, coffee, and tea were ordered from a girl who asked if they knew about the volcanic eruption. Each of them simply nodded. As they ate, Rosita told of the terrifying blast that made her aware that the mountain on which her grandparents had built a home had once again exploded. She discussed the fact that her grandmother was not frightened at first, but she became frantic.

"It was as if Grandmother expected another eruption, even hoped to end her life in a fiery way, something she often talked about with a shaman," Rosita told them. "She told me to get on my bicycle and ride far away, but I couldn't leave her. Her fear came when we went outside and saw the mud and ice headed directly toward us. She shouted that she did not want to be buried that way and collapsed in my arms. At first, I felt her heart beat. Then, the beating ceased. I will forever be grateful that you two came, out of nowhere, so she could be buried in the soil in which she planted so many flowers during her long life."

"What a horrible experience for you," Ramon offered.

"I am happy I was with her to the end. The last few weeks have been happy times for both of us. She told me many things about our family that I had not heard, including stories of the years my father spent tending goats on the slopes of the volcano. She spoke of her regret that her only son had left there to go to work for a timber company, something that was a godsend for me. Father worked himself into positions of authority that provided a good income. That income allowed me an amazing childhood, and the frugal attitude of my father and mother allowed me to go to school."

"Tell us about your education," Derek said.

"I did well in nursing school and decided that I wanted to be a doctor. My grades were good in some of the classes I needed to get into a medical school. Those classes ended when I got word from a caregiver in *Puco* that grandmother needed full-time care. I planned to go back to school, but the money I had saved to pay for re-registering is buried in Grandmother's home under the many tons of material that slid down the mountain."

"We might have retrieved your money," Ramon said.

"You risked your lives to bury Grandmother and to save me. The money was something I thought nothing about throughout the entire ordeal."

"The caring and loving person you are will be rewarded," Derek said. "I am proud to have been of some assistance to you and the many injured in the disaster that you treated."

Derek left the table and walked out of the terminal, took his phone from his pack, and called the lodge. Harriet answered. She mentioned how worried everyone was for his safety, and that of Ramon, since they had been told by Luis that they were going to the site of the massive volcanic eruption being reported. Derek assured her they were all right and gave her the estimated time that their flight was to arrive at the *Puerto Natales* airport, and told her about a female guest who would be with them. The next hour Derek spent pacing in front of the terminal.

Witnessing the obvious mutual love of the couple he was with made him think more seriously about his feelings for Afton. Since they first met, he had held her in high regard and enjoyed being with her, more so than any woman he had ever known. Their common interests, their enjoyment of their work, and a desire for excitement and challenges had caused a strong bond to form at once. He had never been in love, so he didn't know how he should feel if he was in love with Afton, but he knew that he would not be happy without an association with her. More and more she was on his mind and he had often imagined what she was doing when they were apart.

Rosita and Ramon were seated in a departure area when Derek joined them. Rosita voiced concern about her appearance, but when it was pointed out to her that many in the terminal looked like they, too, had survived a disaster, she felt better. Ramon assured her a new wardrobe was in her future when they got to *Puerto Natales*. His mother was a good seamstress.

Instead of hearing their flight called, they heard an announcement that all planes were grounded due to ash in the air. With great disappointment, they returned to the lounge. Although their last sleep was limited and the place where they had relaxed, earlier, was not occupied, they spent the waiting time not sleeping, but in quiet discussions. Derek called Harriett to tell her of the delay.

In response to Rosita's questions about where she was being taken, Derek explained the Lautaro Lodge to her and told her about the owners, staff, and the professionals with whom he and Ramon worked. He provided her with a particularly complimentary description of Afton. Ramon wanted to mention that Derek had told him he was in love with Afton but decided against that. He did tell her that the brother she had met also lived and worked at the lodge. Ramon's mother was discussed in loving terms, and he told her of the loss of his father to heart failure when he was young. Rosita had many questions about Africa and the home Derek had left to come to Chile.

His parents having been killed during a native uprising was something that Derek never discussed, or wanted to remember, but the loss of loved ones being discussed by the others caused that experience to surface in his mind. He told his companions about that incident, about him growing up with foster families, and some things about of his hunting-guide business where he met Roger Richardson. He told them of his relationship with members of the Zulu tribe and said that his best friend was a member of that tribe.

When their flight was called, the three of them rushed back to the departure area and were told the wind had shifted, so flights going south would no longer be in danger. Derek called Harriet again. Each of them slept a little more before the flight landed.

Carrying the two backpacks, Derek and Ramon went to the curb in front of the terminal and stood there, with Rosita between them. Derek was surprised and very pleased to see Roger coming to pick them up in the Land Rover. As they entered the vehicle, Derek introduced Ramon and Rosita. Roger mentioned that he and Margo had arrived the previous day, also on a commercial flight. Driving them to the lodge, Roger asked about their experience with the volcanic disaster. Derek provided a brief summary. Rosita added that they had saved her life and buried her grandmother near her home on the mountain. To explain Rosita's presence, Derek told Roger that she had nowhere else to go when the volcanic eruption destroyed the home where she and her grandmother lived, and that with her nurse training and experience, he thought she could find a job in this area.

Dinner was finished when they got to the lodge, but Harriett had made certain that food was kept warm for them. She told Ramon that Luis was staying at the goat farm, but the room where he and Ramon stayed was ready for him. She escorted Rosita to the room where Doctor Grayson had stayed, which had been made-over for her. She told her to freshen up and come to the kitchen for something to eat. Derek found he could hardly wait to see Afton. The feeling was mutual. She was waiting for him at the door to his quarters. They embraced and kissed. The dancing seemed to have awaken feelings in the hearts of them both. Roger parked the vehicle and joined Margo in their suite.

Margo and Roger joined everyone for breakfast in the dining room. There were no guests staying at the lodge, so Roger considered this a good time to discuss operations. He began by asking Ramon if he would consider organizing and conducting longer horseback adventures that involved overnight camping, explaining that the idea had developed from Josh Wright's descriptions of his experience with camping and his equipment. He assured Ramon that he would be compensated for the use of his equipment. Ramon could not have been happier when he accepted the job offer. Roger expressed a need for him to meet with the owners of adjacent *estancias* before trips were planned.

Rosita was even more excited than Ramon about the plans Roger had for her. She was told that he and Margo were certain that a trained nurse staying at the lodge would reduce their liability and lower their insurance costs. He added, "Margo also reminded me about our meeting with Countess Shirley Rothchild at a social event in London, who told us that she would like to spend an extended vacation at our lodge. Her Private Secretary told me that the age, and health condition of the Countess meant that she would have to have full-time nursing care. With your help, Rosita, we would have as a guest one of the wealthiest women in the world."

Those who had yet to have a chance to brief the lodge owners about their individual projects and activities did so at that breakfast. Afton explained what was happening at the goat farm. Roger asked that she take them there the next day. He planned to spend that day with Miguel at the fish facility, he said.

Chapter Fifteen
The Countess

Seeing Rosita at breakfast wearing a dirty sweater and skirt, Afton realized that she had not been able save any other clothes, so she invited her to come to her quarters after the meal. There she offered a change of everything Rosita was wearing. Before changing into those clothes, Rosita asked to shower again. She emerged from the bathroom in a towel, with wet hair. Afton told her she was welcome to use her hairbrush and pointed to where she could find a new toothbrush. Rosita went back into the bathroom and closed the door.

Hearing a knock on her front door, Afton opened that door to allow Margo to enter. Margo explained that she suspected that Afton was providing Rosita was clean clothes. She repeated what Ramon had told her about him promising Rosita that his mother would make her new clothes. Margo suggested that the three of them find Ramon and go with him to have his mother take the measurements needed. Rosita emerged from the bathroom. She displayed a fine figure in the tightly fitting clothes and her very pretty facial features were framed by long, dark hair that had been brushed dry.

The presence of the woman she knew had been instrumental in her receiving an offer to remain at the lodge and to be a part of the staff surprised Rosita, but the two women who greeted her made her feel comfortable right away. She sat in a chair and joined in the discussion about them going to see Ramon's mother. Rosita expressed a strong desire to do that.

"I'll find Ramon, ask him to take us, and get a coat," Margo said, as she left the room.

Afton took a coat from a rack and put it on. From a closet, she removed the poncho that she had been given when she left the home of Rosita's grandmother and draped it over her new associate.

Ramon's mother was overwhelmed when they arrived, and the women were escorted into her small, clean and well-furnished frame home. Ramon had called to tell her he was safely back, and she was aware of his affection for a woman that he had gone to rescue from a volcano, the woman who had to be the one he held by an arm as they entered. She was surprised by the introduction of the other two women. They were both women her sons had often spoken of, expressing feelings of respect and admiration for them. She said that she was given a long, native name, so they should call her Mia. Ramon explained that he had promised that she would make much needed clothes for Rosita. Afton said that she and Margo had come along to meet Luis and Ramon's mother.

While she took measurements for clothes, they should go to a shop and buy other necessities, she suggested. Rosita said she could contribute to her new wardrobe by making a poncho like the one she was wearing, if she was provided yarn and a loom. When Afton asked if she had made the poncho that she was wearing, she confirmed that she had. "Then, you have work to do back at the lodge where there is a loom and carded, dyed wool," Afton told her.

Margo and Afton left, and Afton drove the Range Rover into the city. Having found that Afton's undergarments and other clothes fit Rosita and she had given them a shoe size, they were able to do a great deal of shopping for her. Included in the items they purchased were outfits for her to wear until the clothes made by Mia were available and nurse's uniforms. Thinking they should give Mia more time with the woman with whom her son had fallen in love, they spent the entire day shopping and eating lunch at a waterfront restaurant.

During lunch, the conversation became personal, as it often did when these two whose friendship continued to grow, spent time together. At one point in the conversation, Afton reminded Margo of her earlier response to a question about her feelings for Derek. She said those feelings had grown, constantly, until she was now certain that she loved him, and she thought he loved her. Margo conveyed how pleased she was about that, saying that Derek was one of the most outstanding men she had ever known.

They picked up Rosita and Ramon, said goodbye to Mia when she came to the vehicle, and were back to the lodge in time for dinner. On the drive back, Rosita asked who at the lodge wove wool. She was told that Heidi once took care of the sheep and goats behind the lodge, something that Rios did now, and made beautiful wool clothes, but that she was now living on an angora farm with her new husband. Rosita asked if mohair fiber was available with which to work. She was informed that fleeces from more than 100 animals were just going to market from that farm, a farm also owned by Margo and Roger.

Rosita informed them she could make fine clothing from mohair grown on young goats, having learned to do that as a child from her mother and grandmother. When asked, she said she could teach others to do so. Margo told her that her contribution to the Patagonia operations that she and Roger were building was going to be much greater than just her role in medical care. The purchases made for Rosita were taken to her quarters and Afton helped put them away. The extent of those purchases Rosita had not expected, nor the nurse uniforms.

At the dinner table, a copy of the local newspaper was next to where Roger always sat. The paper had been folded so that a special article was displayed. Roger read the article, as the food was being served. The paper had been with the mail delivered that day, and Harriett had already shown the article to Derek. It was a reprint of an article published in a Santiago paper that provided an account of the temporary medical care that had been provided to victims of the volcanic eruption on the road to *Puco*. When he finished the article, Roger commented that he was very proud of what some at the table had done, saying the article even mentioned that the men involved were from the Lautaro Lodge, which was great publicity. Derek knew that he had to discuss the article with Roger, because it mentioned that funds for medical supplies had been provided by one of the men. He didn't want Roger to think the trip expenses and the costs of the supplies were from lodge accounts without his approval.

Little more concerning the incident was discussed as they ate. Roger expressed his pleasure with what he had learned from Miguel concerning fish production, and other operations were discussed. Walking alone with Roger later, Derek explained that the expenses related to the trip that resulted in Rosita joining the staff he had paid. Roger replied, "I expected that. It was your funds that saved me, as well. I have known that and should have reimbursed you."

"No reimbursement is necessary," Derek said. "I came here with adequate funds to get me back to Africa if the job didn't work out. The job worked out far better than I expected, and I have been paid well. Having funds to help in emergencies, makes me feel very good." The conversation ended by Roger saying, "My association with you, Derek, I consider an important part of my life."

The next day, a trip to the Andoni Goat Farm was organized. Rosita was invited to go with Roger, Margo, and Afton. Sitting with Rosita in the second seat of the Range Rover, Afton explained to her the planned expansion of the herd that had begun and her role in increasing the forage to allow that. Rosita continued to be amazed by the surrounding countryside and the activities of those she had met since her arrival. Activity at the farm was winding-down, and the shearing crew had left. Raoul and Luis were with the fleece-buyer. He was inspecting the last of the fleece being stuffed into a six-foot long burlap sack.

Roger introduced himself and those who arrived with him to Mathew Fredrick. Luis mentioned Roger was the owner of the farm. Learning who he was, Mr. Fredrick told Roger that due to the condition of the pasture, the quality of the goats, and the new shearing shed, the mohair he was buying would result in his firm producing some of the best fiber entering a growing market. He picked up a fleece, blew into it to demonstrate how clean it was, saying that the absence of dirt, particles or seeds of plants, and burrs was the most important element of a marketable fleece. Roger asked about his firm. He replied that his family business had been processing wool and mohair from the region for more than 100 years.

Margo commented how impressive that was and asked if some exchange of fleece for yarn would be worked out. Mr. Fredrick asked what she had in mind to do with the yarn. She replied, with an arm on Rosita's shoulder, "This young lady will weave some fine clothing in the manner she was taught by her mother and grandmother."

That statement solicited excited comments, "I have been trying to get more women in the area interested in weaving. The items made by the Mapuche woman are world famous. No one can produce better ponchos, jackets, or sweaters. Is your family from around here, young lady?"

"I have no family left," Rosita answered. "I was just brought to this area from *Puco*. My father's mother and at least four generations of Mother's family were sheep and goat herders and weavers. I began working with wool and mohair with family members when I was ten years old, but I have never seen such a fine fleece as the one you are holding. Is it from a young goat?"

"The young were the last to be sheared. If the sacks that Luis will haul to our facility later today contain fleeces that are all as good as this one. This has been a most rewarding buying trip for me," the wool-buyer offered.

Roger had a contribution to make. He said, "The pasture free of contaminating weeds is the result of the good work of our botanist, the other young lady here with my wife and me. During the next growing season, we will increase the herd even more."

"I look forward to the product," Mr. Fredrick said, as he went back to inspecting the last mohair being sacked.

Heidi joined the visitors. She was introduced to Rosita and she invited the group to her new home for tea. Before serving tea, she showed them through the house that she was proud to have redecorating and refurnishing. The thoughts about weaving with mohair yarn discussed as they sipped tea was, of course, appealing to Heidi. She had made many clothes from the wool of the few sheep at the lodge. She told Rosita where to find the loom and dyed yarn that she had left there after Afton commented that Rosita had been forced to flee an active volcano without her clothes, so she wanted to make some apparel for herself.

The concept of Rosita and Heidi working with other woman to create a *cottage industry* producing fine mohair clothing was discussed further on the trip back to the lodge. Rosita told them that she was excited about the concept and would do all she could, but she still wanted to go to medical school, eventually. Margo pointed out that Mr. Fredrick had not committed to providing yarn. Roger replied, "We all heard the excitement in his voice when the potential for garments being made, locally, was mentioned. He will make available the yarn his company produces from our young goats."

The loom and dyed wool that Heidi had left were moved by Rosita to her room, with the help of Rosanne. For the next few days Rosita spent most of her time weaving. Ramon did insist that she take long walks with him to see all that was happening around her and the countryside that she thought magnificent. Ramon was asked to begin to organize overnight camping trips for guests. Roger and Margo traveled to meet the owners and managers of adjacent *estancias* to obtain permission for such trips to go beyond *Estancia Margo*. They learned that the largest adjacent property, owned by a media mogul in the United States, was being given to the government for parkland.

Luis came to the lodge in the farm truck and asked that someone follow him to the farm and bring him back. Before Derek did that, the two of them went with Ramon to get his camping equipment and to buy packs to carry the equipment on horses. To Rosita's surprise, they returned with some clothes already finished by Mia.

Early one morning, Margo called the number that Countess Rothchild had given her to invite her, once again, to spent time at the lodge. The call was answered by her Private Secretary, Faye Wallace. Rather curtly, Miss Wallace informed Margo that she would pass on the invitation. Then, later that day, Margo received a call from Faye to inform her that the Countess had accepted the invitation offered but made some demands: The countess would require transportation that included a conformable bed on a private plane, a ground-floor suite, rooms for a secretary and a personnel assistant, and nearby medical care that included a blood-pressure measuring devise and resuscitating equipment.

Margo assured her those things would be provided. The woman gave Margo a tentative date when the Countess would be able to make the trip; three weeks from then. The date surprised Margo, she expected the Countess would want to come in the spring or summer but was informed that the she had grown up in the mountains of Switzerland and that winter was her favorite time of year.

The company plane was equipped with wide seats that could be reclined for use as a bed. Assuming that would not be adequate, Margo called the co-pilot, Ted Benson, and requested that a single bed in a closed compartment on their plane be added, if that was possible. She discussed with Roger them moving back to the large bedroom upstairs in the lodge, which he did not object to doing, and she met with Rosita. Adding a cabinet for medical supplies and equipment in her quarters, that were already being used for weaving, was discussed. The two women then went of the city to purchase what Rosita thought appropriate, and Rios helped install the cabinet when they returned.

Rios also helped Ramon with his new assignment. All horses at the lodge had carried only people on their backs. Now, three would be needed to carry heavy packs of camping equipment. Rios chose the three he thought most suitable from his years working with the group. Those three accepted the packs without too much kicking or bucking, but it was a different situation when weight was added. Therefore, that was done a little at a time and the new pack animals were taken, tied in a line, on nearby trails for short trips until they became used to the new effort in store for them.

They were hobbled at night outside the corral until they became used to that. Cooler weather indicated the changing season and no one at the lodge, including Roger, thought the overnight camping would become an attraction to guests until spring. However, a group arrived from Bavaria that included two young male naturalists with a special interest in tracking puma on their wide-ranging, territorial movements. The opportunity to do that with a pack-train appealed to them. Still uncertain about the pack animals, Ramon and Rios decided they should both accompany the naturalists in the first, extended trip into the wilderness.

The trip had an auspicious beginning. In late morning on the first day, a puma was spotted, feeding on a guanaco kill. They tied the horses they were riding and the skittish pack horses. For a longtime, the cat was watched through binoculars and photographed with long lenses. The guests recorded distinguishing features and markings. When the carcass was dragged into a brushy area, the group re-mounted and followed. Light snow falling through the night allowed easy tracking. Keeping some distance away from the cat, the puma was tracked until dusk. An overnight campsite was chosen. With Ramon knowing how the packing had been done, he directed the unpacking and the erection of a camp that included a large tent, quite quickly.

Rios set aside the riding gear and packs, and he hobbled the horses in a grassy area nearby. Ramon built a fire and began preparing the evening meal that consisted of salmon, boiled rice and corn, as well as bread baked at the lodge. The guests watched the efficiency of their guides in amazement. Both coffee and tea were prepared to accompany the meal. Second and third cups were drunk as the group sat around the fire chatting in German. Rios, who had carried his rifle over his shoulder until then, was asked if they were safe from attack. He told them that because of the large guanaco herds in the area, they and the horses would not be bothered on the trip, unless the cat thought it was being cornered.

After a big breakfast the next morning, the camp was dismantled. The men and horses were ready to resume tracking soon after sunrise. The cat tracks were located by Rios, but the puma was not seen again until late morning. It had begun circling around them. The consensus was it had reached one limit of its territory. Rios estimated that if that territory included the lodge, and he assumed that it did, the total area would be several hundred square miles. The naturalists recorded those thoughts, very pleased that they now had first-hand knowledge about something they had been studying.

The tracking of the cat continued. It stayed in wooded areas until near the lake on *Estancia Margo*. There it chased and took down another guanaco. Once again, it was under the watchful eye of the trackers for a long time. Riding back to the lodge, the guests expressed their appreciation for a rewarding trip. The trip was explained, in detail, to the two older men who had arrived at the lodge with the younger men. They had spent their time hiking. It was made clear that the group consisted of professors and students from a university.

Because of the demands of her private secretary regarding her visit to the lodge, the owners assumed that Countess Rothchild was now in poor health. Instead, she proved to be a spry, feisty, and friendly octogenarian, with a pleasant personality. Roger drove the Range Rover to the company plane to pick up the Countess' entourage and baggage. The Countess greeted him with a friendly smile and an embrace. When she was taken to the terminal for the required customs screening, she managed that better than Faye Wallace or her personal assistant, Bessie Young. The Countess insisted on presenting her passport herself and spoke with the attendants in perfect Spanish. She wore a silk dress and a cashmere sweater beneath a full-length chinchilla coat.

Miss Wallace was a tall, slim, middle-aged woman with an aristocratic appearance, dressed in a business suit. She carried a wool coat over her arm and acted with some distain toward the customs officials. Bessie was older and slightly overweight. She wore a simple dress and heavy wool coat. Saying little, Bessie followed Miss Wallace, with her eyes downcast.

On the drive to the lodge, the Countess asked many questions about the region. Stepping from the vehicle in front of the quarters prepared for her when Rios opened the door, she walked back to the front of the main building where she stood for several minutes. When Roger and Margo joined her, she told them how impressed she was and embraced Margo.

Rios and Harriett moved the baggage, under the direction of Miss Wallace, into the suite and upstairs to two bedrooms. Bessie began to unpack the Countess' suitcases immediately, putting everything in closets and drawers. Upon her entrance to the suite, the honored guest walked around the suite, voicing her pleasure with the accommodations and the beautiful flowers from the hothouse that Afton had placed in the rooms. Rosita was the first staff member to whom the Countess was introduced when she arrived from her adjacent quarters. She wore one of the nurse's uniforms she had been provided. She was greeted warmly.

Rosita told her that she was staying in adjacent quarters that were equipped with medical supplies and equipment, saying that she would be available to her day and night. The Countess said she appreciated that. However, without regard to what may have been said by her staff, she was in good health, so she did not think that Rosita's services would be needed. She added, "That does not mean we will not become good friends."

The unreasonable and unnecessary demands made by Faye Wallace became more evident when Roger went back to the airport for his flight crew. The bedchamber added to the plane, with curtains enclosing a single bed, was not used. The Countess was happy sleeping on a reclined chair like all other passengers.

Accommodating the Countess and her staff, the flight crew, Margo and Roger, meant that Harriett had accepted no more reservations. She was concerned about making certain that the Countess received first-class service. She had no reason for any concern. No one who had ever stayed at the lodge expressed more appreciation and demanded less. She was offered meals in her rooms but insisted on eating with everyone else on the regular schedule. Bessie helped her dress each morning and accompanied her to the dining room.

After dinner and conversations in the living room where she drank one glass of sherry, Bessie assisted her when she went to retire. No one determined, at first, what Faye Wallace did each day. She spent most of her time in her room. In Bessie's free time, she helped the household staff. Having learned that Rosita was weaving in the room next to her, the Countess spent hours watching her, while carrying on long discussions about Rosita's upbringing and her desires, including her hope to go to medical school.

The requests the Countess made to see the surrounding countryside all involved trips in the Range Rover to see the snow-covered mountains and the ice field. Several trips were made with the Countess in the front seat with Roger, Margo and Faye in the second seat. Whenever the Countess was outside of her rooms at the lodge, she wore a beautiful dyed-wool poncho that Rosita made for her.

To the surprise of everyone, the Countess, who asked to be called Shirley, became sincerely interested in every activity in which those working for Roger were engaged. She asked to be shown the fish operation, the nursery, and the work rooms in the lower level of the main building. One day several rolls of mohair fiber arrived. The shipment included dye of many colors, with a note from Mathew Frederick stating that dying mohair was much easier than dying wool. She became very interested in Rosita's change from making outer garments from wool to mohair, watching her often, and she became very friendly with Ramon who spent his spare time with Rosita.

A new project was revealed, when Josh and Jenifer arrived to begin the preparations for oil and gas exploration. The Countess took time to discuss every aspect of the planning and asked to be explained the mapping project that had led to Josh's recommended drill sites. Her offer to provide exploration money shocked Roger and Josh. Roger explained that oil and gas exploration was far too risky for the investment of family money such as hers, without becoming certain that he had convinced her of that.

Chapter Sixteen
Natural Resources Potential

No one in the business world outside of Chile had learned more about the Ministry of Mines, the Chilean agency that controlled mining, as well as oil and gas development, in the country, than had Roger Richardson. He had studied the regulations under which the agency operated and had profiles created of all the important management personnel. He understood, therefore, what would be required to obtain the right to explore for oil and gas and produce the hydrocarbons found in the country where all such material and minerals were owned by the federal government.

He was aware that the government officials were intent on expanding the dwindling reserves of oil and gas in established fields that were located, principally, in the *Punta Arenas* region, both on-shore and off-shore. To accomplish that, investments from outside the country were being actively encouraged. Rights were being granted through individual contracts and through the issuing of concessions. Roger thought that his company, The Richardson Group, had a good chance to secure a contract covering exploration drilling in a small area that Josh had determined to be the most prospective, and that the agreements he had obtained from the surface-land owners to drill in that area, agreements that called for payment for any damages and the reclamation of all drill sites, enhanced that chance. He knew from previous action of the Ministry that concessions covering large blocks would require a commitment to spend large sums of money on exploration and development.

The first application prepared by Josh and Jenifer that Roger submitted to the Ministry, with approval of his Board of Directors, received a quick, favorable response. It was assumed that the field office of the company listed on the application—Lautaro Lodge—had something to do with that response.

The lodge was only a few tens of miles from the lease area and had developed a good reputation with government officials.

Roger and Josh were flown to *Punta Arenas* where they were able to contract for the services of a winterized drill rig that was inactive. Within two days, the rig and related equipment began the move to a site that Josh had surveyed. The motor-grader used at the lodge and the goat farm was moved and Rios began leveling the site and building an access road. That work had been completed and the Vergara brothers had built a fence around the site, with a wide gate, by the time the drilling equipment arrived.

Within less than two weeks from the time the Special Petroleum Operations Contract had been received from the Ministry of Mines, drilling of the first well commenced. A contract was signed with a 'mud logging' company to analyze the drill-bit cuttings and to monitor natural gas 'shows.' A small travel-trailer was rented for Josh to stay in while directing the operations, and a communication system was created to keep the lodge informed about progress, using a satellite telephone.

The drilling operation was, of course, the activity of greatest interest at the lodge. However, other work on seed preparation, hothouse plantings, and fish production continued. Rosita, with the Countess watching and conversing with her much of the time, began to produce beautiful mohair outerwear. Bessie assisted the Countess, mornings and at bedtime and helped the staff. Faye, the others were to learn, was busy writing the Countess' biography. Margo spent a lot of time with Afton, while Roger tried to say current with things happening at his London office, by telephone. Jenifer kept a daily log of drill-site activity forwarded to her from her husband.

When those daily reports began to include shows of oil and gas, Roger went to the drill site. There, he watched as solid cores of oil shale were recovered from the drill hole, placed in plastic sleeves, and put in properly marked boxes made for that purpose. Roger and Josh discussed the fact that the analyses of those cores at a laboratory in *Punta Arenas* would be necessary to determine if commercial quantities of oil could be produced from these strata, but what they saw was very encouraging. It was decided it would be prudent to acquire a concession covering a larger area.

Discussing the submittal of an application to the Ministry for a large concession that evening with Margo, sitting in the lodge living room, Roger was overheard by the Countess. She had stayed current with all oil and gas activity and read reports that had been prepared. Her contribution to the discussion was very meaningful. That contribution made it clear that she saw a way to help. "The granting of a concession will require a commitment for future expenditures of a lot of money," she told them. "If my money was to be used in that regard, it might never be spent. In that case I would face no risk. Revenues from your first field could be reinvested in future exploration and development."

What the Countess said revealed keen business sense. That was confirmed when she said she would expect a payment on product sold from the concession for which she provided a capital commitment, even if it was never needed. A flurry of activity followed. Roger presented this proposal to his Board, who approved it. Loan documents were executed and funds from an account of the Countess, along with The Richardson Group money, was transferred to an account to back a concession application sent to the Ministry of Mines. The approval of this application took a long time. Before it arrived, the first exploratory well had been completed, core data had revealed that it was possible to recovery commercial quantities of oil, and well-completion, using the latest technology for releasing oil (called fracking) was underway.

Those results were being celebrated at the lodge but were overshadowed by the arrival of representatives of a consortium of a large, Canada-based oil company and a Chilean investment group. These men offered to buy out the oil and gas interests of The Richardson Group in Patagonia and replace the concession commitment with their capital, when the concession was assigned to them. The chance for a quick return on investment was something Roger's Board could not refuse, so the offer was accepted. Roger made certain that the account of the Countess would receive a large, unexpected early increase.

Upon learning of this financial transaction, the Countess told Roger that short-term interest on the money she had provided would have been adequate, but she had a plan for the windfall. She told him had she had been planning for some time to make certain that Rosita was able to become a doctor, and that Rosita had informed her that while she was taking preparatory class at university, she had applied to medical school at Saint George's University on the island of Grenada and had been accepted. She said she had hoped that Roger would allow this employee to take a leave-of-absence to do that and that Rosita could be able to travel with her and her assistants when they were flown back to London in his company plane.

The news was unexpected, but Roger he was in full support of the Countess' plan. When asked if Rosita had been told, the Countess suggested that they do that, jointly, at dinner one night. Roger asked when the Countess wanted to leave. He was told that she was enjoying her stay so much that a trip scheduled to get Rosita to Grenada in time to begin the spring semester should be considered. Roger told her that would be good, for he had other business affairs to conclude in Chile on this trip, and that he and Margo were also enjoying their stay.

Before the plan was announced, Roger discussed it with Margo. She was very pleased for Rosita. She mentioned that an island wardrobe would be needed, but Ramon's mother would have time to make warm-weather clothes for her. She said that the weaving Rosita was doing was being taught to Rosanne, who also wanted to learn about medical care, so a replacement at the lodge was already being trained.

Rosita sat with tears in her eyes at the dinner table when the Countess announced her medical-school plan. The others applauded. Roger commented that it was the hope of them all that Rosita would choose to establish a practice in Patagonia upon graduation. After dinner, Rosita and Ramon discussed this life-changing event for hours, during which Rosita promised to return and marry him.

Margo had taken a special interest in the weaving. She saw great potential in a business that produced garments made by native women from locally grown wool and mohair on a large scale. Such garments were already highly prized items among tourists. With concurrence from Rosita and Heidi, she established weekly training sessions in the conference room of the lodge, solicited the help of male staff members to learn the process of dyeing the fibers, and worked out arrangements with Mister Fredrick for a supply of yarn. She also created a way to sell the product online.

Within a month, Margo had rented a small building in *Puerto Natales* and had hired ten young, native women to produce *Lautaro* brand sweaters, vests, and ponchos. Each of those women had learned weaving from their mothers and grandmothers and had studied the exceptional techniques of Rosita. A store-front was created to sell items to the tourists. Other natives were hired as sales people and to work in packaging and shipping. Rather than the *cottage industry,* once considered, a significant manufacturing business was created, the profits from which were to be distributed to the employees.

When Josh Wright had conveyed to the oil and gas consortium all he had learned in his geologic studies in Patagonia and had delivered copies of all his maps and data, with Jenifer's assistance, Roger asked them to meet with him regarding a new assignment. He began the meeting by saying, "We now need to concentrate on the biggest prize in Chile, a concession from which to produce lithium, the natural resource that will become extremely valuable very soon."

Plans were discussed that involved Roger, Josh, and Jenifer flying north in the company plane. The first stop was to be in Santiago where the plane would be fitted with camera equipment, ordered by Roger from Texas, to take aerial photographs of the *Atacama* Desert, the region that was becoming the most important source-area of lithium in the world. With the equipment installed and the flight-crew trained to operate it, the photographs would be taken. Josh and Jenifer would then establish a base of operations in *Arica,* near the Peruvian border, and from there conduct geological reconnaissance, traversing the desert on all accessible road segments.

Margo had decided to stay in Patagonia and continue her involvement with the Lautaro Wool and Mohair Works. The Countess was happy to stay at the lodge throughout the winter, if necessary. She and her companions would be the only guests after the pilots left.

The pilots had enjoyed their stay at Lautaro Lodge, as they always did, but were happy to be on duty again. The flight to *Los Cerrillos* Airport, near the central of Santiago, was uneventful. The clear weather provided magnificent views of the most beautiful part of Chile. The arrangements made with the camera manufacturer in Texas worked out. The camera equipment and technicians were already there. Installation work began soon after The Richardson Group plane landed. Roger, his flight crew, and companions took rooms in a nearby hotel.

The next morning the flight crew went back to the hangar rented for the plane modifications. Josh and Jenifer spent the day touring the city. Roger called Tomas Ledesma, at his office in *La Moneda*, the presidential palace, and was granted the audience with the man that Roger had long anticipated meeting, again. The meeting with the President' Chief of Staff was scheduled for ten. It lasted until, and through, the lunch hour. As Roger had hoped, the work that his people were doing in Patagonia had come to the attention of many in the federal government, including the President, according to Tomas.

His group's discovery of new oil and gas reserves that were much needed received special commendation. The discussions during lunch in a fine restaurant became personal. The well-being of the Ledesma family and those at Lautaro Lodge were discussed. Tomas mentioned that his son considered Rios a good friend and expressed his desire to do more exploring with him. Roger assured him that Marco and his parents would always be considered honored guests at the lodge. It wasn't until Roger and Tomas were leaving the restaurant that Roger mentioned that the study of lithium resources was his current undertaking.

He mentioned that the geologist who had been responsible for the oil and gas discovery in Patagonia was to open a field office in *Arica* and that his plane was being outfitted with camera equipment with which the *Atacama* Desert would be photographed in the coming days to provide him a base data. Tomas told him that he would be interested in see the outcome of that work. Roger responded that the results would include a request for a concession.

Leaving Tomas, Roger had mixed thoughts about the outcome of their meetings. He was pleased about the complimentary things he had heard about the results of his investments in Chile, but he had received no assurance about the granting of a lithium concession. He wondered if he should have pressed for such assurance but realized that was beyond what Tomas could offer and told himself that a meeting with the Ministry of Mines would be critical. His small investment group was now be in competition with some of the largest natural resource companies in the world.

Before taking a taxi back to the hotel, Roger shopped for something for Margo. He thought a lot about her since she had become such an important part of his life. What he found was a delicate piece of fine silversmith work to wear around her neck. When he returned to the hotel, he found Josh and Jenifer in the lounge. Joining them, he discussed his meeting after they told him how enchanting they had found the Capitol City. They did not see the pilots again until dinner. The long day they had watching the mounting of the camera and learning to operate it was described.

Josh pointed out that the main desert area they were to photograph covered nearly 41,000 square miles east of the coast range, excluding the slopes of the Andes Mountains. He said he had devised a flight path for the first, higher altitude photographs to be taken that was nearly 1,500 miles long and explained that other flights would be required, at lower altitudes, after he had arranged for the surveying of ground control in areas prospective for lithium extraction. Ted Benson gave Josh the information he had received from the camera company for the printing of the photographs.

A more desolate landscape did not exist anywhere on earth than the one photographed on the flight the next day. From the flight altitude chosen, no vegetation nor structures could be seen. The adjacent mountain slopes were nearly bare of vegetation, as well. In the mountains, only small patches of snow could be seen on the highest peaks.

By contrast, the coastal city of *Arica* looked like a paradise. From a curving coastline with sandy beaches, a beautiful city came into view as the plane approached an international airport. Margo had reserved rooms for them in a hotel adjacent to a surfing beach. The setting rivalled any place that Roger and the others had stayed, previously.

Roger and Josh spent the next few days finding office space, furnishing that space, and renting a vehicle. Ned Willis had unloaded the camera. He sent the film to have it developed, as soon as the office could be used for the return address.

For the first time in Chile, Jenifer saw negroes and mulattos, like herself. Much of the service help at the hotel had black skin. In speaking with them, she learned that many of their race had crossed the Andes from the Amazon Basin of Brazil on a tortuous foot-path. Some had traveled on such a path from Bolivia to the coast. One woman, who was particularly talkative, told Jenifer that her son had been crippled from the explosion of a land mine when he wandered off the path. That statement caused Jenifer to ask others about land mines. She found that in the 1970s, the Chilean dictator, fearing invasion from Peru, had caused a strip of land along the border to be mined.

When Jenifer mentioned what she had learned to her husband and Roger, Roger informed her that he was aware of that situation and knew of a fund in England, initiated by Princess Diana before her untimely death, to provide money for governments to remove land mines. He promised Jenifer that when he got back to London he would see if such funds were being directed to this area, and if not, he would try to make that happen.

One evening, Jenifer rode the bus home with Mari, the woman whose son was a cripple, to see how they lived. She was appalled. The hovel in which the boy was laying was made, like at least a dozen nearby, of packing-crates and cardboard. The boy, she was told, was ten years old. He could slide around and crawl, but not stand, so his days were spent within a few feet of the filthy blanket on which he slept. His father, Jenifer was to learn, had found a job at sea, his intent for coming to Chile with his family. His wife and son had not seen or heard from him in three months. The bowl in which Mari had left some cornmeal for him to eat was empty. His mother took, from a cloth bag she carried over a shoulder, scraps of food from the kitchen at the hotel and placed them in the bowl and handed him a plastic bottle of water, half full. The boy devoured the food and water.

Jenifer asked, and was told, that employees at the hotel were given one meal each day, which Mari had eaten at the end of her shift. Looking around her, Jenifer saw others returning from work to these dreadful conditions. Most were women and young children. With tears in her eyes, Jenifer left Mari and her son, who she called Bo. She cried about what she had seen on the bus ride back to the hotel. At dinner with Josh and Roger, she explained her day.

"Was there no help for those people?" Roger asked. "No mission or church people?"

Jenifer replied, "I saw none."

"Tomorrow, I will go back there with you to investigate," Roger said. "It is not like this country to disregard such needs."

Roger and Jenifer drove the rented Jeep back to the slums after dropping Josh at his new office the next morning. The only help they found was four young Chilean women distributing food and water and providing places for people to sleep in a large Quonset that had a faded sign attached, indicating that the building had once been an army barracks. They were told by one of the girls that the facility was sponsored by the church they attended. Driving on to where Jenifer had been introduced to the tragic situation, Roger walked around in a state of disbelief.

"We must help these people," he said. "Our team will create a tent city to replace these hovels and I will provide funds to expand the food distribution."

The remainder of that day, Roger and Jenifer searched the surrounding area for tents to purchase, of all sizes. Roger paid for those they found and asked that they be delivered the next day to the site he described, all except the one small tent they took with them. They loaded that tent in the jeep with new blankets, bottled water, and crutches.

When Mari returned from the hotel that evening, she saw her son moving around a tent on crutches, as Roger was driving the final stakes to hold the tent secure in a high wind. Jenifer took Mari by the hand, and they walked to the Quonset where food that Roger had purchased was being unloaded and meals being prepared by the young women. The two of them, each carrying a carton of food and bottles of water, went back to the tent. At least two of the refugees ate a proper evening meal.

The next day, the pilots went with Roger and Jenifer to the site. Before they left, the tent city that Roger had envisioned surrounded where Bo stood in front of his tent, watching in amazement. They stopped at the Quonset where Roger left a bank draft to supplement the funds the church group had collected for food.

Discussing what had been done for homeless people with Josh that evening, he suggested a meeting with city officials to solicit more help for those people, and he volunteered to go with Jenifer to do that. At the offices of the city government, they had to wait for hours to be seen, and the man who finally spoke with them offered not help. The conclusion he offered was, "Those people should not have come here."

Jenifer responded, "I'm certain they are aware of that and realize the reason for doing so was not worth the suffering. However, those who are fit for work seem to be contributing. As our employer pointed out while we were settling up tents for some of the homeless, it hardly ever rains here, but they need protection from the wind and human beings need privacy. The type of homes the government could provide would be very inexpensive. Furthermore, the two farming valleys near the city produce abundant vegetables and fruit, some of which could become available to them under a charitable arrangement."

"Water. What about water? Our city is in short supply," the government man said.

"We purchased bottled water. It was expensive, but available, and we see surfers showering in front of our hotel," was Jenifer's reply.

"Given a chance, some of these people will make a significant contribution in your society, as my wife has done in the Caribbean and Patagonia," Josh added.

In dismissing them, the man said he would look-into the situation. Neither of them expected that to happen.

Roger had arranged to meet Jenifer and Josh in the hotel dining room for lunch, where he waited by himself. The pilots had gone for lunch on the beach. A man came to Roger's table and sat down without an invitation. He introduced himself as Russ Bouchett and what he had to say was not well-received: "Our people saw you meeting with Tomas Ledesma in Santiago. We checked on you and have conclude that you are seeking a lithium concession. You should not do that. The lithium play is for major companies, like mine. Securing the funds for development and production will be impossible for a group such as yours, and my Canadian consortium will oppose your bid for a concession. The government's limit on the extraction of lithium-containing brine from the ancient lake beds will be met by us. Other concessions are not necessary."

Roger did not confirm or deny his long-held interest in lithium production. He told the man, however, that he did not appreciate him trying to infer with his business, when the man left the table.

Jenifer and Josh arrived. During the afternoon, a strategy was devised. Roger discussed the need for Josh to define the ground-water basins within the desert and to conduct water-balance studies.

"The man who confronted me to express his opposition to our involvement was right about one thing, the government restricts the extraction of brine. That is wise. Mining the ground water would result in less lithium leached from the lake beds. You need to define, as best you can, Josh, individual ground-water basins. That will require all you know and all you can learn about the geomorphology of the desert. There was recently a once-in-a-lifetime rainstorm over parts of the desert. The area has numerous weather stations that would have recorded the rainfall amounts and have years of data on the evaporating winds.

From that data and what you learn about the porosity and permeability of the soil, you can make estimates of the ground-water recharge. We must choose our concession application carefully and have irrefutable information about proper brine-extraction volumes we would expect to withdraw. It is an enormous area. You have been given a near impossible task but do the best job you can. I consider this the best natural resource potential in the world today. While you and Jenifer work here, Margo and I will do everything we can to secure the funds for an extraction and recovery operation."

Roger spent a few hours in the field office with Josh and Jenifer the next morning. Then Josh took him and the pilots to the plane. They were airborne by late morning.

On the flight back over the desert, Roger asked that they do so at a low altitude. They got a good view of the operation of the Canadian consortium and took photographs. It consisted of enormous evaporation ponds, large stockpiles of dry material, and a huge processing plant.

Roger was alone for the first time in a long time. During the hours of flight-time from the *Atacama* Desert to *Puerto Natales,* he contemplated all his efforts in Chile, with a feeling of accomplishment regarding what his people had done to advance concepts and to establish production that would be of benefit to the nation, individuals, and groups for years to come, in some instances. He knew that the things accomplished would continue to be advanced, even if the two people most responsible, Derek and Afton, were to undertake new challenges.

Chapter Seventeen
Funding

Roger found that everything at the lodge was moving along very well when Margo discussed the activities he had missed while they lay in bed, still in a loving embrace. She was very proud of the garment-producing organization she had started and reported a regular increase in sales. When asked about their honored guest, she said the Countess had been very busy.

"She has helped Rosita prepare to leave for medical school, spent time with Afton, observing her work in the nursery, and provided material to Faye for her biography, daily."

"Do you think she has enjoyed her stay?" Roger asked.

"She told me that her stay here was very memorable and that we could expect her back next winter."

"Will she be ready to leave soon?"

"I think so, for she in anxious to see Rosita in medical school. I have assisted Rosita in obtaining a passport and Grenada entry papers. The Countess has forwarded money to cover her registration, room, and board for the entire study period. Rosita has held telephone conversations with her friend from nursing school who is in her second year at the school. That girl plans to meet the plane and get Rosita settled-in. A flight to the Caribbean is in order."

Roger responded, "That's good. You and I need to return to London and begin working on major funding. I think we are on a course to become lithium producers in this country."

At breakfast, Roger provided a short summary of where he had been and what had been accomplished. He conveyed good-wishes from Tomas Ledesma and mentioned, briefly, the plight of blacks he had tried to help, and the route taken by them to get to the coast of Chile where there were many landmines. The Countess said she had previously contributed to a group hoping to have land-mines removed, worldwide, saying she would contribute more when she returned home. A schedule for departure for Grenada and London was set for the following morning.

Margo insisted that Roger go to see the garment operation with her. He was amazed by the efficiency of the manufacturing, the activity in the sales room, and, particularly, the quality of the garments. Knowing that this would be their last chance to visit *Puerto Natales,* a city they both had come to enjoy, for some time, they walked along the waterfront and had a leisurely lunch at a seafood restaurant.

The afternoon was spent by Roger with each of those working for him on *Estancia Margo,* while Margo, Rosita, Bessie, and Faye packed. Harriet and Rosanne prepared an elaborate dinner as a parting gesture. It was greatly appreciated by all and provided for expressions of thanks and well-wishes. As she had suggested earlier, the Countess promised to return during the next winter.

A van from the airport arrived after breakfast. Final farewells were offered, with many embraces, and the journey began. The flight to Grenada was uneventful. Roger allowed Rosita to call her friend, Rachael Vaira, on his satellite telephone. She was waiting at the general aviation terminal. Roger went to greet her and escorted her into the plane to meet everyone. Rachael was an exceptionally pretty, young woman. As she stood next to Rosita, the Countess commented that there could never be two more attractive doctors.

Rosita was overwhelmed by it all. She hugged the Countess tightly, and told her, with tears in her eyes, "What you are doing for me is beyond words of thanks. I promise you that I will become a doctor and serve everyone I meet that is in need."

The Countess replied, "I know you will, my love. Please write to me often. My address is written on this envelope." The envelope the Countess gave her contained a bank draft, with a note describing the large sum as "spending money."

Roger carried Rosita's things to a waiting taxi, hugged both young women, and waved as the taxi drove away. Returning to the plane, he saw tears in the eyes of both Margo and the Countess. All on board sat in silence as the plane was refueled.

During the flight over the Caribbean and the Atlantic oceans, the remaining passengers slept much of the time in reclined seats. The private compartment created for the Countess, but never used, had been removed.

Faye had used Roger's phone to announce their pending arrival at Gatwick Airport. After everyone had cleared customs, this time Faye handing it all for her people, they found a Rolls Royce waiting at the curb. Before the Countess got in the back seat next to Faye, she embraced Margo and Roger, thanking them for a stay at their lodge that she would never forget. The pilots had retrieved Ted's car. Margo and Roger were driven to their home.

Roger's first attempts to obtain commitments for the capital necessary for lithium-brine extraction and processing were made from his office, with the assumption that his group would receive a concession. He made many telephone calls and met with several men who had invested with The Richardson Group before. Margo had made many sketches, in charcoal, of scenes and people while in Patagonia from which she began to create oil paintings. Each evening, the two of them discussed the success, or lack therefore, that Roger was having. One evening Roger announced that his complete success would require him to travel to meet with possible investors to adequately describe the potential of this new venture. Margo understood but did not think it as necessary for her to accompany him.

A flight was made to Zurich a few days later. From a hotel room on the river, where he had stayed many times before, he called Karl Winkley, the son of one of the partners with whom Roger's father had been associated for many years, including in the very profitable venture in platinum mining. Karl invited him to a night club across the river, an invitation Roger tried, unsuccessfully, to decline, having heard that Karl had become a millionaire playboy. He had hoped to meet him for a quiet dinner.

Roger left the pilots after a quiet dinner with them in the hotel dining room and walked, reluctantly, across the river to the club. He found Karl at a table with a beautiful young woman, who looked to be a German. Roger greeted them at the table. Neither stood and Karl did not even introduce the woman, but he ordered more champagne and another glass. Right away, Roger knew he had made a mistake in coming and that Karl was not a potential investor. Before he could excuse himself and leave, another scantily dressed woman arrived and sat next to him in a semi-circular booth, essentially trapping him.

Roger's attempts at light conversation with Karl about their fathers and the times they had spent together as youngsters was lost in alcohol-induced babble.

Eventually, the second woman left. Roger slid out of the booth, told Karl and his companion goodnight, and left the club, without taking a sip of the champagne. As he walked back across the river, he thought it was a shame that hard-earned money of a father was being wasted by a son, thinking his father would be proud of him for pursuing a much different life. He hoped that he would not encounter similar situations when he visited the families of his father's other partners in southern Africa.

The flight the next day was as spectacular as any Roger had ever taken. His plane flew over the center of Africa on a cloudless day, all the way to Pretoria. The contrast between the desert, jungles, plains, mountains and lakes was clearly visible. Roger had called ahead for hotel reservations and provided the hotel with the details on their arrival. He and his pilots were greeted by the driver of a courtesy car from the hotel when the left they plane.

Roger's father's South African partners had assigned their interests in mineral properties to Southern Ventures, a private company, the manager of which Roger had kept in contact with over the years, but he had not seen Eaton Embry for several years. He called Eaton from his hotel room as soon as he checked-in, and he was invited to Eaton's club for lunch the next day. Roger and the pilots spent their time together until then. They took walking tours of the city and ate dinner and breakfast in fine restaurants.

The club was within walking distance of the hotel. Eaton was waiting for Roger in a bar with dividing walls made of highly varnished hard wood, and he seemed genuinely pleased to see him. Over one drink, they discussed previous meetings in southern Africa and England. Then, they moved to an elaborately furnished dining room. At a corner table, they ordered lunch and the discussion turned to business matters. Before Roger could explain his reason for coming, Eaton explained the gold-mine expansion his organization was currently funding, assuming Roger had come to participate. When the confusion was sorted out, it became obvious to Roger that he had made another unsuccessful journey. They parted on friendly terms, and Roger walked back to his hotel, dejected.

On the flight home, it was decided to stop for fuel at Cairo and to spend the next night there. From the plane to a fine hotel, they encountered much confusion, including a near riot at a protest in front of the hotel. Only small, overnight bags had been brought by each of them from the plane. Upon entering the hotel lobby with those bags on straps over their shoulders, they were ordered to drop the bags and move toward other people being held at gunpoint by three men with hand guns. A receptionist who refused to move from behind a counter was shot.

Quickly studying the situation, Roger concluded that the men, who appeared to be Egyptians, were amateurs and seemed to be shaking with fear from what they were doing. As the man closest to him looked away, Roger dove at his legs, knocking him down. The gun the man held fell to the marble floor and Roger crawled after the gun. Bullets stuck the marble around him, but Roger managed to retrieve the gun and move behind a couch. He turned over a table next to the couch and positioned himself, so he could fire the gun over the table. Seeing someone was prepared to shoot back, the men ran from the lobby.

The pilots rushed to the girl who had been shot. Seeing the bullet had gone through her arm, Ted shouted for towels. A bellboy brought towels with which the wound was tightly bound to stop the bleeding. He and Ned carried her to the couch behind which Roger had hidden before he rushed after the gunmen, watching them blend into the protestors. The police arrived, followed by an ambulance. Roger handed the gun he held to an officer and described what he had witnessed. The pilots watched as the receptionist was put on a gurney to be moved to the ambulance. She smiled and reached out with her uninjured arm and grasp Ted's hand. Those in the lobby dispersed. The hotel manager came to the reception counter. Roger and his flight crew picked up their bags and went there to check-in. The manager had watched the action and expressed his gratitude for what had been done. The rooms they were assigned were the best in the hotel. They were to find out, upon departure the next morning, that the rooms had been complementary.

The event in the lobby and the protest in the street was, of course, on the minds of everyone in the dining room that evening. No one expressed sound reasoning for the actions of the gunmen. The best explanation seemed to be that there was a government official staying at the hotel that they were trying to force into the street to confront the protestors.

More police officers where in the lobby the next morning. They insisted that Roger and his crew go with them to their headquarters to file written statements. That took most of the morning, but a police car took them to the plane afterwards, so they were flying over the Mediterranean by early afternoon.

Roger was happy to be again with Margo when he arrived home, but he was in a state of despair, having yet to secure commitments for the capital for a project that he considered to have the potential to become the most financially rewarding of his life. Margo showed him an oil painting of which she was very proud. It was a portrait of Countess Rothchild dressed in a poncho of brilliant colors. Roger was amazed by the resemblance she had created of facial features and the realistic colors of the garment depicted. He told her the painting was magnificent.

In his office on the telephone the next morning, Roger's administrative assistant, Alice Wilcox, brought him a newspaper that carried an article regarding the events in Cairo. The article identified him and his flight crew and mentioned their contributions. Later in the day, he received a call from Countess Rothchild. She had read the newspaper article and wanted to know why he had been to Egypt. Reluctantly, he told her about his unsuccessful trips to Europe and Africa. Once again, the Countess offered him financial support for a project. He told her the amount of money it would take to develop the concession he sought in northern Chile would be very large, much larger than the money she had pledged for oil and gas exploration, and that this investment was too long-term for her to consider, given the country's history of drastic changes in forms of government and absolute control of natural resources by government.

The Countess replied, "You should come to my home to discuss this. I have an idea that you might consider."

"Margo and I would be very pleased to see you." Roger said. "Margo has a present for you."

A date and time for a dinner meeting at the Countess' mansion was set. Roger continued making calls to possible investors. On the evening of the scheduled meeting with the Countess, Margo drove to the office. They decided to leave the car in a parking lot there and take a taxi to the mansion. Margo had the painting framed and brought it, carefully wrapped. In the taxi, with the painting between them, Roger gave the driver the address.

"Bring'n something to a grand lady, are ya," the driver said, obviously recognizing the address.

"We are, and we plan to dine with that grand lady," Margo responded.

The home of the Countess was in the most fashionable part of London. The three-story structure had been constructed from stone, centuries earlier. When ushered into the interior by a butler, they found immaculate furnishing, carpets on polished hardwood floors, and beautiful wall-hangings, much as they had expected. In a large main room, they were invited to relax and were offered glasses of sherry. Margo leaned the package against the couch on which they sat.

"Your home is much more elegant than our lodge where you have been living," Margo remarked when the Countess joined them, dressed in a stylish gown.

"I'll make a trade with you. I became very attached to Lautaro Lodge," she replied.

"I hope, then, that something I have for you will remind you of your stay," Margo said, as she unwrapped the painting.

The Countess was overwhelmed by the gift. She asked Margo to hold the painting while she studied it. She called for the butler to bring a hammer and a wall attachment to hang a painting. It was hung in a prominent place. The Countess, her guests, and butler stood together admiring the painting. The Countess embraced Margo and expressed her appreciation.

More wine was served and the discussion of Roger's need for capital ensued. The Countess told them she knew of a possible source of large capital, "Sir Reginald Tenneson, who was nearly my fourth husband, is an industrialist. His son would like to build a British-made electric car to compete with the Americans and Asians. Surely, his father understands that for the electric-car industry to be successful, there needs to be developed reliable, long-lasting batteries, that, as I have read, require lithium, the material you plan to produce, Roger. You should meet with Reginald. I will arrange for such a meeting."

The dinner that evening was very pleasant. While they ate, the Countess talked a great deal about her childhood in Switzerland and her Swiss ancestry that she had traced back for ten generations. She compared what she had learned of Roger's business propensity to that of her father who was a builder of railroads and tunnels throughout the Alps. Jokingly, she made mention of her efforts to preserve her inheritance, while three handsome and charming husbands tried to spend it all. She also made them aware that she was an active manager of the money that her father had worked so hard to earn, referring to several investments that had worked out very well for her. Again, she told Roger he could count on her for financial backing at any time.

The dinner was followed by brandy served in the Great Room. Roger was asked to describe his project in the *Atacama* Desert, which he did. At the end of their evening together, the Countess again thanked Margo for the painting, told Roger to expect a call from her, and they embraced each other.

The butler had called a taxi for them. It was waiting when Margo and Roger descended the front stairs. On the taxi ride to the office, and the drive home in Margo's car, the evening was discussed and feelings of affection for a grand lady were expressed.

The call to inform Roger of a meeting with Sir Reginald came two days later. The call came from Faye. Roger and Margo were to meet Sir Reginald and Countess Rothchild for lunch later in the week, at a popular restaurant near Piccadilly Square. On the day of the meeting, Margo drove her car to the office. From there, as before, they took a taxi into the city center. They both worn business suits, which was the way they found their host and hostess dressed when escorted to their table. The couple greeted them warmly, with broad smiles on their faces.

Sir Reginald led the conversation as they ate lunch, exhibiting a good understanding of Roger's business background and the particulars of his new project in Chile. Roger was asked pertinent questions, including one regarding how he viewed his success in obtaining a viable concession from the Chilean government. The lengthy and costly effort that had been made to establish The Richardson Group as a viable operator in the eyes of the President of the country was explained. The President's control of natural resource development, through Ministry of Mines appointees, was mentioned. The work underway from a field office in *Arica* was also explained.

Roger provided a conclusion: "With financial backing, I am confident that a viable concession can be secured in competition with the huge, multi-national consortiums. The technology of producing lithium-containing brine from shallow lake beds and extracting the mineral has been proven, so with a concession in the right area, the project has an excellent chance of great financial reward. However, the costs of a processing plant are very large and there is always the risk of nationalization."

"My son has told me that the industry in which he is determined to be a part, the electric-powered automobile industry, anticipates new battery technology in the future, but considers lithium an absolute necessity now. He provided me research that shows that Chile and Argentina will be the principal suppliers of lithium for decades," was Sir Reginald's response.

"That is my long-held opinion, as well," Roger said.

Sir Reginald's next comment surprised and pleased Roger and Margo very much, "This lovely lady and I have formed an investment group, as we have in the past, and we will supply the capital to develop a lithium concession if you are granted one."

Following those comments, Roger expressed his sincere appreciation and assured his benefactors that they would be kept informed at every stage of project development. The topic for discussion changed. The Countess raved about the Lautaro Lodge and the painting of her, dressed like a native, that Margo had painted.

When Margo and Roger left the table, there was a sense of good feelings among them all. As they walked to the entrance, Margo looked back. She saw Sir Reginal kiss the Countess on the check. She said to herself, *Shirley Rothchild is the most amazing woman I will ever meet.*

In the taxi on the way to the office, Roger made plans to go to *Arica.* Margo expressed her desire to go with him. Telephone calls were made in the office to inform the pilots that they should prepare for departure in two days and to the office in *Arica.* Jenifer answered the second call, informing Roger that Josh was working in the field. She was told that Roger and Margo would be joining them.

At Margo's request, a stop was made on the way home for them to purchase clothes appropriate for a hot climate and a beach community. While Margo packed and made needed arrangements with her staff regarding their home during another absence, Roger spent more time in the office and at Barclay Bank. He obtained the paperwork that documented the funds committed to his latest Chilean venture.

The flight was made without any unusual incidents. They landed at the Cape Verde airport for fuel but did not stay overnight. Margo took her turn in control of the plane from the co-pilot seat, while the crew rotated to get some sleep. Roger plotted his next moves to secure a concession, feeling certain that Josh has delineated a prospective area, and slept for several hours.

Checking into the beachfront hotel, they found that the Wrights had checked out weeks before. The pilots settled-in an assigned room, changed clothes, and went to the beach to watch the surfers. The Richardson's left their bags in their room, hailed a taxi, and went to the office, where they found Josh and Jennifer. They were told the couple had rented a small furnished apartment nearby. Before Roger reported his success in securing the needed capital, he asked Josh to report his success. As anticipated, Josh had defined the limits of an interpreted, ground-water basin from detailed mapping of drainage patterns and limited subsurface data acquired from drilling by the government. The area was several miles from an existing operation.

On a map, Josh had outlined the boundaries of the concession he recommended. Roger expressed his appreciation for the good work. He told them that he had brought the documentation of the capital available that was needed to accompany a request for a concession and directed that a formal request be prepared. The remainder of the day was spent doing that.

At day's end, Roger suggested they go to a restaurant for dinner. Jenifer directed them on a short walk to a place she favored that served Chilean food. Over dinner, Jenifer, when asked by Roger, briefed the others on the situation regarding the refugees that she and Roger had helped when he was last there: "I was able to convince men from the black community to build a simple apartment complex for those people for whom you provided tent shelter, using lumber the city, finally, agreed to provide. The tent city is still used as temporary shelters for newcomers, the numbers of whom are not large. Funds from England arrived, and the government's mine-removal team is again working along the border trail."

"That must make you feel very good," Margo suggested.

"It does, and I have made many friends as a result, both in the black and white communities. Efforts are now needed to have the heads of family groups given jobs. Some of the men have experience in river transport in the interior of the Amazon Basin and are finding work at sea. Once they are found to be good workers, jobs for men, women, and grown children should be possible in harvesting and packing the large amounts of fruit and vegetables grown in the area."

The next day, Margo asked Jenifer to take her to the refugee area while their husbands flew to Santiago to keep an appointment at the Ministry of Mines that Roger had made to present the completed application for a lithium concession. They rode a bus to the area, as Jenifer had first done and often since then. It was a busy place. Young girls in the Quonset were still distributing food and water and workers were expanding crude, wooden apartment rooms. Jenifer led Margo to the tent city and pointed out where piles of cardboard, previously used for shelter, and trash had been replaced by trash bins that were regularly emptied.

By chance, they met a man who had interviewed possible agriculture workers. They asked to be taken to the *Azapa* Valley to see the man's farm. He obliged them. Sitting with the man, who introduced himself as Jorge Vinson, in the front of his pick-up, they were driven the few miles to the valley and on a road parallel to a riverbed that was nearly dry for several miles through a narrow valley between sand hills. The produce being grown was extensive. Jorge pointed to groves of a unique, purple-colored olive, from which a bitter oil was being produced, numerous fields where a variety of berries were grown, and orchards of several types of fruit. Jorge drove them to his farmhouse along a side road, through blueberry and raspberry patches. Missus Vinson was washing and packaging blueberries in a shed with their two young sons. She came to meet the strangers and insisted they go to the house for tea.

As they sipped strong tea, Jorge explained that the market for blueberries didn't last long, and the efforts of the family to pick the ripe berries and package them was not adequate, even working more than twelve-hour days, so he had gone looking for help. Jennifer explained her involvement with the refugees and the torturous journey they had made to come to the area looking for work. She told the Vinson's about how some of those she had met had found work and had proven themselves to be very good workers. She suggested he hire the help he needed from the black refugees and to encourage his neighbors to do the same, pointing out that if enough workers were hired in the valley, a bus service would be created to get them to and from their jobs.

Leaving the farmhouse, Missus Vinson went back to work with the boys. Jorge drove them back down the valley, pointing to where other small farmers lived whom he thought could use help. He promised to talk with them about Jenifer's suggestion. When the offer was made to take his passengers to the city, Jenifer directed him to the office. Before leaving the farmer, Margo explained where their husbands were and told him that if they were successful, they would have a presence in the area for a long time. She offered their help, if ever needed.

They had not been in the office long when a call was received from Roger. With the instrument in speaker mode, he explained to the women their experiences during a harrowing day, "The morning was spend at the Ministry of Mines, refuting the untruths that had been told by those opposing us in our attempt to obtain a concession, including the idea that we would only turn the concession to a major company for a profit, like we did with the oil and gas concession.

I explained how my father had developed platinum resources when that mineral was needed by the general automobile industry and that I have long hoped to assist the electric-car industry by developing lithium for batteries. I hated to do it, but at a lunch break, I called Tomas Ledesma and explained our dilemma. We were treated better after lunch and I was able to discuss our financial backers and Sir Reginald's son's interest in electric cars. At the end of the day, our application was accepted, and we were promised an answer in a few days."

Roger then asked how their day had gone. Jenifer explain where they had been and the condition of the refugee camp where Roger had initiated an improvement in living conditions. He suggested they meet for a late dinner at the hotel, telling them the plane was in the air.

It was a significant distance from the office, but Jenifer suggested they walk to the hotel. On the way there, Jenifer talked about the woman named Mari, who worked at the hotel and had introduced her to the camp where she then lived. Having not seen her crippled son that day, Jenifer was concerned about Mari. They arrived at the hotel just as Mari was getting-off work. Margo was introduced to her, and she was asked about her son. Mari told them that she and he son were getting alone well. Her husband had returned from sea with enough money for them to rent a small apartment and to have her son begin therapy.

She thanked Jenifer, again, for the help that she and her employer had provided, including the crutches, saying she hoped her son would one day walk without them. The three women embraced. Mari walked to the bus stop. Jenifer and Margo went to the hotel bar where they waited for their husbands and the flight crew. There, they sipped local wine and further discussed the day's activities.

Chapter Eighteen
Further South

The waiting for word from the Ministry of Mines was going to be nerve-wracking. Everyone, except the pilots went to the office the next morning. Roger received a telephone call informing him that power-generating equipment was scheduled to arrive at *Punta Arenas* that week. He debated with himself about flying down there but decided to continue the wait where he was. A call was made to ask Derek to go down to make certain the small, coal-fired plant construction got off to a proper start, explaining to Derek the reason that he could not go himself and told him that he knew the request was beyond his contractual obligations. Derek, of course, agreed to go.

A day later, Derek drove to *Punta Arenas* in the Range Rover. He secured a room in a boarding house and made a visit to Milo Bartich to inform him that he was filling-in for Roger Richardson during the initiation of the project. Milo spent time telling Derek of the numerous set-backs and delays that he and Roger had to work through for this to happen. Derek was invited to go with him to inspect the site, near his coal mine, that had been leveled and the generating building nearly completed. There was a large stockpile of coal ready to fire the 25-megawatt unit next to the site.

The equipment did not begin to arrive at the docks for another two days. Derek spent that time getting to know the port city that he had heard so much about. Time was spent in museums and where the replica of *Nan Victoria* stood, the first ship to past through the Strait of Magellan, under the command of the man who found and named that very important waterway. He was very interested in reading early descriptions of Rios' people, the Tehuelche, and viewing displays depicting that culture. He ate some of his meals in restaurants owned and operated by Europeans. One afternoon was spent on a guided tour that concentrated on giving visitors some perspective regarding the era when wool production dominated nearly all of Patagonia.

His role as an observer allowed Derek to spend hours with Milo discussing his mining operations and to learn a great deal about fluidized-bed technology, the technology that was to allow the burning of low-grade coal, on a grate with limestone, to produce steam for the generation of electricity, under the strictest of air-quality standards. The manufacturer of the equipment was also installing it. The crew was from the Boston area, so in the hours after work, Derek learned about that part of the United States. The installers had years of experience, so the job progressed rapidly. Within several weeks, the plant was ready to be commissioned. For that event, Milo invited several government officials and politicians, for whom he had a lunch catered by a German restaurant.

Derek remained in *Punta Arenas* for the plant start-up and the period spent in training operators. Milo called Roger to give him regular progress reports, but Derek had not spoken with Roger since receiving the assignment. However, as had become routine, he called Afton each evening.

The night Derek decided it was time for him to go back to the lodge, a man checked into the boarding house that caused him to change his plans. The man, Claude Murra, was a fellow wildlife biologist from Santiago. The mission that he explained to Derek fascinated him. A condor-like bird, that might be a third species, had been reported by a professional, nesting on a cliff bounding a narrow waterway to the south and Claude was going to investigate. Although Derek thought the bird was probably an Andean Condor with unusual markings, he could not resist accompanying Claude on his quest to get photographs of the bird.

The thought that the venture was not a good idea crossed Derek's mind when the two of them got to the dock and he saw the boat that Claude had planned for the trip. The hull had been fashioned from wooden planks many years before. There was a small bridge with a rickety windscreen and a padded bench. It was powered by an outboard motor. Seeing a concerned look on Derek's face, Claude told him the boat was seaworthy, saying he had used it on trips in *Terra del Fuego* before.

The voyage began by mid-morning. It was cold and windy. There were numerous waterways ahead of them as they crossed the shipping channel. It was all new to Derek. Claude set a course and laid a map on the bench between them with a route marked on the map. Derek tried to follow where they were on the map. After a couple of hours, Claude cut the motor and the boat drifted along the base of high cliffs. With high-powered binoculars, he scanned the cliffs.

"Is this where the nest was seen?" Derek ask and received a nod as acknowledgement. They took turns searching with the binoculars for more than an hour. The motor was restarted, and Claude steered the boat across the waterway to a different vantage point and an anchor was dropped. There was a break in the cliffs on that side and a very narrow beach. As the search resumed, the wind became fierce. The boat began to rock back on forth, violently. The anchor-rope broke, and the boat was thrown onto its side, against jagged rocks. Then, half submerged, it floated for several tens of yards until the wreckage reach the beach.

Derek had moved to a position in the bow before the collision. Splintered planks struck him. He was knocked unconscious from a blow to the back of his head. When he came-to, he saw large splinters in his upper right leg and destruction all around him. Climbing through the wreckage in excruciating pain, he reached what was left of the bridge. His companion had, apparently, been washed overboard, and so had his satellite telephone that he had placed on a ledge after making a call to Afton. Derek attempted to locate Claude in the high waves, without success. His backpack was still attached to the peg where he had left it. He took the pack and the pieces of wool blanket he was able to tear from the padded benches and worked his way through splintered planks to the beach.

The pain in his leg was severe, but he knew that he should not begin the extraction of the wood fragments until he was ready to staunch the flow of blood, or he would bleed to death. He thought his first effort should be to build a fire, not only because the temperature had dropped dramatically, but he needed boiled water to work on the leg injury. There was wood to burn all around him, but it was too wet to kindle a fire. Noticing a narrow area of rock overhanging sand at the base of the cliff, he struggled there, dragging part of a plank from the hull. There, he found a few dry twigs. With them and matches he kept in his pack, wrapped in oil cloth, he was able to create a small flame that he slowly fed with twigs and shavings he carved from the plank with a knife from the pack.

Presently, he had a modest fire. The small tin cup in his pack was for drinking. It was set on the fire several times to convert enough ice to boiling water to disinfect his knife, narrow strips he had cut from the bench padding, and a cup-full which he allowed to cool. Holes he had cut in his wool-lined trousers were spread open. When all was ready, he wiped away blood and began to remove large splinters of old wood from his leg. The pain caused him to pass out at times. However, all the wood was, eventually, removed from the leg and it was tightly wrapped. The bleeding stopped, and he laid back under the overhang, exhausted.

The grave situation that confronted him was clear. His leg injury could result in blood poisoning, if not properly treated; he had no food; and not a soul knew where he was stranded. The storm had intensified, and snow was being blown everywhere. It was necessary, he knew, to bring as much wreckage-wood as possible to the protected area and keep the fire burning. He hobbled back and forth for wood. Fortunately, there was an ax attached to one plank which must have been used to cut ice from the path of the boat at times, so cutting the wood was made easier.

Food to sustain him was Derek's next concern. He noticed ice forming at the edge of the water, so spearing fish with a sharpened stick would be difficult, but hunger drove him to try, without success, late that first day. He knew the chance of killing a hare or another small animal on the narrow beach was not likely. The storm raged for another twenty-four hours. Dry and warm under the overhang, Derek was able to sleep a few hours, even with the pain. Lying there when awake, he thought, constantly, about Afton, knowing she would be concerned for him. The calls to her that he had made, at least daily, when they were apart for the past few months, ended with a call just prior to the disaster. The knowledge that Afton and Rios would come looking for him gave him hope, but he could not imagine how they would find him in this vast wilderness.

Derek carved a crutch from a plank with the ax and his knife, so when the storm subsided, he began to move around some. Taking the spear that he had carved earlier, he was able to try again for a fish. He saw several, but they were beyond his reach. To his surprise, a medium-sized turtle arose from the water and moved up the ice near him. Standing still he waited until he was able to turn the turtle onto its back with the leverage from the spear, crutch and slide it along the sand. His first meal since leaving *Punta Arenas* was turtle soup cooked in a shell. The turtle meat in the shell was supplemented, the next day, with fish. Derek worked his way on the wreckage to where he was beyond the ice expanding at the edge of the water. There he sat, quietly, until he saw fish swimming in ice-free water and speared a large salmon. Back in the shelter he cleaned, boned, and cut up the fish.

The swelling of the injured leg became very disquieting. It was packed in ice whenever Derek lay awake in the shelter. He was fully aware that if he was not rescued soon, he would lose the leg.

The first day without a call from Derek concerned Afton. After the second day she was in a state of near panic. Discussing the situation with Rios, he asked from where his last call had come. She replied, "He was in a waterway that he said was one of many trending southward from across the wide channel opposite *Punta Arenas.*"

"I spend my childhood in that area," Rios said. "There are dozens of channels along which he could have been traveling. In what type of boat was he traveling?"

"A small wooden craft with an outboard motor that he voiced trepidation about. The storm that passed through here has reported to have caused damage even to large transport ships. I'm afraid that boat was sunk."

Trying to calm Afton, Rios reminded her that Derek was skilled at survival and assured her they would find him. The situation was reported to Harriett. Afton called Margo in the *Arica* office to inform her and Roger that she and Rios were going to search for Derek. With full backpacks, the two of them took a bus to *Punta Arenas.* Derek had called Afton several times from the boardinghouse where he had stayed while in the city, so they walked there from the bus stop and checked-in. The receptionist gave them the keys to the Range Rover they saw parked in front when she was told they were going to search for Derek Lugard.

In the darkness early the following day, Rios left the boardinghouse and walked to the docks, hoping to find a friend to assist them. The friend, called Rolli, had arisen early and was sitting on the deck of a modern, fiberglass boat, drinking coffee. A banner over the slip advertised sightseeing tours.

Rolli had not seen Rios for years but his appearance was not possible to forget. He waved and invited him onboard. As he did, Rolli got him a cup of coffee. The long-time friends sat on deck chairs and Rios explained his mission to find another friend and associate.

"Why was he in these waters?" Rolli asked.

"I have been told that he was with another wildlife expert searching for the nest of a unique condor."

"As boys, we climbed to see condors in nests, remember. They were common throughout the area. Any of more than twenty channels could have been taken by your friend, and the storm was so bad that I feared for my boat right here. His chances of survival are slim."

"That I know." Rios said. "To make the chances even smaller, the small wooden boat on which they left here was, apparently, hardly seaworthy."

Rolli reported, "I have no charters pending," and added, "When should we leave?"

"I am with a young woman that I work with at a lodge near *Puerto Natales.* We stayed last night at a boardinghouse. I will bring her, ready to leave within the hour, if you are serious about helping us."

"I would do anything I can for my savior from years ago," Rolli said, as Rios jumped from the boat.

Rios walked back to the boardinghouse where he found Afton having breakfast. With a plate of food from a buffet table, he joined her. She was very happy to learn a boat had been located for their search and asked about Rios' friend who he said owned the boat.

He responded, "Rolli and I grew up together in a very small settlement of fishermen far to the south. We have not seen each other in years. He runs sightseeing tours from the dock here but has no charters right now. There is probably no man that knows these waters better than him. If Derek is still alive, we will find him."

The thought that she could have lost the man she had grown to love dearly had not been one Afton had entertained before. She refused to accept the idea that Derek was dead.

With their backpacks, they rushed to the Range Rover as soon as they had eaten. Afton drove. Rios directed her to a parking lot he had passed earlier. Rolli was waiting when they reached his boat. He said he had re-stocked and was ready to leave.

As they left the slip, Rolli suggested that they start the search in a wide waterway that was slightly west of due south, the direction he had been told Derek reported to Afton his boat was headed, and work their way eastward, traversing all significant channels. The search began that way. They traveled every daylight hour for three days, slept in bunks below deck for a few hours each night, and ate meals Afton prepared, returning to the dock only for fuel. The three of them sat together in the wheel house with eyes and binoculars looking for any signs of life or wreckage as they traveled.

As they searched, Afton asked many questions, in Spanish, about her companion's early life. Rios had little to say, but Rolli was talkative.

"We both enjoyed being together, by ourselves, when we were not helping our fathers," he told her. "From age ten, we began to hunt for food for the village. When not hunting, we climbed to the high country and explored whatever we found, including caves with bats, puma, and spirits. We attempted to climb near condor nests, but they were in places too difficult for us to reach. On one of those attempts, I fell. I would have died where I fell if Rios had not spent a day and a night getting to me, and another two days carrying me home."

"He has been saving people since then, Rolli," Afton said. "So, I expect that to continue."

"We will find your friend and get him back to you in one piece," Rolli replied.

Afton changed her questioning one morning and asked if there were not girls in their village in which they were interested. Rolli had an answer, "The prettiest one began pining for Rios as soon as he left the village. I suspect she is still hoping for his return."

"Tell me about her," Afton said.

"Her name is Rae. Her father died when she was very young, so she lives with her mother and an uncle. She is a beauty, the most attractive girl for many miles around and she had eyes for only Rios."

Rios joined the conversation, saying, "I'm sure she is now married, with several children."

"Not the last time I was home, a couple of years ago," Rolli countered. "She had matured into a fine woman, had taught herself to read and write, in Spanish, and was teaching others. When she saw me, she asked me only about you."

The right channel was finally entered by the searchers early one morning. The wreckage was sighted and Afton' heart seemed to miss beats until the small fire beneath the overhang was noticed. Derek crawled out, but found he could not stand, even with the aid of the crutch. He waved, frantically. The boat was positioned near the water's edge. A canoe was lowered, and Rios padded to shore. Derek's emotions overcame him as he watched his friend approach. He began to cry. In his arms, Rios carried him to the canoe. Rolli had lowered a rope that was tied around Derek's chest. With Rios pushing as he climbed the rope ladder, and Rolli pulling, they got Derek to the deck. Afton knelt next to him, raised his head, and kissed both checks several times. From the deck, he was carried to a bunk below. Seeing his swollen leg, they all realized the seriousness of the injury.

In slurred words, Derek asked that his backpack be retrieved and a search for the body of his companion be made. Back on the small beach, the knife and tin cup that Derek had used were placed in the backpack and it was tossed into the canoe. Rios climbed all through the wreckage and paddled along the edge of the channel for nearly a mile. He did not find a body.

Rolli turned the boat and followed the canoe, a few tens of feet away from the shore. He, too, searched with binoculars. Realizing the body would not be found, Rios returned to the boat, climbed onboard, and the canoe was secured on deck.

On the way to the dock, Afton kept cold compresses on Derek's forehead. He was feverish. They discussed hospitals. Derek told her that he had lived in his condition for days, and that he would survive the drive to the hospital he preferred in *Puerto Natales.*

Back in the slip from which the search began, Rolli and Rios carried Derek to the Range Rover, lowered the second seat and carefully laid him on the floor, with his head near Afton, who had backed the vehicle as close as she could to the dock. To Afton's surprise, Rios told her that she should leave at once for the hospital, while he helped Rolli with the boat and paid him and the parking-lot attendant, saying he would ride the bus back. Without hesitation, the vehicle was driven out of the parking lot and onto the new road leading to *Puerto Natales.* With lights flashing, Afton drove the entire distance at a high rate of speed. Derek was unconscious, so she could not comfort him, but kept readjusting a wet cloth on his forehead.

At the hospital emergency entrance, nurses took Derek inside. Afton parked the vehicle and went to the waiting room where she remained for hours. A nurse approached to inform her something that she already knew: Her friend was in a very serious condition. She assumed the doctors were considering the removal his injured leg but could not bring herself to ask. She completed paperwork brought by another nurse and waited some more, finally falling asleep on a couch. When she was awakened, the nurse who had talked with her earlier had good news. She said the doctors had decided they could save the leg. When asked if she could see him, she was told: "Not for a few more hours."

She went to a cafeteria for coffee and much-needed food. At a telephone stand on the way there, Afton called Harriett to update her and asked that she report Derek's rescue to Margo and Roger. Within a half-hour, Afton was back in the waiting room. Following another wait of hours, Afton was escorted to Derek's room. He was awake and alert. She kissed his checks and sat in a chair next to the bed. Her first words were, "I have been so worried that I had lost the man I have grown to love with all my heart."

Derek responded, "You were in my thoughts throughout the entire ordeal. When out-of-my-head, I dreamed you were holding me."

"Once more, Rios became a rescuer," she said.

"Where is our friend, now?"

Her reply was, "He stayed in *Punta Arenas*, to report the accident to the authorities and to settle expenses. However, I suspect that he may talk Rolli into visiting the settlement where they were born to the south of where we found you. We talked about their childhood there during the search."

"I don't know where Claude Murra found the boat we were on, or anything about him. We should try to find a family member to report what happened to us."

"I will do some research when at my computer in the lodge," Afton said.

A nurse entered, and suggested Afton leave the room because she was going to administer more pain-killers which would help Derek get the sleep he needed. The nurse proposed that Afton return the next day at regular visiting hours. She did that the next day and each day, thereafter, for nearly two weeks. One day she was accompanied by Roberto Murra, Claude's father, who she had been able to contact in Santiago. Mister Murra told Derek that he had been notified of the accident by province authorities who told him his son's body had never been found, so the family had held a memorial. He said he was on his way to *Punta Arenas* to pay the man from whom Claude borrowed the boat for the loss and stopped to find out what had happened.

To explain the circumstances of the voyage to Mister Murra, Derek described, in detail, everything he could remember. "He died doing what he loved to do," was Derek's final the comment. After Mister Murra left, Afton said that it was a miracle that Derek had survived. He agreed with her.

When Derek was allowed out of bed, he paced the hospital corridors, using a cane. He had been laid up for the longest time in his life. He longed to get back to doing what he loved to do.

Afton was there, of course, when the hospital released him. She drove him to the lodge, where he was warmly greeted by all the staff, except Rios, who had not returned. A special dinner had been prepared for him. At the dinner table, he mentioned his ordeal, only briefly, to the staff and two Japanese guests. He resumed his routine of spending time after dinner with Afton in the swing on the porch and walking around the compound early each morning. The leg had nearly healed, and the pain was gone.

Derek's first trip away from the lodge was with Afton in the Range Rover. She drove to the Andoni Goat Farm to study the new growth of forage on the land emerged from beneath the ice sheet that they had seeded. Afton walked along the slope examining the growth. Derek managed to walk behind her with Raoul and Heidi and to their home for lunch. As they ate lunch, Afton announced that she recommended the goats be allowed to graze on the new growth. She told the others that when that grazing began, it would be the first truly beneficial use of land in the country that had been buried by ice for more than 500 years and that she was certain it was only a beginning.

On the trip back to the lodge, Afton drove to a place where many more acres of land were visible that could be used by those engaged in raising goats, sheep and cattle. Derek asked about the paper she was writing about the emergence of such land and found she was seeking a publisher.

Chapter Nineteen
Beagle Channel

Rios and Rolli had decided to visit their home village before resuming their busy lives. The initial voyage went beyond the rescue site and along other waterways to a small dock to which Rolli had taken people to visit *Alberto de Agostini* National Park several times. Rather than leaving the boat where it would interfere with other boats doing that, it was secured by heavy ropes to jagged rocks nearby, and they climbed to a trail heading south, carrying backpacks. Rolli lead the way on the trail. He had traveled this route several times, the last time was about two years previously when he went to the burial of his mother.

Rios recalled the only time for him was when he left his village as a teenager. They traversed steep slopes across a high pass. There was still snow on the trail and the terrain through which they hiked. Reaching another waterway, the trail followed the bank for a few miles. A settlement that consisted of a few stone houses with thatched roofs came into view. In two of those houses, the returnees had been born but no family members remained there. Rolli was twelve when his father left him and his mother. She raised him until he went to work at sea, aged eighteen. Rios' parents had died of small pox, like many in the village, when he was ten. He had stayed in the house with his mother's brother until it was sold and he and his uncle parted ways. His uncle went south to work in a village on the wide waterway called Beagle Channel which connected the oceans. Rios went north, all alone.

The first house the two went to was where the village headman had lived. It was empty. In fact, the entire village seemed disserted. Noticing a faint light in the house where their childhood friend, Rae, lived, they walked there and knocked on a heavy wooden door. Rolli had not exaggerated when he talked about the appearance of the young woman who answered the door. Her facial features were striking, enhanced by large, sparkling brown eyes. Long, black hair fell to her shoulders. Her trim, well-proportioned body, nearly six feet tall, was clothed in a tightly knitted short wool skirt and a matching sweater. Her long, shapely legs were particularly alluring. The strong feelings Rios once had for this beautiful woman were rekindled.

It took Rae only moments to recognize her visitors. She asked them inside and embraced them both. The room they entered was spotless. Crude, wooden chairs were covered by dyed wool and there were several, colorful wool rugs on the floor, one in front of a burning fire. A large loom in one corner revealed how Rae had produced her attractive furnishings.

The guests were escorted to chairs next to the fire, and Rae went into a back room, returning with cups of tea for the three of them. During the next few hours, the childhood friends became re-acquainted, speaking the native language that Rolli and Rios seldom used. Rae explained that she now lived alone most of the time. Her parents had died, and the uncle that moved in with her at the time spent most of his days searching along the edges of the Beagle Channel for relics washed ashore from numerous ancient ship wrecks, some of which he sold to people sailing through the channel on pleasure yachts.

Rolli said he had been told that Rae had taught herself Spanish and was teaching others in the village. She corrected him, saying an anthropologist who had lived in the village taught her to read, write, and speak Spanish, but there was no longer anyone who wanted to learn that language living here.

"How do you stay alive?" Rios asked.

"I exchange my weaving and knitting for food, and I have learned to be good at catching fish," she replied. "Also, Uncle Jock brings me food, at times, that he buys in a village on the channel."

"It must be a lonely life for you," Rolli said.

"Very lonely during the last couple of years," Rae responded. "The man who was studying our people left. Many others did, too, and the older generation is dying away. There are only eighteen still living here."

"How do you spent your time when not working with wool or fishing?" Rios asked.

"I read a lot," she answered, pointing to book shelves. "That is the village library. The books have been donated by the anthropologist, a priest who visits, and Uncle Jock. He buys what he can afford, reads them, and brings them to me."

"Would you like to go north with us?" Rios asked.

Rae answered, "I wanted so desperately to go with you when we were young, and I have dreamed, often, that you returned to get me." That comment was followed by a long period of silence.

Finally, Rae asked what the two of them were doing. They discussed the lives they had lived since leaving the village. Both said they were happy with their present situation.

Rae offered to show them the rest of the house. In a small bedroom with two beds, she told them that room was where her parents had slept, and that Jock slept in one of the beds when he was there. She offered the room to them. A smaller room she showed them, with one large bed, was where she slept and worked part of the time. Knitting was scattered around. In the kitchen, she invited them to sit at a small table with four chairs, while she prepared dinner for them. As they talked about the happy times of their childhood, Rae took a large salmon from a wooded ice-box, cut filets, and cooked the pieces over a wood stove, while boiling rice.

Once again, the offer was made for Rae to accompany them when they left, as they ate. She said she would consider that offer, but if she decided to leave, they would have to go to tell her uncle. They talked long into the night, sitting in the kitchen, before Rios and Rolli when to retrieve their packs from near the front door and retired to the large bedroom. Rolli fell asleep right away. Rios laid awake for hours. The image of Rae walking by his side in the wilderness was very vivid when he did sleep.

The men awoke to find that Rae had made cornmeal cakes, with liberal amounts of salmon cooked the night before mixed in. She served them stacks with tea. At Rae's suggestion, they walked around the village talking with everyone they saw. The older people all claimed that they remembered Rae's guests. After that walk, Rae went home. The other two hiked trails they remembered well. Stopping in a glen, they built a trap they had perfected as children, from willow branches, and caught a large hare. Rios cleaned and skinned it with the knife he carried in a sheath, while Rolli dug edible bulbs with a stick. The meal eaten that night in Rae's home was prepared by her guests. Before they retired, she told them that she had decided to go north with them with no idea what the future that would bring. They planned a trip to Beagle channel the next day.

The canoe from which Rae fished was too small for the three of them to cross the adjacent waterway together, so she paddled across with each of them. They pulled the canoe from the water and hiked the three miles, on a well-used path, to the convergence of the waterway with a broad channel and westward along the shore of the channel that was named after HMS Beagle, the ship that used this route to cross between the earth's great oceans with Charles Darwin aboard. A shack with a large canoe in front was seen. Although dressed in heavy, wool trousers and a long poncho that covered the upper portion of her legs, and she wore heavy, leather boots, Rae was able to run ahead to find her uncle. He was not in the shack or nearby.

Rae motioned her companions to follow as she walked toward a steep cliff-face. Before they caught up with her, she had disappeared. Reaching the opening to a cave, it became obvious where she had gone. Rolli followed Rios into the cave. It was lighted with large candles. Rae was seen standing with her uncle, a stout man as tall as she was, with gray hair. Next to them was a long, rickety table. What was piled on the table was a large collection of truly amazing, ancient objects, including, swords, helmets, breastplates and small chests. Many of the objects were badly corroded and bent, but some were in fair to good condition.

Rolli and Rios were introduced, and they began to examine what lay on the table. Jock opened a small chest to show them the coins it contained. He remarked, "I keep this chest hidden and sell coins only when necessary to buy food for me and Rae. Thieves steal things of real value when they learn I have them."

"Who buys other things from you?" Rolli asked.

"The wealthy on yachts like to take souvenirs home with them. When I take things to the slips at *Puerto Williams,* I return with cash."

Rios asked, "How long have you been doing this?"

"For more than twenty years, I have walked and paddled along the shore of the channel collecting what washes ashore. When I was younger, I dived into the icy waters where there was evidence of a ship wreck. Now, I am too old to do that," was his response.

Suddenly, the wind outside increased, dramatically. At the entrance of the cave, black sand could be seen blowing inside. "One of the many fierce storms is upon us," Jock remarked. "We will have to remain here until it lets up a little."

There was a place on one side of the cave where Jock had made fires before. He led them there, carrying one candle, and he extinguished the others. Driftwood was soon burning. Rios smoothed sand that had blown high on the wall of the cave and raked the jagged rock fragments from the sand with his fingers to make a spot for him and Rae to sit and to eventually lie down. Rolli and Jock created a barrier of driftwood and sat behind it. The wind continued to howl and seemed to intensify. Huddled around the fire, the exploits of Jock continued to be discussed throughout the day. At nightfall, Jock decided to make his way back to his shack. They others stayed by the fire, discussing the way that Jock had been making a living for him and Rae.

Seeing Rae nodding-off next to him, Rios took her head, gently, and laid in on his lap. She slept while Rios and Rolli discussed what they had found and what they should do now. After a few hours, they laid-back on the sand to sleep.

At daylight, the wind had subsided and Jock returned. He carried a box in which cooked bacon was piled on a tin plate, and a clay jug of water. When the fire had been built up, and everyone was awake, the food and water were passed-around. Jock reported the storm had diminished and told them to imagine sailing along the channel in a such wind, saying there was no wonder that so many ships were destroyed here.

Shouting was heard. A demand was clear, "Come out of there old man or we will come in to get you."

"They think I am alone and have come to rob me," Jock said, quietly. "All tracks outside, but mine, are covered with sand."

"Rolli and I will take positions on each side of the entrance," Rios said. "When they enter, we will attack them."

Rolli rushed to get a sword from the table and crouched on one side of the opening. Rios removed his knife from the sheath on his belt and moved to the other side. Two men entered the cave. Only one was armed. He carried a rifle pointed forward. The attack consisted of Rios stabbing the unarmed man in the back of his shoulder and Rolli swinging the sword with force. The rifle in the other man's hands was struck by the sword and flew toward Rios, who picked it up.

"Get out of here now, or I will shoot both of you," Rios shouted. The men ran.

Before Rios joined the others at the fire, he wiped the blood from his knife in the sand, returned it to the sheaf, and looked carefully at the gun. He told the others, "There is a chip missing from the front handle of the rifle. The man who carried it is lucky a Spanish sword didn't cut-off his fingers."

Rolli examined the sword he still held and discussed with Jock what he had thought about during the night, "Some of the things you have collected belong in a museum. If I took some items to *Punta Arenas*, I believe I could sell them. At least, you would receive credit for a contribution to a museum."

Rios added, "The chest of coins should be hidden in the stone house that you and Rae share. I'm afraid those thieves will come back."

Jock agreed to both suggestions. He found a torn burlap sack and filled it. With the sack over Jock's shoulder, they left the cave and walked to his canoe. Rae announced that she and Rios would walk home, and that Rolli should go with Jock in the canoe, carrying the rifle for protection.

Following the violent storm, the weather had cleared. It was a pleasant hike back along the tributary for Rae and Rios. They talked, for the first time, about the feelings they still had for each other. Rae asked if he had any idea what she could do if she went north with him. He told her about the wool garment business his employer's wife had started and suggested that her weaving and, particularly, her knitting skills, would be in demand. He suggested she might want to teach again.

Her canoe was where they left it. They crossed the waterway to find that Jock and Rolli had arrived, safely, ahead of them. Jock had prepared a more complete meal for them, with fish and wild greens they had collected along the waterway, and a pot of tea. After the meal, Jock went to visit a lady friend. Rae told the others that she suspected that woman, a widow, would move into her house when she left. She expressed the hope that the coins that she had seen Jock hide beneath a loose stone, where her mother kept valuables, and the chest he brought with him from the cave would allow them to live, comfortably.

Jock brought his friend, Ali, home to meet Rae's friends. They spent the evening talking about how things in the village had changed over the years. Ali commented that she suspected that the few remaining in the village where among the few of their people still living in southern Patagonia.

Rae put some clothes and shoes in a pack, smaller than Rios'. When she tried to add some of her favorite books, Rios took them and added them to his pack. The items from Jock's collection that they were taking with them were placed in a better, large sack with the opening tied with rawhide. Straps were added to the sack to form a large pack. The plan was for Rolli to carry that pack, Rios to carry his and the pack Rolli had brought with him, and Rae to carry her own. After sincere wishes from Jock for a happy life for his niece, and well-wishes for her companions, the hike back to the boat began. The weather conditions continued to be unusually good. Rios told Rae of his feelings of anxiety and loss when he first took this trail to a new life, as they walked side by side. The boat was where it had been left. Soon, they were on a short voyage to *Punta Arenas*.

In the slip rented by Rolli, the boat was secured. Each carrying a backpack, Rios and Rae walked to a boardinghouse and registered. In adjoining rooms, they showered and laid down for some much-needed rest, agreeing to meet at dusk to go out for dinner. Rae arose from the bed in time to fix her hair and change into her best clothes and shoes. The outfit was one she had knitted. When Rios knocked on her door, she stepped into the hall with a poncho over her arm. With admiration, Rios helped her into the poncho and put on a heavy, wool coat over slacks and a sweater. They walked to a German restaurant.

Their outer-wear was taken by a young woman and hung on a rack for them. Standing together waiting to be taken to a table, all eyes in the room seemed to be directed toward them. For the first time of many, the presence of two very attractive, very tall individuals was noticed with amazement. As they walked to a table, they received several friendly greetings.

They ate a fine German meal and sipped local wine. Rae was aware of the attention, but that did not concern her. She felt flattered. Curiosity caused the restaurant owner, a heavy set, middle-aged woman to come to their table. She sat with them and asked if they were new to the city. Rae replied they were Tehuelche, born in a village near the Beagle channel, and that she had just arrived in *Punta Arenas* for the first time. The woman said she hoped her stay would be a pleasant one, as she left the table.

Not knowing what to expect when he left Lautaro Lodge with Afton to search for Derek, Rios had taken all his savings. With what he had left, he planned to make certain Rae had a pleasant stay. He paid the bill and they walked back to the boardinghouse. In the hall in front of their rooms, they kissed for the first time.

Before they met for breakfast in the boardinghouse, Rios asked the owner if she could recommend a seamstress. He liked the clothes Rae had made for herself but knew she would need more. The woman told him that she would have someone come to take his friend's measurements that afternoon, saying he was doing the right thing because clothes to fit his friend would not be obtainable ready-made. Rae was pleased about that development but said she would need to purchase undergarments before the measurements were taken.

The two of them spent the morning shopping. Rios gave Rae more than enough money for the things she needed, as they entered a department store from a taxicab. He purchased a few little things he needed. From years of experience, he had learned ready-made cloth that fit him properly needed the skills of a seamstress, as well. They had lunch in a nearby café and were back in time to meet the seamstress, a very friendly Asian woman. Rios waited in his adjacent room. The Asian woman left, promising to return with dresses made from the material Rae had chosen.

When they went downstairs, Rolli was waiting for them. He told them that a museum was very happy to take the items he had brought them, and he had received a little money that he would take to Jock as soon as possible, but he had a charter beginning the next morning. The friends parted with good feelings and promised to keep in touch.

Rae sat in the front room of the boardinghouse all afternoon where she read a book provided for those staying there and conversed with the owner. Rios went back to his room and called the lodge. He talked with Harriett and Afton. Afton told him how well Derek's leg was healing and briefed him on what he had missed. Rios explained he had made a trip to his home village, but he didn't mentioned Rae. He did tell Afton that he had a surprise for those at the lodge when he returned in a few more days. Lying on the bed after the call, Rios tried to take a nap. Instead, he pondered about how Rae would be accepted by his associates, where she would stay, and how she could become useful and happy at the lodge.

They ate dinner at the boardinghouse that evening with the others staying there. Rae wore the knitted outfit in which Rios had first seen her as a grown woman. That vision was something that he would never forget. Everyone at the table complemented Rae about her appearance. After dinner, they sat on a couch, close to each other in the front room. Rios explained Lautaro Lodge to her, described those with whom he worked, and asked her to accompany him there. Not really knowing what to expect, she agreed to go there with him.

The seamstress arrived as promised. When Rios paid her for the dresses, the woman suggested Rae be taken to see her sister, a hairdresser in the center of the city. Reluctantly, Rae agreed to have someone, besides herself, trim her hair. A taxicab dropped Rae at the address Rios had been given. He asked the driver to take him to see the new power plant with which he knew Roger and Derek had been involved and bring him back to the hairdresser's shop.

The hairdresser introducer herself as Miss Francine. She had never had such a beautiful customer before; therefore, Rae was given a full treatment. That included curling the ends of the hair that she trimmed, a manicure, and the application of light makeup. During a break in the treatment, Miss Francine called her boyfriend, a news reporter, when she learned from Rae her background. As Rae went back into the reception area, the reporter and a cameraman where waiting for her. Rae was overwhelmed and was reluctant to be interviewed, but the reporter asked questions she could easily answer.

By the time Rios returned in the taxicab, the reporter and photographer had departed. He held Rae at arm-length and told her how truly beautiful she was, before helping her put her poncho over one of the new dresses. Rios asked the driver to take them to a restaurant that featured live music. There, Rios ordered expensive meals and they listened to the music, the first live music that Rae had ever heard. There was dancing, but they did not try to dance. It was late when they returned to their rooms. Again, they kissed and embraced as they went into separate rooms.

Going into the dining room together the next morning, the owner handed them the newspaper that everyone was discussing. A large picture of Rae was on the front page above a long article. Before commenting, those at the table gave them time to read the article. It contained half-truths and some untruths, but it described Rae very favorably. It told the reader about her life in a small village, and suggested she was a princess of the Tehuelche people, the tribe of giants described by those in Magellan's time, for which Patagonia was named.

As the newspaper was refolded, the questions from those at the table began. Rae explained that she was a child of an ordinary couple who had lived in a small, stone house her entire life. She did take this opportunity to explain that people of her tribe were the first to live in this vast region, how they were mistreated by Europeans, and how diseases brought by the newcomers had caused so many of their people to die young. When Rios was asked to comment, he said the two of them had grown up together and had recently been reunited.

When the question was asked of Rae: "Do you plan to become a model or a movie star?" she laughed. She explained that she had nothing to do with the photograph in the newspaper and simply answered a few of the reporter's questions. The questioner responded, "You are more beautiful than models in magazines."

Leaving the dining room, everyone took time to tell Rae and Rios how pleased they were to have met them. Checking out, the owner told Rios she hoped the two of them would return often. A taxicab took them to the bus station. With their packs and a suitcase Rios had purchased loaded, Rios presented the tickets to *Puerto Natales.*

During the bus ride, they discussed their futures and joked about the newspaper article. Rios went into the bus station in *Puerto Natales* to call the lodge for a ride. There, he learned that fame had arrived before they did. The photograph and article had been reprinted by the local newspaper and was visible on a news stand. Rios knew that the article would have been read at the lodge when he called to ask Harriett to send someone to the bus station, but he did not mention having the subject of the article with him. Afton and Derek where astounded when introduced to Rae upon arrival at the station. With the small amount of luggage loaded, the Range Rover started for the lodge.

Derek was the first to comment about the surprising guest. He said, "You have some explaining to do, my friend."

Rios described in detail his trip home with Rolli after the rescue mission. His reuniting with Rae and their trip back to *Puerto Natales* was highlighted. He didn't mention the interview, but Rae did. She explained how a reporter had cornered her and wrote an article about her.

"We have read the article and seen your picture in the paper, but never dreamed we would met you, let alone have you join us at the lodge," Afton said.

"The article was not totally correct," Rae replied. "I'm not a princess, only a lonely girl who was living, essentially, by herself, until my prayers for Rios to return were answered."

"You look like a princess, and you will not find loneliness with our group," Derek said.

"Do you think Rae will be welcomed and have a place to stay?" Rios asked.

"You know she will," Derek remarked, "Even if we tell everyone she is not a princess."

Entering the lodge, Harriett recognized Rae as the person whose picture was in the morning-paper, right away. When Rios introduced her, he made the comment that Rae was a friend, but not a princess. As was her way, Harriett treated her as royalty anyway when escorting her to a room on the second floor. Rios left the suitcase and her pack in the room and whispered that she should wear one of her knitted outfits when called to dinner.

There were only staff members at the table when Rae arrived and sat next to Rios. Throughout another meal, Rae and Rios discussed their experiences during the previous weeks. When they finished, Rios mentioned Rae's talent and pointed out that she had made the outfit she was wearing. Harriett recognized the significance of that, having been asked to supervise the operations of the wool garment operations that Margo had established while continuing her duties at the lodge. She suggested knitted wool garments would be in demand.

Rae replied, "When considering trying to make a living knitting, I read a great deal about knitting machines. I learned that I would need a modern machine and learn to operate such a machine."

Afton commented, "If a machine is needed to advance the wool works, Margo will find a way to obtain one." Knowing she had a lot to tell Margo in her regular letters that were now sent to *Arica*, she said that she would ask.

After dinner, two couples sat on the front porch, with Rae and Rios sitting on a step. Derek commented that a second swing needed to be ordered, one with a seat that could be adjusted somewhat higher than the one on which he and Afton sat.

Chapter Twenty
Marco's Return

The voucher that Marco presented to Harriet when he arrived at the lodge, by himself, late one afternoon was from a university in Santiago. It covered his stay for a month. His reservation had been received months earlier. The new hardtop jeep he had driven from his home was parked in the garage. With Rae staying in a guest room, the accommodations were now to be all occupied, except the owners' suite. At the time, Rios and Luis were busy leading tours on horseback. At least once a week, Luis conducted overnight adventure tours and Derek led regular fishing trips. The fish farm was operating smoothly under Miguel's watchful eyes. Afton was busy processing and planting wildlife forage seeds in the plant-nursery.

Marco had ingratiated himself to those staff members and all who had served him in the lodge during his previous visits with his parents. He and Rios had become good friends. Marco went to find Derek and Afton to explain the purpose of this visit, after Harriett had shown him to a room. He found them together. They were walking from the hothouse. He was greeted with embraces and the three of them continued to the conference room. The endeavor for which Marco sought their help was worthy of that help. He had chosen as a Master Thesis a subject that considered the potential use and improvement of wildlife habitat on public lands re-emerging from the ice sheets, something in which Afton and Derek had great interest and that had been part of their professional services to Roger Richardson.

Undergraduate studies, the graduation celebration, and his graduate classwork was discussed. Derek asked about his parents. He was told that they were well, that they had voiced a wish to spend more time at the lodge and that his father was pleased with his choice of a graduate paper and Wildlife Biology as his graduate Major. Marco was offered work space in the area that Derek used as an office. The way Marco thought their assistance would be needed was outlined: "I would like to be shown the results of the re-seeding efforts you have made regarding wildlife forage, of course, and any data you have acquired on the extent of the ice retreat will be helpful. If you have developed thoughts about other forage plants that might be established, I would appreciate being able to include those in my paper."

Afton responded, "I have copies of maps that accurately document the ice retreat in one area, and I do have some ideas about other suitable plants that I will share with you. We might work together on a program that would prove the viability of some of them. I know that Derek shares my enthusiasm about your paper and is as happy as I am that you asked for our help. After dinner, I will begin to assemble data for you.

Rios had returned from a tour and washed up for dinner in his quarters. Walking by the conference room, he saw Marco. Warm greetings followed. The four of them went upstairs. Rios was very anxious for his friend to meet Rae. She was in the living room talking with guests, which had become commonplace. The original newspaper article about her had been followed by others that described more about her people and her association with Lautaro Lodge, so she had become a celebrity that guests wanted to meet. Her stature and beauty added to the delight of those with whom she spoke. Afton's reply to a letter from Margo in which she described Rae's popularity was that she seemed to be a great hostess. Marco, too, was charmed by Rae when they were introduced. He suggested they sit next to each other at dinner to become better acquainted.

Rae sat between Marco and Rios. During the meal, most of the discussion between Rae and Marco centered on their mutual friend. Marco explained that Rios had, literally, saved his life while they were traversing an ice sheet. Rae said that him returning to their home village for her was a life-saving act, too, in her mind. Pleasant times that Marco and Rios had spent together were recalled. Marco did provide them with an explanation about his reason for returning to the lodge and the length of his planned stay. After dinner, there were five sitting on the front step, where their discussions continued. Rae offered her help to Marco in any way possible.

Rios led another tour the following day. As had become routine, Rae went to see if she could be of assistance to those in the lower level after breakfast. She helped Derek and Marco rearrange furniture and organize the books, maps,

234

and notes that Marco brought-in from his vehicle. When plans were made to begin the examination of reseeded areas on the slopes behind the lodge, Rae asked if she could accompany them. They agreed.

Rios had taken Rae on long walks to help her to become acquainted with part of *Estancia Margo,* and he was teaching her to ride, so he could show her more, but she longed to, somehow, be shown a way that she could be assistance to the staff. That happened when she went with Derek and Marco. She was given a measuring tape, shown how to mark one-meter squares with piles of rocks at each corner, and was asked to count the specific plants, that were shown to her which were growing in each square. A notebook was provided for her to record her counts and Derek marked, with surveyor' tape, the arbitrary places where she was to make the count, as he and Marco studied the area, and Marco took photographs. Derek made Rae aware that puma roamed the area, but they would keep careful watch to make certain she was safe, not knowing how they could do that. He had not brought a gun.

Rae saw a puma later that morning. She was moving from one area that Derek had marked to another. The cat ran down the slope a few yards ahead of her, apparently unseen by her companions. She was not frightened, never having witnessed how a puma killed to survive. *What a magnificent animal*, she thought. The sitting was reported to the men when they rejoined her.

Derek didn't want to cause Rae to be fearful but thought he should apologize for them hiking so far from her. He did that at a place with a good view they found to eat the lunch that the kitchen staff had prepared for them. From there, they saw a puma below them hunting in a favorite area.

Marco discussed with them the fact that his interest in wildlife biology was kindled by scenes like this and what he had learned from Derek. He explained further, "The interrelationship of the species and man's involvement I find fascinating. Here we are on a project to expand a primary source of food on which the puma lives. As the deer population increases, so does that of the puma. Then, the more deer remains the puma leaves, the more food there is for condors and other scavengers. The cycles are endless."

Rae responded, "This may be a time for me to ask something that I find unclear. I have read the Origin of the Species and other books describing the survival of the fittest, yet I am not certain how that applies to mankind. Rios has the size and other physical characteristics to survive in competition with wild animals and other humans anywhere. Our ancestors were even larger.

However, other humans arrived who were less fit to survive in our lands and the diseases they brought decimated my people."

"The survival of humans is certainly complicated," Derek said. "I confess that any element of that is far beyond my acquired knowledge." Rae added, "An anthropologist lived and studied in my village. He didn't have any sound explanations for me, either."

They returned to the job of counting plants that survived the winter season. Derek and Marco worked close to Rae during the afternoon until all the plants in the areas marked had been counted.

Rae was asked to take the notebooks with the counts recorded to Afton when they returned to the working areas in the lodge. There she was told that when the average of those counts was compared to those that she had made in that area the previous spring, a survival rate of the individual plants set out could be estimated. That, Afton said, would be important to the work being done from the lodge, and to Marco's paper, regarding the best plant to provide food for deer. That confirmed for Rae that her effort was, indeed, important. Rae mentioned seeing the puma and Afton told her about the time a cat, probably the same one, jumped over her head while she was working in the same area. Marco joined them. He and Afton discussed going to the area planted on public lands the next day.

The drive to that area began at mid-day in Marco's Jeep. He told Afton on the drive that the vehicle had been his college graduation present from his parents. When asked, he informed her that he and his parents were still very close. They made an overnight stop at Patagonia Camp, something Afton enjoyed doing. The only yurt available was a large one, with two sleeping compartments. They took that accommodation.

Going from the reception office to a restaurant for dinner, Afton noticed a car that she had seen on the road behind them at the top of a steep grade. She thought little about that but should have. They discussed many things at dinner, including their time in an ice crevasse. The bottle of wine they shared made them both sleepy, so in the yurt they went to sleep quickly. After a light breakfast, they stopped at a small market to purchase bottles of water and somethings for lunch. The same car that Afton had noticed the previous day was following a few cars behind them when they left the resort. She mentioned her concern about possibly being followed but when they turned toward her test plot, that car did not, so she told Marco she must have been mistaken about someone following them.

The Jeep was parked where the lodge Range Rover had been parked on previous trips. Afton explained her study area and told Marco how she had been injured by falling ice once straight ahead of them. He decided to hide the key to the Jeep in front of a tire in case it would be needed by her in another emergency.

Afton began studying the tiny plants in her test plot on her hands and knees. Marco hiked along the slope to the north. He was out of her sight for some time, then reappeared near the top of the most prominent hill, but he was not alone. She took binoculars from her pack to see who had joined him. What she saw was Marco's hands being tied behind this back and him being pushed ahead by three men down the hill.

She rushed to the Jeep, found the keys, and drove back to the main road. Her intent was to drive to a place opposite the hill to try to see where Marco was being taken. The car she thought might have followed them was seen parked on a narrow side road. At a high point on the main road, she turned the vehicle around and found a place to park where the hill on which Marco was last seen was visible. She called Derek on the satellite telephone he had obtained for her when he got one for himself to replace the one lost in the boat accident. When Afton explained the situation, Derek told her that he would call Marco's telephone, then call her back.

Afton watched and waited, seeing only traffic on the main road. The return call came. She learned that Marco had been taken to exchange his life for the release from prison of a drug-producer captured crossing the border from Peru. Marco's father had been told that unless he arranged for that release within 48 hours, his son would be killed.

Derek asked if the abduction had occurred in an area where he had worked. Afton described the site and told him they had worked there together the previous summer. She was told that Marco's uncle was going to pick him up and Derek asked her to meet them at the heliport at Patagonia Camp.

Afton was at the heliport when it arrived. The helicopter was shut-down. Mister Ledesma, Derek, and two men in uniform walked to greet her. Derek carried a map which he spread out on the hood of the Jeep. He asked Afton if the abduction site was where he had made a mark that he pointed to on the map. She confirmed it was. Derek proceeded to inform the others what he remembered about the area, "In studying the woodlands in that area to define a wildlife corridor, I came upon an old, dilapidated shack just below that spot."

Mister Ledesma asked Afton if she thought Marco was being held there. She said that she thought he must be because the car she thought belonged to the captors had not moved. She offered a plan: "They know I was with Marco, so they will not be surprised if they see me looking for him. I will move along the edge of the woods and find the shack to confirm he is there and to see if I can devise a way for him to get out without being harmed. Your group should secure a vehicle, drive the main road until you see a sedan parked on a side road, and approach the shack from that direction. When I am certain Marco can get away when you storm the shack, I will call Derek."

After considering the plan for a few minutes, it was agreed to by the others. Derek folded the map, hugged Afton, and told her to be very careful. She drove away to do her part.

Afton found the shack, apparently unseen. The back wall was practically falling-down. She crept there. Through broken siding-boards, she determined there were two rooms and saw Marco siting on the floor in the largest room where three men were seated on rickety chairs around a table, playing cards. His back was against a dividing wall. Through a narrow opening, Afton crawled into the small room and to a place behind Marco, carrying a knife from her backpack. In a whisper, she told Marco to move his hands a few inches to his right where she was able to cut the rope that bound him, through a crack between boards. Continuing to whisper, she told Marco to rush to the back of the room when he heard voices from in front of the house, telling him she would create a way out for him there.

Afton crept back outside. In a call to Derek, she said one word, "Go!" She began tearing away broken board. Hearing shouts ordering that the captives be released, then, gunfire, Marco got through the space that Afton had created. The two of them ran. They did not stop running until they reached Marco's Jeep, where he embraced and thanked her.

Marco drove to the main road. There they waited. When a police van and two other marked cars passed, they saw a motion for them to follow, which they did. At the heliport, Marco was greeted by his uncle. Derek again held Afton, tightly. Marco left in the helicopter and Derek drove to the lodge with Afton, arriving in the middle of the night. This new adventure was relived on the way there, and they both expressed emotional strain during their separation.

Derek wondered why that region of Patagonia had been the site of so many of the most eventful happenings during their stay.

Harriett, Rae, and Rios where waiting for them, talking together in the living room. Food had been kept warm in the kitchen. After hearing about all that had happened, the others went to bed. Eating at the table in the kitchen, Afton commented that they were associated with a very caring group of people, and that she thought it was time for her to help Rae find a permeant place among them.

The following day, Afton asked Harriett and Rae to accompany her on a trip into the city to determine how things were progressing at the garment operation, something, she told them, Margo had asked her to do in her last letter. What they found was a very busy place. Two sons of one of the women who was weaving mohair had been instructed to die that fiber and card wool. A woman was engaged, full-time, in a display and sales area and six women were weaving. Harriett asked the woman to take time to speak with her and to meet Afton and Rae. A sign indicating temporary closure was hung on the front door and the women congregate in the front room.

In response to Harriett's questions, several expressed joy for the opportunity to work at something they loved to do. When the subject of Rae's talent at knitting was mentioned, one of the women commented that knitted-garments were in demand and very expensive in stores in the region. When the idea of adding a line of such garments was discussed, that woman said the secret would be in design, saying that she had operated a knitting machine before arriving in the area, but she didn't have design talent. Harriett told them that she was handling the books for Margo and had been depositing the revenue from the beginning of the operations. Further, that in addition to the pay checks she had been issuing, based on their time cards, they could expect their quarterly share of the profits from their work.

A very pleased group of formerly unemployed native women went back to work, the sign was removed, and waiting customers were invited to enter. On the drive back from the city, an arrangement was made between Harriett and Rae to share in the hostess duties at Lautaro Lodge and the supervision of the expansion of garment manufacturing. Afton said that she would write to Margo explaining their day and obtain permission to add a knitting machine.

Derek had received a call from Tomas Ledesma. His thanks for breaking his son out of captivity was expressed and he told Derek that Marco was insistent on returning to the lodge to continue the work on his thesis. When he said he was considering hiring body guards, Derek convinced him that Marco would be safe among those working at the lodge and when he did field work or was otherwise away from the lodge, he or Rios would go with him for protection, adding that the two of them were better marksman than anyone he could send as bodyguards.

Juan Ledesma brought his nephew to the lodge the next afternoon. He was shown the office area that had been created for Marco in Derek's work space. He told Derek and Afton that one the abductors they had helped apprehend was in the hospital, two were in jail, and the drug-producer was waiting trail. When Mister Ledesma left, he gave Derek two of the latest rifles made, equipped the telescopic sights, and boxes of ammunition. The guns were in hand-tooled leather cases. Derek had a thought about how one of the guns could be put to good use.

Rios had told him, earlier, that he had kayaks made for him and Rae, with the hope of spending some time on the waterways with Marco. The previous ill-fated outing of him and Marco, when he had to go in a canoe due to the lack of a kayak big enough for him, was explained. Derek found Rios that evening, explained the commitment he had made to protect Marco, and told him about the rifles they had been given. He suggested the kayak trip be scheduled. He and Afton would stay nearby on Luis Aparicio's boat with a new gun, although there was no reason to expect trouble.

The activity was scheduled. Afton was invited, and she was asked to take Rae to buy suitable clothes the day before. Derek went to the city with them. While the women shopped, he arranged for a charter with Luis and stocked the boat with food and wine.

The morning of the outing, Marco drove the kayakers to the facility where he rented a kayak. Those made for Rios and Rae were there. They left the area slowly while Rae was given instructions. Soon, the three of them where gliding, rapidly, toward the ice field. Derek and Afton drove the Range Rover to a parking lot near the boat dock. Carrying a gun case and his favorite fishing rod, Derek followed Afton onboard Luis' boat. As instructed, Luis kept his boat some distance behind the kayaks for nearly two hours. Derek fished. He kept three large salmon he caught. His new gun was positioned next to him and Afton napped in a lounge chair nearby. When Derek motioned, Luis sped past those in kayaks, who waved.

In a cove, the boat was anchored. Derek prepared a meal of salad, bread, and broiled salmon. Those in kayaks were helped aboard when they arrived, and each craft was secured by a rope. The meal and wine were served. Both Marco and Rae were over-joyed, exclaiming how invigorating they had found the experience. It was late afternoon when they started back and dusk before they reached *Puerto Natale*. Derek paid Luis and asked Afton to drive to the kayak landing. One of Rios' kayaks was tied on the roof of the Range Rover and one on Marco's Jeep. Very happy friends returned to the lodge, not knowing what awaited them.

It was a night of dancing arranged by Harriett for guests and staff. Music could be heard when the late-comers left the garage, after tying the new kayaks above the vehicles. Those late-comers, who had spent the day on the water, went to their rooms to shower and change clothes. Joining the crowd in the converted and decorated conference room, they enjoyed the special food and drink. Rios took it upon himself to teach Rae to dance. He received help from Afton. Many of the guests asked Rae to dance. Without regard to the fact that she was mastered only simple movements, she attempted to follow the steps of all who asked her. Afton danced with Marco, Derek and others. Everyone had a very good time.

Chapter Twenty-One
Lithium

Exploration and development work began on the lithium concession as soon as it was issued. The initial effort involved proving the ground-water basin postulated from surface mapping by Josh. That entailed contracting for the drilling of a series of shallow holes. A drill rig that was not committed elsewhere was not easy to find but the services of CP Drilling, owned by an Englishman named Charles Pennington, was secured, eventually. Roger favored that driller because his equipment would be able to drill large-diameter holes to produce brine after the initial slim-hole drilling. Charles also had a good reputation among those with whom Roger spoke for being reliable and The Richardson Group was becoming accepted as honest competition. Men actively working on other concessions in the region began to communicate with Roger's people. That happened after Tomas Ledesma paid a visit to Roger in the field office that he had set up.

Mister Ledesma brought word of the abduction and rescue of his son, and Marco's decision to continue his studies as planned. He told Roger that he was once again beholding to those at Lautaro Lodge. Hopes of success in this new venture were expressed by him. The visit was short, but its importance was recognized by all who saw the arrival and departure of a helicopter on which a presidential seal was clearly visible. Roger experienced positive reaction to the visit. He no longer encountered animosity among the management of operations near his and some even offered encouragement or advise. Advice was welcomed and proved to be valuable.

Roger and Josh had extensively studied extraction techniques being employed, and they knew the geologic conditions controlling the mineral deposit as well as anyone, but neither had worked where the pumping of brine, and multiple handling of such large volumes would be required. That depended, of course, on the ground-water basin being as mapped and the shallow lake-bed sediments being porous, holding commercial amounts of dissolved minerals. The determination of those factors was the intent of the drilling underway.

A series of holes were drilled, the ground-water flows measured, and samples collected to be analyzed for mineral content. Josh supervised the work of Charles and two Chilean helpers. The work had to be done with protection from a blazing sun and the hot wind that blew constantly. The analyses were done by a commercial laboratory in *Arica*. Roger, being confident that the brine reserve would be defined, spent time studying ways that might increase the amount of water in the shallow sediment to offset draw-down when the production of brine began.

The *Atacama* Desert was the driest place of earth. Mountain ranges surrounding the area created rain shadows. Rain very seldom fell in any amount. Some moisture was carried inland from the ocean in the form of fog. The best way to have that moisture reach the surface was through the installation of what had been called "Fog Catchers." That required the installation of panels of wire-mesh on which the fog would condense into droplets and fall to the surface. At such a site that Roger visited, the surface was covered by sheets of plastic from which water was collected in containers for human consumption. For such water to reach the near surface brine, it would have to be funneled into input wells. Roger carefully analyzed this method of obtaining water.

The conclusion Roger drew from his study of "Fog Catchers" was that such operations may not result in extending the life of the production of lithium, that it would be very costly, and that the success of his proposed operation would depend much more on the efficiency of the recovery plant he would have to install and the manager he could find to manage the plant. He had contracted with a recruiter many months earlier to find a good plant manager. The person whom he considered the right man had yet to be hired. However, before that man was engaged, a great amount of work had to be done and there were contractors available to do that work.

The first contract Roger signed was for the leveling of huge evaporation ponds and the building of surrounding berms with the top layer of ancient-lake sediments from which the minerals had been leached and moved down to the water table. A series of rectangular ponds were built, and an area of prior nitrate mining was reclaimed to form a catchment basin. Shallow ditches were dug so that if enough rain did fall to cause runoff, it would flow into that basin and seep into the ground water. The leveling of areas for stockpiles and the recovery plant were complete by the same earthmoving contractor.

Plans called for delaying the construction of the processing-building for one year, the time estimated for the drying of a significant amount of lithium-bearing material in the evaporation ponds. Drilling large-diameter wells to produce brine was accomplished. Pumps with parts made of stainless steel were installed, as was an electric-power generator. Roger then decided that his involvement in the project would not be needed for a time.

Margo had helped out a little in the office but spent most of her time painting. Roger took her down the coast in a rented vehicle for new scenes to paint before planning to fly to London where the other business affairs of The Richardson Group had been neglected for months. It was a relaxing trip for them both. New acquaintances were made at hotels in which they stayed. One of those was a middle-aged man, traveling alone, whose home was in Tokyo. Roger and that Japanese man sat on an upper-level patio of a hotel with a view of the ocean, while Margo set up an easel nearby and painted that view.

The men discussed mining, including the fact that Chile was now the largest producer of copper in the world, with many of the largest mines on earth in the *Atacama* Desert. The man told Roger he represented a Japanese consortium that owned ten percent of one of those mines and was looking for additional investments. Roger did not reveal his lithium operation, but the man must have made inquiries, because at breakfast the next morning he approached Roger and asked if an interest in his concession was for sale. The response was that he planned no such sale. That was the first, but not the last, response Roger was to make to a possible investor in the lithium operation.

Meetings were held in the *Arica* office with Josh and Jenifer in which progress in the pumping of brine into the first evaporation pond was discussed. Josh reported that a man from the Ministry of Mines had come to inspect the operation and to install a meter on the well to measure the volume pumped, so the government would know if the amount allowed as a condition of the issuing the concession was ever exceeded, although it would be years before that amount could possibly be extracted. From the office, Roger called the pilots and scheduled a departure time, Josh drove him and Margo to the airport, with their luggage.

The flight to London made a stop on Grenada, at Margo's request. When Rosita received a call from the airport, she took a taxicab to meet them. The meeting took place over a meal at the terminal, as the plane was refueled. The report on Rosita's time in medical school was a positive one. Rosita said she was doing well with the classwork and that she was adjusting to the climate. Once more, she expressed her appreciation for all Margo, Roger, and those at the lodge had done for her, saying that she corresponded regularly with Ramon and the Countess.

The Richardson's were very happy when they arrived home. Their traveling and intense activities had been stressful. They needed time to recuperate but both knew that would not be possible.

Waiting for Roger in the office, among a stack of letters and messages, were applications for the job of plant manager. He studied those carefully. The application he found the most promising was from a man who managed a solar-salt operation in the Great Salt Lake area of the State of Utah. He dictated, to his Administrative Assistant, a tentative offer of employment that indicated it was conditional upon Jack Watson coming to London to meet with Roger. The offer was mailed with an airline ticket.

The remainder of the morning was spent dictating responses to the many other business correspondence before Roger went to lunch. Returning from lunch, there was a young man waiting for him who insisted on discussing an important matter. The man introduced himself as Yang Chow and Roger escorted him into his office. The important matter was another offer to buy the lithium operation, this time from a large Chinese company for whom the man worked.

"The operation is not for sale," Roger told him.

The man responded, "You have not heard the offer I have been authorized to make." When that offer was made, it was so much larger than Roger could have imagined that he was shocked. He sat, silently considering, what he had heard for several minutes. Finally, he told the man that he would present the offer to his investors and walked with him to the outer office. Business cards were exchanged, and Roger was told that his early reply to the offer would be appreciated.

Before contacting Sir Reginald or the Countess, a conference call was held with the Board of The Richardson Group. During that call, Roger provided details on the analyses of the brine now being pumped into evaporation ponds, and the work that had been accomplished on the concession. The consensus of the directors was that the offer should be presented for the reaction of the outside investors before a vote of the Board was taken.

Roger had planned to set up a meeting with Sir Reginald and the Countess to provide them with a progress report as well. That meeting now had a much more important purpose. It was held at the restaurant where they had met before. The representatives of the investment group were waiting at a table when Roger and Margo arrived. Following warm greetings, Roger gave them a progress report and told them about the offer. The sale, he assured them, would result in a multiple return of all investments made, to date.

The Countess asked Roger for his recommendation. He provided a long reply in which he told them of his long-held interest in major production of natural resources and his belief that this project would provide that, although he had yet to develop the economic analyses that would project a long-term rate-of-return and that the huge investment in a processing plant was still to be made.

Sir Reginald was the first to respond. He voiced his reluctance to aid the Chinese in their attempt to dominate the rechargeable-battery business, adding that would also give them a lead in the production of electric cars. Countess Rothchild suggested that another investment would have to be found to put the money to work. She said she was happy to see this venture through and was confident that a steady income was likely from lithium production. The opinions of the investors were conveyed to Roger's Board.

Dinner was ordered with a bottle of French wine and the dinner discussion became less business-like. The Countess asked Margo about her painting. Upon learning she had completed several of the coast of northern Chile, the Countess told her that she wanted to sponsor a showing of her working in depicting the beauty of that country.

The showing took place a few weeks later at a gallery that the Countess often supported that was owned by a friend so hers. It was a formal affair, attended by many important people in London society. The Countess, with Sir Reginald by her side, acted as hostess. Margo circulated through the crowd who were drinking champagne and explained the scenes she had depicted. The paintings were found by most to be very good. Margo received many complements. Selling paintings had not been the objective of the showing and Margo had not set a price on any of them. However, several people wanted a painting to hang. Names and addresses of those were recorded and deliveries were made during the next few days. In that most of those paintings were of scenes on *Estancia Margo*, they were considered good advertising for the Lautaro Lodge. Margo was surprised by the amount of money that the people who received the paintings sent to her. She gave that money to a shelter for unwed mothers.

Jack Watson arrived from the United States. Following a long interview, Roger hired him. A place for him to stay near the office was found, and he began work in the office space that Josh had used. In anticipation of getting the job, Jack had made himself familiar with the processing techniques being used to produce marketable lithium carbonate from the material extracted from evaporation ponds in several parts of the world where that was being done. He made drawings of a plant that would use the best elements known for filtration, ion exchange, and chemical treatment, with solvents and reagents. He also created a tabulation of the capital costs by contacting manufacturers and suppliers and projected operating costs. Roger studied all of this, critically.

In discussing the situation with Margo at home one evening, he decided that with what Jack had provided and the confirmed support of his financial backers, they should fly back to Chile and start construction on the recovery plant. He asked Margo to call Jenifer and have her locate Jack, a single man, living quarters. The call to the pilots to schedule a departure, Roger made. The next day, he informed Jack of the decision and a few days later, the office management was once more left to Roger's experienced assistant.

Once again, the flight went from London, to the Cape Verde Islands and then to *Arica.* Jenifer was notified of the estimated time of arrival and she was at the airport to meet them. She took Jack to the apartment secured for him that was within walking distance from the office, in a rented sedan. In a second leased Jeep, Roger drove Margo, and the pilots to the hotel where they had stayed before. Jenifer explained that Josh was staying on the project site in a trailer, monitoring the pumping of brine, so Roger arranged to pick up Jack at the office and go there the next morning. Margo went along for her first visit to the project site, without knowing what to expect.

Margo was amazed at the enormity of the settling ponds, one of which was slowly filling with a yellowish-colored, dirty-looking liquid. They found Josh in a trailer with a young Chilean man he had hired, so he did not have to be there all the time. After introductions, Josh, Roger, and Jack walked around the site. Margo stayed in the air-conditioned trailer, talking to the new hire. She found that he was born and raised on the coast, about sixty miles to the west. Not being able to find work there, he rode his motorcycle around the desert until he was hired by Josh, who needed help. The others returned. Josh and Jack went back to *Arica*. Roger and Margo drove to *Copiapo* intent of obtaining a contract for the construction of the processing plant building.

Copiapo was a city of moderate size, the capital of a province of the same name. It existed because of mining, first for silver and, more recently, copper mining by numerous small miners, whose ore was processed at a local smelter. Deciding to stay the night, they took a room in a small hotel and toured the area. A museum dedicated to mining was found particularly interesting. The population proved friendly, the room clean, and the food good. The next morning, a contractor was found who had equipment that he would move to build the building, the drawing of which Jack had made. From there, they drove west for more than an hour, across dryland with scattered vegetation and some agriculture. Small grape and citrus farms were seen. The coastline along which they drove back to *Arica* was spectacular. Several stops were made to view the ocean. Margo regretted not bringing her easel, paint, and brushes.

At the hotel where they had taken rooms for the month, Margo and Roger hosted a dinner, so that their associates could become better acquainted. Jenifer drove there with Josh and Jack. They joined the Richardson's and the flight crew at a table on a patio with a view of the ocean. During dinner, some of the things about the region were explained to Jack and the building contract was discussed. Margo commented about the climate she found very pleasant. Jenifer informed the others that she had learned that an ocean current moderated the temperatures along the coast and inland considerable distances in places, suggesting that if not for the rain shadows that caused the low rainfall, the region would have one of the best climates on earth. The pleasant dinner ended with plans to continue the development of a lithium production facility.

Josh was to spend some well-deserved time with Jenifer while Roger and Jack went to the site to layout the building the next day. Jack remained at the site to await the arrival of the building equipment and Roger returned to the office, where Margo was filling in for Jenifer. When Roger got to the office, Margo told him he had missed a call from Derek. Roger called Derek back and was informed that he and Afton were planning a vacation on Easter Island.

To that announcement, Roger expressed his hope that they would have a great time. Derek had not mentioned that they were going to get married, but Roger suspected that. When he told Margo about the call, she told him she was certain they planned to marry, having known of Afton's feelings for Derek for a long time. She said that she was sure the confirmation was in a letter from Afton back in London.

The construction of the building went smoothly. While that was in progress, Roger spent time in the office ordering the needed processing equipment from Jack's list. The projected arrival of that equipment was not well-defined. The actual arrival proved to be sporadic. However eventually all the equipment was in place. Orders for the chemicals needed in the processing were not submitted. That would be done when there was enough dried lithium-bearing material in stockpile for plant start-up. The initiation of production and cash flow was now dependent upon hot dry winds. The decision was made to leave Jack Watson in charge of the entire operation, while Roger, Margo, Josh and Jenifer flew back to London. There, another project was initiated.

Roger had been informed by a letter received some time previously about a possible deposit of rare earth minerals in east Africa that was not being exploited. He assigned Josh to investigate. Following weeks of study, Josh reported that the deposit reported was, probably, not as represented. Because other information about mineral deposits Roger had received from this source had been proven accurate in the past, he made the decision that he and Josh would fly to Johannesburg to meet with Johan Weiser, a friend of one of his directors.

The flight was long from London, with a stop on the Ivory Coast. They met with Johan at a hotel and found that the deposit he though had commercial value was on a large property he had recently purchased, with the intent of developing a hunting lodge. Roger explained to him the success he had in creating a lodge in Chile that catered to tourists interested in nature, but not hunting. They were flown, by helicopter, to the property. Roger spent time examining an old building that Mister Weiser intended to remodel, while Josh was flown to the deposit pointed out to him.

The result of the trip to southern Africa was that Josh concluded that the geology of the area he investigated was not one where commercial rare earth minerals would have been deposited, and Roger convinced Johan that a facility such as Lautaro Lodge would be a better investment for him. The helicopter took the three of them back to Johannesburg, where they went to dinner together. Discussions throughout dinner were about the lodge that Roger had expanded on his property in Chile. The concept of professionals and those intimately familiar with the region providing guided tours was the concept that Roger attributed to the success of his lodge. He pointed out that from his days on big-game hunts in the region he was aware that the wildlife that tourists could observe from a facility that Johan might create far exceeded the wildlife in Patagonia.

The discussion resulted in Johan deciding to study the possibilities had Roger had suggested. When he asked if Roger would provide further advise, he was told that was something he could count upon. The next day, Roger and Josh returned to the company plane for the flight back to London. The flight was uneventful.

Margo informed Roger that a letter she had received confirmed that Derek and Afton planned to marry on Easter Island. The letter also announced that from Easter Island they were going to fly to the western United States to visit Afton's family and to South Africa so Derek could show her where he had grown up.

Chapter Twenty-Two
Homeward Bound

Afton and Derek did not make an announcement about their upcoming departure from the lodge. Rather, they met with each one of those with whom they had been associated to tell them of their plans to take an extended vacation and to express their gratitude for the pleasant times they had spent together. Harriett had hired a young girl to help with housekeeping. She was assigned to care for the plant nursery, as well. That work Afton explained to her, but not knowing what the future held for her and Derek, Afton had been concerned about the advancement of the field projects that she had initiated, particularly after their value was documented by the paper that Marco Ledesma was writing.

Those concerns were dispelled after she received e-mail correspondence from Emily Norquist. Emily was a botanist living in Norway that had an interest in what Afton had been doing at the other end of the earth, work that was described in an article, written by Afton, that appeared in the magazine *Nature*. In their correspondence, Afton suggested Emily contact Roger in London, who might want to hire her.

For several months, Afton and Derek had been planning to get married. Neither had strong feelings about any organized religion, so a church wedding was not considered. Nor did they want a formal affair, like others that had taken place at the lodge. They decided that the trip they wanted to take to Easter Island would be a honeymoon and the cruise-ship captain would be asked to perform the ceremony. They left Lautaro Lodge without fanfare. Rios drove them to *Puerto Natales* in the Range Rover.

A stop was made at the bank in which most of the money they had each earned in consulting fees from The Richardson Group was on deposit. A great deal of those earnings was converted to traveler's checks. Rios took them to the dock where a medium-sized cruise ship of the Regency Line was tied. It was a very emotional parting for three who had become exceptionally close friends. They hugged each other before Afton and Derek walked up the ramp, with packs on their backs and Derek carrying a suitcase. They introduced themselves to the purser who escorted them to a spacious cabin.

On the way to the cabin, the man said their request to have the captain marry them had been received and that they would be notified when the captain had time to do that. Standing at a deck rail, the port city that had become an important part of their lives faded from their view.

The voyage along the fjords was enjoyable for both. Derek's voyage to search for his client was recalled and discussed. The scenery with which they had become so familiar and the abundant sea life they observed was still fascinating to them. The wedding ceremony was memorable. It was performed on the bridge deck with the setting sun behind them. The captain who read the vows, in English, and the purser and steward who acted as witnesses where very cordial. A Certificate of Marriage was later delivered to their room. To celebrate, they ordered champagne and a seafood dinner in their room and spent more than twelve hours in loving embraces in bed.

The ship had previously stayed overnight at the re-built dock at *Puerto Montt*, so it entered the open sea directly and headed for Easter Island. The weather was warm, with a bright sun. In deck chairs, the couple spent the daylight hours on that leg of the voyage. They left the cruise at the dock on Easter Island. A courtesy van took them to the *Taha Tai* Hotel, a picturesque, low-profile building. From there, they hiked to examine the *Moai* for which the island was famous and to *Rapa Nui Parque Nacional,* the parkland at the north end of the island, returning each day for a swim in the hotel pool. The stay was enjoyable, with excellent service and good food. The newlyweds were relaxed and very happy at the end of their honeymoon. They looked forward to the next trip, but Afton had some trepidations about going to California so that Derek would meet her family.

They flew from Easter Island to Santiago and took a direct flight from there to San Francisco, arriving early one Sunday morning. There could not have been a better time for Afton to show Derek the sites in the bay area. She rented a car and drove him around San Francisco, across the Golden Gate Bridge, and inland to Cloverdale, her home town. Approaching Cloverdale, Afton explained that she had been estranged from her parents because they totally opposed her decision to take a job in Chile after completing her studies at nearby University of California, Davis. She said that in letters she had written to them, the rewarding work she was doing was explained, but few of those letters were answered, and she had not told them about Derek. "I can't promise you a warm welcome when we arrive," she added. Derek promised to do his best to win them over.

Afton's parents, Betty and Frank Atkins, were home when she parked the car in front of the home in which she had been raised. Afton and Derek left the car and walked toward the front door, leaving their luggage. The parents met them before they reached the front porch. To her surprise, they both embraced Afton. When Derek was introduced, Betty embraced him and Frank shock his hand. The couple was escorted into the house and asked to make themselves at home in a large living room. The mounted head of a large deer hanging over a fireplace, gave Derek reason to believe that he and Frank would have common interests.

He stood admiring the trophy when Frank told him that their son, Frank Junior, had killed the deer when he was young and that he was now a Park Ranger in Wyoming. Sitting on a couch, Afton noticed the copy of the magazine, *Nature*, in which the article she had written appeared. Next to the magazine was a folded page of the newspaper. They were the first things that Betty wanted to discuss. She said that their son had told them about the article, and they had rushed to buy a copy of the magazine. A few days later, she said, the article was mentioned in a section of a San Francisco newspaper that referred to Afton as a botanist who would become famous for the discovery that she described in the article.

The significance of what she had discovered and the work she had been doing related to ice retreat was discussed by Afton, with contributions from Derek. She told her parents that she did not expect to be famous, but she was proud of what she and Derek had accomplished in plant restoration in Patagonia. She explained how the two of them had become good friends and were now husband and wife. That required an explanation of the wedding and the honeymoon.

"We are poor hosts," Betty said. "What can we get for you two?"

Afton replied, "I have become a tea drinker."

"I'll bet you will drink a beer with me, young man," Frank offered as he left the room.

Afton followed her parents to the kitchen where she sat on a stool while her mother prepared tea. Frank returned and gave Derek one of the bottles of beer he carried. It was now Derek's turn to speak about himself when he was asked to do so. Based on Frank's many questions, his life was found to be interesting. He discussed his interests in wildlife from his years growing up in South Africa, through his time as a big-game hunting guide, to his recent experiences in Patagonia. While he spoke, Betty and Afton returned with cups of tea. Afton sat on the couch with Derek, and Betty in a chair next to Frank.

"We will be so pleased for you to spent time with us," Betty said. "But you must go to Wyoming and have our son show you the wildlife in Teton National Park." Derek responded that he would very much like to do that.

Betty mentioned that they had visited through the lunch hour and offered to prepare something for them to eat. She and Afton went back into the kitchen. Before they started preparing lunch, Betty returned with more beer. Frank and the son-in-law, who had been a complete surprise, continued to talk. When he was asked, Frank said he had recently retired from the Santa Fe Railroad, after working for nearly a decade for Southern Pacific before a merger. He said that Betty was a real estate agent.

They ate lunch on a patio behind the house, adjoining a swimming pool. Questions about the future were asked. Derek told them that after seeing where Afton was raised and meeting the two of them and her brother, he wanted them to go to his homeland to show Afton where he grew up. Afton told her parents that they were on vacation from their jobs in Chile, but their future there was uncertain, adding that they planned to visit their client in London to discuss that.

When lunch was finished, Frank offered to get their things from the car. While the women cleaned up, he and Derek did that, and Betty directed that the bags be taken to the room that had been Afton's, when they returned. There, the couple was left alone. They took naps and ended the afternoon with a swim. As they left the pool, Frank suggested that they dress casually for dinner and he would take them to his favorite Italian Restaurant. The restaurant was, obviously, one that Frank and Betty frequented often. Everyone there seemed to know them, and some recognized Afton. The proud-parents spoke with many and discussed the visit of their daughter and her new husband. The meal was authentic Italian, prepared and served by family members. Derek found it the best such food he had ever eaten and told their waitress that. During dinner, they discussed a trip Frank suggested they take the next day.

Betty was required to be in her office, but Afton drove her father and Derek to Willits, an hour away, with the intent of him seeing the white deer that roamed ranches near there. They saw several herds that Derek found fascinating. Knowing Derek would not know much about horse racing in America, Frank only mentioned, casually, that a famous horse, Seabiscuit, was buried on one of the ranches. They toured the area west of Willits and ate lunch at a roadside café, returning to Cloverdale in early evening. Betty had dinner ready when they arrived.

Another friendly family meal was eaten, with local wine. The discussions centered on stories of Afton's and her brother's childhood, many of which embarrassed Afton. It was announced that reservations had been made for them to fly from Sacramento to Wyoming and that Afton and Derek would leave early the next day to visit UC Davis on the way to the airport.

The parting the next morning was tearful. Promises were made to stay in closer touch in the future. On the drive to Davis, Derek expressed how pleasant their stay had been, and that Afton need not have worried about how she would be received. Her response was, "I wonder how I would have been received if I had returned home without having published an article about my work and with an unattractive husband."

He replied, "You would have been welcomed. Your parents love you and your brother."

The tour of the campus was short, as was the flight to Jackson, Wyoming. The brother, who Afton said was called Junior, was waiting for their arrival. He was almost as tall as Derek, with a muscular body and handsome face. In his personal Jeep, he drove them to a nice hotel. They spent the remainder of the afternoon and evening, over dinner, discussing what each sibling had been doing since they had last seen each other. Afton emphasized her work with Derek and their marriage. Junior asked about their stay with the parents in Cloverdale. Derek described it as very pleasant.

"I have been told that you are a wildlife biologist, trained in Africa," Junior said to Derek. "Would you like to see the animals in the wilds around here?"

"That I would," Derek answered.

During the next three days, Junior took them all around the park and surrounding areas. They observed, bison, deer, elk, moose, grizzly bear, black bear, wolverine, and many smaller mammal species. Derek told them that the number of species they had seen was nearly as large as that in some of the areas he hunted in Africa. One evening, hunting was discussed. The two former hunters explained that they now preferred to hunt with a camera, which Derek had done on this exciting outing. No two brothers-in-law could have more in common than Derek and Junior. Their time together, with Afton, was something that neither would ever forget. On the way to the airport, promises were made that they would spend time together in the future.

A flight was taken to Cheyenne. There, the couple boarded an over-the-pole flight to London. Both slept through much of that flight but were awake to see the magnificent sights of Ireland, Wales, and the western United Kingdom, approaching London early in the morning. Roger and Margo had been told in a telephone call of their schedule. Margo was in front of the terminal at Heathrow Airport when they cleared customs with their bags and walked to the curb. Warm welcomes, with tight embraces, followed before entering Margo's car. The drive through London to the Richardson home took more than an hour. During that time, Margo questioned her guest, whom she had sincerely missed, about their adventures since Afton had penned the last letter to her. She congratulated them on the marriage that she said she had expected.

The welcome by Roger in front of his home was as warm. They were escorted to a guest room and invited to have wine or cocktails after they had settled into the room. The apprehension was real. The next few days were to set the future course of two experienced, professional people.

The first evening, during a casual gathering and dinner, and at breakfast the next morning, the discussions included only the way things were when they left Lautaro Lodge and the things that Afton and Derek had done since then. Roger told them that the future would be discussed at the office the following day. The apprehension grew, as Afton and Derek lay in bed that evening. Neither knew what to expect and neither had a clear idea about a future that would please them the most.

Margo and Afton rode to the office together. Derek rode with Roger, who briefed him about the progress at the lithium operation and told him he was certain that project would develop into a highly profitable venture that could become as valuable as his father's venture into platinum mining years before, his objective when he first went to Chile. With the four back together in the office, Roger said he had hired Emily Norquist to continue the exceptional work that Afton had been doing at the lodge. That addition and the training that Derek had given Rios and Luis were adequate, he told them, to assure everything they had built together on *Estancia Margo* would continue to make them all proud. "It is time for new challenges for you two," Roger continued.

From his desk drawer, he retrieved two checks and handed one to each of them. The amount they thought to be unbelievably large. Roger referred to the checks as bonuses. He then discussed a possible challenge: "While you are in South Africa, you might look up Johan Weiser. A few weeks ago, when I was with him, he showed me a property on which there was an old building that I tried to convince him could be converted into a lodge like ours. I'm certain he would need investors and he could use the experience of you two, if he decides to do that. I believe he is an honest man with whom you could work." The meeting ended with Roger receiving sincere words of thanks.

Margo drove the couple into the center of the city to show them the sites and to deposit their bonus checks in Barclay Bank. One of the places they stopped was at the gallery where Margo's paintings were still being displayed. The quality and variety of Margo's work amazed them. Walking, slowly, to study each one, Afton commented, "You have captured the beauty of Chile." Derek offered, "They are as realistic as photographs with more depth." They both realized that Margo had become a very accomplished artist.

At a lunch room near the gallery, they enjoyed a traditional order of fish and chips, with mugs of beer. Walking to the theatre district, Margo picked up tickets to a play that she had ordered. She then asked if they would like to do some shopping. They declined, saying they preferred to continue to visit famous sites, which they did until early evening.

Roger was at home when they arrived there. There was just enough time for them to prepare to go back to the city. Roger planned to take them to dinner before the play. That ended the most heartwarming day that Afton and Derek had ever experienced.

Two more days were spent by the Lugard's with the Richardson's. The highlight of that time was a visit to the home of Countess Rothchild. Upon learning, when she called Margo, that the couple who had been so kind to her at Lautaro Lodge was in the city, the Countess insisted that Margo bring them to her home for tea. That became another experience that would long be remembered. The Countess was her charming self. She asked about everyone at the lodge and told them about her regular letters from Rosita. Margo's portrait of the Countess was admired even more than the landscapes they had seen at the gallery.

Margo took her guests to the Gatwick Airport that was closer than Heathrow. They had reservations to Johannesburg, with a stop in the Cape Verde Islands. The parting was emotional, particularly for Afton and Margo, who had become the closest of friends. They promised to continue exchanging letters on a regular basis. All embraced as Afton and Derek left the car. The flight to the refueling stop was uneventful, but mechanical problems were discovered on the ground, so there was a long delay before the flight resumed. That create an opportunity to spend some time visiting the surrounding area of Sal Island and eating a good meal at a café.

They arrived in Johannesburg in early evening and secured a room in a hotel located in the suburb of Sandton that provided a courtesy car. The area was one that Derek knew well. He had spent time there with foster parents, now deceased, and attended school at a church sponsored school before being accepted at the university. They ate dinner and breakfast at the hotel. At a nearby shopping center, they acquired some new clothes and Afton saw, for the first time, a display of native artwork that she thought both attractive and fascinating.

At a leasing facility, Derek leased a Range Rover. It was like the old one he had sold when last there and the new one he drove in Patagonia. The remainder of the day was spent giving Afton a tour of the city and showing her the evidence of massive mining operations. They ended up in a community where the population was predominantly Zulu. As Derek had hoped, they found the man he considered his best friend in the small house where he lived when Derek last saw him. Kip Abioye lived by himself. Derek and Afton walked, hand in hand, down a path to the front door and rang a small brass bell.

The appearance of Kip startled Afton, although she had been told much about him. He was at least as tall as Rios, but more muscular. The muscles of his upper body were obvious. He wore only trousers. His dark black skin seemed to glisten, and his black hair was neatly trimmed.

Clasped arms were the greeting of these lifelong friends. Kip embraced Afton and invited them into a well-keep large room, with rugs on the floor, two hand-carved wooden chairs, and large pillows scattered about. On the walls was the type of native artwork that Afton had admired in a store. The guests sat on the chairs. Kip excused himself and went to a kitchen. Returning with two cups of tea, he offered them to Afton and Derek and sat cross-legged on a pillow. He spoke words of greeting in a deep voice, with a strong English accent.

Without being asked, Derek briefly explained where he had been since they were last together. He told Kip about Afton and their marriage. Kip explained that he now worked as part of a group that took tourists on safari. The group was different from the one with whom he and Derek had worked together. This group escorted people who wanted only to observe wildlife on the plains and in jungles. Derek asked him for a recommendation of a trip in which Afton could observe wildlife and study the flora, her passion as a professional botanist. They were told a trip was being organized that he was to lead into Kruger National Park.

Derek asked him to reserve a place for them on that trip. Kip and Derek talked about some of the memorable experiences they had together on safari. Afton found it all extremely fascinating. When they left, Kip and Derek again grasped arms and Kip embraced Afton once more. This time the embrace was so tight that she could feel the muscles in his arms. Walking back down the path, Derek told Afton that he now felt at home.

Chapter Twenty-Three
Safari

Derek knew that the largest park in the country and part of one of the largest game preserves in the world could be seen by staying at lodging facilities within the park and taking excursions from there, but he wanted Afton to have the experience of camping in the wilds that had been a part of his life for so long, and the thought of spending time once more with Kip in that setting was something that he looked forward to. Knowing the jacaranda trees would still be in bloom, Derek drove Afton to Pretoria, where as many as 50,000 such trees had been planted since they were introduced from Brazil, while they waited to hear from Kip.

Entering a basin where the highway crossed the Magaliesberg Mountains, the color purple could be seen everywhere. The streets in the city were covered with blooms, in some areas from curb to curb. A few government buildings and monuments were visited on a short walk. Hours were spent in the National Botanical Garden for Afton to be introduced to the flora of the region. In late afternoon, Derek drove into the adjacent hill country, toward Kruger Park, to show Afton the type of terrain to expect on safari. They returned to Johannesburg by way of Kip's home and learned they would be on the next tour with him. A date was set for them to leave their vehicle at a fenced lot in the outskirts of the city and begin the safari in a small bus.

At the starting place, standing next to that small, four-wheel-drive bus, the Lugard's met and spoke with those with whom they would be spending the next week. They were two Americans, Mary and Lowell Taylor, from Austin, Texas; a single young man, Eric Heston, from Los Angeles; and a middle-aged German couple, Hans and Suska Hess. Kip was dressed in a type of uniform that consisted of tan Bermuda shorts, a matching shirt, a bush-jacket and a pith-helmet.

He shook hands with the others waiting, greeted Afton and Derek as before, and invited everyone to get into the bus. He then went to a Range Rover in front of the bus where three other black men waited and signaled the caravan to move out. The bus carried equipment secured on the top and a rear-compartment was stacked high with water and supplies. It was driven by an East Indian boy. A Jeep followed with a colored cook, three black servers and cooking equipment.

Within little more than an hour, the caravan entered the park though one of the southwestern gates. Immediately, wildlife could be seen, including a pride of lions crossing the road. They moved slowly through permanent, overnight facilities, then on a well-maintained road for several miles, before crossing miles of a roadless area to the first campsite, located in a grove of acacia trees.

The passengers left the bus and watched in a state of amazement as a camp was quickly set up. Four small sleeping tents were erected into which cots, with mosquito netting, a night stand, and a lantern were placed. In front of each tent, a camp table and two camp chairs were placed. On the table was set a second lantern. The erection of two large tents, for the staff to sleep, and a food tent followed. A fire ring was constructed from stone lying nearby, and a fire started, next to which cooking tables were placed.

The Indian bus driver showed everyone to their individual tents. They were told to expect someone to take drink orders very soon and described where a shielded latrine was being created. Having been engaged in such activity for years before he became a hunting guide, Derek was inclined to help. Instead, he held a chair for Afton to sit with him in front of their tent, as dusk approached. He felt very good about being back in the wild-country of Africa.

The drink they chose was white wine, when a server with a white cloth around his waist arrived. Within a short time, the server returned with an open bottle for them and drinks for the others sitting in front of their tents. There was little space between the tents. They were close enough to converse with those in front of the adjacent tent, the Taylors. When Mary asked if the safari was their first, Afton answered, "It's mine, but Derek spent years as a big-game hunter."

"What do you do now?" was Mary's next question, to which Afton replied, "We have just returned to where Derek was born and raised. We have been engaged in consulting work in Patagonia and have yet to decide what we will do next. This trip is my introduction to the natural environment of southern

Africa which is of great interest to us both. My training and experience have been in botany and Derek is a professional wildlife biologist, with experience on three continents."

"Do you see yourself involve in hunting safaris again, Derek?" Lowell inquired.

"My hunting days are over." Derek said. "The client for whom we worked in Chile suggested that we help create a facility that provides people a way to observe wildlife and plants in the way this trip will. That was the purpose of the lodge where we worked in Patagonia."

Lowell remarked, "I am strongly committed to wildlife preservation. If you need financial backing for such a venture, I would be interested."

These discussions continued until a dinner bell was heard. The food was set out buffet-style. As each person filled a platter, a server carried the tray to their respective table, with a napkin, silverware, cups, and a pot of tea. Afton and Derek found the food good, drank the remainder of the bottle of wine, and sipped tea. A server returned to clear the table. Kip came to join them, carrying another folding chair. More about Lautaro Lodge and the wildlife of Patagonia were discussed until Afton said it was her bedtime.

The lantern on the table was left lit until Afton changed into a long nightgown in the tent and turned-on the lantern there. Derek extinguished the outside lantern, went into the tent, and changed into light, cotton shorts and a T-shirt. Lying beneath mosquito netting on her cot, in total darkness, Afton became aware of the multitude of sounds. She asked Derek to identify for her the animal that made each cry or roar. He was able to do that for he was very knowledgeable about the twenty-five animals that were most common in the region, and many of the numerous birds. One sound surprised him, the bark of a wild dog. That animal, he told Afton, was now rare.

Breakfast was served in front of the tents at sunrise. Before that, Derek and Kip had taken a long walk around the campsite, where many of the animals heard during the night were seen on the move, including a large male lion. As soon as Kip saw that those in his tour group had finished the meal, he announced the pending departure of the bus. With them all aboard, Kip sat on a fold-out seat behind the driver. Afton and Derek sat across the aisle from the German couple, who were surprised by the greeting in their language.

Throughout the day, the bus was driven on a winding route, avoiding the heaviest brush and around groves of trees. Many stops were made during which the passengers disembarked the bus to view and photographed a wide variety of animals, including a small group of elephants, a pair of white rhinoceros, a leopard in a tree, and a cheetah on the run. It was explained, by Kip, that Afton was a professional botanist and she was asked to explain the dominant plant life at each stop. Box-lunches were distributed at a mid-day stop and blankets spread to create a place to eat under mopane trees.

Kip was asked many questions about what was seen. Questions were also directed to Derek when the word spread that he was a wildlife biologist with vast experience. The day-trip ended back at the camp at dusk. The activity in camp was the same as the previous evening and night time, as was the activities the following day, when several other animals were seen. The most impressive were giraffe and Cape buffalo.

The third morning, the camp was disassembled. A route further to the northeast was followed. That led into a grassland that had been created, Kip told them, where an overpopulation of elephants had thinned the brush and trees. That day many impala and herds of zebra were seen. A new camp was created near the banks of the Olifants River. Before dinner, Afton and Derek walked along the riverbank with Eric. He informed them that he was a financial consultant to people in the movie industry who had invested in wildlife hunting areas near Mount Kenya. The reason he was on this tour, he told them, was to judge the acceptance of safaris that didn't involve hunting, something that was being considered at a resort in which a client was a big investor.

At a low-lying, sandy area, Eric removed his shirt and prepared to dive into the river. Derek restrained him, as he saw a very large crocodile slither into the water from the willows just ahead of them. Eric put his shirt back on and thanked Derek. Some of Kip's crew had gone fishing. The main course of the evening meal was fresh fish.

That night, Afton was kept awake by a strange noise that Derek identified as the chatter of hyenas. The bus was driven across the riverbed the next morning where the crocodile had been seen. This time a hippopotamus was nearly submerged to the west of the crossing. The bus moved further to the northeast. Grasslands again dominated the vegetation and more grazing animals were seen. Among them were sizeable herds of wildebeest and kudu. Elephants were numerous.

At one stop, Kip walked with Afton and Derek, ahead of the others. Kip had a rifle held by a strap around his shoulder, as he did each day, for protection. A shot was heard. Kip and Derek discussed the fact that noise had to have been made by a large caliber rifle. Kip asked that Afton stay with the others. He and Derek walked on. They came upon a scene that they both had seen far too often. They crouched low in the brush and watched two men begin to cut a tusk from an elephant.

Kip whispered that they were near the Mozambique border, across which poachers often came onto park land. Having not seen a game warden on the entire trip, Kip nevertheless decided to call for one on the satellite telephone he carried in a case on his belt. The call was answered. The scene before them was described and an approximate location conveyed. At a place closer to the men, Kip shouldered his rifle, shot over their heads.

In a native language, he shouted to them that they were surrounded by rangers and ordered them to step away from their guns. They complied. Derek ran forward and picked up two large-bore rifles. He held one pointed at the poachers, as Kip removed rope from a backpack and tied the two men to a rear leg of the dead elephant. They left the scene and walked back to where Afton stood with the others. All that they had seen and what they had done was explained. Kip suggested they continue to explore the area with Afton and Derek while he waited for the ranger. He handed Derek his rifle. It was recognized as the one Derek had given Kip when he left for Patagonia.

The group stayed together and came upon a Sable antelope grazing on what Afton identified as buffalo grass, the most common in the area. Later they saw what Derek told them was a rare roan antelope. Everyone was waiting for Kip when he arrived back at the bus. He reported that rangers had arrived and taken the poachers into custody. Eric asked if poaching was a serious problem. The group was told that ivory and the horns of rhinoceros were, unfortunately, still in demand, so poaching over much of Africa was a problem, with hundreds of animals killed just in this region. The trip back to camp took until after dark.

The evening meal had been kept warm and was, quickly, served. After they had eaten, Eric carried his chair to sit with Afton and Derek. As the three of them sipped coffee, Eric explained further the resort on a private preserve in which a client had invested and the consideration of restricting hunting there. Afton discussed *Estancia Margo* and the Lautaro Lodge, where tourists from all over the world came to observe and photograph wildlife. That discussion made Afton realize how much she missed the lodge and the friends she had made there, but she told herself that Africa held rewarding challenges for her and Derek, as well.

The next morning, the camp was once more disassembled, the river crossed again, and the tour continued northward. The populations of several species seemed to increase, particularly elephants, zebra, and impala. At one stop, Kip pointed out a black rhinoceros that he said was much less common than the white rhinoceros. The next camp was to be erected near the Limpopo River, the northern boundary of the park, after a long day of travel with fewer stops. While the camp was being formed, two rangers arrived. One of them was a white man that Kip and Derek knew well. They had worked together on hunting safaris.

After warm greetings and the introduction of others, Rolf Wilson told them that a hunt was underway for a large, male lion that had killed a boy in a Zimbabwe village, across the river, that had been tracked into the park through mud flats. He asked if Kip and Derek would like to join in the hunt. Kip told him that he needed to stay with the people on his tour. Derek knew he should not go, but he could not resist the offer. In an open-top Jeep, the rangers with Derek in the second seat moved slowly along the south side of the river. Rolf stepped out often to look for tracks. Seeing large lion tracks, he followed them a short distance, turned, and signaled the others to follow him. The other ranger rushed to his side with his rifle and Rolf's. The two of them followed the tracks.

Derek walked several yards behind. The lion had cleverly doubled back and was out-of-sight in thick brush as the pursuers walked by. Seeing it attacking from the rear, with a loud roar, Derek dove to the right. At that instance, the rangers turned and fired. The huge cat fell next to where Derek lay. The rangers approached the lion, carefully, not certain it was dead. When it was declared dead by Rolf, the rangers straightened out the body. Rolf's companion said it was the largest lion he had ever seen. Derek said it was as large as any killed in his presence. Rolf asked his companion to go bring the Jeep.

"Don't you miss the hunt?" Rolf asked Derek.

He responded, "Not really. I, now, regret the death of an animal, even one that must be put down."

The Jeep arrived. With difficulty, the lion was placed across the hood and the hunting party returned to the campsite. Everyone in the camp congregated around the dead lion, in awe of its size. Rolf explained why it had to be killed.

There was no discussion about how it had been shot. The others had eaten the evening meal. It was served to Afton and Derek, with beer that Derek had requested. Their companions on the tour gathered around their table after they had eaten. Sitting in the light of the lantern, Derek told them about the hunt, and the state of his mind, seeing the dead lion lying next to him. After the others had gone to their tents, the Hess's remained.

"I have been frightened of wild animals all of my life," Suska said. "But I was losing that fear being around so many that seemed to present no danger during this trip, until tonight."

"A lion, referred to as a man-eater, is very rare," Derek told her. "Unless they feel trapped, members of the cat family will not attack a human. The animal kingdom is dominated by docile creatures who want to be left alone."

"I heard you speak of Patagonia where you both worked at a lodge," Hans commented. "My great-grandfather emigrated to Chile, and I am told that I have family in Patagonia."

Afton responded, "There are many German families living near *Puerto Natales*. We worked at a lodge near that city."

"We have been considering going on vacation in Chile next year," Hans said.

Afton responded, "You could not find a better place for a vacation than Lautaro Lodge." Afton went into the tent, turned on the lantern and wrote-down Margo's contact information, which she gave to Suska when she returned, saying her friend should be contacted to make a reservation should they decide to vacation there.

The last night in camp was an exciting one. A group of elephants lumbered through at sunset. The others followed the lead of Derek. They stood in front of their tents and waved towels to divert the animals away. No damage was done. Afton and Derek followed the elephants and watched them wade into shallows in the river. Watching them drink and spray water, Derek commented, "Now Missus Hess will add the fear of being trampled to death to her fears of wild animals." When they returned to camp things had settled down and dinner was being served. The evening turned out to be pleasant for everyone. Once again, Kip came to spend hours talking to Afton and Derek, this time about the future.

The camp was disassembled for the final time after breakfast. While that was being accomplished, those who had been shown more than two hundred miles of the magnificent parkland and the multitude of animals and flora in the park walked to, and along, the river bank. Two of their companions approached Afton and Derek. As they walked together, Lowell Taylor told them how impressed he had been with their knowledge and told them that should they chose to establish a facility for tourists on land that was dedicated to the conservation of nature, he would provide financing. He handed Derek his business card. Mary commented that the two of them had made the safari more enjoyable than it would have been without them.

A second private conversation was held with Eric Heston. He told them that they should consider working at the facility in which his client had invested, near Mount Kenya, continuing: "Whether or not hunting is discontinued, you two would make great additions to the staff. I will write to the manager and recommend you and report my favorable impressions to my client when I return to Los Angeles." Before he left them, Eric handed Derek a handwritten letter of introduction, directions to the facility, and his business card. Amazed by these developments, the Lugard's walked back to the bus and got onboard.

The caravan left the park through the northwest gate. By the middle of the afternoon, happy travelers were disembarking the bus at the tour company yard. Farewells were accompanied by words of appreciation and expressions of pleasure. Derek told Kip to expect them at his home that evening to discuss the future.

Derek drove to a restaurant. He and Afton ate a leisurely late lunch, during which Afton told him how pleased she was that he had taken her to see what she now knew would always be an environment that was cherished by him. The most impressive things that she had seen were discussed, and experiences relived, particularly the lion encounter. After lunch, Afton was taken by a house where Derek had lived with foster parents and to the school that he had attended before going to university. No one he remembered was seen.

Kip was waiting for them when they arrived at his home and he had prepared tea for them. Sitting together, this time all on large pillows, the safari was discussed, and Kip was thanked for a very enjoyable time.

The discussion of the future began with Derek telling his friend about the offers they had received: "The young man from Los Angeles has a client with financial interests in a large game ranch in Kenya. He suggested we might be accepted on the staff there, and he plans to recommend us. Mister Taylor offered to provide funding if we wanted to start our own business that involved conservation."

Kip responded, "The trip was of value to you, beyond showing your wife our African way of life."

"Indeed, it was," Derek said. "Do you have any thoughts about what we should do? Bearing in mind that I would not be happy doing anything again that didn't involve you."

"The game ranches around Mount Kenya receive a lot of publicity and attract the very wealthy. Some are managed properly and add to the conservation efforts established on huge areas of public lands," Kip said.

"I have read about some of the efforts there," Afton contributed. "At least one was started by a Hollywood actor."

"You and I have never been happy taking orders. It might be good to be our own bosses for a change," Kip said.

The discussions continued after they ate beef stew that Kip had prepared, and Afton helped serve. Derek laid on the floor a map, given to him by Roger, that showed the landholdings of Johan Weiser and the building he thought could be converted to a lodge. Before the evening ended, Derek pledged to carefully study their next venture.

Chapter Twenty-Four
Nature Preserves

Afton and Derek secured a room in a different hotel in Johannesburg. Kip was invited to dinner in the hotel dining room. During dinner, a decision was made for Derek and Afton to fly to Nairobi and investigate the Sisal Game Preserve and Safari Services, where Eric Hess had told them there was a good employment opportunity. Kip cautioned them to be careful while in the city. He said it was called *Nairobbery* because robbery of citizens and tourists had become so commonplace.

"Why is that?" Afton asked.

Kip told her, "The city has nearly a million very poor people living in a slum; it has grown rapidly without building enough police stations; and many police officers are corrupt."

Derek asked what Kip knew about game facilities. He said, "There is a national park within the city limits, other national parkland nearby, and a large park around Mount Kenya. Many private preserves exist throughout the region and it is the largest center for safaris in east Africa. I nearly went to work up there before I was hired to take tours in Kruger."

"I wish you could go with us, Kip," Afton said.

"I do, as well, but I have another tour tomorrow," Kip replied.

The evening ended and Kip left them in a parking lot. He was driving his small pickup truck.

The Range Rover was left at the O. R. Tambo Airport and Afton and Derek took a morning flight to Jomo Kenyatta Airport, near Nairobi. A courtesy van took them to the Nairobi Serena Hotel. Learning that hotel was one of a chain of thirty-six hotels and resorts that catered to tourists that were interested in the wildlife of the region, they decided to take advantage of other van services offered and not rent a vehicle.

After checking-in, they took a long walk around the city, which Afton found fascinating. It was the first time she had been where black people were the majority. She was raised where negroes were a minority. There were few in Patagonia. Many white people were in Johannesburg and they were still the majority in Pretoria. She was apprehensive only because of what Kip had told them about robbery, and rightly so.

Afton seldom carried a purse, preferring a backpack. However, a finely tooled leather purse, attached to a long strap that she had purchased in Pretoria, was on her side as they strolled along busy streets. Two young men approached them from behind. One cut the strap at a place on her back. The knife did not cut her or her shirt, but the second man grabbed the purse and they ran. Derek pursued them until he lost them in the crowd. His shouts were ignored by all he passed.

Afton was lamenting the loss of her passport and an expensive digital camera when Derek returned. No one that walked past where they sat on a bench offered information about where they could report a robbery. Some they asked seemed to have the attitude that they deserved the loss.

They walked for many blocks in the direction the robbers had fled. Finally, they found a small police station. The incident was reported to an officer who spoke English. On their walk back to the hotel, Afton discussed her mistake for not acquiring a laptop computer and transferring to it her many photographs she had taken in Kruger National Park which were still on the stolen camera. The fact that similar photographs were on Derek's camera that he had left in their room was of some consolation.

To preserve the photographs on that camera and for use in the future, they stopped at a store and purchased a Japanese-made, small laptop computer. Before going to dinner at a restaurant near the hotel, Afton made the transfer and Derek arranged for a van the next day. The restaurant specialized in Arabian dishes. Neither had eaten such food before, but they found it enjoyable.

It was a shocking surprise when Afton's purse was returned to her by a bellboy when they went to breakfast. He said a police officer had given it to him in the middle of the night. Her camera was missing, but the purse still contained her passport, visa, and personal effects. Afton, much relieved, took the purse back to their room and left it with their suitcase, before joining Derek in the hotel dining room.

Departing in a van hired for the day, Derek's backpack was all they had with them. The driver took them where vehicles were allowed around the national park in a city. Then he drove for a couple of hours to show them the headquarters of safari companies, ending up at the main gate of the Sisal Game Preserve. A gateman opened a large, wooden gate and waved them inside. Derek had called to announce why they were coming. They were greeted by a heavy-set Englishman with a distinct accent, who introduced himself as William Barnes.

The tour they were given, as the van driver waited for them, was extensive. They were escorted through an elaborate clubhouse with a wood-paneled bar and numerous tables. People were in each area. In a large reception room, they were shown a scale-model of the preserve on a large table. On the walls of the room, there were life-sized photographs of several wild animals. In an office next to the reception room, they were introduced to the manager, Ross Hargrove, another Englishmen. He looked to be in his forties, and in great physical condition.

The interview that followed was seriously conducted. Both were asked many questions about their education and previous experience. The interviewer said he was very impressed by their backgrounds and remarked that he saw advantages of having both a wildlife biologist and a botanist on the staff. As the interview as winding-down, Derek said he had been told the organization was considering discontinuing hunting. Mister Hargrove said that curtailing hunting was being considered, but to assure that the land owned by his company would continue to support the wildlife populations, at least culling would have to be a part of game management. William Barnes was waiting for them outside the office. Leaving Mister Hargrove, he told Derek to call him in few days for a decision on their employment and handed him a business card. Mister Barnes escorted them to the van.

On the ride back to the hotel, Derek brought up the subject of population control. "As we saw in Kruger National Park, too many of one species can change the habitat, completely. Small preserves need to be near huge blocks of public land, where the populations can intermingle, and sound management principals need to be applied in all cases for tourism based on wild creatures to continue to flourish," Derek said.

Afton had told the hotel manager a little about themselves when they check-in and he had talked to the van driver about where he had taken them that day. When Afton and Derek came to the lobby after some time in their room that evening, the manager offered to buy them a drink, telling them he had something to talk to them about. What he had to discuss with them was a job offer: "I understand you both have training and experience with the natural environment, something that most of our guests come here to observe or study. I have been authorized to offer you both positions with my organization. It would involve travel between our various hotels and resorts, where you would be asked to give lectures and guide tours."

Before responding, Afton looked for a reaction from Derek. She detected the positive feeling she felt about such work and said: "That sounds like an exciting challenge. We will consider it."

"Then, stop by my office before you leave and pick up job application forms. Consider drinks and dinner on the house," the manager said as he left them.

The discussions and positive thoughts the Lugard's were having about the job offer, as they ate dinner, were interrupted by a loud explosion. Looking through the window next to them, they saw a fireball near the center of the city. They watched as the fire was brought under-control before going to their room.

Early the next morning, they were told in the lobby that the terrorist group el-Shabaab had detonated a bomb in a government building the night before. This changed their feelings about the job offer. They checked out of the hotel, took an envelope the manager that left for them, and asked a courtesy van driver to take them to the airport for an early morning flight, with little enthusiasm about working in Kenya.

The Range Rover was retrieved from a long-term parking lot at the airport in Johannesburg and they went to the hotel where they had last stayed in that city. From the room assigned, Derek called Johan Weiser. Roger Richardson had called him days before to tell him to expect that call. Mister Weiser informed them that he was tied up with other business, but if they wanted to visit the property that he had shown Roger, they should go to Dongola Ranch where there were excellent camping sites from which they could travel over his entire land holdings. He suggested Derek come by his office to get a map. Derek told him that Roger had given him a map but asked for the office address where they could meet later.

The next day, a tent, other camping equipment, food and water were purchased and loaded in the Range Rover. The drive to Dongola Ranch took eight hours, on a narrow road through primarily brush-covered lowlands. As Mister Weiser had said, very good camping facilities for tents and travel-trailers existed on a ranch that was advertised to cover nearly 4,500 hectares. The spot chosen to erect their tent was beneath an arbor that provided protection from a hot sun. A couple camped next to them was from Cape Town. They appeared to be in their late twenties. The two couples became well-acquainted over the next few days and would, eventually, become good friends. Their names were Gay and Boyd Whitcomb.

When Afton explained their reason for being there, the couple asked if they could go along when they went to the areas they planned to investigate. Their small car did not allow them to travel into the bush, so they had been taking short hikes, always with concern about encountering vicious wild animals. Derek saw no reason not to include them and Afton said she would welcome the company.

The northern boundary of the Weiser property was the Limpopo River, that boundary also being between the Republic of South Africa and Zimbabwe. Derek drove to a point on the river bank, shown on the map to be near the northwest corner of the property that had once been the center of the river. He noticed that the adjacent property at that point was part of the Mapungubwe National Park. That he considered very important, because of the continuation of habitat onto protected land. The river was virtually dry, except when rare, heavy rain fell.

The birdlife along the river was exceptional. Wild animals of several species were seen drinking in the few pools. To the south, the herds of zebra and impala were large. Both black and white rhinoceros were seen. When a large white rhinoceros was spotted in a grove of trees Derek's passengers wanted to take a closer look. "Not without a rifle in case of an emergence," Derek told them. "That animal can be very unpredictable, and my rifle is still with a friend." They watched for several minutes. The animal moved away from them and the trip continued along the river bank to near the northeast corner of the property.

From there, Derek drove, diagonally, across the property in a meandering route so the dense brush could be avoided. At regular stops, Afton studied the plant life. Derek examined the animal tracks, with Gay and Boyd by his side. Back at camp that evening, the new acquaintances could not stop talking about what they had seen that day with Afton and Derek. Afton prepared spaghetti for the four of them and the talking lasted into the night. In sleeping bags in their tent that night, Afton remarked that the reaction of people to nature was what she enjoyed the most during their stay on *Estancia Margo*.

The next day the southeastern portion of the Weiser land was traversed. Giraffe and many of the animals, seen the day before, were numerous. The passengers were just as excited. The third day was spent examining the lone building on the property. It was a large structure that had the appearance of a former barracks. The siding and roof were not in good condition, but the foundation and floors were thick concrete, and the framework had been constructed from thick hardwood that had must have been imported.

For the first time, Afton revealed to their companions the concept of making a lodge from this old building and she described the lodge where she and Derek had worked in Patagonia. Boyd grasped the potential of a fine lodge from where what they had observed over the last two days could be shown to tourists by the two professionals with whom they had toured a vast area. He told Afton and Derek that he was an accountant, that Gay had worked as a bookkeeper, and that they would be available to assist in the formation and functioning of an organization to undertake such a project.

The couples left each other the next morning. Gay and Boyd were heading back to Cape Town. Before they left, they gave Afton their contact information and asked Derek to contact them if they could be of service to him. Derek drove east to see the airport at Musina. There were several private airstrips in the region, but this was the nearest commercial airport to the Weiser land. From that airport, they drove back to the hotel where they had stayed in Johannesburg, arriving late at night.

A call was placed to Hans Weiser the next morning to make an appointment to meet with him. The meeting took place at ten in his office. Following introductions, Derek initiated the discussions. He reported, "We have traversed your property. A significant population of wildlife was observed, and Afton determined the flora to be typical of the region. The only building we saw on the property will require a great deal of remodeling to make it useable for any purpose. Due to a contiguous border with a national park, the migration of big mammals should continue, reducing the chance of habitat destruction by overgrazing. We believe a viable nature preserve there could be established. For such a reserve to be a sound investment related to tourists paying for the opportunity to visit the property, camping or lodging facilities will have to be built at least as good as the others in the region and a private airstrip will, probably, be necessary. It is a long way to the airport near Musina."

"Would you two be interested in supervising the needed improvements and managing the property?" Mister Weiser asked.

Derek replied, "We have received other offers of employment since arriving here. However, the challenge your property represents is of great interest to us. The retreat on the Patagonia property of Roger Richardson where we last worked has become a very popular place for people from around the world to relax and experience an undisturbed natural environment. Such a place would be possible on your property with enough good planning and hard work. We believe we are up to the challenge. We have become associated with someone who represents capital and a couple with business experience that could prove indispensable."

"The poaching, smuggling, and movement of undocumented people from Zimbabwe are concerns of mine. The smuggling of people, drugs, and goods from Beitridge to Musina has become a serious problem," Mister Weiser said.

Derek's response was, "We drove the north boundary of your property, along the river bank. A roadway could be improved for regular patrols. Such patrols might deter some of that."

The meeting was concluded when Hans offered to have a management contract drawn up for them to consider. Leaving the office, they were asked where they were staying.

"We have a room at a hotel in the outskirts of Johannesburg where we have stayed a lot lately," Afton answered.

From a desk drawer in the outer office, Hans retrieved a set of keys, wrote an address on a sheet of paper, and told them they were welcome to stay in the house his son had vacated when he moved to London. From that time onward, Afton and Derek became involved in a challenge that would be all-consuming for many years.

The house offered was on a small estate. The Range Rover was parked in a driveway adjacent to a walled front yard. A wooden gate, when unlocked, provided them with access to a very large garden with a pathway to the house. Although having been unattended recently, the garden was a pleasant surprise to Afton. Numerous flowers and blooming shrubs were growing on a slope. Many of them she recognized as being native to Africa. A courtyard separated the garden and the front door of the house. The courtyard, too, contained many plants.

Derek unlocked the front door. Inside, they walked through a large living room, adjoining kitchen, a pantry, two bathrooms and three bedrooms. There were kitchen furnishings but no furniture. The rooms were clean and bright, with large windows in every room. The house and the settling were far more than either of them had expected. Embracing Derek, Afton commented, "We will be very happy here."

They returned to the hotel, ate dinner, and went to bed early. Lying in bed, they relived what had happened to them already in Africa. Envisioning a lodge on the Weiser property, Derek made a statement that Afton could not disagree with, "For this new venture to be successful, we must make certain that we create something to rival the Lautaro Lodge." They fell asleep in each other's arms, with visions of a very exciting future.

CPSIA information can be obtained
at www.ICGtesting.com
Printed in the USA
BVHW052037271222
655044BV00011B/304